EDGE OF THE TRIANGLE

Δ   *A Novel by*   Δ

d. h. cook

FOR INFORMATION (INCLUDING SPECIAL MARKETS PURCHASES FOR EDUCATIONAL, BUSINESS, OR SALE PROMOTION USE) CONTACT: **WWW.NOVELISTDUANECOOK.COM**

COOK, D. H. (DUANE HAROLD), 1951-

EDGE OF THE TRIANGLE

ISBN-10: 0615461905

ISBN-13/EAN-13: 9780615461908

BISAC CATEGORY: FICTION / HISTORICAL

WEST...

Her fingers slammed into the mud and she struggled to keep her grasp. Her muscles tightened, clawing, straining to hold her prey. She slowly dragged the earth toward her body, lifting. Her moaning could be heard for miles.

Scratching, dragging, digging. Repeatedly slamming her massive fingers back into the water. Deeper and deeper she grasped for the soil beneath the surface and greedily clawed at her spoil.

She groaned and whined under her heavy load. Complaining as she lifted the prize to her mouth. Bewailing the contest between steam and steel's brute strength and the limitations of nature's elements.

She gorged herself with every morsel she pulled to her gullet. Clattering. Chugging. Large chains clanging loose, then stretching taught, squealing under the load. She smelled of sulfurous burning coal as ash snowed down around her. Steam hissed while she sucked up the gravy of silt, sludge, slush, and sewage.

This was no ordinary beast--this marvel in her day. She was *The Thomas*. Twin sister to *The Mill*.[i]

While her gigantic iron fingers gouged the earth under the surface of the water, a pair of forty-eight inch centrifugal steam dredges with forty-foot suction pipes licked up the bottom of New

York Harbor.

Suddenly her fingers stopped. She slowly began to move. She tugged with all her might, pulling away under the heavy load for the short trip. Her straining gave way to calmness as she quietly pulled forward.

Once she reached her destination, she opened her throat and spewed out silt, sewage, and rock. Then she returned to the hourly cycle of gorging and spewing. Day after day. Six days a week, if not seven--trying just to catch up. Season after season-- the unchanging drone sounds of progress. Year after year, ending the nineteenth and bringing in the twentieth century.

After decades of studies and political wrangling in Congress, in 1898 the United States Army Corp of Engineers had contracted to dredge a new east channel in New York Harbor.

Metropolitan Dredge Company ordered a pair of monstrous steam-driven, sea-going, self-propelled dredges from Maryland Steel, which would do the job for ten cents a ton. They had almost delayed too long.[ii]

MEETS EAST

At the same time *The Thomas* and *The Mill* were chiseling the bottom out of New York Harbor, workers an ocean away laid the keel of another type of monster.

For thousands of years, men have gone to sea. The ships they sail are fickle mistresses taking them away from loved ones in search of fortune, honor, adventure, or a new life. Ships carried mastheads of beautiful women leaning forward into the waves carrying with them the hearts and minds of men. What man could resist following her? Ships have been as varied as are women themselves. *The Thomas* and *The Mill* were frumpy, old busybodies--hard to look at for most men, and real beauties to others.

In early 1868, Thomas Henry Ismay had purchased the trade name, house flag, and goodwill of a bankrupt company for 1,000 pounds sterling, and laid the foundation for the White Star Line of passenger ships. With his death in late 1899, his son Joseph Bruce (J. Bruce) Ismay took the helm of the company.

The ships J. Bruce built were glamorous, graceful queens of the sea. The second of his Big Four, the *RMS Cedric*, had a gross tonnage of 21,073 tons, 71 tons more than her sister-ship the *RMS Celtic*. Just sixteen months after the *Celtic* was launched, the

Cedric followed her into the water. The British Empire was built on their command of the oceans. Her massive ships spoke to their strength. Their opulence and elegance reflecting the rewards that go to an Empire.[iii]

Only cities with the largest docks and deepest harbors could reap the benefits of the lucrative business these massive ships brought. The draft of these monsters (depth to which a vessel is immersed) would have made New York Harbor obsolete had it not been for the dredging done by *The Thomas* and *The Mill*. New York would have been left out.

The world was in headlong pursuit of technology and advancement, but at what cost?

QUEENSTOWN

Of course, all the world's technological advances don't mean much if a man can't feed himself. Fortunately for Rory John Millwood, all navies run on two types of liquid.

The first is salt water.

One year after Thomas Ismay's bold purchase, Rory was born at midday on May 8, 1869 in a small cabin on the banks of Cork Harbour, County Cork, Ireland. His mother had little difficulty during the delivery and was up cooking supper a few hours later. He was the seventh son of John and Mildred Millwood.

Cork Harbour is the world's second largest natural harbor. About a dozen miles from the city closer to sea is the sheltered seaport town of Cobh (pronounced 'KOV' and historically known as 'The Cove of Cork'). Most of his life it had been called 'Queenstown', having been renamed in 1849 to commemorate a visit from Queen Victoria.[iv]

At the time, John had asked, "What has the bitch done for us that we should name our town for her?" (In 1922, when the name was changed back, Rory grumbled, "Just when we were beginning to get used to it, the bastards spend our money again to give it its name back. Bastards.")

The second liquid all navies run on is plentiful, foamy beer and ale.^v

John, worked at the Lady's Well Brewery, mainly as a carpenter. Mildred took in mending and tended to her brood of twelve children. Rory was the eleventh child and the youngest son. If the oldest had survived, he would have been fourteen, having been born shortly before the wedding of John and Mildred.

Over the years, the neighbors heard ruckus, laughter and singing. They also heard cries of anguish as eight of the children died young. The two remaining girls were married off young and moved to Queenstown to start their own broods. The two remaining boys were mischievous and playful in and around their home. Not much was expected of them until they turned seven-- their parents thought too much childhood had been robbed from the eight children they had already lost. They gave the boys' free reign to romp and play.

Rory was small but strong; just right for cleaning brewing equipment. When he was eight, he began doing odd jobs at the brewery. On his first day his father leaned over, brushed his son's cheeks with his hands, held him firmly by his biceps, looked him in the eyes, and told him he had better behave so as to reflect well on him. He was always eager to please his father, so he took the words to heart. He took responsibilities seriously, a trait that served him well his entire life.

Rory had once dreamed of life in the navy, but never enlisted. Instead, he found jobs in and around the docks. Merchants always needed help servicing Her Majesty's Ships. The Royal Navy was slow in paying, but had plenty of work. Making deliveries, collecting materials, and tending to the delights of captains and especially their ladies, were never ending.

By his twentieth birthday, Rory stood five feet, six inches tall and weighed 127 pounds. During the day, Rory dressed in blue denim with light, wool shirts. He looked unshaven most of the time, wore a bushy mustache, and had shaggy, brown hair. He knew how to leverage one merchant against another and how to grease the palm of a revenue agent in favor of his clients.

"So, let me see if I got this right. The chickens cannot be considered livestock, if they are dead. So if I kill them before your very eyes, they won't be covered by the import assessment?"

The revenue agent walked away with two prime plucked and cleaned roosters--one for himself and one for his boss. The merchant walked away with no heavy import tax or fee for his imported chickens. Rory walked away with a fat commission, and everyone walked away smiling--except the chickens.

When the pickings were light with the merchants, there was work on the docks of the Royal Navy which always needed a hand loading and unloading commodities. With all that handling, of course, shrinkage or spoilage fell into Rory's pocket to be later turned into cold cash.

The navy had strict regulations, so finding ways under, around, or through certain requirements brought handsome rewards.

Something always broke and messages had to be delivered to iron suppliers, craftsmen, and merchants. Many a heavily scented letter had to be picked up or delivered to Queenstown's fairest, keeping the flames of passion alive. While passing along notes Rory flirted with the girls, including the one he would soon marry.

The civilian side of port business was more profitable; the military side was more steady. Between the two Rory made his way. Some jobs he picked up around the harbor lasted months and others only days. And at night, Rory worked all his adult life behind the taps at one of Queenstown's taverns. He had an easy manner and liked straight pubs--no gambling and no girls. While he never had girls in the tavern, for a small tip he was happy to procure one for a patron.

When he tended bar, Rory put on a clean white shirt and white apron. He was careful to listen to the scuttlebutt around the bar and turned up more than one opportunity for the next day.[vi]

Nothing was allowed to get out of hand in his tavern and everyone liked a place where a husband could hide out. There were never random fights wheeling out of control, leaving the husband with two things to explain.

When sailors were in town, business was brisk and Rory didn't put up with shenanigans. "One misstep or angry outburst and the little man has them out the door before they knew what hit 'em," bragged O'Rourke to his fellow tavern keepers.

"He knows when a man has had enough and tosses out men three times his size with one hand while taking their companions out with the other. If he really gets angry, he leaves them in a sorry state, I'll tell ya."

The owners approved of his approach.

Δ   Δ   Δ

The Millwood's ancestral home was a small cabin east of Cobh. It was out of sight, in a small grove of trees where rocks and the contour of the land make clearing the land difficult.

Since land was plentiful it was easier to cultivate around the eyesore. The land didn't even belong to them; it belonged to the Lord, who was not aware they were there or he would have demanded their forced removal, on principle. After all, you were not very powerful if you couldn't keep squatters off your property. The farmers who tended the land were keenly aware of the Millwoods reputation for using violence when necessary. If they told the Lord of their existence, they would have been ordered to remove the Millwoods, which would have set them up for a beating. But if they didn't report the Millwoods, things would go on pretty much as they had for generations. They didn't see any good reason to upset the apple cart. It helped that the Millwoods didn't steal much.

This was the first home where Rory, like his forefathers before him, brought his blushing bride, Muirne (pronounced MEER-ne), until he could locate better living quarters. Most stayed for years, a few their whole lives.

She took one look at the place; her eyes narrowed and a scowl came over her face. She didn't say what she was thinking: You want me to live here? The honeymoon that should have been beginning abruptly ended.

Rory had a reputation for judicious use of violence at work. At home, he beat his wife at least twice a week, when he came home from the tavern and awakened her with his fists. Always drunk, he apologized the next morning.

At the end of the night working at the tavern, he locked up, donned his Irish cap, and slowly walked home smoking his pipe. If he weren't beating her, he snuggled with his wife and fell fast asleep, to get up early the next morning. It was amazing he fathered any children.

Δ   Δ   Δ

"Ting" went the lock as Rory carefully opened the door as quietly as possible.

"You're late," screamed Mr. O'Rourke every day as he heard Rory quietly close the back door. Rory was not late; he was never late. But after O'Rourke made the comment a few dozen times early in his employment, Rory expected it.

"I'll be there in a minute," said Rory in reply as he opened the cabinet door. It was hinged in such a way that Rory could change his shirt, while any patron's view was blocked.

He removed the shirt he had worn all day on the docks, wiped perspiration from his armpits with it, and threw it into the bottom of the cabinet. Rory put on a fresh white shirt, tied the tie into a bow, pulled up his sleeves, and slipped on sleeve garters. The garters were not in fashion, but Rory didn't care--he wore them anyway. Rory had gotten them from a friend who had seen them in San Francisco.

Then he checked the two main doors to the tavern and made sure the right door wasn't locked. Each heavy, oak door contained a pane of frosted glass, which Rory had once broken. A patron had insulted a regular and Rory grabbed him by the shirt collar and right arm to assist him out the door. In his haste, he had failed to notice the door was locked and pushed the man's head through the window.

O'Rourke was amused, but still deducted the windowpane from Rory's pay at an exorbitant price. The following day, Rory had his father adjust the lock so it locked securely, but when it was unlocked, it could be pushed to open freely. Never again did he pay for a replacement window.

O'Rourke always deducted broken glasses and steins from Rory's pay--even glasses O'Rourke had broken himself. Rory concluded the only way he could ever break even was to sample the inventory, which he did after O'Rourke went home. Even decades later, when O'Rourke's grandson, Roger, watched Rory fall to the ground, he announced, "I'm gonna have to take the cost of those three steins out of your pay." It was a good two minutes before he realized Rory hadn't simply stumbled. He was dead of a massive heart attack.

O'Rourke owned the tavern and tended to it during the light daytime traffic. He opened whenever he happened to arrive, which could be anywhere between eight and four. Most days he arrived before lunch and his wife dutifully delivered his hot dinner, leaving quickly, since women were not permitted in his establishment.

One Saturday afternoon, O'Rourke's wife struggled to push open the door to the tavern. Using her apron to protect her hands from the heat, she carried a glass pie plate, piping hot, piled high with thick, dark lamb stew. She had underestimated its weight and her endurance and found herself at the door to the tavern, unable to open the door and unable to spot anyone who might help. "Oh my."

She ended up standing on one foot, while awkwardly kicking at the door with the other. Rory heard her scratches and came to the rescue.

He welcomed her in and she sheepishly looked around the room for her husband. "I'm looking for O'Rourke."

"Over at the last table." He was where he always was when Rory was behind the bar. While he watched her deliver the plate, he thought how odd it was that even she referred to him as O'Rourke.

She quickly finished. There were no pleasantries or "thank you" from her husband. As she turned to leave, Rory motioned for her to come over. She looked back at O'Rourke, as if to see if she needed his permission, but he was lost in concentration devouring his dinner.

Rory whispered, "What is his first name?"

"His what?"

"O'Rourke's first name. What is it?"

She stood there with a blank stare. It was as if he had shined a lantern into a deer's eyes. She blinked several times before the answer dawned on her. "It's Ruaidhri Tomás O'Rourke." She went on to slowly pronounce his full name--"ROO a ree. tuh MAWS. OH ROAR ark." She went on to explain, nobody had ever called him by anything other than his last name. Nobody. Ever. The family tradition had been to trade the first and middle name for each successive generations first born male child, first 'Ruaidhri Tomás', then 'Tomás Ruaidhri'. It may have been that way for the last two thousand years, for all she knew. In future generations, the tradition would continue to the present, but be Anglicized-- first, 'Roger Thomas', then 'Thomas Roger'.

The one room tavern had large arched windows on three sides of the building. It was dimly lit by gas lanterns. All the glass above eye level was clear and glass at eye level was frosted. There was a stove in the corner, which O'Rourke was too cheap to supply with wood, and a place for a piano, which was never ordered. Rory kept the pine floor well swept. Though instructed to sweep after closing, Rory did it each evening shortly after O'Rourke left. He faithfully wet mopped once a week.

Rory had gotten spittoons from a traveling salesman, which advertised the salesman's wares, and insisted the patrons use them instead of the floor. His regulars faithfully obeyed Rory's rule, but since he wasn't there to enforce his edict during the day and O'Rourke did not care if you spat on the floor, the unfinished pine was stained with tobacco juice.

Rory waltzed by the three tables to see if anyone needed anything and collected many orders, as O'Rourke was never attentive to his customers. Each table had four captain's chairs. Most of the men were merchants and he knew what they liked without asking--another "Murphy's".

"As soon as Rory comes in, you won't see O'Rourke lift a finger around here, even if the place were on fire," Kelley noted. When Rory got behind the bar to fill orders, O'Rourke was done for the day.

The bar itself was about a dozen feet long, with a brass foot rail. On any given day, there were four sailors standing at it when Rory arrived. Most likely they were off their ships conducting official Royal Navy business. Contrary to written rules which stated they were not to drink when off ships for business, they managed to slip into one of the taverns before returning to the shuttle boat. The plum assignment always included the bonus of a quiet stop for a brew. No captain ever reprimanded a man for coming back later than he should and few abused the privilege.

There were a half dozen white towels hanging on brass rings. Behind the bar were a large mirror and a few shelves where the hard liquor was displayed. The mounted head of a single pig hung above the mirror. Nobody remembered how it had gotten there, who had placed it there, or why.

Whenever a sailor showed signs of too many brews Rory, smiling the whole time, grabbed his hat, coat, and official Government pouch for him, and had the man thanking him and out the door before he knew what hit him. After a few seconds standing outside in the light rain, his coat, hat, and pouch in his arms, one sailor shrugged and stumbled toward the docks, saying, "I will have to remember the place where I was treated so kindly."

O'Rourke sat in his chair with his hands on his arms approving of his lucky find. "Rory is a good man. I'll have to give him a raise." Of course that never happened until he heard from his competitor what the going rate was.

"Cock an' 'en shillings a week!," quipped Mr. McCormick, O'Rourke's nearest competitor. "Yer are such a cheap langer! Oi pay Shorty twelve for doin' 'alf av waaat Rory does! Oi aught ter 'ire 'imself meself, yer dumb arse!"

"Thanks for the Murphy's!"

"Any time. Clap yer next week."

O'Rourke walked back to his tavern while deep in thought. He came through the double doors and slowly walked straight up to the bar where Rory was polishing a beer stein. "Might I have a word with ya, Rory?"

He whispered into Rory's ear and Rory's eyes lit up.

"Twelve shillings! Thank you, Sir!"

Shortly after 9 p.m., O'Rourke stood, yawned, stretched, and said, as he did every night, "Ya won't mind locking up, will ya?"

Rory replied, "Not at all," as if a great trust had been laid at his feet.

Before O'Rourke was out the door, Rory had the broom in his hands. "Move your feet" and "Get out of the way," he ordered. There was less talking and less drinking as the evening waned. Patrons slowly filed out over the next few hours.

Rory stood behind the bar, washing up the last of the steins and glasses when the last two said "Goodnight" and left.

Almost before the door swung shut, Rory turned off the lanterns and put the key in the door. He took off his sleeve garters, tie, and apron and placed them in the cabinet, took the old shirt from the bottom of the cabinet, and grabbed his coat and hat. He took one last look at the place, saw a warm, friendly joint, stepped out and locked the door. He always checked the door one last time.

Most nights it was black as pitch. The rain had stopped and the clouds had blown away to the east. His eyes adjusted and he saw bright stars for as far as the eye could see. The Milky Way bloomed overhead. Stars waved in the breeze. It was colder than usual for springtime. Rory pulled his collar up on his coat and reached for his pipe. It was the first time he smoked it all day.

He couldn't see clearly where he was going, but he could tell by the surface: cobblestone, then gravel, then dirt. He had walked the same path home for the last two years. The dogs barked while wagging their tails as he went by. He caught flashes of their tails in the dim glow of his pipe, but he really couldn't make them out. But they could see him. He gave them a nod, and they quieted down.

Rory quietly entered the cabin and lit a candle. His daughter was in her mama's arms asleep on their bed. He dropped his clothing on the floor, blew out the candle, and slipped naked into bed behind his wife.

REVENUE AGENT

His chair slammed back onto the floor, "Like hell you will!"

"What? What did I say?"

"I know what yer tryin' tado!"

"I merely suggested Rory might want to consider applying for the new revenue officer position."

"What are you trying to do, steal me best man?," O'Rourke said, being very protective of his prized but underpaid asset. In fact, Rory was O'Rourke's only man.

Kelley whispered to Rory, "Why don't ya get your own place, Rory? By the way you take care of it, most people think the place is yours already. You do everything--ordering, sweeping, mopping, handling cash and glassware. What the hell do you need O'Rourke for? He doesn't do nothin'. O'Rourke can become your second best customer. Unlike me, he might even pay you for his beer." Kelley laughed.

Rory just turned his head and said, "Mr. O'Rourke, you know I would never leave you."

Rumors have always been rampant in the Navy and the smaller the bit of information the greater the need for man's imagination to fill in the details. Ideas have to be considered, weighed, exchanged, adapted, denied, speculated upon, and refined. Like a stone tumbling down a river, it becomes a new creation--clean and smooth with the rough edges removed.

The rumor of an additional revenue agent was just that--a rumor. But frequently a rumor is the catalyst to consider an issue. The rumor of adding an additional agent spawned the thought of splitting the Cork Revenue Office between North and South operations. As ships became larger, it seemed more captains desired to anchor at White Point or Rushbrooke, rather than take the west passage around the Great Island in Cork Harbour north to Cork. The authorities would see patterns that did not exist and justifications that were not there, in order to draw a conclusion about what they did not know, because it seemed to align with what they wanted.

Man doesn't bat an eye later in coming to the exact opposite conclusion as before from the same facts and data. However, these things take time to maturate, and the rumors that circulated at O'Rourke's Tavern that night spawned a great deal of excitement, even if they were at this point, baseless.

"I have never thought of being a Revenue Agent," lied Rory.

"You're good with numbers," said Mac. Mac and Kelley were regulars at O'Rourke's and Rory's favorite allies.

"You stay out of this!" grumbled O'Rourke, still scared.

"WhatdidIsay?" replied Mac indignantly.

Rory had considered this new position as the ideal way to steal more than his current day jobs allowed. He had dealt with enough revenue agents to know their games and ploys. He knew he would be good at it.

"Well, you've got a good memory," replied Kelley.

"What's that gotta do with anything?" snorted O'Rourke.

"I think you need to have a good memory to be a revenue agent--ya know, to do things the same way each time."

"You mean to keep your lies straight," observed O'Rourke.

"Bull. You just gotta be able to read. Aye."

Rory kept quiet. He could not read a lick.

"--and write."

"Shit, whatahyatalkingbout? You make it sound like he's gotta be the second coming of Jonathan Swift!"

"No, you just got to fill out all the damn-blasted forms the government requires."

"Hey, and you're good with figures. You always know to the penny how much of a tab I got--," said Kelley, realizing then he was bringing up a sore subject. He shifted his eyes over to O'Rourke who had been deep in thought at the loss of Rory and had not caught the admission.

"You just need to study the Revenue Books. All the revenue agents carry with them three volumes with charts of assessments and conditions."

"I guess you could borrow one," said Mac, realizing as the words escaped his mouth that that would be impossible. No revenue agent kept multiple copies, nor could one possibly part-- even temporarily--with even one of the volumes. Agents were purveyors of highly prized information. Widespread knowledge of the actual regulations would cause a cancer of distrust to grow. There would be claims of prejudice and demands for a court of higher appeal to dispute the agents' edicts. The process would sputter and stall.

There was a long silence as the machinery of men's minds ground to a halt.

"I'll get you one," said one of the sailors who had been listening in.

"How the hell are you going to do that?"

The obstacle seemed too large, and yet here a sailor in the Navy, who did not interact with any revenue agent, who never dealt with merchant ships, claimed he could find a copy.

The discussion continued for three more days before the sailor plunked volume one of the Regulations down on the bar.

"How the hell--"

"Actually, I asked one of the agents to explain the finer point of definition concerning Egyptian hemp used for rope. I went on to ask more details about the rope, and he finally pulled out this volume to show me for myself the definition. I scrutinized the text for a while, while he elaborated. At last, I thanked him profusely for clearing up my mind on the situation, making it a point distinctly to hand him back the book. Then I complemented him on his mastery of his craft, the credit he was to his profession, how the Queen was blessed to have a servant of such high moral character, and on being such a wise observer. While he was basking in the glow of his self worth, I took the book back from him, wished him a grand day, and walked off."

Hours later, the agent was scrambling to locate the volume that the sailor had so definitely returned to him, while the sailor had free beer the rest of his days, Rory had his study guide and O'Rourke was none the wiser.

Over the months, the book lay open on the bar and Rory studied along as he worked. Of course, the biggest problem was that he didn't know how to read, but he stumbled along, asking merchants about certain words and sounding out others. Mostly he memorized what he could sound out.

One day, Rory asked the same sailor if he could get him another volume. This time, instead of sleight of hand, he stole the remaining two volumes.

From then on, when that sailor brought in his friends, they also got free beer, Rory had a complete set of study guides and O'Rourke was still none the wiser.

About the time Rory had complete command of the regulations, the Cork district officials announced the port was being broken into two. A new revenue office was opening in Queenstown, for which there would be the need for an additional agent. Any man who could read, write and fill out the application could take the oral examination. The specific date, time, and place were yet to be determined.

Δ   Δ   Δ

A week later, Kelley wandered into O'Rourke's Tavern and slapped down the official Department of Finance application onto the bar. Now Rory had a dilemma, as he had not confessed his illiteracy yet. Even though he had spent months stumbling his way through the regulations, he couldn't see how he would slide through this final hurdle. Nevertheless, Kelley had free beer for a month, Rory had an application and O'Rourke was again none the wiser.

With the assistance of a number of regulars who were all merchants in Queenstown, Rory carefully filled out the application with his neatest handwriting and took the form by hand to the Finance Office in Cork. A few days later, a supervising revenue officer arrived in Queenstown to scout locations for conducting the meetings and oral examinations required for the hiring process. Someone asked the agent to give him a better understanding of his requirements while escorting him to O'Rourke's Tavern. The ale and beer flowed freely.

Senior Finance Agent Mr. Sean Shanahan answered someone's question, "Well, an oral examination, is just questions and answers."

"Do ya make them up aheada time?"

"There are questions we are to ask to ascertain the candidate's abilities, but I have latitude to ask questions on my own."

"So you go by the book?"

"Well, I think through what to ask."

"So you use questions by some jerk, stool jockey who doesn't know crap about nothin' or do you apply your own real world experience and wisdom in asking your questions."

Shanahan took the bait, "I believe it is important to have the candidate satisfy questions based on my experience."

"So, give us an example?"

"Well, let me think. If someone was importing ceramic bowls from Spain, what would the assessment be?"

"Why should you assume it's from Spain?," Rory chimed in for the first time.

"What, I mean the ship has just arrived from Spain."

Rory continued, "Well, Portuguese ceramics get a higher assessment than Spain. So I would ask them to prove the ceramics are in fact from Spain, or I would tell them they appear to be Portuguese to me and assess them accordingly."

The supervising agent was astounded. He had never thought of that swindle before.

"Try another."

"Let me think."

Rory poured him another ale.

Shanahan continued, "Well, fish eggs arrive from Russia in a--"

"Sturgeon?"

"What?"

"I asked if they were sturgeon."

"Well, I ah, let me think--certainly, yes, why?"

"Fertilized?"

"What difference in the world would--"

Rory interrupted, "Caviar comes with a very high assessment value, whereas fish eggs for other uses, such as fertilizer--"

Shanahan's eyes lit up!

The evening continued with questions and ale and answers and ale, until the wee hours, when Rory suggested Shanahan could conduct his interviews exactly at the table where he was sitting. He was certain O'Rourke would find it his patriotic duty to provide all necessary refreshments for this important government responsibility and even waive the cash rental payment allowance his office had given Shanahan.

The following evening, Kelley asked Rory, "What questions are ya expecting and when will ya have his exam?"

"I think I took it last night."

The next few days' steady streams of applicants were summoned for the job interview of revenue agent at the most unlikely place, O'Rourke's Tavern. Each interview started out with the same two questions: One about Russian fish eggs and the other about Spanish ceramics. Most applicants couldn't answer either question and were easily dismissed. In the end, there were only two applicants left. One was the bright son of a revenue agent, a colleague of Sean Shanahan. The other was Rory Millwood.

"How do you know so much about revenue agents?" Shanahan was really probing to find out if Rory knew the unwritten rules.

"I've worked the docks all my life and seen plenty of negotiations between captains and merchants and agents. I have noticed things can come to a mutually satisfactory conclusion when one side gives in on one thing and the other side gives in on a pair of things!"

Shanahan thought, Voilà--he gets it! The agent gives up one definition in trade for the other party giving up a pair of things-- one for the agent and one for his boss!

Still Shanahan stewed and stewed upon this grave decision. How was he going to tell his friend he had chosen Rory over his son? Most of the stewing took place while he was getting stewed at O'Rourke's Tavern. A week went by and he was no closer to deciding than he had been before.

Rory was starting to worry.

Δ   Δ   Δ

"I need to decide soon. The office is to open on Thursday."

Kelley overheard the comment and whispered to Rory.

"Aye. And I know where to find him. Take over, will ya?"

Kelley came behind the bar while Rory left abruptly. An hour later, Rory quietly came through the back door to change out of his bloody shirt.

The next evening, Shanahan walked in to O'Rourke's Tavern. He was very cheery. "I have a most distressing report today. One of my candidates had to withdraw. He seems to have had a most tragic accident and both legs are broken. His father withdrew his son's application with the sad news he would have to take his name out of consideration until his legs heal."

Shanahan went on, "I told him that was most difficult, as he was one of my two top candidates. Perhaps he would consider applying with the next vacancy. He was most excited to hear my suggestion and apologized to me for this carelessness on his son's part that was unlike his typical demeanor."

Shanahan sat quite contented with himself, drinking ale late into the night. He had been considering setting up 'The Ireland Department of Finance, Revenue Agency, Cork District, Queenstown Subdivision Office, Queenstown, County Cork, Ireland' at O'Rourke's Tavern, but was dissuaded by his boss. He suggested the bank in town would be more appropriate.

When only Rory and Mr. Shanahan were left, Shanahan made his announcement.

"Mr. Millwood, I have been appointed to head the Queenstown Office. We will be located at the bank. I believe you are the ideal man for the position. I would like you to come work for me."

Rory feigned surprise, "You want me to be a revenue agent?"

"Yes, I would."

They went on to discuss hours of operation so as not to interfere with his current position at O'Rourke's, required attire and the like, and he offered Rory twice what he had expected for a salary.

"Thank you, Mr. Shanahan for the confidence you have seen in me. I accept your offer."

Rory walked home that evening without a care in the world. "To think I will be making this fabulous salary and be able to steal ten times as much."

Rory quietly entered the cabin and lit a candle. His children were asleep in their own bed.

He dropped his clothing on the floor, blew out the candle, slipped naked into bed and cuddled up to his wife. He noticed something was not quite as usual. Her nightgown was bunched up to her waist. His pulse quickened as he reached down under the covers. Her buttocks were bare as he suspected. He whispered in her ear as her smile broadened, "Aye, this truly is me lucky day."

Δ   Δ   Δ

Once he started the revenue agent job, with Sean Shanahan as his boss, Rory began to change. The first thing anyone noticed was a lot more revenue was being collected. That wasn't to say all of it was being turned in.

The second was also a big one--he became father to his first son. On March 14, 1890, ten months to the day after starting the revenue agent job, Muirne gave birth to a baby boy, to the squealing delight of their two young daughters. He was named 'Rory John Millwood, Junior' and he was known as Junior (or Mill) the rest of his days.

Rory and Sean agreed to a dress code. Rory got regular haircuts, kept his hair on the short side and began wearing a beard, which turned over time into large mutton chops that joined to his mustache.

Learning the revenue books had inspired him to learn to read better and Rory began bringing home books. He asked people for recommendations and took any books offered. He didn't struggle long with any he found too difficult before placing them on the shelf. Those he could read without too much frustration, he took with him for slack times in the office, and they were frequently found open at O'Rourke's.

After starting in the new position, he took a lunch break and often brought in dinner when he came to work in the tavern. He drank more as well, sensing O'Rourke would never fire him. Rory put on weight--lots of weight. He wore larger, more stylish dress shirts and nicer slacks at the tavern.

Rory either went to work very early in the morning or very late, depending on when ships needed to be processed. If he did not have ships early in the day, he sat and read over coffee or tea following breakfast. Many mornings he spent a few minutes teaching his wife to read. This turned into the most pleasant part of the day. She not only learned to read, she memorized each lesson (which book he had used, which page numbers he had her read) and in future years she taught each of her children.

Rory saw himself as more important and expected others to see him in the same way. Even when he bartended, which he really did not need to do any longer, he was more reserved and set down the expectation that his infant son follow his example. After all, he was making Mr. Shanahan (and himself) wealthy. The least he expected was a position for his son when he came of age. He had found the key to success, and, come hell or high water, his sons would follow in his footsteps.

Δ   Δ   Δ

Rory smiled and sympathized with his patrons on the hardness of life as he pulled the tap or poured a shot, always ready to serve his guests. Friendly, with a chipper, "What will you have, mate?" and "So how was your day?"

"I'll tell ya, I got screwed today!"

"Oh, how's that?"

"We got into port this morning, and I had to wait three hours before getting permission to unload."

"Three hours!"

"Bastard revenue agent was taking his sweet-ass time."

"Is that so?"

"Yeah. Prick came in as if he owned the port. Demanding this paper and that. My Gosh, you'd think the money he was collecting was his own."

"Is that a fact?"

"Spouting this rule and that regulation."

"I hear they can be bastards alright."

"You know it."

"So what happened next?"

"Well, he got through his inspection and asked for more papers, which I didn't want to show him, but he insisted. Could have made me stand there three weeks if I had not gone to get them. Then he taxed me for twice what I had expected, spouting this rule and that."

"Is that a fact?"

"Bastards."

"Yes they are. I don't know one of them that would leave me a tip."

"Well, I got even; because he didn't see a few things I had hidden, so I made out alright."

"Good for you! Have another beer?"

At the end of the evening the patron left having blown off some steam, leaving Rory with a big tip and never realizing Rory was the agent he had dealt with earlier that day. On the next trip into port, Rory would look for the contraband he had mentioned.

He taught Mr. Shanahan it was not how much your salary was that made you rich. If you have no expenses, you can do well for yourself. No discussion with a shipping agent was complete until the personal benefit to Misters Shanahan and Millwood was clearly understood. Mentioning specifics was dangerous, but walking away with a few chickens, eggs, milk, clothing, or tobacco went a long way toward determining a lower assessment. The art was to make sure the assessments were high enough, so that once reduced they didn't spark alarm at the Department of Finance.

Rory's command of the regulations was superb and he played the game well. So well, in fact, the main office became concerned. The "revenue per agent" clearly showed the two men were being overworked. The higher-ups demanded to know what additional assistance they could provide.

Rory thought for a moment and decided accounting assistance would help. After a clerk was brought in to handle the checking and cash transactions with the bank and all associated paperwork, it eliminated three hours of work per man each day. The other impact was that this required cuts be split among three men, instead of two. Hard-wall offices without windows were then also needed, so nobody would observe Misters Shanahan and Millwood asleep at their desks, having worked less than five hours per day.

Rory did not see anything wrong with stealing. As a revenue officer, he observed the government stealing all the time. He was being rewarded for applying rules in unique ways--making up taxes, fees, and such. There was little a merchant could say, and as long as costs could be passed along to the supplier, why should he care? The intermediary showed value as he minimized the taxes due, and who was to say what was truly due?

Δ   Δ   Δ

After a late evening at the tavern, Rory quietly entered his new home. His children were asleep, and unlike most nights, none had fallen asleep in their mama's arms.

He dropped his clothing on the floor and slipped naked into bed behind his wife. She stirred momentarily, smiled at his warm body against her back instead of being awakened to a beating, and quickly fell back to sleep.

He drifted off, exhausted from being on his feet all day.

Rory soared in the clouds above Cork Harbor, wearing a tuxedo, starched white shirt, black bow tie, golden cummerbund, black silk top hat, and carrying a black cane with gold trim. He wore spats on his highly-polished black leather shoes. He was looking down upon the merchant ships. One after another, parades of ships swam into the harbor. For as far as his eyes could see, a steady stream of ships, closely spaced, pulled toward him. He could see bags filled with gold piled high on their decks.

He continued to float above the ships, clouds, and birds. He looked down to see an army of his assistants walking from ship to ship picking up ten bags of gold from each. They took eight bags of gold to the customs office, kept one for themselves, and dropped one bag off at a special office. He looked at the door and it was marked: Rory John Millwood, Sr., Esq., Inspector General,

Revenue Office, Cork Harbour.

He swooped down to enter his office, which overlooked the harbor. Through a large window he saw a steady stream of ships pulling into the harbor and an ever-steadier stream of junior revenue agents, dressed in tuxedos, walking briskly with two remaining bags of gold in their hands, each dropped off one bag in his anteroom.

He saw Junior, also in a tiny tuxedo and a diaper, crawl on the moneybags, squealing in delight.

MOIRA & JUNIOR

One morning, Rory announced to his wife, "I'm tired of this small cabin. A man of my position should have a proper home."

Rory had not considered the additional expense renting a house in town would entail.

"You want how much?"

Despite the surprise, he had already set the wheels in motion with his wife, and he figured he couldn't reverse his decision without showing weakness.

Once they moved into town, he became suspicious of the men who lived nearby, who tipped their hats and said hello to his wife. He figured nothing good would come from that which a few beatings wouldn't prevent. He ignored her cries of innocence. He was not punishing her for what she had done--he was preventing it.

They rented and saved enough money to buy a house for cash. In late 1894, they moved a few streets to the east to their own home. Rory loved owning floors beneath his feet.

Even before the second move, Junior had met Moira. Moira, three years younger than Junior, was a wisp of a girl with pale skin and eyes so large and dark brown, you could hardly tell where the irises stopped and the pupils began. They spent leisurely days playing with their friends near the water. The bay was well protected and there was always one of the neighbor women outside to watch over them and break up their squabbles.

By the time Junior was six, most of his playmates went off to work and others to Catholic school. Junior and Moira did neither. Their families allowed them a bit longer to remain children.

Over the next few years, when the school children joined them after class, Junior and Moira would slip off by themselves hearing chants--"There go the lovers", "K-I-S-S-I-N-G", and "Juniors Got A Girlfriend." They were immune to the taunts, mainly because the kids were just stating the obvious, what was to be embarrassed about that? They slipped out of their clothing and into the cool waters of the bay.

Junior taught Moira how to swim. "It's easy. Trust me." She lay on her stomach on the surface of the water, being held up on his arms. "Kick!" He showed her how to point her feet back and kick each leg in rhythm up and down, opposite each other. He taught her how to extend her arms forward and pull herself through the water. She choked and sputtered until he showed her how to roll her head up to get a gulp of air. He tossed her out away from him and she swam back. Soon they were running together to take a big jump into the water and swim back to shore. They swam until twilight, dressed and went to their homes, tired and happy. Junior was a natural swimmer--it was one of his favorite activities.

One of the boys teased Moira when she was about seven, and learned a painful lesson. Like his father, Junior was never afraid to take on boys three times his size. He learned early that a bloody nose put an opponent on the defensive quickly, and the best way to accomplish this was to get close enough to do damage before the opponent was aware you were there.

Only once had he taken a full swing at another boy. He had been close to a fence, and when the other boy ducked he had fractured the little finger on his left hand. He masked the pain by going home, lying on a bed, and biting a pillow. At supper that evening, he didn't mention the injury and acted as if nothing had happened. The swelling went down, the pain disappeared in a few days, and the finger healed with a distortion to the knuckle.

"Stay away from that slut!" barked Rory when Junior entered his teen years. "She is no good for you. Whatdoya think will come of this?"

Junior remained silent.

"You're becoming a man now. Put away the things of a child. You need to be working. By the time I was your age, I had been working for five years."

Junior was devastated. He thought to himself, how could he not see we were meant for each other?

"Do you know what her ma is?" Rory boomed. "What do you think you are doing?"

Night after night, Rory badgered Junior. "She could be my daughter, don't ya know?," Rory lied. "I have known a slut or two in my time. They are nothing but trouble."

"I am an important man of the community. I know it is just puppy love, but you need to stay away from her. You need to grow up to fill my shoes. You won't do that by carrying on with that slut."

Rory resolved to resist Papa's orders with every barb and insult.

By the time he was fourteen, Junior was hearing, "Find a girl of your own race. The slut is a Catholic. How can you bear to be with her?"

Over time, Junior learned to tune out the taunts.

"You're not listening to me, boy! I am gonna smack you twelve ways to Sunday!" Rory slurred after an evening at the Tavern. He had woken him up to insult him about his behavior.

At least when he is screaming at me, he isn't beating Ma, Junior thought.

"Go ahead, ruin your life! I am an important man in the community. You need to follow my example. Son, I will teach you to read and write and you can become my assistant. You'll become just like me."

Junior could not think of any reason he would ever want to become like his Pa, who could never love the way he loved. Perhaps he saw a man who could never love at all.

At hearing of the way Junior was verbally assaulted by Rory, Moira wanted to release her sweetheart from his pain.

Δ   Δ   Δ

"Maybe he is right. Maybe we shouldn't be together."

"He's not. Don't ya think God made us to be together?"

"All I know is that I cannot stop thinking about you. I see you everywhere I go. I can't think of being without you."

Junior remembered the latest blast from his father: Rory had screamed, "Get work, you bastard. Who raised you to be so lazy? Do you see me skipping work? Do you see me talking all day? All you do is eat and play. You're probably fucking that slut every day."

Junior was devastated. Moira was the sweetest girl he knew. To violate her would be unforgivable. Not until they were married. He could wait.

"What can I give you to show you my love?" Junior asked.

Moira didn't know what to say.

Moira's mother, Anne, was a barmaid in Queenstown. She was five feet, four inches tall and 100 pounds. Her hair seemed always dirty and unkempt. Small, meek, quiet, but with a great wit—-she shocked patrons whenever she would burst in with a comment at the bar. More than one sailor sat at the bar thinking he could have her if he wanted, by force if she resisted. She would never be able to pick out Moira's father in the sea of sailors she had served.

In one evening of loneliness and weakness, she had given in to an insistent sailor. He was gone before morning, never to be recognized again. He had probably been back through that port, but hadn't remembered the saloon with the young barmaid he nearly raped. That he might have fathered a child never crossed his mind.

When Anne had found herself pregnant she felt lonelier than she had before. She didn't know how she would have made it without the few neighbors who were loving, patient, and understanding. Once her precious daughter was born, Anne did not regret the minutes when passion swept her childhood away. She knew the price she would have to pay. But she also knew God would help her. He had to. God is a God of mercy and love and forgiveness. He would see her through. How could she ever give the baby away or seek someone out to kill the new life stirring in her womb?

Moira grew up to be the spitting image of her mother. They could have been sisters.

Anne worked hard as a barmaid, seamstress, and cleaner to

provide for herself and her daughter. She and Moira lived on the east end of Queenstown, further east from the Millwoods, but close enough to be in the same collection of kids.

When it was her turn to watch the children play, she noticed Moira and Junior were always together. It seemed they were just infants the first time she had seen it. Over time, Junior took on the role of protector. Anne saw Junior's tender touch and gentle manner with Moira as a blessing and a matchless gift.

Anne grew to love Junior as if she were his own mother. She was happy her daughter and Junior were together. She saw something she would never experience herself, a genuine love between them beyond their ages. There was a purity and sacredness to it. She noticed Moira's love for Junior by the tilt of her head as she paid attention to him as if she were hanging on every word.

Δ   Δ   Δ

During the dead of winter, when the water and air temperatures would both stand near 45°, and their friends were sitting by a cozy fire, they still went to the bay--so happy to be together, they hardly noticed the cold.

When they were young, the ships and boats paid them no mind. As they grew older, they attracted greater attention. As teenagers, they still slipped away naked into the summer waters. The light breeze and heavy boat traffic kicked up breakers on the shore of the harbor. Once when she had developed, he stood in a few feet of water looking at her. For the first time, he noticed her well-formed, full breasts and erect nipples. He saw the sweep of her waist and her delicate shoulders. He felt a love for her in a new and different way--he had never known this feeling before. He felt himself become erect and for the first time, was embarrassed and surprised. That only happened to him when he woke up in the morning. What was wrong? He slipped into the deeper waters and turned away to watch the ships.

She sensed something was wrong and swam up behind him. She hugged him from behind to console him, not recognizing the increased effect her breasts pressed into his back was having. He told her everything was wonderful, but she did not believe him. She pressed her questioning further, and he became quiet and still. Finally, she became quiet and slowly left the water. He stayed a few minutes longer, quiet, and motionless. Thinking.

As they swam every day among increasing hoots and hollers by the boisterous sailors, there were yells of "Hey, beautiful, whatyadoin'there?" and "You can swim with me any time!" They may not have noticed, but Rory heard of it.

"You have been with that girl again, boy?"

Junior startled awake.

"Idiot. Don't ya know what you're throwing away?," Rory barked in a drunken slur. "I have plans for you."

Junior sat up in bed.

"Was that you swimming naked with a girl the whole harbor is singing about?"

Junior looked down, but did not speak.

"I guess you're just not working enough. Me? I work two jobs to feed you, ya little bastard. You're gonna get that poor slut pregnant and then where will you be? The three of you will starve to death, because you are lazy."

Junior was a good, solid, quiet worker. In addition to his chores, he worked in town, usually odd jobs. Economic times were tough and many a man was looking for work and willing to take just about anything to feed his family. Even odd jobs were hard to come by.

Many nights, when Rory got home generally around midnight, the barrage of insults would begin. Sometimes, Junior would be asleep, but usually he was either already awake or awoken by Papa's entrance.

"You're no good, you little prick. You are probably not me own son. I never thought she would cheat on me, but I am looking at living proof."

Junior's mama stood by unable to help and dare not say a word. But Rory had crossed the line. In an instant, Junior caught his father in the throat with both fists and drove hard. Rory, taken my surprise in his drunken state, was slammed to the ground. He lay there stunned among the knocked over furniture.

Junior packed his things. "Mama, I'll be back soon, but I cannot be here now." He kissed her on the cheek.

He trotted off to Moira.

BITTERNESS

"You know you can't marry her. She is my daughter by blood. Her mother gave it out at the tavern for free," Rory lied in his drunken slur.

Junior remained silent, once again trying to ignore the insults.

"I got it all laid out for you. You need to learn to read and write better. When you turn eighteen, Sean is all set to make you a junior revenue agent. You will be an important man, just like me. Then you can think about marriage. Until then start thinking with your brains instead of your pecker."

Sean owed Rory innumerable favors. It was just about finding the right time to collect.

"The Millwoods have been trying to get a leg up for generations and now that I have succeeded, you need to join in. Take advantage of what I have built. Generations of Millwoods can live off my coattails now, provided you don't screw up a good thing. Follow in my footsteps. Be like me."

Each time he heard Papa say, "Be like me", he was reminded to never let that happen.

Junior startled awake to the sound of the door closing. Sitting up in bed and looking outside, he spotted his papa briskly walking away from the house. The first rays of the sun reflected on a cloud to the west, so early the birds were not yet chirping. The cloud was so brilliant white at first he thought it was the moon. He scanned the room to see his brothers and sisters sound asleep in two small beds. Their threadbare blankets were pulled tightly to their throats. None of them stirred. He turned back to watch papa disappear from sight and then let go of the old cloth used as a curtain. He linked his hands together behind his head as he lay back down.

He wondered, why is my papa different? He tried to think of any other man who worked every day. Shops he swept out for a few coins didn't stay open every day--their owners took Sunday off and most took off half day on Saturday. His uncles didn't work every day. Men in the neighborhood didn't either. His did. Seven days a week he worked--he never missed a day. The Church frowns on staying open on Sundays, but Papa goes to work.

Junior thought about other men who took their families to Church on Sunday and spent their afternoons picnicking, fishing, boating, and resting. Couldn't he take us boating, just once?

Of course men worked long hours, but they still made time to be with their families. Why not my papa?

Junior thought, he brings things home at night. Things he has gotten. No, things he has stolen. He's proud when he steals things. Proud he has gotten away with something. He struts around like a peacock with his treasures, "I brought you a prime rooster this time to feed the little bastards."

Mother was never happy about what he brought home. Rory called them "a benefit of my position." She told us never to steal. She cooked the rooster for our dinner, of course, but she didn't have to like it.

Junior looked around the room. His brothers and sisters hardly moved. The room was a patchwork quilt of faded, worn blankets, rising and falling with their silent breathing. A gray kitten nested in his sister's arms.

When Junior was young, he lay in bed listening to his parents argue late at night.

"He was one sorry Captain when I got through with his assessment." Rory laughed.

"But, Rory--"

"You said you wanted chairs."

"No, Rory. Don't you see this is wrong?"

Not listening to her comment he said, "He gave me these two chairs to bring home to you."

"You mean you made him give you the chairs."

In his drunken state, it took him a few seconds to realize what she had said. He slapped her hard across the face. "Don't you tell me what is wrong!"

Junior had looked around the room. His sisters eyes were wide open. He quietly jumped down to the floor to peek under the door.

"How do I explain this to our children?"

"Tell them I bought them for you."

"I won't lie."

He grabbed her by the arm. "Listen, bitch. How I provide for my family is my business. You tell them whateverthefeck you want."

"How can I teach them not to steal, if--"

"I don't steal,--"

"You're hurting me."

"--I trade."

"Trading for something you don't own, to get something you want is the same as stealing."

He slapped her again with the back of his hand. "I didn't make him do anything he didn't want to do."

"He had no choice."

"Yes he did. He could have paid more taxes if he wanted to." He twisted her arm.

"You're hurting me."

"I'll show you hurt."

"No, Rory!"

He dragged her into the bedroom.

Junior scrambled back to his bed and turned on his side. He tried not to remember the screams he had heard next.

Some nights, Junior lay in bed asking himself, why does he beat my mother and me? When he was younger, he did not understand why it was that he picked on him alone to beat—never the other children. As he got older, he was pleased Papa didn't beat his sisters and brothers--why should they suffer?

He lay there, trying not to think any more, but remembered the awakening he had the night before at the back of Papa's hand. Juniors head had banged against the wall, his left cheek instantly on fire.

"You little prick."

"WhatdidIdo?"

"What didn't you do?"

"Wait!"

"What is that tramps name again?"

Junior remained silent.

"Oh, yeah. Moira. Sweet little tramp."

"What?"

"Were you with her again?"

It was no use remaining silent. The beating was coming, no matter what. "Yes."

Rory slapped Junior. "After I forbade it."

There was nothing to say.

The furious beating ended quickly when Rory lost his balance and fell on his side on the bed. He got up and staggered out of the room. Rory always left after the beating was done. He wouldn't be back. But for Junior, there would be no more sleep tonight. Sleep brought terror. Junior's brothers and sisters' eyes peeked over their blankets, staring at him.

The children had quit asking Junior what he had done to deserve the beating. He never had an answer for them. They wondered when it would happen to them, but it never did.

Junior took his blanket with him to the main room of the house and lay on the floor, thinking. If I talk back, he slaps me. If I remain quiet, he goes on with his never-ending rants. The night was filled with thinking, but no answers.

"Junior?," said Anne.

"Yes, Ma'am?"

"As God is my witness, your love for Moira is one that most people hope to see just once in their lifetime."

"How's that?"

"Most people settle. They want to raise a family, or they just want to get married for security. Some marry to stop the loneliness. Some just want sex."

Junior blushed.

"What I am saying is if you really love someone, you want what is best for them and hardly think of yourself.

"People like you get married, not because they just want to. They get married to feel the fullness of it."

"Ma'am?"

"When people like you marry, well, it's as if God is putting his arms around you. I imagine it was like that for Adam and Eve."

Junior hadn't heard many Bible stories.

Anne went on, "I learned in Sunday School that God walked in the coolness of the day with them. He had made Eve for Adam, and she was exactly what he needed. A rib was taken out of him. God then molded the woman to fit back in the empty place that had been left behind."

"I think I have always loved Moira."

"Maybe so. I do know you were meant to be with her and she was meant to be with you."

"But what about you?"

"Don't mind me. Knowing you two are together brings me all the joy a mother could ask for."

Moira said, "We couldn't be without you!"

"Yes you can. I hear you talking about America. I hear your dreams of jumping on one of those big ships. You'll go."

"Oh, not without you."

"Never you mind. Ya gotta world to conquer. I can make do. You might think I won't be in the way, but trust me, I know better. Man is suppostta cling to his wife and make a new family. He has gotta leave the old behind. Sez so in the Bible."

Δ   Δ   Δ

Junior picked up work wherever and whenever, and began to save for the day they would leave. After he inquired about the cost of tickets, word got back to Rory.

"What's amatter with you, idiot? Don't you think I know everything that goes on in this village? You been asking about buying passage out of here.

"Don't you know only Catholics leave? Real men don't run away, so I should have guessed that is exactly what you'd do!"

Junior was quiet, but his eyes gave away the rage he was feeling on the inside.

"They call them 'coffin ships'. Ain't 'cause their coughing. It means your dead. They get half way there and start throwing the bodies to the sharks."

Junior said nothing.

"Nobody ever sees you again. Got it. Might as well be in your coffin."

Bitterness between the two increased over the next month. Rory then changed his tactic--"Go ahead. Give away your good prospects on a whore. I knew you would come to nothing. Go ahead. If you are so stupid, go ahead."

Junior dreaded nights at home. His days were filled with hustling extra work. He saved every pence he could, but it would take years before he could collect enough. He thought of stealing it. That pulled him up short--even with the thought of stealing he could see himself following the path of his father.

Junior also changed. He started shouting back--attack and counterattack, night after night.

Junior's days were filled with work, but by late afternoon, he slipped off with Moira to the still waters of the bay. They splashed and played. When it was sunset, they dressed; he walked Moira home, rushed to his own house, ate supper with Mama, and prepared for the evening battle.

Always, he thought more and more about leaving for America.

"No son of mine is going to run away!"

"Who's gonna stop me?"

"I'll beat the tar outta you."

"We'll see about that."

Junior dreaded going home each evening. He thought of running away. But remembered what he had learned--the quickest way of saving money was to take from the hand who beat him, endure the pain and the hurt, and look to the day he would end it.

TEA

"I'd like to invite your friend and her mother over for tea."
Junior was shocked. "What? Why?"
"There is something important we need to discuss."

"We'd love to," was Anne's response. A date and time was agreed on and Muirne busied herself cleaning and polishing. Rory didn't even notice. She got out a small set of chipped china she had found discarded. She treasured it and used it only for holidays.

An hour before the set time, Junior returned from work and nervously awaited their guests. Muirne ran her fingers through his hair. Her love for him was enough to allow her to do the hardest thing a mother can do. She had thought about this long and hard, during many shouting matches and assaults. This was the way it had to be.

Promptly at 3 p.m., there was a light knock on the door. "Won't you come in? I am Mrs. Rory Millwood; call me Muirne. You must be Moira. So happy to meet you. I have heard so much about you."

She had looked forward to this day for a long time. She had known Moira since she was young, but didn't peek into this corner of her son's life. She said she had heard so much, when in fact, she hadn't heard much of anything and never anything other than what Rory told her.

The ladies were dressed in their Sunday best, including hats. Anne introduced herself.

"So nice to meet you, Anne! Please be seated."

They sat in the parlor on chairs Rory had stolen in trade for a reduced assessment and had their tea on a small, dark round wooden table with a lace tablecloth, also taken in trade.

They chitchatted about the weather and the town's people. Small talk was painful for Junior. Then there was a long pause.

"Well, I am not sure how to start, so I will be most direct. I need to send my son to New York City to live with my brother."

Junior's jaw dropped.

"I have saved enough for his passage, though I am not sure the accommodations will be to his liking."

Junior objected and Moira looked at him puzzled. There was a long pause.

Anne smiled knowingly. She broke the silence. "Junior, your mother is not sending you away from Moira. She is sending you away from your father."

"Does he know?"

"No."

"I can't do it."

"You must."

"You can and you must," added Anne.

"I have barely enough to send Junior. But that is all."

Junior thought a long time. "It will be years before I have enough for Moira."

"It will be quicker if you go now and save money there. Work is more plentiful in America. It will be no time."

"I can't do it. Don't I get a say?"

"You have had your say. You say it nearly every night. There is no other way. He will kill you some day. Or you'll kill him. He would rather have no son, than a son that will not do things his way."

"I don't understand. What did I do?"

"You didn't do anything. Your father has a dream he cannot let go of. He sees he has been lucky. He made a step up in the world. It was mostly just luck and it came early to him. He wants you to make the next step, and you will, but it will not be the next step he is looking for you to make."

"I don't understand."

"You will. When yure a parent. We all have dreams for our

children. Sometimes those dreams can become so real to us they seem to be our childrens destiny. But they're not. We can'na live a life through anyone else and we can'na make anyone live the life we want for them. Each has to set his own course." She pulled out a small roll of cash.

She continued, "Besides, even if you stay here, he will never be satisfied. You could become just like him and still not live up to his expectations. He'll always be the big revenue officer and you will be his junior. Nothing you can do will ever stand up to his standards. They can'na. Not even he can live up to the standards he has built for you."

Moira began crying, "Don't I get a say?"

Anne spoke softly, "Moira, trust Junior and trust God. He must escape before tragedy befalls him. The waiting will be hard, but his love for you will not lessen one speck in the months you are separated."

After Moira and Anne said goodbye, there was silence in the Millwood house. Junior knew he had seen the most courageous act he had ever witnessed. He hugged his mother. He knew what would happen when his father figured it out.

In his heart, he knew he had to leave. But he determined to wait to see if he could find a way to take Moira.

Δ   Δ   Δ

One night, Rory had a particularly bad day and came in slamming the door. A merchant had objected to his assessments and complained to Sean. When he didn't get satisfaction there, he went to Sean's boss. There was an accusation of soliciting a bribe, which Sean squashed, but not before damage was done to Rory's credibility. He was told he would be watched more carefully from now on, and he didn't like the sound of that. There was more paperwork to fill out and more meetings to determine why this complaint had occurred.

"It occurred because the bastard doesn't know how the game is played. There is a negotiation--everyone gives a little and everyone gets a little. Bribe, my ass! Next time his stuff goes through, he'll learn his lesson. I can hold up doing an assessment until after the ship has sailed."

"Now, now. Get ahold of yerself. Everythin' is gonna be fine. Just cool off. Don't do anything to attract more attention. Those green gills in the office don't know nothin' about how the real world turns."

Rory stewed all day in the office and was so foul at the Tavern that evening that everyone left early. Rory locked up and stormed home.

"And I don't need any guff from you tonight!," was his greeting to both Junior and Muirne.

"What did I say?," asked Junior.

Rory sat at the table facing away from Junior and rattled off a string of insults. Junior tried to ignore him, but Rory just kept on.

"Now I know you get this from your mother!"

Junior had enough. Without thinking, he grabbed the chair next to his father and smashed it on his neck.

His mother ran in screaming, "Oh, what have you done?"

Rory lay on the floor. There was no blood.

The chair was in pieces, legs everywhere. The back of the chair was still nearly intact in his hands. Junior dropped it on the floor and then caught his image in a windowpane across the room: his face was distorted with rage, his eyes filled with hate. He was becoming his father.

Junior piled up the pieces of wood and checked Pa. He was still breathing. He moaned, groaned, and tried to stir. Then he passed out.

Junior walked briskly to Moira's house. I could have killed him, he thought. Mama was right.

The house was dark. Anne and Moira were asleep. He knew where the key was kept and let himself in. Exhausted he laid down on the floor. What have I done? He sat up and rocked himself on the floor. What have I become? Finally, he lay back down and fell asleep.

Δ   Δ   Δ

As long as Junior could remember, he had watched Irish Catholics move to America for a new start. He didn't know why.

The Great Famine (1845-1852) was the match; British Penal rule was the tinderbox. By British law, Irish Catholics could not own or lease property, vote, hold office, live within five miles of important cities, obtain an education, or enter a profession. On paper, the intent was to prevent Catholicism from challenging the state Church. In reality, it created a ready class of slaves out on the farms.

When the Great Famine devastated the potato crops, Irish Catholics faced starvation. As many people starved to death as migrated, most to America where prospects were not much better. In Ireland, you could starve to death: In America, you were equally at risk of dying from malnutrition or diseases malnutrition brings. Either way, you were dead.

Junior had seen families torn apart--the older generation fearful to move and the younger fearful to stay. So each made a choice and each lived or died with the consequences. The anguish was frightful.

Junior had seen it play out on the docks dozens of times when he worked near passenger ships.

The man scratched his whiskers. It was too hide the tears welling up, as he thought to himself, men don't cry. His wife leaned over to kiss their grandchildren. She had hugged them all that day and the day before. Getting one last touch. Implanting the feeling into her memory. Now, she could hardly let go of them. The decision had been made. It was not the one she would have made, but she did not have a say. Their pa was doing what he thought was right.

"Safe trip."

"Thank you, Papa."

"Write to us when you get settled."

They knew it was likely they would never see them again. All except the children; they thought their grandparents would join them soon. Their parents had told them as much. They said they would bring them over or we would all go back for a visit. They promised they would.

Father and Mother herded their children aboard the waiting packet boat, waving and smiled bravely. The grandparents waved back, holding onto each other, waving back and holding back their tears.

Δ   Δ   Δ

Junior dreamed he and Moira were hand in hand standing on the dock overlooking a luxurious ship. They were dressed in white and black. Everything was in white, black, or gray. Suddenly they were transported, hovering, above a large ship filled with immigrants. Their ship was floating in front of them. Clean, happy. The ship's captain smiled broadly, as he moved the ship easily through the harbor. They were joined on all sides by dozens of ships, all bright and clean, with people dancing jigs on the decks. All the ship's captains were smiling and waving to one another. There were platters of food being passed around and a beer mug in every man's hand. All the other ships were in white or sepia, cream colors. The children had new toys and played games. As they moved out into the ocean, they joined a stream of hundreds of ships, all bright and clean, all with smiling people, all with waving captains, all with platters of food, all with joyous children.

Like a stream of ants, the ships carried their human cargo. Instantly they were there. America! The ships pulled into various harbors, where they unloaded people to welcoming arms. Officials received people and assigned them to homes in the country and to plentiful jobs. Stacks of welcome baskets overflowing with fresh fruits, vegetables, and plump, beautiful potatoes rose in piles on the docks.

A minister on the steps of a church, his hands quietly folded, waited patiently to marry Junior and Moira.

As their feet landed on the ramp of the ship, everything around them turned from whites and grays to bright pastels. They had arrived in a new world of milk and honey. They had arrived in a land of plenty.

BITTERNESS

One day in the early dawn, Junior awoke in a panic. His mind raced, how can I live without Moira? I don't know if I can go. Isn't there a way we can go together? What would it be like not to see her every day? I can't imagine not touching her skin or looking into her eyes every day. I have never been without Moira--ever.

Maybe I should try to find his stash. That would be justice, wouldn't it? Buy Moira's ticket using his money!

He began thinking of killing his father--making it look like an accident. No, I could never seriously hurt him.

But even if he was in jail for killing Papa, he might as well be dead. One of them was going to die if he stayed.

"Oh God, show me what to do!"

Δ   Δ   Δ

At dusk one evening, after swimming, Junior walked Moira home. Anne greeted them at the door. He said he needed to get home to see his mother and eat dinner with his family.

Anne thought about the visit they had together. "What a wonderful mother you have!" said Anne. "She is so wise, Junior."

"If she is so wise, why did she marry Papa?" he blurted out.

Anne laughed. "Yes, if we could only do the wise thing each time."

"I'm sorry I said that."

"We all make mistakes. I am sure your father is not the same man he was then. He's trying to do as well as he can."

There was a pause as Junior thought through what Anne said.

"I let a man take advantage of me once. I was young and would tease the sailors. It was nothing more than that. I knew some day the right man would come along, but I was tired of waiting. He spoke so sweetly. He seemed to care about me. And when we were alone, it seemed like I was missing something. There was something I hadn't yet experienced. I didn't understand. I thought men had to express their love in different ways than women. It was exciting. I could see he was excited. I thought it was because of me."

There was another pause as the experience played out again in her mind.

"Yet it wasn't about me. It was about a natural, physical reaction--any woman could have fulfilled what he needed, but I was stupid." She paused. "I didn't exactly say yes, and I didn't exactly say no. And there he was. And I was so confused. My mind was telling me one thing and my body was telling me something different. When he entered me, I was scared and it hurt. Was this right? Was it supposed to feel this way?

"When I missed the monthly, I was so scared. I didn't have any family here and I didn't know where to turn. Should I end it? Oh, you hear such terrible things. Should I give the baby away? I didn't know how I would make it through. I went to the Church and some of them were so kind and some of them were so hurtful.

"I half lied and told them I had been raped by a sailor, and it went better for me.

"My neighbors were more understanding. At least most were. They would see me through this, though they knew that my life would be forever hard.

"I went day after day, hoping "Aunt Flo and Cousin Red" would come for a visit, but they never did."

Anne didn't speak.

When she could finally continue, she said "When I first felt the life in me, I had no one to share it with. It was so exciting. I knew then I could never give that baby away. It was impossible. I made up my mind with Moira's first kick."

She stopped when tears dropped from her eyes. She pulled her sweater around her shoulders, wrapped her arms around herself, and bent forward, remembering the feel of her first kick.

"I'll never forget the day I went into labor. It hurt so much. Soon it was over and I was overcome with joy.

"Your mother is right. She knows you and your father better than anyone else. She has already lost you. She knows that. She can't think of what you might do to one another, but she has lost you already.

"The best outcome for her is that you go on to America. If you were to run away to Dublin or Shannon or London, she would expect your return every day of her life.

"When Moira was in my womb, it was my job to keep her safe. And now I will keep her safe for you."

"Will you come with her?"

"I am not sure that I can, but I will try."

He didn't dare ask what that might mean.

"You go. Make the way for her, for both of you. There is no other way."

Δ   Δ   Δ

In late winter, talking with his mother over supper Junior said, "I know what I must do now. I'm ready."

"I know you are," she said.

"I have been talking with friends whose husbands are in the know. It seems the best ships are the large ones; they're steady even in the worst weather. And they understand the Royal Mail Ships are the most reliable."

Her mouth went dry. She seemed excited by the prospects of his leaving. In fact, she was near tears, contorting her face to smile with every forced word.

"When should I go?"

"Soon!" She thought to herself, let us get this over with as soon as we can!

She knew the White Star Line had a ship leaving soon: *The RMS Cedric.* The largest most stable ship, protected by the Royal Navy--what mother could ask for more?[vii]

"How will it be when I disappear? You need to protect the children from Papa."

She had nothing to say.

"I'll see about a ticket tomorrow."

She whispered to herself, "Oh, Gawd, that sounds so final." She went to the kitchen to retrieve the bundle of money she had hidden for his passage.

As she handed him the envelope, she knew once Junior walked through that door, there was no turning back.

Δ   Δ   Δ

Junior stood outside the office of James Scott & Company in Scott's Square, Queenstown looking at the papers in his hands. He had booked and paid for passage on the *RMS Cedric* to New York City. It was scheduled to depart from Queenstown on Wednesday, March 14, 1906 at 3 p.m. sharp, his sixteenth birthday. He was to report to the pier behind James Scott & Company offices by nine that morning. He had been warned mail ships were required to leave on time, and that he should not be late. He passed inspection, meaning the agent thought him fit to pass the medical inspection that would take place on Ellis Island.

He was given a flier explaining he needed to bring "all necessary and appropriate wearing apparel, articles of personal adornment, toilet articles, and similar personal effects." These items would need to be declared on a form distributed by the stewards during the voyage. It detailed how much tobacco could be brought and which items were prohibited: "intoxicating beverages, cuttings or seeds, plants except vegetable and flower seeds, smoking opium, seal-skins or garments made therefrom, aigrettes, osprey plumes and feathers or parts of wild birds."

Another sheet of paper explained the physical limitations of the baggage he could bring; a release of liability by the steamship company; and an official notification that his baggage could not be accessed during the trip.

There was a card on which to write his name, country of origin, destination, and sponsoring contact information, with a short string to tie to his clothing.

Lastly, he looked over the ticket with his name, address, nationality, destination, ship information, dock, time, and date of boarding neatly printed.

"I know we have never talked about marriage, but I kinda always thought we would."

"Of course!"

"So, if I asked you to marry me, would you marry me?"

"Well, are you asking to marry me?"

They both giggled.

"Of course, I will marry you. I've known that since the first day

I met you."

"You met me? I don't remember ever not knowing you."

They giggled again.

They agreed as soon as she joined him in New York City, that they would get married, even before they set up housekeeping.

"Should we wait until we have money for both you and your mother to come?"

"I don't know. Do you think we should?"

"Yes, I think we should."

"That will be twice as long."

"I know. I don't know if I can wait that long."

There was a long pause.

"I don't know either."

They decided once Junior had saved enough money for two steerage tickets, he would send it to her using a money transfer arranged through the White Star Line office in New York City to the White Star Line office in Queenstown.

He pulled her over to face directly in front of him and looked into her eyes, "We can do this." Slowly, reassuringly, he placed his hands on her shoulders. Still looking into her eyes, he placed his left hand on the back of her neck and pressed her head toward him. They kissed slowly.

In the late afternoon the day before he was due to depart, they spent as much time together as they could. He did not have much to pack and could not risk raising suspicions with Papa.

"You know, I can't bear to see you off at the dock."

"I know."

"But that makes this goodbye, then, doesn't it."

They embraced in Anne's parlor until dawn.

A SAD BIRTHDAY

By 8:45 am, mother and son were standing at the dock behind James Scott & Company. Over a hundred people were already in line.

"After this blows over with Papa," Junior said, "I'll see you again," knowing it probably was not true.

"Of course," she said, fearing she would never see him again.

"I love you."

"I love you, too. I have always been proud of you, Junior."

They embraced. Moira watched them from the streets above.

"How will you tell him?"

"I won't have to."

"Watch out for Moira for me."

"Of course. And Anne. Have a safe trip."

They stood together, silent.

Mother was thinking, I'll never see him again.

Moira was thinking, I'll never see him again.

Junior was thinking, will I see either of them again?

Junior grabbed his two cases and with a quick "Goodbye" stepped onto the dock and into the long line. He turned away so his mother wouldn't see the tears streaming down his cheeks. She stepped away from the dock to watch him go. She thought, I endured pain at his birth, sixteen years ago today; I'll endure this pain.

Vendors walked up and down the line of passengers, hawking crafts, creams, ointments, books, games, puzzles, tissues, drinks, snacks. Getting everyone in line six hours before departure was a wonderful way to sell items they may have forgotten. James Scott & Company saw a tidy profit from this ploy.

At last, a packet ship named *PS America* took on the 115 Third Class (steerage) passengers who had been waiting. She pushed off and proceeded down to the Deepwater Quay a few hundred yards away, on the west side of the village. Moira came down to stand and hold hands with Junior's mama.

The *PS America* met up with her sister ship, the *PS Ireland*. Both vessels loaded mailbags from the mail train and the *PS Ireland* took on three First Class and eight Second Class passengers. Those passengers waited in a special area next to the Victorian railroad station and transatlantic terminal. Both tenders pushed off together for the outer anchorage of Queenstown Harbor, Roches Point, one hour before sailing. At 3:03 p.m., an exchange of whistles indicated the tenders' business was complete. As the *RMS Cedric*'s anchor lifted from the floor of the Harbor, water splashed down from the chains. The ships horns blasted twice as the anchor was pulled up on deck. The powerful engines pounded. The propellers stirred the waters behind the ship. The mournful strains of 'Erin's Lament' played on bagpipes, floating up from steerage. The ship slowly moved forward.[viii]

When Rory got home that evening, he surveyed the house, sensing something was wrong. It took him but a minute to realize everything belonging to Junior was gone.

ELLIS ISLAND

As Junior walked up the gangplank onto the *RMS Cedric*, he felt dwarfed by her tremendous length and girth. There wasn't a cloud in the sky and the breeze from the west was biting. His nostrils were so cold they ached, so he buried his nose in his sleeve. As he stepped onto the ship, carrying one of his two bags (he had dropped off the other when boarding the tender), he was greeted with a comment and a chipper question, "If yer weather 'olds, 'e 'll 'ave a fine v'yage. Sec'on Class?"

He replied, "Steerage."

The steward pointed to the stairway down. As Junior clumsily descended deeper and deeper into the bowels of the ship, he recognized his rank in life in the eyes of the crew and other passengers. He was one in a long line of steerage passengers trudging down, as if to their grave. As the pace slowed, a deck hand bound down the passage, pushing aside travelers left and right, barking "Move along lively" and pointing the way around blockages.

The passages became tighter and tighter as they fitted around fixtures of the ship. Junior finally arrived at Steerage Number One, the place reserved for single, English-speaking male passengers. There were similar compartments in every direction. The room held twenty-four passengers. As Junior entered, most bunks were piled high with someone's earthly treasures, usually a bag or two, with musical instruments, books, apples, birds in cages, hunting gear, cooking utensils, tobacco pipes, and flags. For most, these and the shirts on their backs were all their earthly possessions. He saw the dim compartment was lit with gray light through the dirty port holes. Up close, he saw that each bunk had straw mattresses and horse blankets.

He found an empty bunk on an upper berth and sat with his legs swinging over the side. The mattress was hard and lumpy. He made the mistake of moving back from the edge of the bunk. The straw had absorbed so much moisture it felt clammy and smelled stale. When he pulled the blanket over, his nostrils were assaulted by the rancid smell of human sweat. The blankets were continually used, but never cleaned.

Tin plates and cups, edged with rust, and crude eating utensils rested at the foot of each bunk. The bunks were attached to the ship with cables that could catch a man by the throat while he walked in the dark to relieve himself and made navigation in the night lethal. Short wooden benches were attached by cables in the crowded seating area. Deckhands kept the floors scrubbed clean and the walls were scraped of rust and slopped over with lumpy, gray paint.

Δ   Δ   Δ

"Gran' day ter yer," was the call from the next bunk. "'owaya!"

Ronnie, an elderly man escaping the hard life of rural Ireland, was an Irish Catholic with a good sense of humor beneath the scars. He was seventy-two years old and looking to find comfort in the new home his daughter had made in western New York.

"Grand, I guess. I am going to America, but leaving my sweetheart."

"I scon leavin' me sweetheart, too. Though she 'as been in de groun' dees score years." Ronnie told Junior about their life together, their one daughter, his wife's death and how he missed her.

"I buried 'er at Saint Matthews, wha oi can visit 'er every Sunday. But oi jist cud not clap digger 'er up ter take 'er wi' me," Ronnie said with a wink. "Oi raised spuds 'til they quit comin' an' me bottle av water said it wus time for me ter join 'er in a Fairport they 'av in New York, America. De lassy sent me a ticket, so 'ere scon are."

When Junior saw Ronnie's quick wit, he thought how he would

be a good man to talk with during the long hours on board. He chatted with him for a good while. Then he decided to stretch his legs on deck, climbed the steps up, while others descended in increasing numbers. Before he made it all the way to the top, a clear voice announced, "Move along down. The baggage boats have just departed, and all passengers are to return immediately to their assigned area." Stewards enforcing the order informed the passengers, "The ship's surgeon will be down shortly."

He did not appear for another three hours and when he did, he wandered and crawled through the steerage spaces as if he didn't have a care in the world. He smoked his pipe, in disregard of rules for everyone else, looking over each person without a word.

Junior heard a mother with a baby complain to the doctor at the entrance to the men's quarters, "It is so crowded in with the women, I can'na find a place for my children," and another woman asked, "When will we eat? My children have been standing all day," but the surgeon ignored them all. He pulled off hats and looked in eyes. Junior saw people holding their breath. That seemed odd, but he didn't know what that was all about. He listened to a father whispering to his son, "Don't cough! At the least cough, the surgeon can nod to the stewards, and we will get pulled off the ship."

After a while, passengers noticed another character in their midst, silently watching them all. Junior figured out this was the ship's detective, on the lookout for unsavory characters escaping the long arm of the law or ruffians who would be rejected at Ellis Island.

Once the doctor departed Steerage Number One, Junior returned to his bunk to find Ronnie sitting asleep. He wanted to talk and Ronnie aroused as if Junior's eyes had seared him. "Doctor gone?"

"Yep."

"Oi clap de detective didn't catch yer," winked Ronnie.

"Yer either," replied Junior.

Both laughed.

"Well, settle in." Both did.

"Waaat puts yer on de vessel?"

Junior told his life history, while Ronnie sat nodding. Occasionally, Junior thought Ronnie had nodded off to sleep, but then quietly Ronnie asked a painful question, "'Oy did it fale ter leave 'er?" It was as if Ronnie knew that someday, when they were reunited, he would want to recall how it felt at this very moment.

Almost imperceptibly, the passengers noticed the ship was moving, as tugs pushed the ship from her mooring across the bay to take on the first- and second-class passengers from their respective salons. They heard the squealing of the gangplank and ropes stretching tightly outside, feet rumbled and carts rolled above them.

At last, a warning bell rang and the ship's horn bellowed a response. They heard the rumblings as the screws began turning. The faint sound of cheering from the dock was answered by a spontaneous, explosive noise from all the steerage areas. Their adventure had begun! As the cheers in steerage faded, the passengers became melancholy. Disembarking meant finality. Reality was striking them that loved ones left behind would never be seen again. Not speaking of it did not ease the pain.

Δ　　　Δ　　　Δ

Twilight shifted through portholes on the starboard side, as they passed the lighthouse by Roche's Point.

The monotonous droning of the screws lasted through the entire voyage. Activities around the ship were carried out with precision and punctuality. Within an hour of leaving they were served a plain, tasteless supper of soda bread, butter, and tea served black. There was just enough to give everyone in Steerage Number One a slice of bread, which settled their stomachs, and set low expectations for the meals to come. That night, the water was smooth on the lee of the Irish coast. Most fell asleep easily under the light rocking of the ship, the drone of the screws, and a little something in their stomachs. There was little noise from the rest of the ship that first night.

The first morning light filtered through the portholes early, but it was hours before breakfast was served. Men slowly meandered through the spaces to relieve themselves and return to their bunks. Some played music on harmonicas, Jew's harps and fiddles. At eight, breakfast was carried in--sticky oatmeal, soda bread and butter, and coffee. The coffee was warm, watery, and tasteless. The oatmeal was hot and plain. Ronnie turned his spoon upside down and the oatmeal clung to it, "Dis 'ill steck ter yisser ribs!," he laughed.

After breakfast, Junior meandered up to the deck. It was cold, but the fresh, salt air was a relief. People squeezed onto every inch of space and Junior wandered around, watching the crew manning their stations. Passengers spoke quietly among themselves, enjoying a rest from the noise below. Seagulls watching the activities of the ship hoped something would bring them a morsel. As the ship moved further from shore, the seagulls lessened and the swells increased. The ship rocked more and steerage passengers reluctantly moved down below. The skies grew darker and colder.

As water washed over the starboard rail onto the deck, the few remaining steerage passengers put out their tobacco and descended the steps. Junior was the last to go. The stench of vomit blasted his face and he gagged and tried to return to deck, but the stewards pushed him downward and sealed the door. He moved down the steps as quickly as he could to his room as other stewards delivered dinner of watery soup, some form of meat, and boiled potatoes ladled onto plates from a slop-bucket. He found burying his nose in his dinner brought relief from the stench all around him.

As the days went on, the weather became better and the ship rocked less. Seasickness decreased as people became used to the motion of the ship or the various remedies took hold. Irish stew was served every few days at breakfast. Fish replaced meat a few times at dinner and warm pudding was served for dessert twice.[ix]

Δ   Δ   Δ

In the evening, Junior heard music from the salons above and he watched the dancing and singing in steerage.

For most people the passage took longer than they expected and there were two reactions. Some accepted it and became more reserved and quiet, while others became belligerent and vocal. Junior made the best of the situation by talking with Ronnie and other young men, spending as much time as possible on deck.

On the fourth morning, after breakfast, everyone had to line up for vaccination. Grown men whimpered at the thought of getting stabbed in the arm. Those without a pockmark from a prior vaccination were assumed to need one for fear the first one had not taken. When told they couldn't leave the ship without it, they tearfully pulled up their sleeve, pushed their arm forward, and looked away.

After lunch on the fourth day, the stewards came through steerage, "Who can read?"

Anyone who answered was handed a large card. "You'll need to help the others." The cards had the twenty-nine questions all passengers would be asked, once they reached Ellis Island. They were simple questions, but not everyone knew the answers.

The next day the stewards asked, "How is it coming with the twenty-nine questions?" The questions had been the hot topic of conversation the previous afternoon and evening, a welcome relief to the monotony of the trip. "Better study. You'll need to answer them all."

The further the ship sailed the more conversation revolved around two subjects: Life in first-class and life in America.

"Lucky bastards in first-class. The food we get goes to them first, and the next day is given to second. Then the crew is fed. Then we get it, if there is any left."

"Yeah. They probably feed the seagulls before us."

"I hear they catch the seagulls, give them our slop for a few days, and then cook them up for our dinner."

Ronnie leaned over to Junior with a wink, "Don't yer believe any av dis. Dare are sum things even seagulls won't ayte."

"Aye, there will be a plenty when we get to New York."

"I hear they got beefsteaks a plenty in every pub. And fer cheap, too."

"Yeah, we work a few hours and have plenty to eat. I hear they got potatoes and cabbage just growing wild in the city for anyone to grab."

"They don't call it the land of plenty for nothin'."

Junior noticed more ships as they approached New York harbor. Specks on the horizon, turned to clouds of coal smoke, as the *Cedric* maneuvered toward the harbor. Seagulls increased and the decks were abuzz with excitement. As they got closer, Junior began to make out the shapes of ships. Below decks, passengers collected their belongings into their bags. Between the fog banks, Junior was puzzled whether he was seeing land. It smelled different, he thought, as they got closer and the water became greenish.

He had been told what to look for, but Junior was not quite sure what he was seeing. A deck hand who was coiling up a rope, overheard what he had been muttering to himself outloud. He pointed to the horizon in the west, "There it is--Sandy Hook."

The end of the trip took forever. Finally, they made out the towering buildings of Brooklyn and Manhattan as they approached the channel beneath them, which had been cut by *The Mill* and *The Thomas* years earlier. When green, tarnished copper of the Statue of Liberty rose before him, Junior stood on deck ready to jump into the water. Tugboats bumped alongside and guided the *RMS Cedric* to Chelsea Piers. They stood on deck, looking up the streets to see horses, wagons, and trolleys in truly a new world. They saw the pier below them and watched the first- and second-class passengers disembark. Carts filled with baggage came off next.

They strained to hear a steward below, "Anyone who can prove he is a United States citizen can now leave." A few people left steerage, climbed the stairs, and passed through the heavily guarded passageway to the gangplank.

"If you are not a United States citizen, go back to your assigned place. Dinner is coming soon. You will leave the ship in the morning."

It was dead quiet in steerage, which turned into a long, restless night. With the ship no longer moving and the decks all sealed to prevent escape, there wasn't a breath of fresh air below.

Breakfast was served at eight and the wait continued. Around eleven, the stewards announced, "Bring your belongings, up on deck." In what seemed like a final act of cruelty, they were pushed away from Chelsea Piers and Manhattan to the opposite side of the ship, where they were loaded onto a barge containing their checked baggage, and pushed by tugboat back beyond the Statute of Liberty to Ellis Island. The tugboat captain yelled, "Here is where you get off. Take everything with you up to that big building. You'll be processed there for possible admission to the United States. Good luck to ya."

Δ   Δ   Δ

The Department of Immigration worked well with the shipping companies to complete much of the documentation prior to passengers disembarking. Most people who would not have passed muster were eliminated before the ships set sail.[x]

The admission interviews had been honed to twenty-nine questions, which were provided in writing prior to or during the voyage. Once the immigrants were before the standing desks at the Registry Department, they were usually asked most of the twenty-nine questions. If there were no inconsistencies and no missing information, the process went smoothly.[xi]

Fraud was a common problem for hoodlums and convicts seeking to escape justice, but most were found out because of their inability to tell the same lie twice.

Agents were thorough and took their time to make sure questions were fully understood and answers fairly given. One complicating issue was the large number of illiterate immigrants who had assistance in filling out their forms. Most immigrants had nothing to hide and all to be gained by truthful, accurate responses. Any hesitation or evasive answers were a tip off to problems, which were handled directly and efficiently.[xii]

Those considered criminally insane were routinely returned.

An immigration agent rushed the man through the crowded entrance to the main building. "Make way!" Two agents, each dragging baggage behind them, maneuvered through the crowds. The first agent stopped to wait for his partners to catch up, holding the man by his collar.

"Poor bastard. You'd think he could wait until he was off the island before he'd start picking pockets."

"Hell, he can't help himself. It's the only way he knows. He ain't got the sense to come in out of the rain."

"Amazes me that he made it all the way here."

Once the agents dragging the baggage caught their breath, they took the thief back to the empty barge where an armed guard stood over him before returning him to the White Star line for transport back to Ireland.

There were accusations their native countries were attempting to rid themselves of problems, but it was more likely they had slipped through the cracks in the great wave of immigrants.

Δ   Δ   Δ

Inspectors ferreted out all medical conditions that could become a charge to the government. Illness contracted on-board or symptoms that did not show up until arrival caused passengers to be isolated and treated, or returned to their home country.

Young women traveling alone were closely examined to make sure they were not white slaves being sold into prostitution. Agents were also careful to make sure passage had not been provided illegally by trading future labor against the cost of their ticket.[xiii]

Customs declaration forms were required from passengers for items not being worn upon arrival. Most passengers consumed any offending articles before disembarking, but a few insisted on trying to smuggle items in a favorite plant from the homeland.

"What the hell have you got there?"

"What?"

"Fool. Hand over the tin." He looked inside the tin before he continued, "Just as I thought. Potato eyes. When will they learn? See that. See that corky, rotten part. That's blight. Blight. Fool. That is what killed off the potato in Ireland. We told ya, ya can't brin' it here, didn't we? Bringing it here could cause it to spread here. Is that what you want? So why did you try to bring it here? You've earned yourself another long ocean voyage home."

At other times, limitations on tobacco became a problem as immigrants under-counted their cigars and cigarettes, at the risk of being denied entry.

$$\Delta \qquad \Delta \qquad \Delta$$

As tugboats pushed the barge past the Statue of Liberty, the massive main building of the Ellis Island Immigration Station came clearly into view.

Junior's mouth dropped open. He could not believe what he was seeing. The Station was the largest, most grand building he had ever seen. Enormous windows and arches graced the sides and entrances.[xiv]

Designed in French Renaissance style, it consists of brick laid in Flemish bond, trimmed with limestone and granite.

Ronnie said, "Whow, luk at dat cathedral!"

Junior started to correct him. Truly, the barge was approaching a new type of cathedral. Old world cathedrals were for funerals, weddings, and baptisms. Junior wondered which of the three this new world cathedral would represent: Perhaps all three.

He just said,
    "Something old, something new,
Something borrowed, something blue,
And a silver sixpence in her shoe.
This marriage is creating a new America."

The day was beautiful as Junior stepped off the barge. He held one bag in each hand and his all-important papers tucked into his shirt: Passport, Visa, Alien Identification card, customs declarations, and immigration documents. He lumbered up the entrance and into the long queue of the Registry Department. He didn't know it would take him four days to pass through.

There seemed to be some confusion over his name. On paper, his name was Rory John Millwood, Junior. Apparently, Junior couldn't keep his own name straight.

"Drop your baggage here."

He took his two bags and dropped them off in an unguarded, common area.

An old man told his wife, "I'll stay 'ere wi' our things."

One of the agents came over, "You can't stay here. Get in line."

He looked at his wife, but did not budge.

The agent repeated, "You can't stay here. Get in line."

He looked at his baggage. It was everything they owned. He slowly got in line.

Junior wasn't worried about leaving all his earthly possessions; he hardly had any. Lines were long and roped off between areas. His line led into another room, but he couldn't see much. The line inched forward slowly. There was little chatter.

Junior finally made it to the doorway of a cavernous hall. He could hear the scuffling of feet and quiet conversations. Occasionally he heard, "Next!" or directions being given out.

As Junior first stepped into the Great Hall, he was impressed with its beauty and size. Large windows graced the room on all sides. As he got further into the room, he saw his line led to a standing desk, where a uniformed agent sat on a stool and asked questions. The agent was in no rush.[xv]

The agents decisions could send a man and his whole family to another waiting area, a medical examination room, or a group of benches. Their decisions could send a man to a warm meal and bed, or back to the barge.

Interpreters talked quietly to the immigrants and translated their replies back to the agent. The agent looked over all the documents, and asked questions. The agents were the last bastion. A bad decision would admit criminals and undesirables into the country, which could have far-reaching consequences. Many had been immigrants themselves a generation earlier.

Junior's documents were mostly in order. But he slipped up on the easiest question: "What is your name?"

"Junior Millwood."

The agent eyed the forms cautiously. "Your full name."

"Junior John Millwood. I mean, Junior Rory Millwood. Rory Junior Millwood."

"I see."

He hit Junior with a barrage of questions. He repeated the questions. He asked the same questions in different ways.

Everything checked out. So, why didn't this person know his own name? Had he memorized all the answers? Was he stupid? Criminally insane? A compulsive liar? What was he trying to hide?

He was sent upstairs for another long wait and was told to sit until his name was called.

"MILLWOOD!"

Rising he called back, "Aye!"

This agent went through much of the same routine again, with the same result.

He was assigned a bunk in the single men's dormitory--a room with a series of bunks hanging by chains close to one another. It was cool in the room and a skimpy blanket did little to warm him.

The following morning after breakfast, he was told where to sit and wait. The third time an agent went through the questions, with exactly the same result.

"How come your immigration application and other papers don't match?"

"Whatdoyamean?"

"They don't match. Your name doesn't match your application."

Junior looked it over. "Well, I'll be damned!"

"That's my father's name, Rory John Millwood. I'm his son, Junior."

The agent blinked at the obvious, crossed out his name as written on the application, and wrote in, Rory John Millwood, Junior.

He pointed to the stairs and said, "Get over to medical."

Δ   Δ   Δ

The uniformed military surgeons could tell whether a person was fit or not by watching him struggle up the steps with his belongings. Back, Feet, Hernia, Lameness, and Neck injuries were easy to diagnose. Many surgeons merely stood at the top of the stairs awaiting their patients' arrival to mark their condition in chalk on their clothing. A quick look at the eyes and teeth were all that was typically required. More extensive examinations were conducted when the cursory six-second exam raised suspicions.[xvi]

On the fourth day, the senior agents determined that Rory

John Millwood, Junior was not a threat to the well-being of the country and granted him admission to the United States of America. He was asked if he had thirty dollars, and he joyfully pulled out a wad of bills from his pocket, far more than the thirty-dollar minimum. His British bills were exchanged for United States paper money.

A lawyer who had been attending the hearings, and watched Junior fumbling with his cash, slipped up to him.

"A word of advice."

"Yes."

"My associates would be pleased to assist you when you get to the other side of the harbor." He slipped an oversized paper shamrock in his top buttonhole and slapped him on the back.

Junior's mother had arranged, for a modest sum, for her brother to sponsor him. Junior had never met his uncle, but he did have a letter of confirmation (not mentioning any gift of course) and a valid address. He also had sufficient cash to get there and enough money to sustain him for the few weeks until he got himself settled. With all his documents in order, he got back onto a barge for transport to Castle Clinton, where he finally stepped onto the soil of Manhattan Island.

THE LESSON

As he stood for the first time on the street on the lowest tip of Manhattan, Junior was met with a dazzling array of choices. He was greeted by a blast from the Salvation Army band, with drums and brass, flags and banners. They wore gray suits with gray and red hats. There were runners from everywhere calling to him. Men from pubs beckoned him to join them. People from hotels were there to carry his baggage. Street vendors sold pretzels and sausages. Paperboys hawked editions in all known languages. Porters from the railroad companies dragged away steamer trucks. Large signs advertised beer and there were girls from dancing shows in scandalous attire. Junior thought he must have stumbled upon a holiday parade. The colors, noises, and odors assaulted his senses. Families hugging and kissing were a great joy to witness.

There was also disappointment as many walked through the parade without anyone to greet them. Heads down, they trudged to their next destination. Their travel was not yet done. It was too early for their celebration. Or there was never a celebration. Some men walked through the welcoming barrage to a pub for a beer. Others sought the gambling houses and bordellos.

Junior was taking all this in, when he was grabbed by two men and dragged out of the cloud of gaiety. With a flourish, they showed him the shamrocks in their own buttonholes, which matched the one he had been given.

"He has sent us too many today," one man said to another, holding Junior by the collar with his left hand and another man with his right.

"Yeah, well don't complain, tomorrow may be different," was the reply as he grabbed Junior by his arm as if to restrain him.

"What is your name?," said one, ignoring the answer.

"We're here to show you how it is done in New York."

"Let us help you with your bags."

They briskly helped him up the street and around the corner.

"You'll like it here. Everyone is so friendly."

The other laughed.

"You need to protect yourself at all times. Until you get established."

"See ya in a bit," the other said as he left with the other man.

"Yeah, I got him." He turned to size Junior up. His cheap, charcoal gray wool suit was wet with perspiration, and his sweat smelled of alcohol.

"Education is expensive, but worth the cost in the long run."

Junior thought, what a curious thing to say. It was the last thing he remembered. From behind, a piece of lumber caught him squarely in the right temple. When he awoke, he was in a narrow alley. He never remembered his head hurting so badly. There was dried blood on his scalp. His bags were gone, his pockets were empty, and his shoes were missing. His stomach tightened with convulsions, and he turned to the side to vomit, but most landed in his lap anyway. He lay there a long while with his back against the wall. He did not think at all. Slowly he sized himself up. Nothing seemed to be broken, but everything hurt. Was it early morning or twilight? Seagulls flew by. Where was he? He tried to remember. His clothing was torn and his favorite scarf gone; a parting present from Moira the night before he left.

He struggled from the alley back to the street. He looked both ways, not recognizing anything. Some instinct told him which way to go, to get back to where he had come from. He turned the corner at the next block and looked both ways. Yes, this is the way, he thought. He could now see the water. The parade had been here! Right here! Where are they? They could help.

He walked down to the waterfront. The sun was just rising in the east. Seagulls trailed the fishing boats out on the harbor. It was quiet and calm. Two fishermen sat on a small, grassy knoll just a few feet up from the beach, on a dirty blanket.

A few yards away, a pathway where men carried down small

fishing boats led to the water. A knife and the remains of a small fish rested between them on the blanket. Their hats were pulled down and their coats wrapped around them. They watched the man stumbling around.

"Drunk?" one asked.

"Hope he doesn't disturb the fish," was the reply. They had not been there long. Each had a cup of steaming hot coffee and hoped to catch dinner before they needed to get off to work. Most days were kind to them. One of the fishermen noticed the dried blood on the man's head. He watched him long enough to see he was neither drunk nor hung over. He could see he had been hurt. He noticed he had no shoes. He reached out his hand with the coffee cup.

Junior looked at it for a few seconds. The cloud was beginning to lift. "In a minute," Junior replied. Then he walked, fully clothed, into the bay.

As was their tradition, the Salvation Army showed up by the middle of the afternoon to welcome the immigrants, divert them from the paths of destruction all around them, and point them to the path of life.

For Junior, they were a salvation. They quickly found dry clothing and shoes and gave him scraps left over from their lunches. They collected as much information from him as they could. They gave him a hot meal and a place to spend the night. They preached that night about the ways of the world and the need to choose the right path. Boy, did that ever resonate. The following day they pulled strings and tracked down his contact information from the Department of Immigration. "Small miracle we hadn't filed this yet."

It included a name he never remembered seeing. Under "Name and address of relative you are going to join", it read: Mr. Robert Charles Boyden, 107 Charles Street, Manhattan, New York, United States of America.

Δ   Δ   Δ

"Who the feck are you?"

"I'm your nephew, Rory John Millwood, Junior. Everyone calls me 'Junior'."

"Who?"

"Junior. Your nephew."

"Come on, Charlie. It's your sister's boy," replied his wife from inside the house.

"I use to have a sister, but she abandoned me."

"Knock it off, Charlie, you know you're not gonna turn family away. Besides, you already spent the money she gave you to look after him for a few days."

She pried the door from her husband's hand. Pushing Charlie aside, she said, "What was the name again?"

"Junior."

"I'm Betty. He is kinda like a blister; once you get used to him, you can ignore him. It's a wonder what the mind can do."

"Shut up."

"We were expecting you earlier."

"First, I got hung up at Immigration."

"Yeah, that happens. Do you need a baaaa--WHAT THE HELL HAPPENED TO YOUR HEAD?" It was the first she looked at him.

"That would be the second delay."

"Come in. Come in. Can I put something on it?"

"No. Aspirin helps."

"I'll get you some."

When she returned he noticed she was wearing a light, pink sleeping gown and matching robe. She pulled them tightly around her as she handed the aspirin and glass of water to him. "You're just in time for supper."

"Figures he would show up for dinner."

"Shut up."

"Thank you. I could eat." In fact, Junior hadn't eaten most of the day.

She quickly set an additional place.

"This is most kind of you, Mrs. Boyden."

"Betty. Call me Aunt Betty."

"Aunt Betty."

"Charlie, supper!"

Charlie was wearing boxer shorts, an undershirt, and socks.

"Sorry we're not dressed for company, but we really didn't know when you'd arrive."

"If you'd arrive," corrected Charlie. "I thought you said supper was ready."

Aunt Betty ignored him.

She returned with plates of leftovers for the two men and turned back to get her own. Charlie dug in.

"Don't we say grace any more?"

"Guess not," Charlie replied.

Betty stared at Charlie until he began to pray.

"Dear Jesus, Thank you for this food. Amen."

Betty continued on, "And thank you for safely bringing Junior to our home. Thank you for blessing his trip. We pray for the quick healing of his injuries. Amen."

Charlie ate quickly, while Aunt Betty quizzed Junior. "Tell me about your trip."

"How did you get injured?"

When Charlie finished he got up and left to read the afternoon edition of the *New York World* newspaper.

"How old are you?"

"How is your mother?"

"Do you have a girlfriend?"

Betty and Junior sat at the table for two hours talking about the trip and his experience.

Charlie got up and went to bed.

"We don't have much room. Let me get you sheets and blankets and you can make yourself at home on the sofa."

"That would be grand."

While she went upstairs, Junior slipped out the front door to urinate off the front porch. He had been too shy to ask about their facilities.

As he came back in, buttoning his fly, she asked, "So, what kind of work do you do?"

Junior explained he worked at the shipyards.

"Charlie is a pressman for the *New York World*. He works the afternoon edition."

Charlie operated a four-color printing press used for department store advertising supplements and the funny pages. Most of the work was for the weekend editions, which was printed during the week. Charlie told her he printed the afternoon edition rather than explain to her why he did not have to work the odd hours necessary for a morning paper. It was the least of the secrets he kept and lies he told her.

"Maybe you can apply there?"

"That would be good."

"You can also try the piers. They are always building something around here and the street works are always hiring. The garment places are always looking for strong, young men."

Aunt Betty left and returned with more aspirin and water. "This should help you sleep."

"Thank you."

"You know, your Uncle Charlie--well, you know, when you get to know him--you'll find out what a real bastard he is."

They both broke out laughing.

"I'm glad you're here. Good night, Junior." She kissed him on the forehead.

The following morning Charlie rudely woke Junior.

"I don't know what she was thinking. Don't even think of applying at the *World.* I don't want you here with her alone. Get your ass out and find some work. There is plenty around here. Then you can find yourself a new place to live."

Charlie sat down, ate his oatmeal, and drank tea. He waited until Junior had dressed and showed him the door, before going off to work as if he did not have a care in the world.

Junior spent the day wandering from place to place. Really, it felt more like from sign to sign: 'Help Wanted. No Irish Need Apply'. He spent a few hours doing day labor work and returned home soiled and tired. It was just a matter of finding the right job to get started, he told himself. I can do many things.

Each day he went out, he found some manual labor to do for a few cents—-usually digging or carrying bricks. He returned each night with a little change, half of which he turned over to his aunt. She held up her hand to refuse his gift and reminded him, "You really do not need to give us anything." He insisted. He stashed away the other half.

Each night was the same: A light supper, ignored by Uncle Charlie, interviewed by Aunt Betty. Every morning was the same.

"What work did you find yesterday?"

"How soon will you be moving out?"

Aunt Betty would slip him a little extra oatmeal.

Finally, the words he had been waiting to hear, "You're hired. Report here at 8 o'clock sharp on Monday morning."

Δ   Δ   Δ

"Great! How soon can you leave?"

"Charlie, really! Junior, this is great news. What will you be doing and what is the name of your employer?"

Junior gave her all the details he could remember.

"Don't think I have ever heard of them."

The clothing trade in Manhattan was three times larger than the second largest industry, sugar refining. Up until the Civil War, most Americans made their own clothing. The clothing trade concentrated on uniforms of all shapes and sizes, from sailors and soldiers to slaves on plantations. Mass production and cheap labor changed America. No longer was tailor-made clothing the privilege of the wealthy. Mass produced clothing became affordable, so the middle class could buy, rather than make, their own. Soon the skills necessary for sewing disappeared in many American families.

An essential skill one generation before was disappearing from the American landscape and Junior was the benefactor of the change. Cheap, Irish labor, scorned elsewhere, was readily accepted for the mindless tasks of the garment district. Much of the work was done in homes converted during the daylight hours into mini-factories, called sweatshops. Large factories purchased partially completed pieces from these Mom-and-Pop shops at low rates.

But large, efficient factories ruled the trades. They had the power to negotiate with the department stores for large orders and with suppliers for materials. Contracts for large volumes kept the factories humming. Modest changes in styles from year-to-year kept the workforce busy. Wrong guesses in style changes or soured relations with a department store buyer could turn a profitable business on its ear. But that's why God made fire insurance. Mysteriously the excess, unsalable inventory disappeared in flames and the insurance checks allowed owners to return to full production in a matter of weeks. After a few weeks off, the most valued employees returned, and the hiring frenzy for cheap labor began. This is how Junior found a job.

Junior and his Aunt talked well into the night on Saturday.

"We need to celebrate. I'll make a big dinner and bake you a cake."

"But won't Uncle Charlie be mad."

"Don't worry about your Uncle."

Δ   Δ   Δ

Betty made a special trip for lamb and ingredients to make mint jelly, red potatoes, biscuits with fresh butter, and chocolate cake. It just so happened that each item on the menu was Charlie's favorite.

The dinner went along peacefully, until the end.

"How did you pay for all this?"

"Junior gave me some of his earnings."

"You're getting awful familiar with Junior."

"Charlie, he's your nephew."

"Could a younger man keep up better with you in bed?"

"How dare you!"

"Well, you have been so happy since he has been here!"

"I have had someone to talk to for a change."

"I'll bet he has been slipping back in here after I leave for work every day--"

"That's ridiculous!"

"--getting his fill of home cookin', if you know what I mean."

"How dare you!"

"I ought to throw both your asses out. You deserve each other!"

"He is your sister's son. I'm showing him the kindness due a family member making a new start."

"You have been showing him more than your kindness, I'll bet."

"Bullshit! What would you know?"

So the argument raged for the next hour, with Junior at the table, his jaw hanging open, not knowing what to say. Would defending her help? Or just get her beaten? Would anything he say help? Probably not. Why would he believe him anyway? It was best to begin work on Monday and find a new place to live.

His mind began to wander, until Junior caught her shift in tactics. "Of course we've been sleeping together, you with the 'Irish Disease' and all, who would blame me. Why don't we go to court! After inspecting your limp noodle, the judge would throw the case out for insufficient evidence--that you're a man."

Since it was impossible to prove their innocence, there was no use defending themselves against Charlie's absurd charges. As long as there was no real threat of violence, Junior decided to excuse himself from the table and the bickering soon stopped.

Charlie cleared out and began to read his paper.

"I'll be out as soon as I can. I start work tomorrow and will begin asking around for a place to live. I'll be gone in a few days."

Charlie snapped his paper to the next page as if he was not in the least bit interested.

"Your wife and me are innocent of your charges. She is a good woman. Better than you deserve."

STARTING WORK

Junior was not sure how long it would take to walk to work that first day. It was less than two miles, but he didn't want to be late for his appointment. When he originally walked to his Uncle's house he had gotten the streets and avenues all mixed up. He didn't understand the difference between avenues, drives, boulevards, and streets, and using the number for street names was no help.

He was walking on Fifth Avenue, when he came to Fifth Street. "What the hell?" He looked at the Fifth Avenue street sign. Then he looked at the Fifth Street sign. Then he looked at the Fifth Avenue street sign again. He shrugged and continued walking.

He asked directions a few times and really wasn't sure he had arrived at the correct house when he got there. When he found his job on Washington Place in the garment district he had not walked directly there from his Uncle's home and had not gone straight back afterward.

On Monday, he was up by 5:30 a.m. after a restless night. He ate Aunt Betty's oatmeal and black coffee. She had been embarrassed by the encounter with her husband the previous evening and did not quite know what to say. He was too nervous to listen. She tried to find the words a few times, but kept stalling. His stomach was unsettled and he thought a brisk walk would help. He told her he should be leaving, and she gave him a hug.

After walking to work in under a half hour, he sat in Washington Square Park watching the pigeons in the cool of the morning and the flowers, especially the roses. There was little activity when he arrived, but by a quarter to eight, things began to pick up. He meandered over to the building and told the security guard he was there to begin work.

"Take the elevator on the other side of the building. Tenth floor."

Δ   Δ   Δ

The tenth floor contained pressing and shipping areas, a showroom, and a few offices. A receptionist/telephone operator pointed Junior to the right office.

Junior waited for Mr. Bernstein to get things going downstairs before coming up to meet him. There was little paperwork before Samuel Bernstein "made a price." He told Junior he would be making six dollars a week. It was a 59-hour workweek. He took him across the main room to meet Oscar Stern, foreman of the packing department.

Oscar was five feet, eight inches tall and weighed 127 pounds. He wore a gray wool suit, black bow tie, white shirt, and vest. His black hair was oily and slicked back. He wore wire frame glasses and tilted his head back whenever he inspected a garment. He carried around his neck a cloth measuring tape, which nobody had ever seen him use. Many of the foremen wore a cloth tape, but they had legitimate reason to do so--their areas sewed shirts they would need to measure to make sure of the correct size. If Oscar were to measure something, it meant he would have been checking some other area's work. This was an unwritten taboo.

On the way over, one of the owners, Mr. Harris, stopped Bernstein, "May I have a word with you, Sam?"

"Excuse me."

Mr. Harris and Mr. Bernstein huddled together.

"What are ya doing hiring Irish?"

"What?"

"Irish."

"No. British."

"You sure."

"Yes."

"I tell ya, stick to Jews and Italians. You can't go wrong. Carry on."

Junior had gotten tired of the "Irish Need Not Apply" signs. It helped that he did not have a particularly Irish last name. "My ship sailed from London," he had explained. It was not exactly a lie. His ship had sailed from London. He just was not on it. He had gone aboard when it stopped at Queenstown, Ireland.

"I don't have my Alien Identification Card. It was stolen when I was jumped." He had to be careful about this one. You were required to have your card at all times and the employer was expected to see the card. The card would have shown his port of departure in Ireland. That he was jumped also might raise suspicions about the applicants' judgment and ability to defend himself. Junior would point to the still visible knot on the side of his head, "Smacked from behind with a four by four."

If the interview were going well, he would ask about the nearest Anglican Church. Most people assumed that if you were Irish, you were Catholic. If he needed, he pulled the "I've never even been inside a Catholic church" line. No outright lie had been told.

Δ   Δ   Δ

After a week of work, he received his pay. Three dollars minus expenses.

"They told me six."

"It's training wages. This week and next." Actually, that was not true. Wages were handed out from the owners to the foreman to the worker. The foremen would extract whatever additional they could. The justified expenses were taken out of the pay by the company. The unjustified were taken out by the foreman. The training wages for such a simple job as packaging was half a week, not two weeks. Oscar pocketed the balance.

It was standard across the garment industry for companies to rent to their workers the equipment they used, and charge for maintenance and repairs. Even though the seamstresses would have long since paid for their sewing machines, the fees continued. If the mechanical drive mechanism that ran all the machines snapped, it was surely determined to be the failure of one particular machine and charged accordingly. Workers were also charged for errors.

The packing department had little in the way of equipment, but there were handcarts. Junior's cart cost him 35 cents a week.

Junior started his career in debt. He had borrowed money

from Aunt Betty (behind Charlie's back, of course) to buy work clothes and shoes. He had also borrowed money for food while he was out looking for work and fares on trolleys and the subway. He insisted on keeping a close accounting of those expenses and paying Aunt Betty back promptly. However, things were going in the wrong direction. He also learned the amount that had been taken from him when he was mugged was enormous.

Δ   Δ   Δ

This Irishman was a good catch, thought Oscar Stern after Junior's first day. Cheap. Smart enough to outwit the bosses into hiring him. He worked hard and didn't complain. He was in and out of the toilet in a flash. He did good work. Strong and wiry, just the way I like 'em.

Before lunchtime, Oscar could see Junior's pace was greater than the men around him.

Oscar was good-natured, when he was not picking your pocket, which turned out to be most of the time. He had worked his way to his current position by keeping a close eye on things. Mostly, he pressed for good quality work. You could always get a man to work faster, but you couldn't get every man to work better. Better meant fewer customer complaints. Fewer customer complaints meant happy owners. If the owners were happy they did not come to bitch, and you kept your job.

He was Jewish and in earlier times, would have been orthodox, but the six-day workweek and career advancement made working the Sabbath a must. The higher foreman pay and the ability to skim off the top of his workers were too much of a lure. He was twenty-nine years old, had been married for eight years, and had no children.

He owned an apartment a few blocks south of the plant at 172 Thompson Street in Manhattan. It was almost new, modest, and quite modern with modern gas heating and indoor plumbing. His wife, Teresse went by the name 'Rose'. While Oscar worked, she was at Temple most days praying to have children. She knew it was the curse of God, from Oscar's sin of not keeping the Sabbath, that prevented her from getting pregnant. Why was she the one to suffer? She did not understand.

Rose decorated the apartment with roses everywhere, except in the flower vases. There were roses woven into the throw rugs, on the linen, on the towels, on the silverware, in the frosted glass windows--everywhere. Well, except in the flower vases; Rose was allergic to roses.

At the end of his first day, Oscar had a few words for Junior. They were not really meant to encourage him as to give him a message: "Continue to do good work, and you may be able to keep your job."

"I need to find a place to live. My uncle's place is too far," he lied.

"Is that a fact? I just might know of a place". He wanted to think over having an Irishman in his house.

"Please look into it for me," replied Junior.

The following morning, Oscar announced he himself might be interested in taking in a boarder. In reality, the $90 per year mortgage was killing him.

On a handshake, they agreed that Junior would move in in a few days. Oscar told him it would be a bargain at $3.00 per week, not including board. He would have to pay extra for his meals. Oscar assured him it was the 'going rate', and Junior believed him.

Junior solved one problem and created two others. He no longer lived with his Uncle and continual demands to get out. Now his boss had not one hand, but two, in his pockets.

11

MANHATTAN

As spring turned to summer, Junior settled into his new routine. He was up early each day buying fresh bread and fruit for his midday meal. He loved the smell of the loaves coming out of the nearby bakery oven. He often bought soup, cheese, and butter from a neighbor woman.

Returning home, he made himself oatmeal and coffee for breakfast. Oscar would already be gone for the day by then and he returned well after Junior arrived back. Junior slowly walked to work admiring the neighborhood noises in the crisp mornings-- the dogs barking, the chickens squawking, the newsboys, the wheels of carts on the pavement, and horses neighing as they stretched their legs to the new day. He admired the beautiful roses in the park and their sweet fragrance. Suggesting Rose walk with him to the park sometime raised her husband's eyebrows, and it never happened.

For ten hours a day he packaged shirts, which had just been ironed, into cardboard boxes with tissue paper. Sometimes there were multiple shirts to a box and sometimes they went into the department store's specific box. The individual boxes were then packed into shipping cases and marked for delivery.

He was so good at his job, and it required so little thinking, he could watch the people in the offices nearby. The buyers bustled with sheets of paper, placing orders, negotiating for materials, getting signatures from the two owners when required. Salesman hung out by the display rooms, drinking coffee and flirting with the typists, before going off on their rounds to pick up orders. The phone operator served as receptionist to guests, mostly people from the department stores there to see plans for the new lines of shirtwaists.

Shirtwaists were versatile, high-necked blouses made of crisp, light, translucent cotton or sheer linen. They were easy to mass-produce and ranged in price from a few dollars for simple designs for common workers to a few dozen dollars for elegant attire for society women. There was the usual mix of vendors selling buttons, ribbons, cartons, cloth, and tissue paper. Occasionally the owners' wives and children dropped by for a visit and lunch when in the area shopping.

Δ   Δ   Δ

Everywhere he turned, he was reminded of Moira. He saw her in the secretaries the salesmen flirted with. He heard her voice in the telephone operator. He thought of the family they would have together when he saw the owner's children.

Junior had to pick up the ironed shirts from the Pressing Department and move the completed cartons to Shipping. Others around him did the same mind-numbing work, mostly silently. After his ten hour shift, if there was no overtime, which was rare for his department, he got into line to be checked out. Each day he and all his co-workers were searched. Rarely was anything ever found. He began making a few friends at work, but most people were standoffish to an Irishman.

He took the freight elevator down to the street and walked south toward home. After being on his feet all day, he was tired, but walking felt good. The wind that whipped through the area was filled with ash and soot, but he didn't mind. It smelled better than the manure and sewage along the streets.

He relaxed with a drink of water, sat on the front steps, and watched the day draw to a close.

Soon after Oscar returned home, Rose served supper. Junior was not aware of it initially, but Oscar charged him an exorbitant amount for meals. Oscar just took it out of his pay, with all the other trumped up expenses.

Oscar's wife was delightful and strikingly beautiful. Junior wondered what drew her to Oscar. Her hair was pulled back and tucked into a bun. She had a wonderful figure and smelled of perfume. She wore the most elegant shirtwaists her husband's plant produced and beautiful wool skirts. Her hands were beautiful and graceful and she had large, expressive green eyes.

Rose cooked simple, pleasant meals. She sat at the table after supper, describing each activity of her day, and Junior listened quietly. She found ways to reach out and touch his hands or arms whenever they talked.

Δ   Δ   Δ

Most evenings Junior excused himself to take a walk alone after supper. It was during these walks that he felt most lonesome. Oscar smoked his pipe and read before retiring early. Rose frequently followed him to bed shortly, but just as often she waited up until Junior came back from his walk. Over time, she became more relaxed around Junior. He noticed when she wore flimsy clothing that showed her beautiful breasts and ankles. She gave Junior coy looks and batted her eyes. She began flirting with him; his senses were becoming aroused.

Was he just imagining things? Soon she left stockings and underpants where he would see them. Was she doing this on purpose? Once she left her brassiere on his bed. He held them up, looked at the cups which were meant to suppress her ample breasts, and could smell her perfume on them. He lifted the brassiere to his nostrils and closed his eyes imagining her in it. She startled him when she came up from behind him, pressing her breasts into his back, and snatched the brassiere from his hands, whispering in his ear "Sorry, did I drop that there?"

Three things ran continuously through Junior's mind. First, how could Oscar not notice? She was brazen enough to do this even when Oscar was in the next room! Second, would he lose his job and home on the same day? Where could he turn? Third, how would Moira feel if he gave in to temptation?

He spent as little time at home as possible to avoid Rose's advances. Sunday was the worst. He had never attended church before, but began in order to get away. After church services at Trinity Episcopal Church in lower Manhattan, he found a place to swim. He had missed swimming each day so much. He walked to places where the water was cleanest and swam for hours, returning exhausted late in the day. Junior was in a financial bind. He didn't realize how much he was being ripped off. He thought Oscar was his friend and benefactor.

Oscar was always cheerful around him, with a broad smile, and welcoming hands. Oscar actually saw Junior as his meal ticket and the longer he dangled Junior along the better. After all, this was America. How would Junior know whether this was the custom of the land? Oscar thought of this in the broadest possible terms. Each new generation of immigrant lifted the previous generation up. They took the lower jobs, which allowed the previous to move up the social and economic ladder. One day, Junior would lead men and could duplicate Oscar's pattern of success.

Junior set aside a jar to save money, to drop in the few cents he had at the end of the week. He quickly suspected the few pennies he saved were being stolen and began to hide them instead. He still owed Aunt Betty money and missed her, but did not know how to reconnect with her other than to take her money back personally. He wanted to talk with her about Rose's behavior, how he might protect himself, but he could not find the courage to discuss such a delicate matter with anyone.

He missed Moira desperately. All his thoughts revolved around missing her or failing her--failing to get the money they needed. He wrote to her a bit every evening while in bed, and mailed it once a week. Many nights tears streamed down his cheeks. Hearing Oscar and Rose making love in the next room added to the sting. Outwardly, he clung to the belief that things would get better, but couldn't see how they would.

Δ   Δ   Δ

Weeks turned into months and a year. Not much changed. Moira sent a wonderful letter that arrived on Junior's seventeenth birthday. Almost weekly he received letters from her that only made him miss her more. He had heard from his mother twice. She said she was well and did not give much information.

Oscar was still squeezing him for every cent, but he had been able to save a little each week and hide it away. After his dreadful trip, Junior had his heart set on buying second-class tickets for Moira and Anne, making his goal twice as far away. Questions kept running through his mind: What if she died on the voyage? What if she were assaulted or raped in the bowels of the ship? He couldn't bear the thought of her in steerage, but couldn't see how he could be without her any longer. Rose's advances didn't help.

She was so beautiful and elegant. Everything about her was appealing. How much longer could he evade her? How much longer did he want to?

Δ   Δ   Δ

"Want to go downstairs?" Oscar barked one morning shortly after the workday had begun.

"What?"

"They are short downstairs. Need boys to move waists around."

"Does it pay more?"

"No," Oscar lied. "Hey, this is just for a day or two."

"Good."

Junior quickly reported to Mr. Samuel Bernstein, the man who had hired him a year before, on the eighth floor.

"Millwood, we are short runners to take partially completed garments to different workstations." Bernstein turned Junior over to Mrs. Farnaugh who showed him the ropes. It was easy work, much easier than packaging. Each station had a specific task, such as sewing a hem or attaching a sleeve. The completed garments were stacked at each station and he had to keep everyone supplied with work from the previous station.

He did this work for two days, and returned to packaging. He enjoyed the variety the change brought being with more people. Back upstairs, he guessed there were two hundred people on the eighth floor. The room smelled of cloth and tissue paper, cigar smoke, ozone, and machine oil. The noise from the sewing machines filled the air in short bursts, but there was also chatter and humming. The sewing tables didn't leave much aisle space, but there was enough room for people to get through.

He liked being around people, especially so many young women. There was always something happening. Someone was always getting up to use the restroom and get a drink. The bosses ran around monitoring things. Clerks kept counts of garments completed. Runners like him took partially completed garments upstairs to the next floor and finally to the top floor for pressing.

The windows to the south gave greater light and the twelve-foot ceilings added to the feel of being in the sky. He liked watching seagulls and pigeons flying around outside.

Junior also found his legs hurt less when he worked on the eighth floor. He was still on his feet all day, but did less standing in one position.

Mr. Bernstein asked Oscar if Millwood would be interested and capable of working downstairs full time. Oscar told him he would ask, but really, he wanted to consider the impact it would have on him. Junior would get higher pay from this job, but would also learn how much Oscar had been skimming off the top. He would be paid from another boss and this complicated things. He never asked Junior what he wanted.

The next day, Oscar told Mr. Bernstein he did not think Junior was ready for a change on a permanent basis, but should have him fill in as necessary. In reality, Oscar saw filling in downstairs was the best of both worlds, for him. Junior got higher pay, but didn't know it, since his pay still came through Oscar. A few days a week, Junior would find himself assigned to the eighth floor for relief when short-handed.

$$\Delta \quad \quad \Delta \quad \quad \Delta$$

That September, Junior was working on the eighth floor, when he heard and smelled something odd. A sewing machine drive cable had snapped. Suddenly oil squirted from the shaft onto the cloth and sparks were flashing. He looked for a drive disconnect, but couldn't see one. The rattle of the still spinning drive had frightened the operator away. He reached for the cable to steady it, just as an oily garment burst into flames beneath his hands. Flaming oil squirted onto his hands from the broken cable as he tried to both pat out the flames and find a way to shut down the out-of-control cable. The cloth caught in the cable and wrapped around his hands. The cloth tore at his fingers, squeezing out feeling.

As someone reached the master drive switch and slammed it off, all the sewing machines stopped suddenly. Buckets of water splashed onto him from different directions. The fire was quickly out. While one of the Cutters came over with his knife to free Junior, a mechanic quickly replaced the broken cable to get the sewing machines running.

They walked Junior to the washroom and applied wet towels to his hands. The pain got worse after they freed him from the tangled cloth and the shock wore off. He was taken to the company doctor who applied ointment and bandaged his hands. Instead of being a hero for trying to put out the fire and rescue the sewing machine operator, Mr. Bernstein said, "How foolish! Do you think we should even bring him back once his wounds heal?"

Only thinking of himself, Oscar replied, "I think we should give him another chance."

Δ   Δ   Δ

Pain the night of the accident was excruciating. The only thing that seemed to help was cold water. The Doctor had given him an opiate for the pain and when he finally decided to take it, it allowed him to sleep. The extreme pain eased over the next few days and Junior became accustomed to having both hands bandaged. He could dress himself, if he took it slowly. Using the toilet was difficult, but he managed. He could eat bread, which he did not bother to butter, and fresh apples.

In the month before Junior returned to work, he found himself walking a great deal during the day. Frequently he walked up to work in the morning and stood outside the building, greeting employees. It was just to get out of the house before Rose went off to Temple. Much of the day he spent sitting on the front steps watching the neighborhood. He began smoking cigars to pass the time.

The doctor had told Junior to change the bandages every three days. On the days the bandages were to be changed he would remove the bandages himself, and spend the afternoon wading up to his neck, keeping his hands in the water. He could not actually swim, as the motion of his hands through the water stung too much. Afterward a neighbor, Lydia, wrapped clean clothes around his hands and pinned the cloth in place with small safety pins.

He talked frequently to the neighbors and, for the first time, began to get to know them.

Without an income, he spent the little he had saved and skipped meals. The last week he lived on fruit he could find. Oscar cut him a break by reducing his rent for the month by twenty-five cents per week--a sacrifice in Oscar's mind, as he was not able to swindle him for expenses, such as charges for wheel wear on the carts used to transport the cases to shipping.

Junior did not feel he was of much use during his convalescence, but what could he do? He befriended a young neighbor, Naomi, and her newborn baby, Ruth, who was listless. She didn't respond to her mother's sweet voice. Naomi confided to Junior that she had been told her breast milk was not rich enough, and she needed to supplement with cow or goat milk. Her own malnutrition was being passed along to the child. Her husband gave her change to purchase milk from the vendors, but she found that difficult with a newborn infant. Could he help?

"Yes, of course."

Naomi reminded Junior of Moira with mousy brown hair and brown eyes, but formless. A young girl, with hardly any figure, and a newborn daughter on her hip.

He remembered a milk vendor who came by each morning. Slim was tall and lanky. He had sad gray eyes and spoke little. Junior tracked him down, though it took a few hours to find him.

Morning after morning, when Junior was purchasing his bread and fruit for lunch he also waited for Slim to come by to get a pint of milk in a small pail for Ruth. Naomi shared that her husband was a construction worker who drank away the rest of their money. Even with the milk, Ruth was not getting better.

Slim got his milk from the dairies in central Pennsylvania; the further from New York City the cheaper the milk. Slim added a little ammonia to the milk to kill the souring smell it had acquired while being transported. In eastern Pennsylvania, there were great deposits of calcium carbonate and plentiful streams of fresh water. Doctoring the milk on the way from the dairies was a time-honored method of stretching the milk being delivered to the children of Manhattan. It was killing Ruth.

Δ   Δ   Δ

Junior's burned and twisted hands were swollen and raw from the third degree burns on his palms and the tourniquet twisting of the snagged cloth. The frequent changes in bandages helped to keep them clean and the swims in the oily East River coated them with a soothing balm. After three weeks, Oscar began pressing him to return.

"Mr. Bernstein wants to know when you can return," Oscar lied. He was thinking about his lost revenue. Junior knew he needed to return soon, but he did not see how he would manage because of the blisters. He also knew that if he wanted to eat, he had to get back to work soon. His savings were quickly being exhausted.

Oscar had been pumping Bernstein about letting Junior return. Sam was non-committal. He could not afford to put a young man back to work who could not do the job. What kind of example would that set? At the same time, he heard from the women downstairs about Junior's heroic act and daring that may have saved them from worse injury or destruction. The only response Bernstein would give to Oscar was, "We'll see."

Three days later, Junior reported back to work. He arrived early on a Monday morning at Mr. Bernstein's office. Bernstein was actually happy to see him. "How are you doing, Millwood?"

"Good. I'd like to go back to work, Sir."

"How are the hands?"

"Much better, Sir." His hands were still very tender, especially in his palms. He believed he could fake his way through the days until the calluses returned and he was back to normal.

"Millwood, the ladies told me of your brave actions. Thank you for trying to put out the fire."

Junior did not know what to say.

"The cable snaps on occasion. Better to get away from it than to contain it. You didn't need to try to grab it to put the fire out. Go for the fire buckets next time. I guess we all have to learn."

Mr. Bernstein reached into his desk drawer. "Thought these might help." He handed Junior a pair of soft, elegantly stitched cotton gloves. "I had them lying around the house." Junior gingerly tried them on. It was painful, but they fit perfectly.

Mr. Bernstein got up and walked Junior from his office through the Shipping Department to the Packing Department.

"I know Mr. Stern said you would like to stay here in packing, but I think you would do better downstairs."

Oscar tried to intervene, but Bernstein continued on "Would you be interested in working on the eighth floor?"

"Well, he, he--," Oscar trailed off not knowing what else to say.

Junior said "Yes."

Bernstein escorted Junior downstairs using the executive elevator. Mrs. Farnaugh greeted him as if she were a long, lost aunt welcoming a soldier back from the war. The women referred to him as their hero, and he blushed until he could feel the burning in his face.

Mr. Bernstein announced, "Everyone back to work." Returning to the elevator, he whispered to Junior "Your rate will be $8.00 a week."

Junior was almost giddy at the thought of a two-dollar per week raise. He did not realize that was the standard starting rate for this job and he had been given that pay when he worked downstairs before. It just had ended up in Oscar's pocket.

His hands were sore and blisters begin to develop, but he ignored them.

At the end of the day, he pulled off his cotton gloves and washed his bleeding hands before walking over to be checked out.

He puffed on a cigar as he dragged himself home that evening.

Oscar returned to his house in a disgruntled mood. He had lost his meal ticket and had to hire and train a new employee. At least he would get a few dollars back during the training period.

"I need to have a word with you, Millwood. I am going to have to raise your rent."

"If you must, you must."

RUTH

During the fall, Ruth was not gaining weight and still limp in her mother's arms. Naomi would coax her to eat and she would halfheartedly take her nipple, but lose interest quickly. Junior continued to get milk from Slim and, more importantly, encourage Naomi. Junior and Naomi looked at each other in a bewildered way, unable to conjure up the right answer. She seemed to be doing all the right things. She tried everything the neighbor women suggested. In the morning, they passed along their advice, and then returned to their homes. Over time, their words of encouragement and advice dried up as they sensed little Ruth was fading. Instead of their words of advice, Naomi would now hear, "How is our dear Ruthy today?"

"About the same," was all she could mutter.

Behind her back, the women would say to each other, "Would be a blessing if she goes quickly."

But she didn't. She lingered.

At last, the candle that was her life flipped from a slight flame to a whiff of smoke. She was gone.

It happened during the night while Naomi was alone and her husband was out drinking. She lay there with the baby at her side in the candlelight, stroking her hair, thinking what a blessing Ruthy had been to her. It was hard to watch her child die, but Naomi knew it was coming for weeks. She shed tears for her lovely child.

Her husband came in well after midnight. "Why are you wasting candles?"

"Ruth is dead."

He laid down next to Naomi. He was rigid. All he said was, "God's will. You'll have another," and fell into a drunken sleep.

Naomi continued to stroke Ruth's delicate hair until dawn.

Δ   Δ   Δ

The next morning the tenement was alive with the news.

"Did you hear about little Ruthy?"

"So sad."

"Yes, but God's will."

"'Tis really a blessing."

The neighbors began collecting the twenty dollars they figured would be needed for the burial. Junior gave all he could; more than Ruth's father had.

A small, unfinished white-pine coffin was delivered, and Ruth's frail body was washed, dressed in what was to have been her christening dress, and placed inside. The lid was closed and it seemed to be the size of a jewelry case.

For the next two days, neighbors and family, in their best attire, visited Naomi and her husband to pay their respects and drop off food. On the second day, a priest came by and prayed with the family. Every man who came was offered a drink and a smoke in the main room of the small apartment. The women gathered in the next room to console Naomi. Near the end of the second day, an underling of the Manhattan Tammany boss came to have a drink, share a smoke, and chat with the men. He casually asked how they had done collecting money for the funeral. Disheartened, Ruth's father announced they were five dollars short.

"We'll take care of the balance." He then whispered in her father's ear, "Just remember us when it comes election time."

Standing up, he said, "Part of us being neighbors is looking out for one another and helping each other through our grief. The Republicans will not be there to help you out, but you can count on the Democratic ticket to take you through the hard times. We are with you in the loss of your cherished girl."

He then whispered something in an aid's ear, who went to

Calvary Cemetery and told them to reduce the price from the standard $20 to $15, but send the bill to the family showing the Democratic Party had paid five dollars. The order was instantly obeyed.

The following mid-morning, an undertaker from Calvary Cemetery arrived to take the casket away. No prayers were said and no funeral service was given. He carried the little casket in two arms--the jewel now in the jewelry case--back to his wagon. The horse plodded away, clicking its hooves on the cobblestone brick, sounding taps for Ruth.

Δ   Δ   Δ

The build-up to Ruth's death was long and torturous. However, the aftermath was quick. Once the hearse pulled away from the curb, Naomi's husband returned to his work and his drinking. Neighbors went back to their normal patterns and Naomi was left alone to mourn. She slipped into a depression that kept her confined to bed for the next week. Her husband, expecting his life to be unaffected, demanded his meals and conjugal relations. Naomi needed to cry and to talk out her feelings.

After a week, she forced herself to get up, but was haunted by loneliness. Eighty people lived within 120 feet of her. She could hear their laughter and their cries. She could smell the meals being cooked and the manure on the street. There was life all around her, but she felt alone. Nothing penetrated the dark curtain that fell down around and enveloped her.

Her husband couldn't help her, even if he tried. And he didn't. All she could think about was how she had failed Ruth. She had not found the answer to her illness. She had done everything she could to restore her health. She could not understand a God whose will it would be to let her baby die. He may have allowed it, He may have stood by during her time of greatest need and not answered her, but she could not believe God would be so heartless as to will Ruth to die. It would be the easy way out to blame God. God would not answer for Himself, so one could never really know.

If God was not to blame, Naomi felt she was. Her guilt didn't ease up, but she forced herself out onto the front steps to watch people. Junior had been quietly talking to her on the steps after supper each evening. They both heard of accounts on their street of babies suffering similar fates.

Junior was good at listening to her.

"It's not your fault. You did all you could."

Naomi cried on Junior's shoulder.

Junior often came away from their times together feeling guilty. For all his great love for Moira and his tender feeling toward Naomi and her loss, he could also feel himself being attracted to Naomi. He wrote openly to Moira about what Naomi had gone through and how he tried to help. He had been able to resist the beautiful Rose, could he resist the homely Naomi? As fall became winter, their talks moved indoors. He had pledged himself to remain pure to Moira. Could he know the feelings of compassion and resist them turning to passion?

Naomi's need for comforting went beyond her feelings about Ruth. She had lost her daughter to illness and her husband to the mistress of the bottle. Was it his way of coping with the tragedy? Perhaps. When she needed him most, he was less available than ever.

Δ Δ Δ

One evening near Christmas, while standing together in the kitchen, she thanked Junior for being there for her. "I don't know what I would have done without you."

Her hands moved up his arms as she looked into his eyes. She grabbed him by his biceps. She missed the tender touch from her husband when they had first married two years before. "You are a dear friend."

His blood stirred at her touch.

She pressed forward to hug him.

He pressed his hands upon her back and she pressed her small, firm breasts into his chest. They embraced for a long time unable to let go of each other. Slowly she pulled away until their faces were inches apart. Her mouth hanging open, she lingered there looking into his eyes.

He could not help himself--he kissed her. She responded eagerly.

He felt himself become hard a few seconds before she noticed. In a fury of tossing away clothing, they were locked together. That first time, on the kitchen floor, was over in a few seconds.

"I'm sorry I did not mean to--"

"Yes, we did."

That night, alone in his room, feelings of guilt and questions flooded his mind. How can something so natural be wrong? How could he have betrayed Moira? Will she understand? Will she forgive me? Can we resist that feeling again? Can we resist making love again?

The next night Junior tried to apologize for his failure, which led to them making love again. They continued nearly every evening until spring. Junior began to justify that the feeling Naomi received from him was exactly what she needed for healing. He kept telling himself he could break it off for Moira, but he never really tried.

One night, when they were nearly caught by Naomi's husband, it became clear they needed to stop. For Naomi's sake. For Junior's sake. For Moira's sake. The neighbors were whispering. They agreed they must refrain. Most nights they succeeded.

Δ   Δ   Δ

For the next year and a half little changed. Through the different seasons, he walked the few blocks to work in the early morning after shopping for his lunch meal and eating his breakfast. Junior worked hard on the eighth floor and at the end of each day, walked slowly home smoking his cigar. He avoided Rose as much as possible. She stopped her advances once she got wind of Junior's romance with Naomi. Most evenings he spent at least a little time talking to Naomi on the steps or in her apartment. On Sundays, he went to church and swam. His father would have a fit if he knew his son was spending time in church. At least it was not Roman Catholic. He spent his Sunday afternoons exhausting himself in the East River.

Every day he wrote a small bit to Moira and mailed it once a week. The only time he had skipped this ritual was during recovery from his burns. He received letters from her about every week.

Naomi had another baby in the early fall of 1908. He was small, undernourished, and slow to develop, but generally healthy. There were rumors he belonged to Junior, but Junior didn't pay them any mind.

Since there were fewer ways for Oscar to steal from him, Junior began saving money. He was frugal. His only luxury was cheap cigars. He passed the halfway point of saving enough money for

Moira and Anne to travel second-class passage from Ireland by the following spring. Junior considered telegraphing the money and allowing Moira and Anne to decide whether to come on steerage. But he thought better of it and continued to save.

After his affair with Naomi, he felt guilty and thought of sending a gift to Moira to show his love for her and cement their engagement. He asked the women around work what he should send and they all thought it was a romantic idea. Some said a ring. Others said a photograph. One of the girls offered to sell him a favorite item. She explained she was short on the rent money and it would do them both a favor. They agreed she should bring it in and he would make her an offer. One woman came forward to warn Junior that it was probably stolen. The next day the girl placed in Junior's hand a Victorian amethyst pendant brooch crafted in solid fourteen-carat gold and weighing over ten grams.

Junior mumbled, "It's stunning! I have never seen anything like this."

The deep violet amethyst in the center was surrounded by seed pearls. It measured over one inch square.

It was the perfect piece and Junior asked her to set a price on the spot. He was surprised by how low she set it. He asked how she had come by it, and she nervously explained, "It was in my family--an engagement gift for a marriage that was never consummated. The man died and left no one to which to return it." The story was at least plausible.

One of Junior's friends in the Shipping Department arranged to package, insure, and ship it for him. Junior was making many friends at work.

Δ   Δ   Δ

Around the time of Junior's nineteenth birthday, he noticed a new hire on the eighth floor. She had been working at a sweatshop south of Washington Square Park. She had beautiful red hair, which she kept in a bun to accentuate her high cheekbones and fair skin.

Helena made it a point to be clean and well dressed. She attended church each morning and frequently she was the only one there when the candles were lit by the yawning altar boys. She wandered through the park in all seasons, before going in to work. Junior often saw her there. Whether the roses were withering from the heat, just beginning to bud, or had been cut back to sticks in the snow, she was there to enjoy each transition. She anticipated and appreciated each season and watched for the minutest changes in the roses.

She was nearly always the first worker in the building, often waiting for the security man to open the doors. She walked up the first flight of stairs, so as not to draw attention, and then ran the remaining flights, even though she would spend her day on her feet and her legs would be exhausted by evening.

She stood in the middle of the room, at her workstation preparing for the workday. She welcomed people as they passed by her. She often prayed for the workers and their family as they entered the room and kept tabs on the events in people's lives. Over time, she remembered all the birthdays and anniversaries, the pregnancies, births, illnesses, and deaths of her co-workers and their families.

She looked forward to seeing Junior each day. She admired his easy manner and his athletic, trim body. He arrived on the floor at the last possible moment each day, but always had something to whisper to her on his way to his work area. Junior was just teasing, but Helena was falling in love.

LABOR PROTEST

Because Junior was paid so little, he was always one of the last people to be let go. Besides, Oscar had to take care of his investment.

During the steamy days of summer in 1909, labor unrest mounted. Most workers had not seen a raise in two years and some had seen a reduction. Since workers were not unionized, wildcat strikes occurred, pitting workers against owners in winner-takes-all battles. If the workers were the first to give in, wages were often reduced as punishment. While hired thugs kept workers in line, police turned their heads away.

Without unions, there was never enough money to hold out in an extended strike. Workers got fired for merely suggesting some form of labor action. Junior steered away from the protestors, concerned that without a steady job, he ran the risk of being deported.

Many of the women began attending meetings and rallies of the Women's Trade Union League. Most listened to the socialistic speeches, cheered the rhetoric, and proclaimed the catchy slogans, but few joined the union.

Junior went to a few rallies to see what was going on. Since it was a Women's Union, he felt there was no place for him. After he heard during one of the rallies it was "run by women and for women with a minimum of male intervention" he had no interest in joining.

One September day, a hundred and fifty workers at his plant were fired to rid the company of suspected union sympathizers and those having attended a rally.

A walkout at the Rosen Brother's plant, demanding a twenty-percent wage increase, electrified garment workers throughout the city.

"Do you think we could, too?"

"If they can keep from caving in, we can."

The strikers' tenacity and perfect timing caused the owners to cave in and grant increases to all their employees. Newspaper reports commented on the strikers "steadfastness and militancy." Competing firms were angered by the action and galvanized together against future worker unrest. They stepped up firing ringleaders at the first sign of trouble and roughing up of supporters.

Junior had witnessed some of the problems, especially among the Cutter's Assistants. Unlike the Cutters who were highly-paid men, treated well, respected for their work, and could get a job any place in the garment trade, their Assistant's were a lesser class. The disparity between the pay levels of these two groups created sore feelings. Assistants were often the first to be let go, physically escorted off the premises at the smallest whiff of unrest. Junior had already seen this happen and felt uneasy. There was increasing pressure to strike every day. As summer reached its peak, so did the labor unrest.

One afternoon, Junior was summoned to the office on the tenth floor. A most unusual thing had occurred. The company received a telegram addressed to 'Rory John Millwood, Junior' from the White Star Line. The telegram read: ANNE DEAD. SENDING MOIRA 30 SEPT ON ADRIATIC.

MOIRA

Moira was as uncomfortable thinking of being in second-class as Junior had been physically in steerage. At sixteen years old, she listed herself as an orphan. She stood five feet, four inches and weighed one hundred pounds. Her large, dark brown eyes took in all around her. She was meek and quiet. For proof of her engagement, she had a stack of letters from Junior and the pendant he had given her as an engagement present.

"Best keep that item private, Miss." The agent marked a special note concerning the engagement on the papers. He did not know if it would do any good, but it certainly would not hurt. The Immigration Officers on Ellis Island were always on the lookout for girls coming to New York City as white slave prostitutes. The agent's note indicated this was not the case with this girl, "as ample documents indicate". He added, "Please process her application swiftly." He gave both Junior's home and work addresses, which could also be helpful.

Junior's mother provided most of the details to the White Star agent when she paid in cash for Moira's passage. Everyone involved (Junior, Moira, and even the White Star Booking Agent) knew where the cash for the trip came from-- Muirne had stolen it from Rory's hidden stash. Mr. Millwood was a prominent man about town and the booking agent was sticking his neck out by being helpful. He looked at Moira and this mother's sad eyes and knew what he had to do. The documents were as impeccable as any he had seen. Every detail matched Moira's story. Everything was in order. He could do a lot for Moira, but he could not do a thing to help Muirne. Another beating was in store for her when Mr. Millwood found out, and they all knew it.

Both Moira and Junior felt same emotions: joy, jubilation, pain, and panic. For Moira, she was finally setting sail on her new adventure. The plan they worked out so long ago, the plan they had waited for, was now beginning to come true. She was jubilant at the thought of being back together with Junior. Moira believed her mother died of a broken heart during the torturous wait. In fact, a large, fast-growing aortic aneurysm had taken her quickly, quietly, and painlessly, while she slept.

The grief of losing her best friend in the world was often more than Moira could bear. She longed to be in Junior's arms, to know she was once again secure, but panicked at the thought of being on the ship among the wealthy. She mainly wore cotton smocks and had a single set of good clothes. She knew she'd have to dress for dinner every evening for a voyage that could be ten days long and that she didn't have the training or manners necessary for second-class. Muirne helped her out with the clothing, but this shy, young girl would have to pull off the rest.

The agent had already been thinking ahead. He summoned a wealthy, elderly businessman who traveled extensively between New York and Queenstown who had booked his passage on the same voyage and asked if he could come to his office at his convenience to speak about a situation where he may be a blessing to a young woman. He knew him to be of good, Christian character.

Δ   Δ   Δ

"Mr. Erbacher, thank you for coming in."

"Certainly."

"I have a most unusual request."

"Is there something wrong with my ticket?"

"No, it is more of a personal situation." He explained from the beginning.

"My wife and I will be traveling together. We will need to meet the young girl before we can solidify my answer, but I can give you a tentative yes."

At the arranged meeting, Mr. and Mrs. Erbacher were charmed by the urchin and her wide, dark eyes. Mr. Erbacher returned to the White Star office and made three demands, "She will need to be assigned to our cabin, put us all in second class, oh, we will also have a maid, and Mrs. Erbacher will need to take her shopping beforehand."

Junior's joy and jubilation were similar, but his panic was different. He didn't want Moira meeting Rose or Naomi or Helena. He began asking around for places to move to and found a three-room, four hundred square foot tenement apartment in the 100 block of Congress in Brooklyn, suitable for newlyweds. He was astonished how inexpensive it was, compared to what he had been paying!

On September 30, 1909, *RMS Adriatic* sailed from Liverpool to New York City, stopping briefly to pick up passengers in Queenstown. Few travelers were in the second-class salon when they were motored out to the ship that afternoon. All assumed Moira was the Erbacher's grandniece or the like. She had a single trunk that Mrs. Erbacher had purchased for her.

Δ   Δ   Δ

The ship slipped out to sea in the calm of the evening, as dinner was being served in the second-class dining room. Moira came to this meal the same way she would come to all meals aboard, on Mr. Erbacher's arm with his wife trailing behind. She was wearing a beautiful, white blouse, simple wool skirt, and patent leather shoes that Mrs. Erbacher had purchased for her. She had gotten three sets of blouses, two skirts, and a simple, full-length white wedding dress. Her engagement pendant looked stunning against the white blouse. She had been told to hold onto Mr. Erbacher's arm with her head held high. The Erbacher's maid washed and brushed Moira's long, dark hair and fixed it into a bun. Her transformation was amazing.

"Do exactly as we do," whispered Mrs. Erbacher. By prior arrangement with the stewards, Mr. Erbacher sat at the end of the table, with Moira to his left and Mrs. Erbacher to his right. This placed Moira directly across from Mrs. Erbacher, where she could mimic each of her motions. Frequently, Mr. Erbacher would lean forward to speak to Moira, mostly just to reassure her and make sure she felt comfortable.

They walked around the promenade deck together, smiling, chitchatting, and nodding to acquaintances. Many of his friends noticed Mr. Erbacher seemed more reserved and less social than usual, but passed it off as him being around his granddaughter, or grandniece, or whoever that girl may be. And why were they traveling second class?

The two-bedroom cabin was exactly what Moira needed. Mrs. Erbacher talked to her more like a sister than a mother. She was elegant and proper, with the correct amount of curiosity. The Erbachers were giving Moira a real gift of themselves. They placed her at complete ease.

As the seas became rougher, Moira became seasick. Mrs. Erbacher held her head as she vomited in the chamber pot and sponged off her neck, forehead, and mouth. "That's all right, dear. None of us is exempt." Mr. Erbacher gave her a little wine and she eventually fell asleep.

Δ   Δ   Δ

One evening, Moira said to Mr. Erbacher that she wanted to see steerage. He raised his eyebrow, but complied. He took her down to the bowels of the ship and let her experience the music and the chatter. She didn't stay long as the odor made her nauseous again. They returned to the promenade deck.

"How did Junior live down there for ten days."

"How indeed? But most survive."

"It's so cramped."

"Yes, but they make do. Many spend as much time on deck as they are able."

"I am not a delicate girl, but--"

"Nobody should have to endure that treatment."

Between meals, Moira spent most of the time in the cabin. She sewed, read, and talked for hours with Mrs. Erbacher.

"Will you stand up for us?"

"But, we have not even met Junior."

Jabbing Mr. Erbacher in the stomach, Mrs. Erbacher replied, "Of course we will, dear."

She had been hoping to be married in a church all her life and Junior said he would arrange it. He had been attending a church in Manhattan since he had arrived, principally to get away from Rose. He spoke with the Deacon and told him they would be living in Brooklyn. He asked if he could arrange a wedding once Moira arrived.

As the tugboats arrived to push the *Adriatic* up the river to Chelsea Piers, she looked out amazed at the size of Manhattan. There were people and buildings for as far as the eye could see.

Being United States citizens the Erbachers were able to get off the boat quickly, while Moira was still headed over to Ellis Island. Unlike Junior, she was whisked there by a fast boat.

Mr. Erbacher gave Moira his contact information and let her know how they could be reached for the wedding, or if she needed anything. It was expected the wedding would take place within a few days after she passed through Immigration, but that could take a while.

Her departure from the ship was delayed longer than usual, when Mrs. William Tevis of Bakersfield, California and her four sons, declared the largest customs amount recorded to date. Mabella Pacheco Tevis--daughter of California's first Hispanic governor, Romualdo Pacheco--declared $10,000 in customs, which nearly brought the customs office to a standstill, was reported in newspapers across the country, and stranded passengers until officials could decide how to handle such a large amount. Moira's launch finally arrived at Ellis Island, shortly after 2 p.m.

Δ   Δ   Δ

While Moira was walking into the Great Hall on Ellis Island, being helped with her trunk, Junior was beside himself. The women at work had been amused at this nineteen-year-old boy as he counted down the days until his love arrived. Unlike his normal way when he was Johnny-on-the-spot, he could hardly keep a thought in his head. They called out to him to pick up their completed pieces of work, with "Over here, lover boy!"

Even though she wished it was her he loved, Helena was happy for Junior. She could put her love for him behind her, knowing this would make him happy, even if it made her sad. Perhaps a love for her would appear someday.

The wait was killing him. Friday, October 8, 1909 was the worst. By all measures, it was the second day she could arrive and the most likely day that she would. What pained Junior is that she could arrive over the weekend and he would not know it. On the other hand, she could be over at Ellis Island for many days after her arrival.

He coaxed the telephone operator to call the White Star Line office to get periodic updates soon after the *Adriatic* departed. They did not have helpful information until that Friday at mid-day. The *RMS Adriatic* had arrived in New York Harbor. However, had it arrived during the night? In the morning? At mid-day? Was it even at the dock? Nobody knew. From the southwest windows, Junior could see ships in the East River. He wondered which one she was on.

Mr. Erbacher had slipped his business card into Moira's papers: Mr. Russell J. Erbacher, Importer of Golf and Tennis Equipment. Agent for the Harry Vardon line of golf clubs. On the back, Erbacher had written: Please extend to Moira every possible courtesy. Please return this card and you will be rewarded with $10 off golf equipment at any major outlet in New York City. It was signed: R. J. Erbacher.

The booking agent placed a similar card in Moira's papers asking for favorable treatment. The agent who reviewed her passport, visa, alien identification card, customs, and other documents, was suspicious at first. After looking over the papers and asking her a few of the twenty-nine required questions, he sent her along for her medical examination, while pocketing Erbacher's card. She passed the medical examination with flying colors.

Normally single women were not released late Friday into the city and she would have been held over to Monday morning as a safety precaution. The immigration agent noticed both Junior's home and work addresses were on the forms, as was his work telephone number. This was rare. At the booking agent's request, he decided to go the extra mile and call. When the call came in to the switchboard for Junior, the operator asked what it was about. After the agent explained, she said, "We'll get him there! We'll get him there!" and she left the phone dangling off the hook as she ran downstairs to tell Junior. The agent should have spoken to Junior personally, but thought it would be safe to let her go. She was released to take the launch, with her trunk, over to Fort Clinton.

The switchboard operator arrived out of wind in the middle of the eighth floor. "Where is he? Where is he? He needs to go." Instantly everyone knew what she was talking about. They pointed over to the windows where he was craning his neck to identify any ocean liners arriving in the port.

"Quick! They are letting her go!"

He looked at her puzzled.

The women at the nearby sewing machines broke into laughter.

The switchboard operator grabbed him by the arm and began dragging him to the executive elevators, while she explained, "They are letting your little darling off the Island. You need to greet her." It was still two hours before quitting time.

She told the elevator man, "Lobby! Quick!"

When they arrived at the lobby, she spotted Mr. Harris' chauffeur. "Take him to Fort Clinton immediately and come right back." Junior got into the back seat of the limousine that was sitting at the curb. The driver jumped into the front seat and hurriedly left.

Only on the elevator ride back up to the tenth floor did it strike her what she had done. She had left the switchboard unattended. She had let an employee leave work early. She had used the executive elevator. She had commandeered one of the owner's personal limousines. As the elevator doors opened at the tenth floor, she nearly fainted.

$$\Delta \qquad \Delta \qquad \Delta$$

Mr. Harris' chauffeur dropped Junior at the entrance to Fort Clinton well before Moira left Ellis Island. Junior searched, but couldn't find her. He was sweating and his heart was pounding. He thought he must calm down. He wandered over to the area where he had come out of Fort Clinton and noticed one or two people coming through with their trunks, chests, and bags. There was no big parade.

He looked around to see if he could see the men who had roughed him up, but did not spot them. He wondered what he would have done if he had. He noticed a launch pull up to the dock and disembark a few passengers, one a female, but could not tell if it was Moira. In all his excitement, he needed to urinate, and went off to relieve himself. When he returned, he wondered if he had missed her. Deciding he had not, he walked over to a nearby lamppost and leaned against it to wait.

Things kept crashing through his mind.

"How foolish!" he thought to himself, "Stop tormenting yourself!" He waited for over an hour.

Then she was there right before him, more beautiful than he

had remembered. They stared at each other in disbelief, broke into a broad grin, hugged, kissed, and pulled each other out to look at one another. They heard and saw nothing else.

When they got back to his new home in Brooklyn, they stood on the front steps with the trunk at their side. They honestly could not remember how they had gotten there (he had hailed a horse drawn cab and handed the driver the address and cash).

They hugged, and kissed, and whispered to each other as they sat on the floor of his sparsely furnished tenement apartment all night. By five the next morning, Junior realized he was hungry. "You must be famished?"

"Yes! I guess I am!"

Junior did something he had never done before and did not quite know how to do. He went out to find a place to eat breakfast.

Δ   Δ   Δ

Junior should have been at work on Saturday morning, but Mr. Bernstein was not expecting him. Bernstein chuckled when he heard about Millwood being whisked away in one of the owner's cars and that everyone had kept the secret. It became a legend in the company's history.

After breakfast, Junior asked a simple question, "Tomorrow?"

"Why wait?"

"I'm not sure we can arrange things so quickly!"

"Oh, and we must notify the Erbachers!"

"Who?"

"You know, the people on the ship I wrote you about."

"Right," he answered; still not certain he remembered who they were. Perhaps he had not yet received that letter. They walked hand in hand to All Saints Episcopal Church in Brooklyn after breakfast.

"Seven is my lucky number," Moira said as she noticed the street signs where the Church was located--7th Avenue at 7th Street. The Church was in the Park Slope neighborhood in western Brooklyn that slopes down from Prospect Park.

"Mine, too!," Junior laughed.

Moira stood in front of the church admiring the two massive, ornate towers, the large arch bridging the pillars at the entrance, the gray stone steps and the immense wooden doors. The doors were unlocked at this early hour on a Saturday. She stepped inside and became entranced by the Romanesque-Moorish basilica of yellow sandstone brick and terra cotta. The large windows gave the church a bright, airy feel. She stared in awe at the beautiful Louis Comfort Tiffany stained-glass windows, the ornate altar, and exquisite pipe organ. What a perfect place for a wedding!

Rector William Morrison was there praying when he heard their hushed footsteps. "Good morning, may I help you?" He had not been expecting anyone, but was an early riser and was there to prepare for communion the following day. Junior removed his cap.

"My name is Rory John Millwood, Junior and this is Moira."

"Have you been here before?"

"We just moved to Brooklyn. Well, I mean, I just moved from Manhattan, where I attended Trinity, to here. Moira just arrived yesterday from Ireland."

"I see."

"I asked the Rector at Trinity--"

"Oh of couse, yes, I remember now, the couple that wishes to be married."

Relieved, Junior replied "Yes!"

"Reverend Dix from Trinity contacted me about you."

Δ   Δ   Δ

They sat in the front pew of the empty church.

"Could I see your alien identification cards?"

They handed Rector Morrison their cards, and he examined them.

"How long have you known each other?"

Junior said, "I don't know."

Moira clarified, "He means we have known each other for as long as we remember. We grew up together."

He asked more questions about them and finally asked, "Should I assume you have already consummated your relationship?"

Junior looked puzzled. "What does that mean?"

Rector Morrison looked at Moira and looked again at Junior. Finally, he leaned over and whispered into Junior's ear.

Junior blushed. "Oh no, we have been waiting until now."

Satisfied with their answers, and based on the earlier request from Reverend Dix, Rector Morrison said, "Alright then. When would you like the wedding?"

He chuckled when they requested the wedding be tomorrow, but agreed to a late afternoon wedding. The time was set for 4 o'clock.[xvii]

They returned to Junior's home and were discussing how to contact the Erbachers when a messenger arrived at Junior's door with a hand written note: "Dear Mr. Millwood, Please contact us upon Moira's arrival at BUtterfield-8-636." It was signed 'R. J. Erbacher'. Since Junior did not know how to schedule a telephone call or where to make a private call from, he returned the messenger with a handwritten note of the date, time, and place of the wedding and encouraged them to attend if they could.

Δ   Δ   Δ

Both Erbachers laughed at Junior's note. Instead of coming to the church at four, they arrived two hours early at his tenement in an elegant black-and-tan horse drawn coach, decorated with ribbons and red roses. They greeted the bride and groom in their four hundred square foot apartment as if they were meeting Queen-Empress Consort Alexandra in Buckingham Palace. Both had on formal attire and Mr. Erbacher had the driver bring in his grandson's suit--a black tailcoat with silk facing and horizontally cut-away front, braces, piqué white stiff-winged collared shirt, black bow tie, black silk stockings, black velvet Albert slippers, and white gloves. He also had a red rose boutonnière for Junior.

Junior was shocked, but at Mr. Erbacher's insistence, dressed quickly. "Bad luck to see the dressed bride before the wedding. Let's go!" The two men left by carriage for the church, where they smoked cigars in front after having sent the carriage back to pick up the ladies. The driver picked up the women a short while later, much to the amazement of their new neighbors. Junior was hustled into the church as the carriage approached.

The bride wore the simple wedding gown Mrs. Erbacher had purchased for her in Queenstown. The stunning deep violet amethyst pendant brooch hung elegantly at her neck. She carried a bouquet of red roses.

Mr. Erbacher gave away the bride and served as best man and witness. Mrs. Erbacher was Matron of Honor. After the service, Mr. Erbacher slipped Reverend Morrison more hundred-dollar bills than he had ever seen and thanked him profusely. For dinner, Mr. Erbacher took them to the Waldorf-Astoria Hotel and after dessert, Mrs. Erbacher handed Moira one final wedding present. When she began to open it, Mrs. Erbacher touched her hands lightly and whispered, "You need not open it here. It is a negligee for your boudoir."

Δ   Δ   Δ

Their first night together in the apartment they lay naked in bed.

"Do you believe that hotel?"

"It's more beautiful than the ship."

"Aren't the Erbachers lovely?"

"What a gift they have given us. How will we ever repay them?"

"We can't and shouldn't even try. They were delighted to do it."

"Too bad about your negligee?"

"Whatdoyamean?"

"You only got to wear it for three seconds!"

"Oh, you!"

They laughed, tickled, and made love all night.

Exhausted, she said, "This is better than I had dreamed."

Coyly Junior answered, "I know I was."

"Oh!"

With the dawn, Junior got up.

"Do you have to?"

"Yes. I must."

"You can't just take off one day for me."

He jumped back into bed. "I did already, Saturday. If I take more time off, they'll find a replacement."

Junior miscalculated how long it would take him to get to work that first morning and arrived, running, a few minutes late.

He was whisked up the freight elevator and ran onto the eighth floor. Everyone was busy and ignored him, until wild applause broke out in his section. There were broad smiles, hugs, pats on the back, and jousting. Mrs. Nettleton soon coaxed everyone back to work and all settled into their routines.

He left in such a hurry that he had not eaten breakfast, nor had he bought anything for lunch that day. Junior left Moira with two puny apples, but little else. He walked to the park during the short lunch break and saw Helena waving to him. "Would you like something to eat?"

"Yes! Thanks! I'm famished."

"What have you been doing to work up such an appetite?" she teased.

Junior told her about the wedding and how nice the Erbachers had been to them. Quickly their time was up and they needed to return.

Moira settled into a new routine. She and Junior shopped for meals in the morning and collected the few household items they needed. At the end of the week she asked, "Do you think I will be able to get on at your workplace?"

This made him smile. "I'll see."

Δ   Δ   Δ

"Mr. Bernstein, may I have a word with you?"

"Yes, of course."

"As you may know, I was married the other day."

"Yes, I understand you still owe me a few hours for leaving early last week."

Junior blushed. "Well, I'm sorry."

"Only joking, Millwood! Consider it our wedding gift to you."

"Thank you, Sir."

"I was wondering if it would be possible for my wife to work here."

Bernstein had anticipated the question. "What type of experience does she have?"

"She has been doing mending for as long as I can remember."

"By hand or machine."

"Hand."

"Well, have her come in so that I may speak with her and we'll see what I can do when I have an opening."

In fact, they had an opening nearly all the time. Between illnesses, accidents, pregnancies, labor unrest, and firings they were always hiring.

Moira brought in samples of her work, and not just mending.

"This is quite fine work. Well done. Now, I am not going to have any trouble with the two of you working together, am I?"

"No, Sir."

"Of course, we will not have you in the same group."

"If you say so, Sir."

"Can you begin tomorrow?"

ASCH

From the moment Moira began work, Junior noticed changes in the workplace. He had been aware labor unrest had grown throughout the summer and into the fall. Many of the seamstresses complained loudly about low wages, overbearing bosses, long hours, and little tolerance for error. They had been branded by management as malcontents and dealt with swiftly and sometimes violently. There had been wildcat walkouts, but it had been limited to small groups of people. Some returned shortly afterward and others were never seen again.

This had never been his concern. He had been focused solely on saving money, so Moira and Anne could join him. With Anne's death, all had changed.

Finally, Junior started to notice when large groups, even whole tables of people, went missing. The company filled the gaps as best they could, shifting work and hiring replacements quickly, in order to keep the product moving. Now they had to shut down whole areas. Somehow, they kept shirtwaists going out the door and the required deliveries made. If someone wanted to work, and would not create a fuss, they always had room.

It was surprising Mr. Bernstein treated Junior as nicely as he had. He was under enormous pressure with employees walking off the job or not showing up for work. This is exactly what Junior had done the previous Friday and Saturday. If a woman seamstress had done that, she would have been shown the door. Junior did that and was not only excused for his absence, but paid while being gone two hours on Friday--then given a promotion, of sorts.

Mr. Bernstein did not want Junior and Moira working closely together. He had recently fired a Cutter's Assistant who had gotten too big for his britches. He needed a replacement and Junior fit the bill. He worked hard, was strong, and had demonstrated he could keep up the fast pace. Junior was delighted; the job paid $12 a week, had more prestige and privileges.

Moira's adjustment was much harder. She now worked in a plant, where previously she had worked at her home in Queenstown, near the peaceful water. Now she lived in a crowded, major city. It was hot, tiring, boring, dirty, and noisy work. Now she was surrounded by Italians and Jews, when she had never met any before. She had new neighbors and a new country.

"Junior, it's just so different."

"What do you mean?"

"Well, it's so noisy. People are so different here. It is not that I don't like it, it's just--I don't know."

Moira talked about losing her mother and being a new wife with Junior as they walked to and from work. He puffed on his cigar and listened patiently. It was a tiring life for each of them, yet their times at home were filled with laughter, teasing, and lovemaking. On Sunday afternoons, they enjoyed their favorite pastime--swimming.

They celebrated their first anniversary with people they had not seen in quite some time. The Erbachers suggested a picnic at their Long Island summer home and sent a car to pick the Millwoods up. They feasted on roast lamb and French champagne. The Erbacher's home was decorated for the occasion and they were the perfect hosts.

Mr. Erbacher escorted Moira around on his arm and Mrs. Erbacher treated Junior as if he were her own son. The servants were alert, attentive, and enjoyed serving the young couple. Mr. Erbacher had aged. After dinner, the two men smoked on the porch and drank lemonade. Junior had cigars and Mr. Erbacher smoked his pipe.

"You are a lucky man, Junior. Why, look at your wife down

there. She is having a grand time. How beautiful and full of life she is."

"Yes I am lucky. And you are a lucky man as well, Mr. Erbacher."

"That I am. My dear wife has been a joy and a blessing more than any man deserves. Just look at her skin. She is as beautiful today as she was the day I fell in love with her--sixty years ago."

"Sixty years! I had no idea."

There was a long pause.

"I am afraid we will not see sixty-one, Junior. My chest has been hurting me and the doctor says it's my ticker. Time has taken its toll and my clock is about run out. I have no complaints and I am looking forward to seeing my Maker. His grace and mercy allow me to go home to Him, without the burdens of all the wrong I have done here on earth. I will miss my wife. But, truth be known, I had to see your wife one last time."

Junior began to protest, but Erbacher stopped him, "No use complaining about the world's natural order of things. Man is made to wear out. It has been that way since Adam sinned."

They had anniversary cake and coffee to finish their day. Mr. Erbacher called for his car. They all kissed, hugged, and wished each other well. Mr. Erbacher called Junior aside for one last word. "Please don't tell Moira how ill I am. My time is almost finished. My wife will be ten years behind me. But you, you and Moira, have a full life ahead of you."

He couldn't have been more wrong.

Δ   Δ   Δ

The Cutter's job was simple: Cut through a 120-layer mattress of cloth and tissue paper with exacting precision and without waste; do it quickly so hundreds of people relying on your work were not delayed, and keep the machinery running smoothly with the manual activities needed to support it.

It took strength, patience, excellent eyesight, dexterity, and coordination to do the job. But it took more than that-- Cutter's needed to be leaders. Just as old masters of Renaissance art had their collection of assistants to carry out the work, the Cutters had theirs. They did their work with such panache, it created an esprit de corps among their Assistants. They made their Assistants better; well-trained, experienced Assistants made them better.

Cutters commanded respect and power, and they got it. They

received privileges like no others in their workplace who were thrown out on their ear for the slightest infraction; owners snapped their heads to look the other way when a Cutter drank, returned late from lunch, kidded around with the other Cutters, and smoked around their tables and in the stairwells.

When explaining all this to Moira, Junior said, "Even the Five Points Marauders in the slums of Manhattan from seventy years ago couldn't handle a knife better than the Cutters in the lower East side."

Moira asked, "What's Five Points?"

"A place not far from here where five streets come together."

"Did they make shirtwaists, too?"

Junior laughed. "No, the Marauders were bandits and thieves who terrorized anyone who crossed them, at the point of their knifes." He swirled his knife in front of her nose as if to attack.

"Gosh."

Then he grabbed her, turned her around with his hand on her shoulder and his arm across her chest. He whispered into her ear, "They could pick your pocket and slit your throat and not think nothin' of it."

The Cutters may not have been as swashbuckling as Junior made out, but they were very good with their knives. They were a lively and boisterous lot, worked with precision and speed, and were paid accordingly. They could go to any garment shop in the city and get a job. Their skills were always in demand.

Junior was assigned to apprentice under the skillful hands of Isidore Abramowitz. Junior and one other Assistant were the second pair to run out cloth upon the long tables for Isidore. They then covered the cloth with a layer of heavy tissue paper and smoothed out the sandwich of cloth. The edges had to be precisely aligned, for one single ripple, one slight wrinkle, rendered many pieces unusable. It was essential the sandwich be smooth as silk. They repeated this process sixty more times, making sure the layers were perfectly aligned and perfectly smooth. Any adjustment caused wrinkles in the layers below, so it needed to be constantly rechecked.

The Cutters placed steel-edged sheets of paper as patterns for the shirtwaists, moving the patterns around to make for maximum use of the cloth, as if working on an oversized jig-saw puzzle. The tissue paper served to stiffen the sandwich of cloth, 120 layers thick, so the powerful Cutter's Knife--an electric-powered rotary knife--zipped through with minimal bunching. A skilled Cutter could turn a tight radius without skipping a beat, the better to reduce waste.

Junior watched them finish off the work by manually cutting the few places the machines could not reach, carefully handling the extremely sharp knives. The Assistants then removed all excess material, dropping it in bottom trays of the specially designed Cutter's tables to await the ragman's bi-monthly visit. Finally, they removed the finished pieces, handing them off to the runners and supervisors.

At the end of the day, while the Assistants prepared the first mattress of materials for the following day, the Cutters cleaned and sharpened their knives and adjusted their tools.

Junior's apprenticeship went well and within a few weeks, he was fully trained and dreaming of the day when he would wield a knife. Under Isidore's tutelage he hoped to move from Assistant Cutter to Cutter. He needed to be patient, learn from the master, and wait for the day his opportunity could come.

Δ   Δ   Δ

Soon after their October wedding, reality set in for the Millwoods. Theirs was a life of hard work and long hours. Junior had never gone out exploring the city much at night, but the two of them together had discovered there was much to see in New York. There were always dances and music, or a different play at the theater every night. There were eating-places everywhere. However, everything cost money and they had little to spare. Mostly, they found themselves on the outside looking in.

Within a month of their wedding, the level of labor unrest increased. There were more wildcat walkouts, more picketing in front of their building for better wages and working conditions, more talk about what they would do. On a Monday evening in late November 1909, there was a rally held at Cooper Union, four blocks from work.[xviii]

Moira said, "I would be happy to go home," but Junior took her hand, "I want to see what will happen". She complied. There had been rumors of this sort of large meeting for weeks and the talk was of a general walkout among shirtwaist makers throughout New York City.

For two hours, the speakers droned on. More than a hundred were seated on the stage eager for their turn to speak. The place was packed and overflowed into the halls. There were socialists and idealists talking about this and that. Should they be more cautious or bolder? Were they really prepared for an all out strike? Late in the night, a woman got up and demanded a vote. It was clear that those who had remained until this late hour would support a strike. When the vote was taken, thousands of hands shot up. Junior and Moira looked at each other and decided it was time to walk home.

Δ   Δ   Δ

The following morning thousands walked off the job during the first shift, but that was just the tip of the iceberg. The trade unions expected five thousand. The socialist daily newspaper *New York Call* estimated fifteen thousand workers walked off the job. Garment makers employed more people, by far, than any other industry. Over the next few months, many more walked off the job. There were always some people giving in and returning to work and replacement workers being found. Through it all, the Millwoods kept working. The hardest part was coming into the factory each morning and passing through lines of picketing friends. For the most part, they understood each was doing what they considered they must.

The union was demanding a 20 percent pay increase, a fifty-two hour workweek and recognition of the union. Through it all, the shops kept rolling, but at diminished capacity. As time went on, the strike became bloodier. The police sided with the factory owners and arrested or assaulted strikers at the least provocation.

Finally, the Cutters decided to honor the strike, which crippled the owners. Their Assistants could never do what the Cutters were capable of doing and without the raw input to the sewing machines all shirtwaist makers quickly came to a standstill. The smaller shops caved in to the union demands within days. The larger shops settled by early February 1910, with the last being the largest--the Triangle Waist Company. The workers achieved higher wages and a shorter workweek. But the closed-shop proposal, which would have given the workers an on-going process for improving conditions, died with the bitter strike.

The Millwoods enjoyed seeing the fruits of the strike they sat out. As the busy season in the garment district arrived, normal life resumed. The long hours were not quite as long. The pay was less bad.

Toward the end of 1910, while making love, Moira gasped at

the tenderness in her breasts. She wondered what she had done. The following morning she came down with the flu. It passed quickly.

When the neighbors commented to her, she replied, "I can't be!"

"Why? You have been playing with fire haven't ya! Don't ya expect to get burned?"

She kept it quiet from Junior, but her missed period was the final straw.

Her neighbors made her dangle a wedding ring above her stomach to see if it would swing in a circle (boy) or a cross (girl). They hid wooden spoons, scissors, and pink bows under her bed to influence the sex of the baby according to their conflicting desires. They checked her feet and the hair on her legs. They warned her against the full moon.

Her announcement to Junior was met with joy, delight, and surprise. She teased, "What, you thought you could play with fire and not get burned?"

They began dreaming of what their life would be like and picked out names together, settling on Anne for a girl and John for a boy.

FIRE

Saturday morning as Junior and Moira walked hand-in-hand up Greene Street, Moira was talking about swimming after church on Sunday. "Water 'tis a bit too cold still, I'm afraid."

The air was warm by 7 a.m., unusual for a twenty-fifth day of March in Manhattan. The wind was beginning to pick up from the west. The busy garment season for 1911 had just begun. Junior was already looking forward to going to the park for their forty-five minute lunch break.

Saturdays were always a bit different. For one thing, it was payday. Even if the amount was dismal, it lightened the heart. There was nothing like cash in hand to help the spirits soar. The second thing was that there was no work the next day. Actually, most people did plenty of work on Sunday--they cleaned, cooked, and did their laundry. The work that was done on Sunday was work done for oneself, which made it easier to bear.

That "Saturday feeling" permeated the shop floor; there was more chatter and more laughter, and it increased as the day went on. There were fewer people at work since many Jews observed the Sabbath (Junior noticed most did not). There was both a greater desire to leave at the end of the day and a great allowance to that feeling. After all, the bosses were getting to leave for a day off as well. There were more practical jokes on Saturday and less chasing people back from restroom breaks. Every day there was some sneaking off to get ready to leave, but not like Saturday. People took a late restroom break and conveniently picked up their coats to go home at the same time. Many jockeyed for position, getting early into the inspection line everyone was required to pass through, as quietly as possible.

A time-honored tradition among the Cutters was to end the day near the northeast exit, cleaning and oiling tools, and sharpening their knives. They kidded each other, especially if one were to arrive late. "Can't keep up, huh?"

"I cut two for every one you did today, and you say I can't keep up?"

"Yeah, cut two farts for every one of mine."

"Yeah, well I cut three times as big a mattress as you!"

They peeked at the pretty girls who were coming from their sewing tables and teased each other.

"Ewe, she is lovely. I'd like to get some of that."

"She'd give ya a heart attack, Casanova!"

"Ewe, but I'd die a happy man!"

They laughed, teased, and smoked cigars or cigarettes they kept in their coat pockets on pegs in the area. Smoking was forbidden, but these were the Cutters after all. When they were done, they threw their butts into the closest water buckets that were kept everywhere.

While the Cutters enjoyed their end-of-day ritual, their Assistants raced to complete their final mattress for the day. They prepared the alternating layers of tissue paper and cotton cloth, perfectly aligned and smooth.

The winning pair of Cutter's Assistants had bragging rights for the following day and the honor to assemble with the Cutters as they completed cleaning their tools.

The Cutters kidded them about their speed and prowess and offered them the rest of their cigarettes, which were crushed out butts by then. There were always jokes about circumcision and sex. That day, Junior and his partner won.

As if out of nowhere, Junior produced a small cigar to the roar of the Cutters. Many offered him a light as if he were royalty. "Thank ya veer much! It was a pleasure once again puttin' all your boys down."

"Next one done gets to be made a Jew first!," said Max as he fingered the sharpened blade on his knife.

Izzy responded, "Let me give you my glasses so you can try to find it."

All laughed.

"Hey, Joey, how they hangin'?"

Joseph Zito wandered over from the open doors of the freight elevator, laughing. The warm breeze blasted up through the stairwell and open elevator shafts. He wanted to join in with the boys, but his work transporting people down to the street in one of the freight elevators was just beginning.

"Bet they'll feel better after all your ups and down with the girls in the elevator!"

"I wish, Izzy."

The assembly area went from the freight elevators through the double doors next to a partitioned area and ended at Isidore's cutting table. The Cutters and their Assistants roamed around, smoking, teasing, and peeking at the girls on the other side of the partition. The girls were waiting for their personal items and clothing to be inspected before they would be allowed to pass through to the freight elevator by the night watchman.

"I'd like to inspect that one!"

"Henry has the best job. Checking their bags and their blouses."

"Hey Henry, if you find hair or a nipple, you've gone deep enough! Good job!," Max yelled over the partition. All the Cutters laughed, while the women in line blushed.

In reality, unless a girl was desperate, she would not steal from the company. The cost was too high. If word got around, she was blacklisted at all other shops. If that happened, she would be looking at prostitution to stay alive. Nevertheless, some tried and Junior's heart went out to those few who were inevitably caught.

Isaac Harris had told Junior about seeing Mr. Bernstein fire a man on the spot when caught with a cigar butt, so he was cautious as he puffed on his cigar, blowing the smoke down into his shirt, or only exhaling when he was over by the elevators. Isidore saw his chance to spook Junior as he wandered back toward his cutting table with the cigar clinched between his teeth.

He yelled, as if in warning, "Bernstein!"

Junior didn't even look, taking a headfirst dive to duck behind Izzy's cutting table, to hide from the boss. Banging his head on the edge of the table, Junior was stunned.

Isidore Abramowitz and Max Rothen clapped each other on the back laughing at Junior sprawled on the floor with his mouth gaping open, his eyes searching for Mr. Bernstein.

Their laughter was short lived.

Δ   Δ   Δ

Helena was one of the first persons to see the smoke. She had been standing near her new friend, Robyn, as she spoke with Mr. Bernstein and Dinah Lipschitz.

Samuel Bernstein, short and stocky, looked at a sample of Robyn's work and listened to the numbers Dinah whispered to him, "Make it fourteen."

Robyn turned to smile to herself and winked at Helena as she walked away. Fourteen dollars a week! She had just started that week and they had been too busy to set her pay rate. Since this was payday, the day of decision had arrived. She would not leave until the decision had been made and Dinah returned with her pay envelope.

Helena yelled, "Look!" and pointed east. Eva ran up shouting, "Fire! Fire! There is a fire, Mr. Bernstein." Bernstein took off on his squat little legs.

Helena thought, I had better get out of here. She was not particularly worried, but this was men's work, and she did not want to be in the way. She walked calmly in the opposite direction from Bernstein to the door. The door was wood with a large wire and glass panel on top. That's unusual, she thought, Why would it be locked? She looked down at the knob to see if it had a bolt or lever of some sort, and saw a string wrapped around the knob with a key dangling from the end. She began to reach for the key, when she was knocked into the glass, cracking it. Instantly she was pressed into the door and she could not move. There was screaming and crying behind her. She could hardly breathe for the press of women. It was becoming more intense and she felt strength leaving her.

Finally, a man began tearing the women off her back and tossing them aside like rag dolls. "Let me through!"

Helena was able to squeeze out from behind the mass and press back through the hole the man had just made. She gasped, trying to catch her breath, but her lungs filled with smoke. She ran away from the door and saw light off to her left. People had opened a window to access the fire escape, and she saw her opportunity. She jumped on top of a sewing table and leaped to a second table, before jumping down to the floor, stumbling as she landed. She got up and shot through the window and onto the fire escape, gasping for air. Crowds were pushing behind her as she negotiated the narrow iron steps.

The fire escape creaked and moaned under the load. She could hear the bolts straining against the cement as she quickly descended the stairs. The iron stairs began to sag as she looked down from six stories up. She had to jump off, but to where?

There were walls in every direction and a skylight below.

She thought she might be able to hold onto the windowsill of one of the offices, but she knew she could not do that for long. She opened the shutters, but could not budge the window. She lifted her arm up letting the sleeve protect her face and jumped onto the window. It gave way and she tumbled to the floor, shocked at what she had done. She checked herself for cuts and found none.

Immediately, others climbed through the broken glass window to join her in the sixth floor factory of another garment company. It was dark, but she found her way into the main room. It was also a shirtwaist factory, with a large open space. It must be owned by Jews, she thought, closed for the Sabbath. She climbed over some sewing tables, and then walked down an aisle to the southwest exit. This door was also locked, and she could not see a string or key. Dozens of screaming, crying, clawing, moaning women were right behind her and they began banging on the door, again pressing her into this door.

They could hear people running down the stairs. They began to pound and yell louder. Those running down the stairs could not hear them. They could feel the door being pressed back into them and they backed away a few inches, in wonder. Then the door casing and door splintered, the lock fell to the ground, and a police officer fell on his back through the doorway. He looked up, stunned to see so many women, surprised to see no fire or smoke. He scrambled to his feet, announcing "This way, ladies!," and pointed them to the stairs leading down.

Helena arrived at the lobby door, only to be pushed back into the building. She heard, "Not safe yet. They're throwing bolts of cloth down."

Δ   Δ   Δ

The Cutter's tables were really just very large boxes with legs extending up a foot to hold the tabletops. This allowed the Cutters to do their work, slipping any scrap pieces of cloth under the tabletops. The boxes accumulated scrap for eight weeks before a ragman came to empty them.

Cotton is more flammable than paper, because the weave leaves pockets of air in the cloth. The Cutters were always trying to eliminate as much waste as possible, so most of the scraps of paper and cloth were under an inch on any side. With a mattress of 120 layers, just a square inch of scrap made for sizable waste.

Everything was flammable. The desks, tables, and chairs were made of wood, held together by nails and screws. Carts were made of wood, with wood or rubber wheels. Knives had wooden handles. The patterns were made of paper edged with a small strip of metal. The sewing machines and drive shafts were the biggest things made of metal. If all the metal in the place were melted down it would probably not fill a drum. There were thousands of garments in different stages of completion, stacked on tables and in wicker baskets for transfer from assembly point to assembly point.

Δ   Δ   Δ

Junior's head hurt and he was stunned. Isidore Abramowitz and Max Rothen walked over to help him up, laughing all the way. They brushed him off.

Max was the first to notice the smoke, "What the--"

He ran off to grab a pail of water.

Isidore was next, "Oh shit!"

Off he ran for another.

By the time Max had gotten back and splashed water on the flames, the fire had doubled in size.

When Isidore got back, it had spread throughout the whole table. Flames were now leaping up over the tabletop.

Bernstein arrived on his short, stumpy legs from across the room in a flash. "Fire! Quick, get more buckets."

Junior, still dazed from the bump to his head, ran toward the nearest window where more water pails were sitting.

Bernstein grabbed the pail from Junior and tried to figure the best angle to line up to get the water beneath the tabletop. Black smoke was bellowing out. People were screaming, pushing by, going in every direction. The cloth on the top of Isidore's table burst into flames. The patterns hanging above the table on a string were next. Flaming ash from the burning bin was flying through the air in all directions.

People in the partitioned area pushed their way beyond the night watchman and opened the doors to the stairwell and elevator. The wind came swirling up the eight stories in an instant, driving toward the fire. As if a hurricane had struck, ash and sparks went everywhere.

Bernstein ordered Junior to get the fire hose in the hall. Junior ran back to find his friend from shipping, Eddie, turning the valve to start the flow of water. No water came. Eddie turned it back in the opposite direction; still no water. Bernstein yelled, "What's going on?"

Eddie hollered back, "No water."

"Turn the valve."

"There's no water with the valve turned either way."

Bernstein grabbed some of the girls who were running back to get their coats and purses, "Oh, no you don't. Get out! Now! Listen to me, run for your lives!"

Eddie ran up one flight of stairs and pulled out the hose. He tried the valve from both positions. Nothing.

Bernstein grabbed Junior, "Run for your life." The stairwell down was blocked with flame. Junior started to descend the stairs through it, but Bernstein grabbed him by the collar, "To the roof!"

As they arrived on the roof, they heard and felt a rumble as a barrel of machine oil stored in the vestibule exploded. The intense flames burst the windows on Greene Street, showering glass onto the street eight floors below. Large volumes of air were now being sucked into the loft.

Isidore Abramowitz looked back through the building. He could still see people there--running, clawing, screaming. There was nothing he could do. He walked through the vestibule and up the stairs, holding a garment over his face to protect himself from smoke and headed to the roof.

The top three floors of the building were fully inflamed. It was sunny outside without a cloud in the sky, except for the heavy, black smoke belching out of the broken windows, the staircases, and elevator shafts creating a huge mushroom overhead. Those who made it to the roof could hear fire trucks and people screaming below. They heard metal collapse near the back of the building and each wondered if the building was about to fall.

Smoke choked Junior and his eyes burned. People staggered in disbelief and shock, with their clothing and hair smoldering. Embers glowed in clothing, hair, and skin.

Next door to the west, NYU students attending class in the American Book Building heard sirens and mournful cries for help. Some students found two ladders on their roof that painters had left. The top of their building was fifteen feet higher than the roof of the burning building. They placed one down from the roof of their building to a skylight. The second ladder was then placed from the skylight to the Asch Building roof. It was rickety, but they managed to help a few workers escape. Junior was helped up the two ladders and then walked fourteen staircases down to the American Book Building lobby.

Δ   Δ   Δ

Moira was never in a rush to leave at closing time. She found that Junior enjoyed cavorting with the Cutters and their Assistants, so she let him have his fun and when he was ready, he had always come to get her. She sat at the sewing machine where she had spent most of the last nine hours. It smelled hot from the day's activity. It growled hour after hour, and at the end of the day, once the main drive was turned off, it creaked and moaned as it cooled. She sat back to catch her breath, and let others scamper from their workstations to get out the door. They found most people were still standing in line when they were ready to leave.

The west doors were locked each day by this time, so the bottleneck of one exit should have been expected. Even so, people rushed out as if today would be the day when there would be no inspections and no line. Moira found if she waited ten minutes, they generally made it up by getting home at about the same time. She sat back at the third sewing table, in the middle of the room and closed her eyes. She may have drifted off to sleep.

She thought there sure seems to be a lot more noise today. People were yelling. Must be some birthday celebration going on. She noticed people were running. That's odd, she thought. Then she heard the word, "FIRE!" Her eyes sprung open. Next she heard an explosion. It was near where Junior worked. She saw smoke and then flames, as if awakening to a nightmare.

The air from the elevators and staircase drove the smoke and flames, from the northeast corner of the room, south along the windows. The windows along the east side of the room burst at the same time a window on the north side of the building was opened to gain access to the fire escape. Instantly air was sucked in one window and hot gases exploded out the far end. The effect was a hurricane within the room, swirling around her.

She didn't immediately know what to do. Run? Where? Go to Junior! was her only thought. Get to Junior! See that he is safe.

Moira looked across the room for him. She might have spotted him tossing a bucket of water on the flames. It seemed to have no effect.

She yelled his name and thought he may have looked back at her, but the heat waves distorted her view. One last time she yelled her love's name and was engulfed in smoke. She grabbed her brooch tightly in her right hand. I can't live without Junior.

The superheated gases singed all the hairs from her face and nostrils, sucked the air from her lungs; gasping, she refilled them with hot gases. In an instant, her lungs were cauterized, completely sealed.

She never had a chance to run. She slumped to the floor, where embers of floating patterns and cloth rained down on her, igniting her clothing, hair, and skin. When they recovered her body from the ashes, there was not much left.

$$\Delta \qquad \Delta \qquad \Delta$$

On the day of this fire, some made their choices too slowly. One person turned left and lived. Another person turned left and died. One went up and lived. Another went up and died. Some made intelligent, well thought out decisions. Some just reacted. Call it luck; call it chance; call it fate. Most people, around 75%, made it out alive.

Many fell when a freight elevator gave way. Many fell when the fire escape, designed for just a few people at a time, pulled its mounting from the wall, and plunged to the ground.

As the flames got closer to them, workers stood at the windows watching the firefighters' ladders being extended up toward them. The tallest came up more than two floors short.

The choice narrowed: Burn to death or jump to death.

The "bolt of cloth" that prevented Helena from exiting the building, was a woman cheating death by fire. She stepped out the window and into eternity three seconds later.

Close to eighty made the choice not to be burned alive and walked through the windows to their death. It would all be over quickly.

Jumper nets were tried and quickly abandoned. They had never been used for people jumping from this height before. Thousands of people have survived falling from that height--it did not happen that day.

In eight minutes, fifty people said their goodbyes and perished by jumping--about one every ten seconds. A few walked up to the windows, peered down, then walked back to be burned to death.

The coroner, overlooking the scene remarked to one of his men, "The human body is not made to land on a concrete sidewalk at sixty miles per hour. Legs become spears rammed into the torso. Internal organs splay through splitting skin. Brains are severed from spinal cords. Hearts smash into pulp in an instant".[xix]

The sidewalk and cobblestone street was so littered with bodies, the New York Fire Department reported having trouble getting fire trucks close to the building.

Moira never knew the choice to rest her eyes and wait for Junior would place her in the center of a storm. She never knew she didn't have a few seconds to spare searching for him.

It happened so quickly, she never realized what hit her. One moment she was staring through the smoke to find Junior, the next she was falling to the floor. Unwittingly, she would give up the oxygen in her lungs to feed the fire. Then the fire would ravage her body in its endless search for fuel.

Thirty minutes after sparking to life, the fire was under control. The top three floors were a total loss. But, for a few thousand dollars it was ready to be reopened within a few weeks. After all, it had been built using the latest technology and was fireproof.[xx]

The Triangle Waist Company factory fire is one of the largest industrial disasters in U. S. history, causing the death of 146 (six burned beyond recognition) and physical injuries to 70 more. It remained the worst workplace disaster in New York City until September 11, 2001.

Δ   Δ   Δ

Some of the seventy injured found their way by themselves to Saint Vincent's Hospital, a mile away to the northwest on 7TH Avenue. A few were taken as far north as New York Hospital on East 68th Street. Shortly after the fire was declared under control, a dozen horse-drawn carts started a two-mile parade northeast to the morgue. Slowly their hooves clicked on the cobblestone under the weight of their lifeless cargo.

When the Bellevue Hospital morgue was quickly overrun, bodies were taken to Charity Pier, adjacent to the hospital where 26th Street bends north along the East River. The Pier had been used for a disaster once before; seven years earlier when the side-wheel passenger steamship General Slocum burned to the water line.[xxi]

Homeless men were dragooned to handle the coffins and corpses. They arranged the coffins in two long rows with the corpse's heads propped up on the back of the coffins to aid in identification. The bodies had been numbered by the police, but were renumbered by the coroner's men. Minimal attention was paid to exact details that may have aided identification or fire investigation. Little was done to clean the victim's faces. The pier warehouse was poorly lit.

Family members arrived at all three hospitals and at the pier, hoping against hope that their family member was disoriented, lost, wandering, or injured, instead of among the dead. Seven hours after the fire began, the doors were opened for the families to identify their loved ones and arrange funerals.

After leaving the American Book Building, Junior wandered through the streets. He thought about Moira and all his friends. He knew hundreds had made it out, as he had. About eleven he decided to walk home to see if Moira was there. She was not. Maybe she was still walking around like he had been. He didn't know where to go next. He was exhausted. He smelled of smoke and felt gritty. He had not eaten since lunch.

He walked back to work. The fire was no longer smoldering upstairs, but there were a few firemen standing outside. The last of the bodies from the loft upstairs had been brought down a few minutes before. They had just finished rolling up their fire hoses, after having used them to rinse the debris and blood from the streets. It had just turned midnight. He was stunned to see the streets looked like there had been a rainstorm. If you did not look up or pick up the smell, you would not have known there had been a fire. A string of lights was strung from the second floor windows of the Asch building. It reminded him of one of the department stores Christmas decorations.[xxii]

A night watchman was back inside the lobby at the main entrance on Washington Place.

"Where did they take the injured?"

"Try Saint Vinnie's."

"Thanks."

"They have taken the rest of them to Misery Lane."

"Where?"

"You know. Misery Lane. That's what they call Charity Piers."

Δ   Δ   Δ

The decrepit pier hosted a mournful four-day parade. Gawkers crowded alongside the heartbroken to see the dead bodies lined up in two rows. They looked at the pretty, young girls who had come to an early and tragic end.

The police dealt, as best they could, with those who could not come up with the name of the person for whom they were looking. They chased out pickpockets who sought to prey on distracted family members. However, not before one thief came alongside a man as he looked carefully at a woman, not feeling the hand on his hip that was swiping his wallet.

The line was long and slow. The shuffle of shoes matched the rhythm of the waves outside, as people went from coffin to coffin. They looked closely at the bodies. They were methodical. Nobody wanted to go through this a second time. With the life taken out of them, the bodies looked so different. The lighting was poor, so police officers stood with lanterns every few yards. The swinging of the lanterns gave distorted motion to the faces propped up in the boxes. The silence was broken by a cry of agony. There was fainting and quick dashes out the door to vomit. There were tears and there was stoicism.

Face after face was closely observed. Burns had marred features. The families pondered over every detail and huddled together to discuss what they had just seen.

"Her shoes were like those."

"Her hair was redder."

Six bodies were never identified. Either they were burned beyond recognition, or nobody came for them. Engagement and wedding rings, shoes, odd clothing features, and dental work were used to identify the victims. Some people walked away, not sure whether they had seen their loved one. Others identified a body, but were never really certain and carried those doubts to their own graves.

Δ   Δ   Δ

As the victims were identified, their coffins were taken out of the lines. Undertakers carried them away to their mortuaries. As the coffins became fewer and fewer, the lines got short. After four days, there were just over a dozen corpses remaining. All were badly disfigured, with the agony they had endured burnt into their contorted faces.

Junior had been through the line twice and could not identify Moira. Thousands of people had looked at her destroyed face. Junior returned to her coffin a dozen times. Maybe he was just holding out hope. He looked at the remains of her hands. He just could not decide. He reached into the coffin, turned her right hand, and saw it. The pearls were missing, the setting and pin had melted, but fused into her palm was the amethyst from her brooch.

MOVING ON

Triangle Waist Company was back in operation three days after the fire, three blocks away on the sixth floor of the Sailor's Snug Harbor Corporation building at 5-11 University Place. The following day, Wednesday, the city Building Department inspected and found that building was not fireproof and a fire exit was blocked by sewing tables. The owners were cited. The fine was $20.

On Thursday, before going up to Charity Piers and finding Moira, Junior stopped by the new factory. He could have started work that day if he wished. He was handed a flier telling him Mr. Issac Harris and Mr. Max Blanck were offering one week of wages to the families for funeral expenses.

The city had turned black. Black bunting was draped everywhere in mourning. The spring-like day of the fire gave way to rain and drizzle. Every hour, funeral processions with black horses, black hearses, and mourners dressed in funeral black passed by. Memorial services were held at churches, synagogues, civic buildings, and the Metropolitan Opera House. The daily reminders were like a scab being scratched and picked at and the bleeding just continued.

Rumors raced. Finger pointing and innuendo went in every direction. One *New York Times* front-page headline read "Blame Shifted on All Sides for Fire Horror."xxiii

Investigations were begun and indictments called for even before conclusions were reached. Political maneuvering took place everywhere. Most of the eleven major English broadsheet Newspapers despaired that when all was said and done, more would be said than done.

The International Ladies' Garment Workers' Union suggested an official day of mourning for the city, but the closest thing to that was the funeral march for five unidentified and unclaimed bodies. Ten days after the fire, on April 5, 1911, flower-filled carriages preceded hearses taking fire victims to their resting place at Cemetery of the Evergreen in Brooklyn.

Four hundred thousand mourners marched silently in the rain and the mud. Perhaps a half million more lined the parade route. Before internment, Catholic, Protestant, and Jewish rites were said. Rain pounded umbrellas; someone remarked, "tears of the angels."

Junior marched in the parade. He had a blank stare and trudged forward unthinking the unthinkable.

After the march, Junior did two things. He never smoked again and he started drinking. He found a bar and didn't remember how he got home that night.

That Friday, Junior buried Moira. He turned funds over from Harris and Blanck to Calvary Cemetery to have Moira and her unborn baby, buried near the children and infant's section, where they would be near Ruth, the other baby he had loved and watched die.

Junior didn't know how to contact Naomi to invite her to the funeral, nor did he know if he wanted her there. The Erbachers attended. Rector Morrison said a few words. It was simple and over with quickly.

Everyone promised to get together soon. Each person walked away quietly as the cemetery crew assembled to lower the casket into the ground. Junior went to the closest bar.

Δ   Δ   Δ

The Triangle Waist Company factory fire gave common ground to all workers--well beyond the garment district.xxiv

Junior had attended a handful of evening union events in the past, but he usually left early. He often heard what he wanted to hear and left expecting others to guide the process toward improvement. He heard, during the meeting where the workers ultimately voted for a general strike, that it would be understandable for those struggling to survive to cross the picket lines. When he heard "struggling to survive", Junior figured it applied to him. He heard permission given for him not to participate, and so he did not. Others could earn his wage increase. Others could earn his reduced hours.

After the fire, Junior stayed at the union meetings until the benediction and then made his way over to the nearest bar for more rigorous conversation. He continued to work at Triangle Waist Company during the day. He was not exactly vocal yet in the union, but he attended sessions, became a member and paid his dues.

He blamed God for what had happened to Moira. Why would a loving God allow this? He could not reconcile his beliefs and quit attending church.

Soon he could no longer "see" his wife--he struggled to remember what she looked like. Even though he had grown up with her, he could not conjure up her face. The few pictures he had of her didn't help. When he tried, he always saw her distorted, burned body and face lying in a coffin. It was driving him to distraction. Why was she slipping away from him?

His frequent times in bars, led to an evening job as a bartender. Unless he had a union meeting, he worked most nights. He had nothing else to do and nobody else to come home to. His evening job soon led him to Tammany Hall.

SULLIVAN

Junior stumbled into the Gas House District during the spring of 1911.

Manufactured Gas Plants (MPS) have been used since the 1850's.[xxv]

A byproduct of MPS was the constant stench from the manufacturing process and continuous leaks, leading to naming of the area: The Gas House District.

The area chased out residents and drew in criminals, saloons, theaters, gambling houses, and bordellos. The area became the mixing point for businessmen, gangsters, and politicians. There was a freedom to the area--people from all classes came there.

Workers in the gas house had been compelled for decades to give generously to the Democratic Party machine. The politicians kept the police out of the activities of the saloon owners and madame's. Tammany Hall showed up nightly to monitor the area, as well as indulge in her delights.[xxvi]

Work was plentiful. Quickly he moved to the area, as much to get away from the painful memory of Moira as anything. He could not approach their apartment in Brooklyn without choking up. Attempts to picture her in his mind haunted him. He would arrive home with the vision of her racked and broken body with no hair and the distorted, anguished face in his mind. Sleepless nights were the only thing that prevented nightmares.

He started simply enough as a bartender, but quickly became a waiter. He was good with people, always teasing them. It didn't matter to him who it was he teased--his patrons loved him for it.

Early one morning, Tim Sullivan walked in with a floozy on his arm and Junior told Tim he was a pastor, and was permitted to perform wedding ceremonies on the spot.

Surprisingly, Tim roared.

Junior explained that his membership in the waiters and bellhops union granted him that privilege. He teased the girl that this would allow her to maintain her respectability and reputation.

Tim roared again. He liked Junior instantly and demanded Junior wait on him every time. Most times with a different girl, but sometimes with his wife.

When Junior found out the woman he was serving was Sullivan's wife, his teasing changed. He was brutal. "We don't usually serve the likes of you, but since you are here with Mr. Sullivan, we'll make an exception."

She blushed and was furious, but Tim was delighted.

Junior said things to her like: "You should have seen the dame your husband was in here with last night. What a looker! A little advice: He probably would not be in here as much if he got better service at home, if you get my drift."

Tim roared. It was probably the first truthful statement he had heard all day. The owners and bartenders were baffled by how Junior got away with it. Junior didn't care. He did not have the slightest idea who Tim Sullivan was.

Δ   Δ   Δ

In 1911, Timothy Patrick Sullivan was in his second term as a New York State Senator. He had already been a United States Congressman and had resigned saying, "In New York, we use Congressmen for hitchin' posts." It was undoubtedly true. In Congress, he was one of hundreds of congressional representatives, and "Big Tim" was swallowed up and lost. But in the New York State Assembly, he was a big fish in a small pond, with money, power, graft, and influence.[xxvii]

Junior had once quipped to him, while serving him his third gin and tonic, "If guns are outlawed; only outlaws will have guns!"

It was meant as a joke, but an essence of it must have struck home. Tim introduced a piece of legislation, the Sullivan Act, which required a permit to carry a concealed weapon. By virtue of the steep registration fee, crooked cops on his payroll, and moral requirements expressed in the legislation, he influenced who had guns. His men did; his political opponents did not.

With a grin, Tim told his men, "It is a wonder how my influence grows, while discussing political matters with a colleague, when there is a revolver pressed against the man's ribs."

By the time Junior met Big Tim, he was losing his mind from tertiary syphilis, caught when he was in his late teens. The telltale signs were clear up close--the continual rash on the palms of his hands and the reddish papules and puss-filled nodules on his neck around his shirt collar as the bacteria worked its way up to his face.

Tim spent his days at the Occidental Hotel in the Bowery, the charming face of political corruption. He spent evenings enjoying the delights of the Gas House District.

Through Big Tim, Junior met some of the most influential men in America. The politicians who joined Tim for dinner thought Junior was the owner of the place. At a table reserved for Big Tim, Junior met Charles Francis Murphy and Alfred Smith. In the future, both men were to have a large influence on Junior.

There was never a bill for Tim when he left in the evening, but there was always a generous tip for Junior.

Δ   Δ   Δ

Late one night, Junior was kidding Big Tim: "How can you be in politics? It's all so corrupt."

Tim laughed, "Corrupt? Corrupt? Are you serious? So, take a piece of iron and leave it out in the open air. It rusts and soon 'ya got nothing. But if you take that same piece of iron and put it into a building it supports the whole thing. The building keeps the iron from rusting and corrupting.

"Same way with politics. We hire an architect, a construction crew, and a painter. They do their work and exact a fee for their labor. Isn't that fair? The city gets the Brooklyn Bridge instead of a pile of rusted-out iron. A bridge is something, but a pile of rusted iron is nothing. We exact a fee for bringing all those people together.

"The city is too big and doesn't have feelings. A department for this and a department for that, but nobody to figure out what people really need. That's where we come in. We get things done while the city is still trying to figure things out with their blue ribbon panels.

"My boys take a little from the city, the unions, the painters, the architects, the construction workers and--get things done! The city charges taxes to do all the things they're suppose to do. So we just kinda tax the city right back.

"We then take that money and buy turkeys for Christmas to give out to good folk like you. And when the law is being unfair to you, you come to us and we make things right. When you need a job, you come to us and we get one for you. Is that so bad?

"Ya see, one political party is in power at any one time. They get to decide what is acceptable. In a hundred years, we'll be out and somebody else will switch everything around. Of course, they won't do it as good as us, so we'll get back in and switch it back.

"We manage government contracts and patronage jobs and swing the popular vote to those with the power to get things done--us. The hippo gets to wallow in pools called government business and we, the little birds--the wagtails, flutter around getting this and that done. Without us the hippo would be besieged with minute details, bog down, accomplish nothing. For the price of bird feed, we relieve the city of irritation of not getting anything done."

He took a big swig of his gin and tonic. "Yes, the Hippo has his wagtail, and this city has me--and we are all the better for it."

Δ   Δ   Δ

The last time Junior served Tim Sullivan, in the summer of 1913, Tim ran away from the table claiming he was being poisoned. Within a month, his delusions of being poisoned and spied upon landed him at Incompetency Hearings. The judge ordered him committed to a sanitarium.

Big Tim had made many enemies. One of them arranged with an orderly to take Tim out to breakfast. Since he was delusional about being poisoned, what more fitting way was there to kill him?

"I want $10,000 for my 'Magic'!"
"Seems awful steep. Why are we going to these measures?"

"Shut up," said his associate. It had been decided it needed to look like an accidental poisoning. Anything else would bring retribution. Tim had many enemies, but also many friends.

"$10,000 for my 'Magic'."

"Why is it worth it?"

"Raw, it kills almost immediately. Cooked it takes a bit longer. The person thinks he's sick. Wants help. You can help him get to wherever you want before he collapses. See why I call it magic? It's worth the money."

"We will pay you you're ten grand if it works. Otherwise, it will not be very pleasant when we return." The man started to reach forward.

"NO! STOP! Use these." The scientist handed him heavy rubber gloves. He continued, "After you are done, throw these away as well as the fry pan you use. I suggest steak sautéed in a liberal amount of these mushrooms. Serve it with the cooked mushrooms, eggs, and coffee."

His magic was an especially virulent strain of "death cap" mushroom.[xxviii]

Δ   Δ   Δ

On August 30th, Tim attended an all-night poker party with the orderlies. In the early morning, he escaped. Later that morning, an engineer slammed the brakes on his locomotive. On railroad tracks at Pelham Parkway near Eastchester Road in the Bronx, the engine slammed into Tim's body. He was taken to a local morgue. He was wearing an expensive suit and an exquisitely tailored white shirt with "TPS" monogrammed diamond-studded cufflinks. He had no wallet, no money, and no identification.

The coroner, Thomas Reigelmann, a long time friend and political appointee of Tim, failed to recognize him despite his large size, expensive clothing, and undamaged face. His family took a week to report him missing.

In Sullivan's weakened state from syphilis, his kidneys and liver shut down quickly. He was dropped on the tracks to make it look like an accident.

Δ   Δ   Δ

Police Officer Peter Purfield, assigned to the morgue detail, identified the body thirteen days later. Over 25,000 people attended his funeral at St. Patrick's Old Cathedral, including Junior who could not believe he was dead. He had been a favorite customer and, over time, Junior had learned of the great power and influence of the man who loved to be kidded.

At the funeral, someone leaned over to Junior and said, "It is sad to see such a young, vital man die. Did you know he was only fifty-one?"

Junior spoke briefly with Tim's wife, Charles Murphy, Harry C. Walker, and Alfred Smith.

Al handed Junior his card. "I understand you were at the Triangle Fire. If you get tired of the restaurant business, look me up."

MURPHY

Al Smith is best remembered as a crusading progressive Democrat, four time Governor of New York State, and Presidential candidate. However, first and foremost, he was a pragmatist.

He was born within sight of the Brooklyn Bridge and left school at fourteen to support his family after his father's death. He never attended high school or beyond. His education consisted of observing people at the Fulton Fish Market and carefully reading legislation. He was known for spending long hours after work in the New York State Assembly, reading over every word of legislation, and he became adept at writing legislation for his efforts. He was only surpassed in this regard by his protégé, Robert Moses.

He was also adept at working both sides of an issue, collecting funds from both ends. Moving forward with one side, while telling the other side the "time wasn't yet right" to present an issue. He could keep both sides of an issue involved, engaged, and, of course, funding their efforts. All the while managing what came in and out of committees and what went to be voted on upon the floor of the chambers of the New York Assembly.

On October 10, 1911, committee transcripts show the

Honorable Alfred E. Smith gaveled open public hearings of the Fire Investigating Commission Concerning the Triangle Shirtwaist Factory Fire (FIC) in New York City. He had been elected Vice-Chairman of the FIC under his friend and Chairman of the Committee, State Senator Robert F. Wagner, President pro tempore of the New York State Senate. They had been charged with completing a preliminary report on the fire by February 1912.

Smith was both a renowned reformer and a product of Tammany. Tammany Society, named after an Indian chief and dating to the American Revolution, wielded tremendous political power in New York State and had since the Civil War. He owed his position to Charles "Silent Charlie" Francis Murphy, who trained him to be his eyes and ears in the state Capitol in Albany, while he personally ran downstate. There was no question Murphy was the boss, but Al Smith exercised great influence.

Smith succeeded by playing a delicate balance between insider and outsider to Tammany Hall. He was never tainted by the widespread scandals that periodically rocked Tammany and was instrumental in helping move it to a position very different from its past (and which endured for another three decades).[xxix]

The Asch Building, where the Triangle Waist Company had been located, was a common example of what money could buy. The building should have been required to have three full stairways. There were only two. In the place of a third stairway, Joseph Asch submitted plans to place a 17 1/2-inch wide fire escape that descended, not to the ground, but to a skylight. The City required changes for the fire escape to go to either the ground or a platform. Asch agreed to the changes, but never made them.

For all practical purposes, the fire escape was worthless. This was proven when an actual emergency took place and dozens of people plunged to their death when the fire escape collapsed under the weight and detached from the building.

A few dollars passing to Tammany Hall, greased the wheels of government in permitting the variance.[xxx]

Al Smith recognized the Triangle Waist Company factory fire was a sea-change event. Voters would no longer tolerate conditions in factories that permitted such a wanton disregard for life. In the past, a politician might align with the business owners and drag his feet toward real reform. This time, there was only one side of the issue to be on.

FIC Hearing and New York State court documents are filled with accounts of systemic failures that allowed the Triangle Waist Company disaster. Fire drills were not conducted. Fire sprinklers were not required. Wood floors and fixtures were everywhere. When buildings were required to make changes, nobody followed up to see if they were done. Weasel words in regulations eliminated enforcement (for example, doors were required to swing out "where practical"). City departments were compartmentalized in their work. The Fire Department pointed to the Building Inspectors. The Building Inspectors pointed at the Sanitation Department.

Junior served dinner to the Fire Chief and his assistants one evening after the Chief had testified. He stayed near their table pretending to fumble with some papers, so he could overhear their discussion.

"Nothing has teeth."

"Manufacturers pay the low fines, but they don't make no changes. They blocked fire exits with materials. Our inspectors come in and cite them. They just move the material, pay the fines, and next time we are through the materials are back to their original space."

"It's cheaper and less hassle for them just to pay off one of our guys."

"Or complain to Tammany Hall from the get-go".

Al Smith and Charles 'Silent Charlie' Francis Murphy had a problem. Tammany Hall was "too efficient". That is where Al Smith thought Junior Millwood might come in.

Δ   Δ   Δ

When Al Smith passed his calling card to Junior Millwood at Sullivan's funeral, it was mid-September 1913. The State Commission Report on the Triangle Waist Company factory fire had been completed twenty months before. Al Smith had introduced sweeping legislation and forced it through the State Assembly and Senate.

Smith told Murphy, "Now comes the hard part: Making it stick."

Murphy nodded his understanding and agreement.

With the legislative reforms the Triangle Waist Company fire prompted, Tammany was giving up large sums of graft. In exchange, it was gaining large numbers of patronage jobs. Even so, all the legislation and regulation would be for naught if Tammany went its normal, natural way.

Smith and Murphy understood that if bribes were permitted for bypassing regulations, the effect would devastate the Democratic Party. They would be exposed as not having the leadership and discipline to pull off what voters were demanding. They needed "free agents" to make sure the various New York City Departments followed the law. It was imperative that rogue elements be squashed. It would be easy for a single Building Inspector to take a bribe and pocket it. But, if any disaster occurred again, it could be overwhelming. Tammany needed to be fully committed to the changes. There was no other choice.

Al Smith thought Millwood was the owner of the saloon and restaurant Sullivan frequented (in fact, Sullivan was the silent owner.) He believed he was a successful businessman. Junior personally escaped the Triangle Waist Company fire. He lost his wife in the fire. He had slaved under inhumane conditions. Junior Millwood was the ideal candidate.

Smith thought he would be diligent in enforcing the new laws. What he did not know is that Junior would be ruthless in dealing with both regulators and owners who did not toe the line.

Smith wanted Junior, and other men like him, to be his eyes and ears in New York City, while Smith was in Albany. He would have Smith's ear in Albany and a direct connection to "Silent Charlie".

Charles "Silent Charlie" Francis Murphy was the right man to transition Tammany from the course methods of William Magear "Boss" Tweed and flashy, boisterous "Big Tim". He brought education and respectability to the position. He was not a teetotaler, as many thought, but he drank modestly and out of public view. His accessibility to the masses was legendary. He stationed himself nightly on a well-known street corner to receive his patrons, and they loved him for it. He rewarded the poor with child safety laws and labor regulations. He installed dozens of progressive politicians in prominent positions (including Al Smith) and wielded power at the national level.

Junior was the first of a few men hired by the city to the position of Mayoral Inspector. On paper, he had authority to inspect each and every department of the city. The salary was modest, but the position made him a wealthy man. He quit working at Triangle the next day.

Democrat Mayor William Jay Gaynor was not consulted when the position was created, nor did Junior report to the mayor or any future mayor, ever. Smith told him he could have any government office he wanted (as long as it was not located in Tammany Hall).

He chose City Hall and forced a staffer out.

He was given instructions on how to contact Murphy's office to help with enforcement and how to contact Smith's office with ideas for regulatory improvement. In addition, he met with Smith regularly at his saloon.

Murphy had what he needed for Tammany's transition. He had more power than "Boss" Tweed ever dreamed of, and he held his position longer than any predecessor. Junior would enjoy his coattails.

Δ   Δ   Δ

After taking over the office of one of the Mayor's staff, Junior located the printer used for the mayor's official stationery, gave himself a promotion, and ordered calling cards reading: R. J. Millwood, Senior Mayoral Inspector.

"How soon can you have them ready?" Given an unsatisfactory answer, he said, "That's not good enough. Do a partial printing by Thursday."

He ordered an expensive desk pen set, fountain pens, a small safe, hardbound ledger books for note taking, and other office supplies. "Charge them to the mayor's account and deliver them to my office on the fourth floor."

He spent the first few days in his office carefully reading legislation and regulations related to building codes, building safety, child labor, general labor, food, health, and sanitation. By the time his business cards were delivered, he was ready.

Junior was the first of a dozen men picked as Mayoral Inspectors. It was an interesting job title. Was his job to inspect on behalf of the mayor? Or was his job to inspect the mayor? It was likely Smith and Murphy had the latter in mind.

Smith told Murphy, "I have carefully selected men for the position based on various skills and experiences. I just hope they won't be too greedy in their work!"

Murphy just smiled.

With freshly-printed calling cards, including the raised Official

Seal of the Mayor of New York City, Junior walked down to the city motor pool and commandeered one of the mayor's chauffeur-driven limousines (the Mayor had three for himself and his staff).

The mayor's chief of staff was livid, but he could do little as his hands were not exactly clean. He was also livid the following day when the extraordinary bill came in for stationery and office supplies.

When he contacted Murphy's office to see if they knew anything about "these Mayoral Inspectors", he was told to mind his own business.

Junior conducted widespread inspections in every area of the city and in every type of business. Inspectors were reprimanded for their lackadaisical oversight. Those caught looking the other way due to laziness or accepting bribes were either turned in or forced to quit on the spot.

The New York *Globe* first caught wind of the roaming Inspectors and the Mayor was lauded for his "insight, resourcefulness, and crusading spirit". "Businesses are on notice there are new sheriffs in town."

Murphy told Smith, "I'm pleased. Things are going well with the new Inspectors".

"A good start."

$$\Delta \quad \Delta \quad \Delta$$

Junior did one thing the other Mayoral Inspectors had not thought of--he inspected them and over time, he eliminated most of them.

There was one Inspector he suspected of bribery, but could not prove. He walked into his office, ordered a visitor out, sat down, and held out his hand. He never said another word. He just sat, holding his hand out.

"What?"

Junior was silent.

"What?"

Junior remained silent, sitting with his hand out.

The other Inspector sat there for a long time, staring at Junior.

"How did you find out?"

Junior did not say a word.

The other Inspector turned in his chair, worked the dial on his safe, extracted cash, and placed the bundle in Junior's right hand. Then he took out a single piece of paper, wrote out his resignation letter in longhand, signed the letter, grabbed his hat and coat and left, shaking his head.

There was $50,000 in Junior's hand--a handy down payment on a house.

He could quote regulations verbatim to his opponents, much to their shock if they decided to look them up. When he calculated he would not be caught, Junior made up rules and regulations on the spot. It was something his father had done often and well, so it must have been an inherited trait. He let himself be bribed into not citing the accused (for regulations that did not exist) and collected "fees" left and right. He never spoke to Smith or Murphy about any of this. He just pocketed the money and kept no records.

He was never caught by his clients, although he was questioned by one once. He explained, "Well the reason you cannot find that regulation is because I had it rescinded on your behalf." The businessman smiled, pleased with himself and with Junior after hearing the explanation.

Restaurateurs and saloon keepers were very happy to pay for his meals, in return for a non-inspection. Never again did Junior pay for a meal, drink or theater ticket.

Once a waiter presented a bill to Junior by mistake and within seconds, the owner snatched the bill from the table and fired the waiter on the spot.

Soon, Junior had come up with a saying, "It's not what you make that counts, it is what you don't spend."

Δ   Δ   Δ

Junior worked all the time, relentlessly. He might show up anytime and anywhere to inspect a building, sanitation condition, or public health situation. This was difficult for many businessmen to accept, but they were forced to comply. Of course, he limited his work to anything the city might inspect, but that still was extremely broad. He did not interfere in the activities of Tammany Hall, so Murphy gave him wide latitude.

The Mayor was terrified of him. He certainly was not in a position to explain to the press why Mayoral Inspectors were not part of his organization. The Mayor's staff was indignant. The public had no way of knowing the Mayoral Inspectors were on the city payroll as well as part of Tammany Hall.

A few of them worked as if it was business as usual with corruption, bribes, and violence. They never lasted long. He made examples of the violators among their peers and drummed them out. One fellow Mayoral Inspector was caught having accepted a bribe.

"I demand your resignation."

"You're not getting it, Junior!"

"Fine. You're fired!"

"You can't fire me. We'll see about this when Smith comes to town."

Junior grabbed him by the collar and pushed him off his chair to the ground.

"Get up, you bastard." He dragged him to his feet and had the man staggering to the door, unable to gain his balance, and into the hallway.

Doors to adjacent offices, sprung open and startled city employees came out to look at the commotion.

"What the hell are you looking at?" They retracted like heads of turtles back into their shells.

The man was wearing a tweed coat and long sleeve shirt. Junior pushed up the suit coat sleeves and spun the man around so he was facing down the stairs, leaning forward, with his hands behind his back.

"What are you doing back there?"

"Getting rid of you." Standing at the top of the stairs, Junior tripped the man into a headlong fall. With his sleeves attached together behind his back and unable to brace himself, he broke his collarbone when he landed and never reappeared at City Hall.

Privately, Smith and Murphy were delighted and a bit surprised by how well the arrangement was working out. The only concern they had with Junior's work is that he had eliminated most of his co-Mayoral Inspectors. They also wanted a better way of keeping in touch with him during the day.

Weekly, Smith was on the train between Albany and New York City and frequently met with Junior.

"I want you to have a secretary."

"Why, Mr. Smith?"

"It is imperative I know of your whereabouts. Or, I will need to know what you will be inspecting ahead of time."

"Why, Mr. Smith?"

"Let's just say, neither Mr. Murphy, nor I, want any surprises. We may need to direct you to a certain place, because it would be helpful to our goals."

"I see."

"We certainly would not want you to show up at a place where either of us could be embarrassed or compromised."

"Yes, I can understand that," replied Junior, though he had not a clue what Smith was driving at.

"If you would use a secretary through whom I could contact you periodically during the day that would be sufficient."

Junior agreed.

"Also, I want you to develop a team of people to do the same work you have been doing."

Junior nodded. Over time, he brought in people who served as his Assistant for a period, before being allowed to venture off on their own.

Most were perplexed as to what they were to do. Some thought they were to be muscle for the organization. Others could not understand that they were free to investigate anything they wished. He finally settled in on the theme of them being crusaders to right wrongs done in the inspection processes of the city, whether that was in building, sanitation, or safety.

Junior was of the opinion that everyone knew of someone who was doing something wrong. When he got wind of milk sanitation bribes in the Health Department, he became curious. A name kept coming up that he was familiar with from his old days in Brooklyn--William 'Slim' Ehring.

Δ   Δ   Δ

His old acquaintance had moved up in the supply chain since he had last seen him. Instead of procuring and peddling his own milk, Slim began getting more milk than he needed for his own sales. He soon learned how profitable and easier on the legs this could be. After discontinuing peddling milk on his own he became the distributor to dozens of peddlers, under the name "Slim's Dairy".

He still got his milk from dairies in central Pennsylvania, but started to push further west. He still added ammonia to the milk to kill the souring smell it had acquired while being transported.

However, since he was not selling the milk himself, he did not know the amount of ammonia required to kill the smell, so he was more liberal in his doses. Adding calcium carbonate and water was done in a factory setting now near the state border. No longer was it a quick stop at the creek near the calcium deposits of the eastern parts of Pennsylvania. Now it was a full-fledged component of the manufacturing process.

The Health Department annually reported widespread deaths of children, as it had for decades. All the newspapers reported numbers, as they had done for more than twenty years, but it was just considered by most people a consequence of living in any big city. The Health Department maintained an "on-going investigation," but gave it little attention. Since malnutrition had always been a problem, it was difficult to pin down exactly what was occurring that was causing the bubble of deaths. There were periodic investigations of Slim's Dairy, but nothing was ever proven. Slim began to frequent better establishments and dress better. He no longer was carrying a dour expression and sad eyes. While he was given a "clean bill of health" from the Health Department, all fingers kept pointing back to Slim's Dairy as the common thread.

It was obvious something was amiss in the Health Department. One of the Health Department officials, who Junior was squeezing for a lead, suggested Junior take a look.

At the same time Slim was prospering, Junior found out a particular Health Department Inspector was living beyond his means. It happened to be the same Health Department Inspector who had signed off on Slim's clean bill of health.

Mr. Stoutenberg married. Then he moved to a much better neighborhood. There was no indication his wife's family had money; quite the contrary. Stoutenberg now always had money in his pockets and was flaunting it around town--buying drinks at every corner. He had never done that before. He bought a beautiful fishing boat. On Sunday afternoons, he took his friends out on excursions and there was lots of drinking.

Junior, who still enjoyed swimming in the East River on Sunday afternoons, saw the Health Department Inspector's boat regularly. The last straw was when he saw Slim fishing from it.

Δ   Δ   Δ

Junior showed up one evening at the Health Department

Archive Office.

"You want ALL of Stoutenberg's records?"

"That's what I said."

"And who are you again?"

He spent the evening and into the wee hours looking them over.

"The Mayor will gladly pay extra for you to stay."

"I should have been home hours ago. My wife will be worried."

"You have two choices. Stay with me or leave me here."

"Both are against the rules."

"Which choice will it be?"

He left Senior Inspector Millwood behind locked doors.

It was a great surprise to the staff person the following morning when they unlocked the door to see a man at a central table with enormous stacks around him.

"And who are you?"

He had discovered the anomaly in the test results, the eraser marks and corrections that were made to the records. It was quite a feat for an uneducated man. His next stop was at the New York University Chemistry Department.

Δ   Δ   Δ

"Well, it is used widely in agriculture. Mainly as a fertilizer. Also, as an insecticide and fungicide. Even explosives."

"Would you pick it up in milk from cows?"

"No. It would be long broken down before then."

"Could it kill a child?"

"Are you kidding--ammonia is one of the most lethal commonly occurring compounds in nature. You could kill an army with it."

"Slim. Slim."

It was Sunday evening and Ehring and Stoutenberg were enjoying a pail of brew between them on the fishing boat.

"Who said that?"

It was eerie.

"I'm right here."

"Where?"

"Never mind that, I know what you two have been doing."

Panic set in. Stoutenberg said in a quivering voice, "Come out now. Who are you?" They were still trying to understand where the voice was coming from.

"I am an old friend of Slim's. Past customer. You can call me Mr. Reaper."

Stoutenberg and Ehring's skin began to crawl.

"What do you want?"

There was a long pause. "Justice." After another long pause he continued, "I know all about what you have been doing, the two of you."

They finally began to understand the voice was coming from the water.

"We will pay your demands?"

"Yes you will, but I haven't made any."

"We don't have any cash here on the boat."

Junior continued, "My demands are not for money."

Slim felt his knees going weak. Suddenly he fell to the deck, "Oh, Jezz-us, I will repent! I'll not do it again! I will reform!"

"I know you will reform. I am going to reform you this very night. I am going to reform you into food for the fish and food for the worms." There was a long pause. "I am your judge, jury, executioner, and I will reform you."

They were petrified. Stoutenberg positioned himself to fight off any intruder. They had not heard Junior climb up on the deck, only the small waves slapping against the hull.

HELENA

The next day, Junior was waiting to meet with Al Smith at the late Tim Sullivan's saloon. After Tim's death, it had changed hands a few times before Murphy acquired it. The supposed teetotaler owned restaurants, saloons, and pubs all over town. It made conducting business easy and flexible. There was not anything particularly urgent on Al's mind, but he liked Junior, and liked to monitor Junior's adventures. More than once Junior had passed along a political advantage, beyond his grasp, to Smith or Murphy. Al was in town and it had been three weeks since they had met. Catching up was long overdue.

That night, Junior was a bit nervous. One could never know if anyone had seen him the previous evening when he slipped aboard Stoutenberg's fishing boat and paid Slim back for what he had done to Ruth and countless other children. He was concerned someone investigating the deaths would stumble upon the research Junior had been doing and put things together. Not likely, but it could happen. Junior didn't feel particularly guilty about what he had done. He thought he had done a great job terrorizing the two men before sentence was carried out. He thought about the phrase that came from the Bible, "Vengeance is mine; I will repay, saith the Lord." He concluded he was just helping the Lord complete His work.

He had been nursing a beer, shortly after Smith arrived, when his jaw dropped open. "Is that? Could that be?" Her name had not been on any of the lists of the dead, but she had dropped out of sight. He thought to himself, Oh my gosh. Of all places, Helena walks into this joint on the arm of a politician.

He kept looking to see if it was really her. She had transformed herself after the fire, had gotten more education and refinement at Union sponsored events and classes, and began working in the theater district. She went to dinner with men infrequently. She enjoyed their company, but would not let them get far. She still attended Mass early each morning.

Was it her or was it just a mirage? He kept staring, trying to make out her features, when it happened; they saw each other. In less than an instant, their eyes locked and there was no one else in the room.

They ran to each other, pushing past people, knocking into tables and drinks as they went. There was grumbling, until people saw what was happening.

Without kissing or speaking, Junior and Helena were locked in an embrace. They pushed each other away to arms distance to have a better look. They were beyond speaking.

As certainly as there were 146 dead from the fire, many more were dead to each other. They had scattered to the four winds. Some had returned home. Some had moved out of the area. There were still six unidentified bodies that could be any friend. Yet, here they both were. For him, their relationship had been more teasing than lustful. For her, it was love. An unattainable love, as her beloved was saving every cent to bring the woman of his dreams across the ocean.

The politician who had brought Helena tried to get her attention to join him for dinner. For her, dinner no longer mattered. Nothing else mattered than the man who stood before her. Unable to break through to Helena, he finally left.

It was much the same way with Al Smith. He was not used to being ignored. As he watched, his anger turned to humor. He had never seen Junior this way.

"Why, he is a man after all!," Smith mumbled under his breath as he watched. "Our business can wait until next trip." He giggled, threw down some cash, picked up his coat and hat, and left.

Junior and Helena stayed until the saloon closed. In the early morning hours, they wandered arm in arm through the streets of the Gas House District.

Δ   Δ   Δ

For the next week, Helena and Junior took long walks, sat at her Church, in libraries and in parks. They ended the week not remembering eating or sleeping.

They walked through Washington Square Park and enjoyed the roses. They walked down to the Asch Building and talked about the fire.

"How did you get out?"

"I threw a couple of pails on the fire, but it didn't do anything. Then I tried to get downstairs. I ended up going to the roof. The students next door got two ladders, and we went over to their roof and down."

"You mean one of the ladders was over the street between the buildings."

"Yes, but there was so much smoke around us, we didn't even notice."

"Where did you think Moira had gone?"

"I didn't know. Everyone was going every which way. On the eighth floor we were lucky," he looked up to the building, "most of us made it out."

"Yes, more people on the ninth were trapped."

"How about you? How did you get out?"

"As soon as I saw the smoke, I knew it was going to be bad. I went to the doors and they were locked, so I ran to the fire escape and went right down, then got back into the building and down. To think, a few minutes later the fire escape fell."

"What did you do that night?"

Helena explained, "It took a while before we got out of the lobby. We were told it wasn't safe because they were throwing bolts of cloth and furniture out the windows. That wasn't it at all. People were jumping."

Junior couldn't say anything. After an awkward pause, while the scene played out in both of their minds, Helena continued, "I couldn't finish reading through the list of names, so many people I knew. I checked for you--and Moira."

"I kept going back to the list, to see if your name was on it, too. Where did you go that night?"

"I went home. Sat up all night."

"I walked. After a few days, I went up to Misery Lane to look for Moira. All that was left were the unrecognizable. Those so badly burned--." He could not continue.

Helena stared into space. Finally she said, "I cannot imagine."

"If someone is burned beyond recognition, do you think it is so frightful--what I mean is, do you think some people could not or would not identify their loved one? Because they could never stand the thought of them being gone, having suffered such a death--if they did not identify them, they were not really dead. Am I making sense?"

"I know what you mean."

He talked about the restaurant, meeting a few politicians, and his job. He didn't give her much detail. He did not want to lie to her so he said, "I work out of the Mayor's Office" and "I am an inspector"--not exactly lies.

It was all right in his mind to be as honest with her as he could, but he would not be brutally honest. She needed to know some things from him, but not everything.

"There is something very important I need to tell you, but I want to make sure you are ready."

She looked at him and shaken by the look on his face replied, "I am not sure I am."

"Tell me when you are." She never could.

He concluded by saying, "I have a good job, which I hope to hold for quite some time. The people I am working for seem pleased."

She talked about her struggle recovering from the fire. Her head tilted forward as she spoke. Her face looked hollow and her shoulders drooped as if straining under a heavy load. "I had to get away. I couldn't go back to Triangle."

"I stayed at Triangle a little while after, but my heart was broken and then this came along."

They both just stood there, in front of the building, for a long time, unable to talk more about it. Finally, he asked, "How did you come to work in the theater?"

"It's hardly a glamour job. There are always costumes that need to be stitched. I was helping out in other ways. I even got to say a few lines in a play when somebody didn't show."

During the middle of the week, they were enjoying coffee together. He had not read the newspaper all week and thought he would see what was going on in the world. He browsed through *The New York Union* and visibly stiffened when he saw a headline. It carried a three-sentence article. "The bodies of two fishermen washed up on shore in the East River. They have not been identified. It appears to have been an accident."

At the end of the week, he popped the question, and she immediately said, "Yes, but I do not want to rush the wedding. We still need to heal."

Junior had been thinking of building a summer cottage for himself. He had even looked at property on the water in Long Island. One particular place appealed to him: "Beautiful Baldwin" the real estate agent was calling it. Now, instead of a cottage, he was thinking a proper home for him and Helena, where she could be a proper wife, and they could raise children and never think about the fire or their days at the Triangle Waist Company ever again.

BEAUTIFUL BALDWIN

Shortly after becoming engaged, Junior purchased a twenty-acre piece of property in Beautiful Baldwin. There was room in the area for an additional five or six houses within walking distance, but not within sight. The land was forested on both sides with a shady, sylvan glade in the center and land gently sloping to Middle Bay.

When he told Helena about the property and he asked about what type of house to build, she said, "Surprise me!"

A few days later, she handed him a magazine article on the recently completed Yellowstone's Old Faithful Inn. "A hundred rooms should be adequate for all our kids," she teased.

That winter, he hired a leading architect in the city to design and oversee construction of their home. He told him his requirements and left him with an enormous amount of cash with the parting words, "I trust you. Have fun".

The architect called in his assistant to count the money, prepared Junior a receipt, and contacted the bank to have armed guards come pick up the deposit. He was dumbfounded by the pile of dollar bills on his desk. What has just happened? he thought. Every architect dreams of the day a client will walk into his office in this way: Here, have unlimited funds, go build your masterpiece.

Δ   Δ   Δ

By early spring, one year before their wedding, barge deliveries of Pennsylvania Bluestone from Catskill Park, Ulster County, New York were unloaded onto the back of the property.

A few days later, Douglas fir, Lodgepole pine, and Western Red cedar from western Washington State arrived and were transported by Clydesdale-drawn wagons from the Long Island Railroad Station at Baldwin. The fir and pine were used for beams and posts, and the cedar for paneling the closets. Two days later those same Clydesdales delivered Northern California redwood for interior paneling, decking, and siding.

Over the spring and summer, the timber frame, five-bedroom home (not including servant's quarters), topped by a tin roof painted bright blue, was completed. The center section was an A-frame, a triangle of large windows providing an exquisite view of the bay and the hills on the other side of the water.

One of the requirements was not to disturb existing trees. So the position of access roads was carefully considered. The back of the house needed to have large windows to maintain views of the forests, bay, and meadows. Another requirement was the house be fully furnished--tables, chairs, picture frames, cabinets, window frames, dressers, bed frames, and nightstands were all to be made from red cedar, the redder the hue the better. Each bedroom was to be in a primary or secondary color, except for green. Kelly green was reserved for the main floor, including living room, dining room, and kitchen. The master bedroom was to be yellow.

Even his and her gardens were planted; flowers for her and fruits and vegetables for him. The house was to be completed by their wedding day.

Junior met with the architect a few times, early in the design. He then decided he had given him enough direction and trusted him to make this his finest work. The result was a rustic palace in an unspoiled, sylvan, pastoral setting.

Helena was athletic and trim. Her clothing accentuated her hourglass figure, well-formed breasts, sleek waist, and broad hips.

Junior was also trim and athletic. He continued to swim every Sunday, but in addition started swimming during the week. He looked forward to the new home on Long Island, where he could swim to his heart's content. For Junior, it was returning to his roots.

Δ   Δ   Δ

The Erbachers were aghast when they received an invitation to Junior's wedding. The time seemed too short since Moira had died. Actually, it had been almost three years. It was common for a man in his twenties (or even later) to remarry after the death of his wife and start a family. Junior was already twenty-four and Helena was nineteen. But, of course, the Erbachers needed to admit to themselves that Moira was gone, which was easier said than done. The loss for them was as if she had been their own daughter.

They had just about decided between the two of them not to attend the wedding, when they received a four page handwritten letter from Junior explaining many things. How hurt he was. How he needed to move on from the disaster. How he had known Helena for a long time as a co-worker (of course, his version was highly edited). On the last page, Junior asked Mr. Erbacher to be his best man.

They were stunned. How could they possibly say no under the circumstances? Mr. Erbacher had outlived his prediction of being dead within a year, but he still was in poor health. He was so honored by the request; he said he would do it, for Moira. She would want Junior to remarry and get on with his life.

Helena attended church daily at St. Patrick's Old Cathedral on Mulberry Street. She had moved nearby after the fire and loved the church that was a jewel to the city of New York. Joseph-Francois Mangin had designed an edifice of simplicity, grace, and stately beauty with enormous walls around the central feature of a marble altar. Henry Erben's glorious organ resonated throughout the chamber.[xxxi]

"Oh, Junior, isn't it beautiful! Look at this altar. Look at the carvings. Oh, this is heaven. This is where I want to be married."

Helena dreamed of a stately wedding in this beautiful place, and Junior did not disappoint her. Their wedding was simple, but their apparel was elegant. On the first full day of spring, Saturday, March 20, 1914, Helena made her long-awaited walk down the aisle. It had been rainy, but unseasonably warm, leading up to the wedding. The sidewalks were damp and clean. The flowers were in full bloom.

Their architect, dressed in a long-tailed tuxedo and wearing gloves, stood in the Church vestibule before the wedding. "Per our agreement, Sir, I have everything you requested." He handed

Junior the deed, financial documents, and a ceremonial key to the house, to begin the wedding ceremony.

Guests included friends from their Triangle days, from the theater, from the restaurant, and from Tammany Hall. All of Junior's staff came to the wedding. As promised, Mr. Erbacher served as best man and Alfred E. Smith gave away the bride. After the wedding, they boarded the Empire Corridor train for their honeymoon in Niagara Falls.

Neither Junior nor Helena had seen the house, so when they arrived back from their honeymoon at the railroad station they were met by their realtor, Charles Luerssen, who drove them. He had arranged to have their clothing and personal belongings brought from their two homes in the city and put away while they were on their honeymoon. A chilled bottle of Champagne awaited them, as did a full icebox.

Their train arrived at Baldwin by way of Albany and Penn Station in the early afternoon. It was sunny with a slight breeze.

They were stunned when they rode up and stood in front of the house with their mouths hanging open. Birds chirped their welcome and squirrels danced on the railings. Deer grazed in the glade.

Luerssen said he would call on them in the morning and make any transportation arrangements that were required.

They spent the rest of the day running through the house naked, trying to make love in every bedroom. They laughed and kissed. They fed each other berries and drank the entire bottle of Champagne. They nestled in each others arms and took catnaps all day and all night.

Late the following morning, they started talking about their future. He planned to continue work in the city. She wanted to do Catholic charity work in the theater district on behalf of children and to help union workers. They also looked forward to filling the house with children.

Δ   Δ   Δ

Soon after the homecoming, Junior returned to work and some normalcy. Helena was not clear exactly what he did for a living, but was quite proud of his accomplishments and the income he generated. She believed he was on the mayor's senior staff somehow and a successful restaurateur and saloon owner. She had been told the saloon where they reconnected belonged to him. He never corrected her.

Helena settled in as best she could. She found a church nearby, gardened, put away the groceries she had delivered to her house daily, read, and cleaned house. There was so much to clean they closed off unused bedrooms and the servant's quarters. She had expected to begin working with Catholic Charities and the Women Worker's Unions right away, but she did little during the first year, except enjoy her home, her husband, and the seasons.

The fall was glorious with all the rich-colored foliage and migrating wildlife. Winter was a wonderland with frozen creeks and ponds. Spring started rainy, but ended with an explosion of flowers and lilacs.

The new living arrangement was costing Junior much more than he planned. He was out less in the evening, so fewer free meals and drinks. It cost much more to heat his home. The daily commute was also expensive. Using the Long Island Railroad to get to and from work was costing him more in time and personal funds.

Δ   Δ   Δ

In 1914, the Mayor's office passed from the "caretaker" Republican administration to the Fusion Party platform. Mayor William Jay Gaynor had died the previous September and Ardolph Loges Kline, President of the Board of Aldermen, served out the remaining 113 days of Gaynor's term.

Thirty-four year old John Purroy Mitchel, "The Boy Mayor of New York" was elected on a platform created by the fusion of factions within multiple political parties. His claim to fame had been murder and corruption investigations he conducted against two borough presidents and the chief of police, which had implications up to the Governor's Office. He was able to consolidate factions against Tammany Hall, but was not politically perceptive. Shortly after taking office, he became hopelessly mired. He alienated his base in the Catholic Church and was not prepared to defend trumped-up charges that came from the Tammany camp. He seemed surprised by it all. He died a few years later by falling out of his single-seat training plane from 500 feet when he failed to fasten his seat belt. A mechanic seemed to sum up both his political and his military career. "It makes my hair stand on end to see Major Mitchel fly. He takes risks and seems to think nothing of it."

It came as a surprise to Mitchel that there were such things as Mayoral Inspectors. He looked at their expenses and everything appeared to be in order, but he could not understand why one Inspector required the full-time use of a chauffeur-driven limousine. He wrote a letter to R. J. Millwood to complain. "Do you really need one?" was his closing line.

As if by divine inspiration, Junior remembered his old saying, 'It's not what you make that counts; it's what you don't spend'.

"By gosh, he is right!"

Junior ordered a second limousine and hired another driver. He then had door-to-door service from his home more than twenty miles away and could inspect things at all hours of the day and night, and on his way to and from his office. He could spend even more time with Helena.

Junior developed his own staff and began requiring them to turn in any fees they collected directly to him instead of to his secretary. They were afraid to ask him what fees he thought they should have been collecting, but quickly cash began rolling in. He was making far more now than he ever had before.

Δ   Δ   Δ

Helena had to admit that during the days she was lonely. She looked forward to when Junior came home. They planned to have servants some day, but were able to get by with seasonal help for heavy cleaning and on special occasions. She noticed she really enjoyed having servants around, but could not justify the additional expense that would entail. She decided they would wait until they had children to have full-time servants.

She was relieved when she saw surveyors out looking at land nearby. Within a month, a house went up about 200 yards away. The day the family moved in, she made a pie to take to them as a housewarming gift. They made fast friends with the couple that moved in and with their children. Neil Comstra owned a delivery business; Jan raised their children and taught Sunday school.

Soon there were three more families in their neck of Eden. The Brown's were second. Thomas was a distinguished science professor at Columbia University. Theresa was very involved in their church and raising three active children.

Next came the Fragnolli clan, with three rambunctious boys. Ronald was an engineer. His wife, Martha, loved to garden. She had her hands full with the boys.

Finally, the Bennetts built their home. William was a doctor and medical professor at New York University. Donna was a retired opera singer. They had two daughters who were a joy to their parents and, when they got a little older, a distraction to the Fragnolli boys.

Between the five families, there were always parties, dances, and charity events. Every Saturday evening they had dessert and coffee together and discussed religion, politics, and their children (and to sing around the piano, if they were at the Bennetts).

One of their favorite activities was to picnic in the meadow behind the Millwood's home. Everyone loved Aunt Helena. She held the little ones by the hour. She baked with the older girls and played ball with the young men.

The Millwood home was ideally situated to host their picnics. They barbequed on their deck and cooked and baked in the kitchen. They feasted on the deck or under the shade of a large maple tree and played games from the back of the house all the way to the bay. They boated and swam until they were exhausted and held large bonfires near the water in the evenings. Each family had a dog or two that would run, wrestle, and play to the point of exhaustion.

The five families cared for each other with a bond stronger than with their own extended families.

$$\Delta \qquad \Delta \qquad \Delta$$

On May 5, 1920, Helena turned twenty-five years old. The neighbors brought over a birthday cake that evening. The children came in their pajamas, squealing with delight at the thought of Aunt Helena's birthday. Junior arrived home a bit later than normal to find his house filled with guests. He poured himself a scotch and enjoyed the fun.

That evening after their guests left, Helena turned quiet and introspective.

"Is something the matter?"

"I guess I am just tired."

For the balance of the week, she was quiet.

"Is it something I did?"

"No. Really, I'm fine."

On Saturday, she put on a brave face for the evening dessert and Sunday they had a picnic. The children were running all over the yard having a grand time. They teased Helena about not being able to keep up with them because she was so old.

Junior read and napped in the hammock in the shade of the maple tree in the early evening. He had been swimming most of the afternoon and was exhausted.

As twilight fell, it became cool out and Junior went into the house. He heard a noise, but was not sure where it was coming from. He looked all through the house and could not find Helena. At last, he heard the noise distinctly from the blue bedroom.

Helena was crying.

He knocked on the door, "Oh, my gosh, are you hurt?"

"Well, no, not really." She continued to sob.

He sat next to her on the bed.

"I love our neighbors."

"I know you do, Aunt Helena the elderly." His humor fell flat.

"They have lovely children." She paused. "Why don't we?"

"Oh, dear." He tried to comfort her.

She kept weeping.

"Why, God?"

"Maybe you should talk to Bill," referring to their neighbor, Dr. William Bennett.

"I already have. He examined me on Wednesday. He couldn't find anything wrong or any reason we have not been able to conceive. He said just to keep trying."

"You know, I am always ready to do my part."

She smiled and poked him in the ribs.

"He would like to see you. To see if you are medically able."

"That sounds fine. I will go talk to him right now."

"No. Tomorrow. Stay here with me."

All he could do was sooth and console her. They talked late into the night.

Δ   Δ   Δ

The Millwoods fell into a rhythm. They took long walks together. From April to November, they swam together almost every evening. During spring and summer, they gardened together--she with her flowers while he tended the fruits and vegetables. They loved to boat and picnic. Junior would send one of the limousines to pick her up and they went to dinner, the theater, and a nightcap before coming home to the dogs.

He was still getting up early each day and off to work, but he didn't work as late and started skipping Saturdays entirely. Corruption had changed a bit, not eliminated; become different and better hidden. Incompetence was rooted out. Established city bureaus figured ways of staying out of Junior's sights.

Junior had less contact with Al Smith. He helped on all his campaigns for Governor (four two-year terms) and the 1928 Presidential Campaign in Manhattan, Brooklyn, and Long Island. He arranged fund raising events and speaking opportunities. His staff was pressed into handing out campaign buttons and holding placards at his campaign rallies.

He also heard less of "Silent Charlie" Murphy. Neither realized the machine Junior built right below their noses or the fortune he amassed.

Saturdays and Sundays were reserved for their neighbors. As the kids got older, Aunt Helena proudly attended every event in their lives. Graduations came and then weddings, including a Fragnoli boy to a Bennett girl. There was college for some and work for others. One day it became 'great' Aunt Helena and 'great' Uncle Mill.

Helena finally got involved with Catholic charities, not in New York City, but in Baldwin. There was plenty to do right in their own backyard. She was also busy with church. At Donna's suggestion, she joined the choir at the Free Methodist Church that the Bennetts attended. Helena enjoyed it very much. She had never sung before, but she had a lovely alto voice. She could not read music, but with Donna's coaching, did well.

She never did go back to work with the Women's Union.

They had full lives and yet there seemed to be something missing.

They rang in the 1937 New Year by going into the city for a night on the town with all the neighbors. Junior was forty-seven and Helena was soon to turn forty-three. It was Junior's treat to take them to 'Junior's'--a steak place he had purchased the previous year. They saw a special showing of Robert E. Sherwood's Pulitzer Prize winning drama *Idiot's Delight* at the Shubert Theater starring Alfred Lunt and Lynn Fontanne.

After the theater it was cocktails and dessert at 'The Mill' which had officially opened December 5, 1933 (the day prohibition was repealed). To laughs all around, Junior told his guests, "This place is one of the 100,000 successful speakeasies in New York City and I've been a silent partner in it since the mid-20's." They had a grand time after the play. They were in a festive mood and dressed to the nines.

As the evening wore on, they talked about how the Fragnoli

boys were into construction and automotives. The Bennett girls were married and raising families. The Brown kids had followed in their parents footsteps with college and careers. The Comstra kids moved on to parenthood and professions. The neighborhood was indeed blessed.

That night was the last time that Junior and Helena talked of any regret of not having children of their own. They delighted in being the Aunt and Uncle to such a wonderful group of kids.

After nightcaps, Junior's two limousines whisked them to the Waldorf Astoria. None of them came out of their hotel room for brunch until after 2 p.m.

Δ   Δ   Δ

Something was terribly wrong. Helena was feeling fatigued. More tired than normal. She had cramping and a light period.

Junior was amorous one evening. He noticed how beautiful her breasts were. He tenderly kissed her nipples, but she moved away. "I'm sorry, but I am not feeling well."

"What is wrong?"

"I am just tired and a little sore."

"I know what would be good for you."

"None of that. I just need to get some rest."

When she still was not feeling better after a few days, she made an appointment to see Dr. Bill Bennett.

"You have got to be kidding."

"No. I am not."

"How sure are you?"

"Three quarters. We will know soon enough."

"You must keep this secret, Bill."

"Why?"

"You must. Until we know for sure."

"He'll figure it out soon enough."

"Perhaps. I don't want to upset him. I could not stand it if the worst were to come true."

"As you wish, Helena. Let's make an appointment for one month."

When she was sure, she could not bear not talking to anyone about it any longer. She confided in her neighbor friends and they confided in their husbands.

In the sixteenth century, the French created a parlor game they called Petit Jeux (Little Game). It was composed of intellectual exercises to guess a name or phrase based on one person acting it out. The person acting was silent, but everyone else was attempting to guess the phrase. The game was hardly silent. It began being called by its French Provencal word "charrado" meaning, "chatter." We know it today as charades.

On the next Saturday evening, all the neighbors were gathered at the Millwood's house to play charades.

For the last game of the night, Helena began acting out the phrase. The guesses kept coming fast and furious. However, nobody was getting it. First Junior got *In*--and then *the*, but was very perplexed when he got the last word: *oven*.

"What does that mean?"

They all just looked at each other, as if they couldn't figure it out. They could not contain their giggles.

"What does it mean?"

"What do you mean, what does it mean?" They looked at him, smiling and giggling, as if he were from another planet.

He ran into the kitchen and looked at their stove. Everything looked just fine. He opened the door to the oven. There was something inside. He reached in and pulled out a bun, wrapped in a small tea towel arranged to look like a diaper with one blue and one pink pin.

Δ   Δ   Δ

Junior's perplexed look turned to wondrous realization. Junior turned to Helena, "Does this mean what I think it means?"

"'fraid so, Pops!"

The room exploded into laughter and cheering.

It was unbelievable! Too good to be true!

Helena looked radiant. Her dream had come true.

During the week, Junior came home one day in the middle of the day to check on her.

"What are you doing here?"

"Well, I, uh.."

"Go back to work. I'm fine."

The next day he showed up again at noon.

"What, you again?" She smiled and he returned a sheepish

grin.

"I am sorry; I just cannot get enough of seeing you."

"Go tell the driver to take the rest of the day off."

They laughed until they cried. They lay on their bed, talked, and held hands.

During the week, Junior started calling her Sarai. He kept this up throughout the weekend, but it seemed only Helena and Junior got the inside joke. He just kept calling her Sarai.

Ronald replied, "I knew you had it in ya, Mill!"

Neil patted his groin and whispered among the men, "Maybe she got a little help from a friend!"

Junior played along, calling over his shoulder, "Sarai, you did not happen to get any help from--oh, never mind, what's done is done." He broke out laughing.

"Mill, why do you keep calling her Sarai?," asked Thomas.

"Oh, I get it!," screamed one of the women. Jan Comstra got up to find Helena's Bible, looked in Genesis and found the account in Genesis 17:15, "And God said unto Abraham, As for Sarai thy wife, thou shalt not call her name Sarai, but Sarah shall her name be.'"

Jan explained, "The name Sarai means "contentious"; but the name Sarah means "princess". Once she got over being contentious with God, He blessed her with her heart's desire, a son."

Jan went on to read a footnote, "She was ninety years old and barren when she conceived through Abraham, her husband."

"Or maybe it was a neighbor named Neil." Everyone smiled, shook their head, or booed.

"Yep, ninety years old, contentious, and barren pretty much sums up Helena."

$$\Delta \qquad \Delta \qquad \Delta$$

Dr. Bill was concerned about her age, but thought to himself, many women her age deliver without problems. She is healthy and strong. I'll keep a close watch on her.

The neighbor women were delighted with her blessed news and shared their maternity clothing, baby toys, and diapers. Junior ordered a redwood crib made and planted a special row of roses all around their deck. He tended to both sides of the garden, as he did not want her to strain herself. He also arranged for a housekeeper.

Helena spent long stretches of time wading in the bay where

the buoyancy of the water took a strain off her back and the cool water refreshed her. Junior did not want her in the boat for fear they would capsize, but she absolutely put her foot down when he wanted to eliminate their long walks together. She shortened them as the months went by, but the summer and fall were filled with strolling along the banks of the bay.

Helena had beautiful skin, but there was a radiance about her now. She pulled her long, red hair back and clipped it. She spent long stretches napping in the hammock by their large maple tree, with lemonade on a tray nearby.

Junior loved to watch her. In the dead of summer, she slept naked on the bed and he sat next to her for hours, watching her slow breathing. Her breasts were less tender now, but she had backaches.

A peace had settled in at the Millwood home, with joy, delight, and contentment everywhere.

As she got bigger, she became fatigued at each activity, and Dr. Bennett carefully watched her. The housekeeper and her neighbors were always nearby. Friends were careful not to overextend their visits. The kids, with children of their own now, returned home to have a visit with Auntie Helena. They swapped stories of their pregnancies and asked her about names they had selected.

"Boy or girl?"

"Healthy!"

"Have you picked out names yet?"

"If it is a boy, Mill is fond of the name, Carl. Now, if it is a girl, I like Clarissa. Mill is holding out for Moira, but I think that would be too painful for both of us. Recently he mentioned another name, Anne. Do you like that?"

"Yes, but I like Clarissa better."

"Then Clarissa it must be!"

CLARISSA

December 10, 1937 was a gray day. It was mostly cloudy with the sun breaking through now and then. Snow had fallen a few days earlier, but none stayed on the ground. The leaves on the maple had long since disappeared.

Shortly after Junior left for work, Helena called for her housekeeper, "Janet, go fetch Bill."

"Who?"

"Dr. Bennett. I think my water just broke."

"Well, it looks like this is going to be your big day!"

"Oh, Bill."

"Everything is fine. Your water broke, but you are not very far along."

"Oh, my back hurts."

"I will send for Donna to come and rub your back. That always helped her."

"Mill wanted to be here."

"I'll notify his office right away."

"Ohhh."

"Having a contraction?"

"Yes."

"Have you had many?"

"No, just a few, but they take my breath away."

"You are doing fine."

"Here comes another one," she grimaced.

"I want to deliver from the blue bedroom."

"Why, want a boy?"

"No, it doesn't matter to us. I can see out into the back. I want to look at the maple tree and the bay."

Donna rubbed Helena's back and kept her drinking water. Dr. Bill checked her again, "You're progressing nicely. Things will be fine." Suddenly Junior appeared at the door.

"May I come in?"

"Of course."

"How are you, dear?"

"Fine."

"Why did you come in here?"

"I wanted to see the bay and our maple. Plus I really messed up our bed when my water broke."

"Oh, we have already taken care of that," piped in Janet.

Helena was gripped with a severe contraction, which startled Junior. "Is it alright?"

Bill laughed, "Women have been doing this for thousands of years. It all comes with contractions."

Bill checked Helena. "It will not be long now."

"I'm going downstairs."

"Good idea. A man's place at times like this is at the hearth with a good brandy and cigar."

She had been in labor a little over seven hours and had steadily progressed. It seemed to be going smoothly.

"Bill, I am feeling faint."

"That is not uncommon. It is a big stress on the body to deliver a baby."

When the time came, Dr. Bennett got into position, with his wife at his elbow.

"Now push!"

"I can't!"

"Push!"

"I am."

This repeated a few more times until Bill announced, "Here it comes! Ahhh. Beautiful. Let me look. It's a girl. Helena, you have your healthy, beautiful baby girl. Let me clean her up." The baby screamed.

"Let me see her."

"Would you like to hold her?"

"Not yet. I am not feeling well. Like I am going to faint."

"Just lay back and relax. I'll get Mill."

"Mill, old boy, congratulations! It's a girl."

"Can I see them?"

"Yes, of course, get up here."

Dr. Bennett returned to the baby. "She is so beautiful," he said as he handed her to Donna. Then he stood next to his patient. Helena was motionless. Resting. Gray.

When Junior stood at the end of the bed, Helena opened her eyes. Exhausted, she could not smile.

Donna showed Junior, "And here is your daughter!"

Junior said, "We are going to name her Clarissa Anne Millwood."

The Doctor moved up along the bed, closer to Helena. She was so pale. When he pressed against the bed, he felt warm, dampness against his leg. He screamed, "Oh my Gosh!" He tore back the sheets to see the bed pooled with blood. As Helena delivered the baby, her own life was streaming away.

Δ   Δ   Δ

The death certificate listed obstetrical hemorrhage as the cause of death. The uterine ruptured causing internal bleeding until finally, shortly after birth, the blood just poured out of her body. There was nothing anybody could have done.

Dr. Bennett was beside himself. He had to put it aside to attend to his other patient and make sure all was well with Clarissa. She was healthy. Junior never blamed Bill. He could see it was not something Bill had done.

He, himself, was responsible.

He stood in the bathroom with the water running in the sink. "She was just too old to get pregnant, what was I thinking? I am all to blame." He looked into the mirror, "My God, what kind of monster am I, that I have killed both of my wives."

Bill ordered a coffin delivered from the undertaker and had a place for Helena prepared next to the maple tree she loved. The women cleaned her and dressed her in an emerald green short sleeve velveteen dress. The men lifted her into the coffin. The ladies arranged her hair, not in her usual bun, but flowing down to her shoulders. They placed her hands gently on top of a small, black hymnal that lay in her lap. There were no flowers on her casket, as the roses had long since dropped their pedals.

On Sunday afternoon, they lowered her into the ground. There were few words said. Junior could not speak. Father O'Keefe gave a wonderful eulogy. He worked alongside Helena, saw the woman she was, shared his thoughts, and read some passages. Donna wanted to sing for the service, but was too stricken with grief. She could hardly choke out words to speak, much less sing. Helena's friends from the church choir sang two traditional hymns and the service was soon over.

Junior turned over the first spade of soil, and then marched into the house. That was all he could bear. The workers covered the coffin with soil and replaced the grass.

The women took turns holding and caring for the baby. They went into the house to check on Junior. He was sitting by the fireplace with a glass of scotch, staring into space.

Jan was holding Clarissa, "I think it best we take your daughter home with us tonight."

There was no reply from Junior.

"We'll send over some food later."

Still no reply.

"We will check in on you."

They did. Every hour or so, one of the neighbors walked through the door to see how he was doing. He sat staring out the back, looking at the maple tree and the bay. He had a glass in his hand, but drank little.

He never responded to their questions all night long, nor did he eat.

Δ   Δ   Δ

The neighbors took care of Clarissa for the next two weeks. They passed her from home to home, caring for her, and loving her. They checked in on Junior to make sure he ate. He was able to go back to work, returning home to his scotch and his dark mood. He was foul with his employees, customers, and clients, and dark and moody with his neighbors and even Al Smith. Everyone gave him space.

Junior retreated from the world. The neighbors met together to see what should be done. They bought a pair of goats to graze in the yard and provide plenty of milk. They hired, on Junior's behalf, two Italian sisters to care for Clarissa, named Marta and

Maria. The housekeeper, Janet, who had been helping during the pregnancy, was hired on full time to cook meals and clean. The three women lived quietly in the servant's quarters and shared care of Clarissa twenty-four hours a day, and Junior when he was home.

As he brooded, Junior convinced himself even more that this was his entire fault and his punishment. It was well deserved.

There was no denying to himself any longer; it was his cigar that started the Triangle Waist Company factory fire. He had been able to push that thought out of his mind most of the time. To admit he had caused the fire was to admit he killed Moira. He was being punished for killing Moira and 145 others. He was being punished for being so stupid as to buy tainted milk for Ruth. He was being punished for killing Slim and Stoutenberg, even though the bastards deserved it and, given half a chance, he would take pleasure in killing them all over again.

Why did God have to take Helena, and not he? Why was Clarissa even born? That was my punishment as well--an ongoing reminder of what he had done to everyone. Clarissa was a stock upon his neck; a feeling God had him by the throat and would slaughter him for his wrongdoing one day.

Junior decided to kill himself. He certainly deserved it. He began to write out his confession in long hand. It detailed all his past sins from the time he assaulted his father in Ireland, through his infidelities, the fire, all his business misdealing, murders, lies, cheating, and extortions. It came out to forty pages long, in fine, small script, from his youth up to the present day.

He sat back to reflect on his life and finish the scotch bottle before he would kill himself. He thought of all the ways he could do it and decided hanging himself on a limb of the maple tree would be best. He could be near Helena as the rope snapped his neck. He could gasp her name as the rope choked off the oxygen, asking for her forgiveness.

"Oh God, why did you take Helena and not me?"

Δ   Δ   Δ

He found a rope and chair and took them out to the maple tree. He discovered it would be impractical to kill himself right now, with three women in the house. He thought more about when he would do it. How could he get Janet, Marta, Maria, and Clarissa out of the house?

He made a noose, threw the rope over a sturdy limb, adjusted the height above the chair, and tied off the rope to another limb. He tested it with his hand to make sure it was sturdy and taut. As he stood before the chair, he realized killing himself would be cheating God of the punishment he owed Him. He pulled the rope off the limb and untied it. He took the chair back to the house and threw the rope down on the deck.

God's punishment for him was to care for Clarissa, waiting out his time until God was ready to deal with him face-to-face, and cast him into His fiery hell.

This would be his lasting legacy to Helena, partially atoning, until his judgment by God.

No, he would not kill himself.

He looked up to the sky, "Okay, we'll do it your way."

He decided to have Moira exhumed and buried next to Helena. As he thought some more, it came to him that he could have Ruth buried next to his wives as well. He did not know what it would take to get permission. How could he contact Naomi? There was no way of knowing where she was living by now.

He decided there was an easier way; bribe someone at the cemetery to have it done. His misdeeds would be lined up in their graves before him. The continual reminder of all he had done to the ones he loved. Just one more thing to add to his forty-page list.

Δ   Δ   Δ

Junior held a funeral for Moira and Ruth. Only he and a priest attended, though his neighbors and servants looked on from afar with curiosity. He ordered headstones for the three that were buried, plus one for himself and one for Clarissa. He would confront the demons of his past sins every time he looked that way.

In the spring, he planted flowers and shrubs at the graves. There were red roses for Helena, yellow roses and shamrocks for Moira, and baby's-breath (Gypsophila) for Ruth.

It took him a few months before he was functioning well. He provided for all of Clarissa's needs, but ignored her most of the time. He provided cash instantly to meet any need Clarissa might have. During her early years, she was raised in affluence but without affection from her father.

She had large, brown eyes. They reminded Junior of Anne and Moira. She received great care, love, and affection from Marta and Maria. She had twice the mother and none of the father she needed.

Junior worked long hours, frequently leaving before dawn and returning near midnight. He resumed working on Saturdays. When he was home, he swam a great deal. Returning from the water, he stopped at the gravesites in the shade of the maple tree.

Clarissa was curious about her father, and he began to watch her from afar. She maneuvered from chair to chair until she got near him. She would stop, get down and crawl away, trying to get him to chase her, but he never budged.

When she was eleven months old, she was standing with her hands on a low table trying to walk. She lost her balance and fell down with her chin hitting the table. Junior sprang to his feet, alarmed. At the same moment, Clarissa sprang to her feet and ran to her father, launching herself into his open arms.

He hugged her and kissed her. He held her close while Maria and Marta stood by in amazement. They had never seen him hold her. They thought that perhaps he blamed her for her mother's death. Yet here he was, at last, holding his dear child for the first time.

The tears poured from his eyes. "Oh, Clarissa. My Clarissa. I love you, Clarissa." He kissed her and hugged her and she quit crying.

She never crawled again. When she walked, she walked in looping circles back to her father almost every time. He gently bent down, took her hands, brought her to his chest, and whispered to her.

$$\Delta \quad \Delta \quad \Delta$$

His neighbor, Ron Fragnolli told Junior, "Now you need to, and can, be a father to Clarissa." He took the advice to heart.

She was loved by all the neighbors. Though they no longer picnicked in the Millwood's backyard, they still got together on Saturday evening. Junior came only about once a month, but when he did, he brought Clarissa who was passed from person to person all evening.

He was non-committal when they asked him about dating or marrying again. He saw women from the theater in the Gas House District for dinner on occasion and sometimes for sex.

After killing two wives, he was afraid of what he might do.

Clarissa was ordinary looking as a child. Though she had a few of their features, she did not really look like either her father or her mother. She had large, dark, brown eyes and curly, auburn hair, where her mother's hair had been bright red and her father's was black.

Junior had a sandbox built for her. Next, he had a wooden swing set built and another swing hung from the maple tree. They kept a few goats, and he bought her a miniature horse. Junior had a small barn and corral built, tucked into the woods, out of sight of the house.

When she was five, Junior sent her to the best private grade school in New York City, having her delivered and picked up in one of his limousines. She studied hard and was curious about many things. He insisted his drivers now be qualified to take defensive action against kidnapping or assault. Junior had many enemies, and the best way to get to him would be through his daughter.

He worked fewer hours during the week and stopped working on Saturday and Sunday entirely. He now made time for his daughter. He taught her to swim and they were out in the bay together daily, except during the dead of winter. Once she could swim to his satisfaction, he began taking her out on his sailboat, eventually teaching her to sail on her own. They walked around the yard often.

VACCINATION

After puberty, Clarissa grew to be tall, with a good figure. She never went without make-up, though she used it sparingly. Her moniker was the large handbags she insisted on carrying, even as a teenager.

In 1952, Jonas Salk engineered an inactivated polio-virus vaccine in his laboratory at the University of Pittsburgh. *National Geographic* reported, "Three wild, virulent reference strains grown in monkey kidney tissue culture and inactivated with formalin would change hundreds of millions of lives". Most were changed for the better.

Poliomyelitis was terrifying. Parents called summers fearful. A small, summer vacation would exponentially increase risk of exposure. Water (swimming holes, swimming pools), unsatisfactory hygiene (especially by care givers and food service people), even flies, can pass the pathogen through the fecal-oral route into the blood stream. Between 90-95% of polio infections were asymptomatic (without apparent sign), but within two weeks could progress to paralytic stage. Polio was the most dreaded childhood disease of the 20th century.

The 1952 polio epidemic was the worst in the nation's history; 58,000 cases were reported, 3,145 died, and 21,269 were left with paralysis. The public was desperate for anything that would give them hope.[xxxii]

Salk's vaccine was field tested, led by Thomas Francis. The largest medical experiment in world history to date involved 1.8 million American schoolchildren in forty-four states, including Clarissa near the end of the trial.

In 1953, when Clarissa was 16 years old, she had a side effect from the polio vaccine. There had been few side effects from these vaccinations and Clarissa's was one of the rarest.

For two weeks, she was fine. Then she suddenly lost her appetite and began vomiting. Initially, Dr. Bennett didn't even suspect the vaccine, thinking it was a case of the flu. The flu-like symptoms gave way to persistent crying over the next week, and she struggled nearly the rest of her life with overpowering emotional distress at events around her.

Dr. Bennett searched for answers, consulting with the premier research scientists and medical doctors in the nation. There were none.

When Dr. Bennett could not find answers, Junior took things into his own hands. Perhaps seeing the doctors face-to-face would trigger a better response. He took Clarissa on a train trip to various clinics and research universities. There were just no answers. The standard reply--"It is just a minor side effect; a small negative in the shadow of a greater good." Those responses were of little reassurance. Junior saw it as further punishment for his lifetime of sins. Clarissa missed a great deal of school with the illness and was held back two years.

On October 1, 1955, CBS nightly television news anchor Douglas Edwards reported, "Actor James Dean was killed in an automobile accident yesterday. He was driving a Porsche 550 Spyder west on U.S. Route 466 near Cholame, California. A black-and-white 1950 Ford Custom Tudor coupe driven by 23-year-old college student Donald Turnupseed crossed into Dean's lane from the opposite direction at a fork onto State Route 41. They collided head-on. Turnupseed and a passenger in Dean's car sustained minor injuries. According to the passenger, Dean's final words were, 'That guy's gotta stop--He'll see us.'"

Clarissa was hysterical. Doctor Bennett was summoned to give her a sedative. She did not even know who James Dean was. She had never seen one of his movies.

Junior ordered the televisions removed from his house and the newspapers discontinued.

A month later, in Montgomery, Alabama, 42-year old Rosa Louise McCauley Parks refused to obey bus driver James Blake's order to give up her seat for a white passenger, sparking the Montgomery Bus Boycott. When Clarissa heard about it at school, she flew into a rage and had to be hospitalized for a few days to prevent her from hurting herself.

She was released, spending the remainder of her high-school years tutored at home. She missed her high school graduation.

Through tutoring and counseling, she overcame the traumatic episodes that required sedatives and hospitalizations. Over the years, and generally in hindsight, others continued to recognize her reactions to world events as triggers to her behavior.

Δ   Δ   Δ

During Christmas vacation in 1956, at age 66, Junior decided to retire. He was set for life and could pay cash for Clarissa's college education (including advanced degrees) and still live comfortably. Even so he worried about how she would do in college. He decided he must do whatever he could to help her.

She had always been a good student, but her social skills were few. She tended to be highly analytical and had decided to get an undergraduate degree in Political Science or Pre-Law from Radcliffe, Stanford, Vassar, or Cornell. She eliminated NYU and Barnard because of their closeness to home; the very reason Junior wanted her to attend there. Based on how she liked it she might go on for a law degree, if they would accept a female.

Clarissa recognized her father was willingly setting aside his work life to be available to do whatever was necessary for her. It was a deep act of love. He had come a long way in the nineteen years of her life, from nearly rejecting her into being her biggest supporter, fan, and comforter. He had mellowed.

His impending retirement was proclaimed by the Democratic Party and lauded by all the New York City newspapers. He was credited with being a hero for his work following the Triangle Waist Company factory fire. "His personal experience in the flames led R. J. Millwood to become a crusader for the city." There were long exposés about the Triangle Waist Company factory fire and interviews with victims. The owners were once again vilified in the press. The unions published articles on the success of their movement for better working conditions. The

Democrats claimed the work of Alfred Smith as their own and pledged a greater push for the future of worker's rights.

Junior's refusal of every request for an interview was chalked up to his great humility. He would only say, "I cannot speak for fear of jeopardizing continuing investigations." He was really thinking, with a smile, "I cannot speak for fear of indictment."

They asked about Junior's replacement. Mayor W. Averell Harriman said, "We are still considering all organizational considerations," meaning he did not have a clue what they were talking about. When asked to comment on Junior's career, the Mayor said, "Millwood instilled fear and trepidation everywhere he went."

Of course, he meant himself and his predecessors. The Mayor's press secretary added, "The City will never be the same after Millwood is gone." Meaning: Perhaps we can get more of that good, old-time graft back. "Millwood will be hard to replace." Which, of course, meant we would finally be rid of him, so why would we ever want to replace him?

There were Rotary and Lyons Club luncheons, testimonials, plaques, speeches, and honors galore. After a few weeks of the falderal, Junior returned to running his restaurant and entertainment business interests part-time by showing up some place, Clarissa on his arm, eating lunch or dinner, checking things out quickly and superficially, praising the staff and management, and then returning home. He stayed out of his managers' way and let them run the business.

The only draw back to retiring was no longer having a pair of City Hall Limousines and drivers at his disposal. He found hiring a car more inconvenient than he liked; he could no longer immediately go wherever he wished. He decided both he and Clarissa should learn to drive. However, he could not decide whether to buy themselves a pair of Bentley's or Rolls Royce's. He bought one of each, giving his daughter the Bentley.

Δ   Δ   Δ

Through all four years at Radcliffe, Clarissa had a private room, which gave her the luxury of the way she liked to dress in the morning (though the much-limited closet space severely reduced her wardrobe). She would awaken, sit up in bed and stretch. Then she made her bed.

She took long showers and washed her hair. She dried herself with an oversized towel and stood naked before the closet patiently looking over each individual item. When she was home, this ritual could take more than an hour. She searched through her closets item by item, handling each piece, feeling their textures, looking at them, observing each detail, smelling them. She had a wonderful figure, but did not care to highlight her best features. Instead, she chose simple cuts with lots of pastels.

Once she selected her attire, she dressed quickly. Because of her height (5' 11") she wore flats or tennis shoes. She enjoyed wearing large sun hats in the summer and wool caps in winter. She wore little make-up. After brushing her hair, she put on dangling earrings, a pearl necklace, and gold rings. She frequently placed wooden hair combs in her hair. Her last task before going out was to select and load a large handbag for the day. Caught up in her thoughts, she walked alone to her morning classes.

The day was bright and sunny. Students were crossing paths as they pressed along to their first sessions. A few were chatting as they walked. They seemed oblivious to one another as they went about their routines. Clarissa reached the Social Sciences Building for her U. S. Constitution political science class. It was on the top floor and, after dodging students propelling themselves down the staircase, she arrived at her classroom. It was two-thirds full and she found a seat in the second row. The seats were unpadded wood with a built-in desktop. She set down her handbag on the floor and rummaged for a notebook, pencil, and textbooks. Nobody seemed to notice her as they all engaged in similar preparations for class, or were sitting back yawning and waiting.

The Professor came in, acknowledging the class by whispering, "Good morning, ladies."

He set his dried-up leather valise on the desk in front and peeked inside for his notes and textbook. Grabbing both he was ready to begin his day without having given his students or the subject matter the least thought for the last twelve hours. Well, except for some lustful thoughts about Clarissa. He thought she was brilliant and beautiful. The only reason he taught at a woman's college was for the benefits that came with it. Something about Clarissa in particular was a continual distraction he could not explain.

Clarissa, a brilliant student but a bit on the quiet side, thrived at school. She worked hard and was always prepared. Able to resist behaviors that had sent her to the emergency rooms a few years before; she was ready for anything the world might throw at her. At least, she thought she was.

JOHN

Who would not find John Michael Atwater attractive? He stood 6'2", weighed 185 pounds, well tanned, without a single hair out of place. He was drop dead gorgeous. He had taken a few years off to spend time in Europe after high school and returned to attend Harvard during Clarissa's freshman year. They did not meet until their junior year--she at Radcliffe and he at Harvard.

She had been invited to a fund-raising brunch at The Country Club in Brookline, Massachusetts. The morning she walked in, he was going out to play a round of golf. He played every day and he made it a point of walking through the entire clubhouse on his way out and back from the course. What better way to observe, and be observed by, women who noticed his impeccable tastes in clothing and decorum?

He said "Good morning!" to the staff that was externally stiff and formal, and internally fawning over this ideal country club member.

Though not love at first sight, it was close, for both of them. He had come to expect the kinds of reactions he received from charming young women in the clubhouse. This was different. He walked away with her telephone number and was unable to get her out of his mind.

Unbeknownst to the Atwater family, John's birth on January 20, 1935 was three hundred years to the day his ancestors arrived in New England from Kent, England. His family had been merchants since those early days and generation after generation followed their footsteps. A second 't' had been dropped from their name (Attwater), but otherwise the family had not changed. Both father and son had the same physical appearance of their ancestors. They had always been involved in a church, which for the last two generations had been Methodist.

While they were not prosperous for most of those three centuries, they had grown their businesses in good times and bad, to a point of moderate prosperity. At least until John's father, Jack, got involved at an early age and pushed the business in multiple directions at the same time. During the Depression, he had gotten into arrangements with the government, which gave them a foothold in war industries and positioned them perfectly for the post-war baby boom. But they were not as wealthy as they proclaimed with their expensive homes, cars, country club memberships, and bevy of servants. They were actually living month to month to keep up appearances.

Still, Jack had a good, solid appliance business. By the late 40's he was resisting favorable overtures from Sears and Penney's, and concentrating on major appliances in New York City, New Jersey, and Long Island. He always seemed one and a half steps ahead of other retailers in thinking up financing and service schemes.

Jack's word was not only his bond; it had become legendary in the business world. His memory over minute details in agreements with consumers gained him wide praise and prevented him from falling to deceptive schemes. Jack could "make it right" for a good customer, but one could never pull the wool over his eyes.

His claim to fame came through his business dealings, and his family always came second. When John was born, it was his wife's duty to raise him. There were more interesting distractions with the business--new ventures, new stores, new ideas, keeping one-step ahead of the creditors, and maintaining appearances.

John's parents had recently moved to Brookline, Massachusetts. John had been told it was to explore business opportunities in Boston. In fact, their home in Manhattan was on the brink of foreclosure when they left. The move to Boston was to save face. John was unaware of any of this.

While Jack talked as if he really wanted John to take over the business, he did nothing to prepare him for it. In fact, he did everything he could to keep from preparing him. There were no summer or part-time jobs, or internships for John when he was in high school or college. His only inclusion in the business was an occasional limousine ride to the opening of a new store with his doting mother.

After high school, there was no pressure to attend college immediately. Golf at the country club and travel in Europe stalled the inevitable for some time, though Jack never spoke in those terms. His mother never disciplined him--in her eyes, he could do no wrong. It was a credit to all the nannies, menservants and tutors who had cared for him over the years that he turned out as well as he did.

Clarissa was not sure he would call as he had promised. She had gone on a few dates, but considered herself homely. She felt that if he called her for a date at all, there would be only one reason. She was not prudish, just not ready for that. When he did call to invite her to a picnic dinner at the beach, she felt shocked and nervous.

That Saturday, John picked her up at 3 p.m. sharp in a brand new, robin's egg blue Cadillac convertible. His father insisted he receive a new one every model year. He brought a picnic basket with chicken dinners, biscuits, coleslaw, and unsweetened lemonade. Casual and attentive to her every need, they spent a wonderful afternoon together and ended the day on a blanket watching the sunset.

He invited her to church the next day, followed by lunch with his family at The Country Club. He was wonderful and charming at lunch.

When he had invited her, he told her he had a golf appointment he could not get out of, so his father would drive her to her dorm. Before he left after lunch, he asked her to have coffee with him on Tuesday evening, and she said yes.

On the way back Jack told her it was more than merely 'a golf appointment', "John is playing a sectional round he needs to win to qualify for the Massachusetts state amateur golf tournament. I thought he was gonna wait until after the tournament to give you a call. Guess he couldn't wait."

She did not know what love felt like, but she could not keep John off her mind.

Δ   Δ   Δ

Each morning, John was awoken by his manservant, Jeffery, who literally went to college with him.

The shades were opened if the weather was good. His slippers already placed beside the bed, Jeffrey patiently held John's robe. John stood up and turned around extending his arms backward so Jeffrey could slip John's arms through the robe. Yawning, John walked to the bathroom, urinated, and then walked to the hall, down the stairs and into the dining room. As usual, his favorite foods had been assembled by his personal chef. Coffee was already in his cup; black and piping hot. John liked his bacon hot and very crisp. His eggs were ready to come off the burner precisely as he walked through the doorway.

He sat down and adjusted his bathrobe tightly around him. His favorite newspapers had been stacked to his right and spread in a manner so that he could pick out any newspaper and section he wished without rummaging through the entire stack. Everything was exactly as he liked it. Exactly the way Jack taught him to like it.

When John was nearly finished, Jeffery came into the dining room to discuss the schedule for the day and make suggestions for his apparel selections and times for changing. They came to agreement on his attire for the whole day. Jeffery quipped, "Excellent selections, Sir," and left to prepare clothing in the dressing area.

Of course, all clothing had already been cleaned and neatly hung in the closet. The selections were placed on dressing tables and furniture in the shower area, right down to the jewelry. With each change of clothing, Jeffery placed the next set of clothing in their proper location, all day long; through to the matching silk pajamas, robe, and slippers he wore that night.

After eating, he combed through a fraction of the newspapers, mostly the sports reports on golf, while finishing his third cup of coffee.

Weekly (usually on Wednesday) his hair was trimmed and he was straight shaved by Jeffery. Normally he shaved himself. After showering, Jeffery assisted him in dressing and brushed off imagined lint on his coat.

On that particular day, there was more money in Jeffery's checking account than in either Jack's or John's. It was not that his father was broke, just that every cent was tied up in the business. Jack had mingled company and personal funds for so long, he could never turn all his affairs over to an accountant. There were irregularities everywhere. He did not want to think about them.

Jack's job was to make money. John's job was to enjoy it, marry an exquisite beauty as high on the social scale as possible, get a good education, and make grand Atwater babies. At this stage of life, his job was to charm women until making his selection.

Clarissa was not as high on the beauty scale as Jack thought reasonable for his son, but if she had exceptional wealth, as it appeared she might, he would certainly make an exception.

Δ   Δ   Δ

John was good looking and dated frequently, but still believed in love and marriage. He could not put his finger exactly on what he was looking for, but the romantic in him told him, he would know when she came along. She did not have to be beautiful, but he would not object if she were. She did not have to fawn over him. He wanted a woman who would not love him for his family's money, so it would help if the woman of his dreams also came from a privileged background. He wanted a woman who would also not be afraid of his good looks and be jealous all the time. He wanted a woman who would understand his imperfections and not ridicule or embarrass him. It would be wonderful if she could even love him for these imperfections and compensate through her abilities.

From the beginning, they studied together, ate together, and attended some classes near each other, as many of her classes were on the Harvard campus.

Both wanted to change the world, so they joined the John Kennedy presidential campaign. The feeling on both campuses was electric. One of their own could claim the highest office in the land. There were plenty of opportunities for them to help, while the Democratic Party staffers' eyed their parents as potential major donors. They knew all about Junior, but Atwater was a fresh opportunity.

One morning Jeffery was surprised, upon awaking John to find Clarissa in bed with him. If they had slept together before this, Jeffery had not known about it. Without making any moral judgments, he made a note to be sure condoms were part of John's accoutrements, like lip balm and tissues.

Jack Atwater, becoming aware of John's constant companionship with Clarissa, decided he needed to check into her family. He started by doing credit checks through his business. Finding nothing of concern, he hired a private investigator to dig deeper. He dug, but not enough to find the real Rory John Millwood, Junior. He found out about the Triangle Fire, crusading, work on the mayor's staff, his restaurant and bar businesses, and his home on Long Island. If he had dug deeper, he might have wondered how Junior acquired such wealth. He did not. He reported what he could easily find, let the rest lie dormant, and cashed Jack's check without any remorse.

John saw that his life's work lay somewhere other than in his father's business. His involvement with the Kennedy presidential campaign started him thinking about politics. Perhaps an ambassadorship would be in his future. His father could certainly buy him that. A law degree would be his next likely step, and it would not hurt because Clarissa was talking about a law degree as well. They could help the unfortunate. He had not known any other way of life than privilege, so giving back might be in order.

They were two lovers in their senior year of college, volunteering in a campaign that was exciting. They had achieved a milestone in their work and were in a mood to celebrate. The craze that year was to make love at "Longfellow Triangle" and not get caught. Longfellow Triangle is a piece of grass where Concord Avenue meets Garden Street in Cambridge, near the site of the Henry Wadsworth Longfellow National Historical House. The Police Station was across the way. According to legend, over the last two hundred years the signage on the statue had been changed back and forth from Longfellow to various other heroes to prevent the practice. The joke was about using your "long fellow" at her "triangle". John had his car packed with a picnic lunch, champagne, and blanket. They were headed to The Triangle. That there was two inches of snow on the ground didn't bother them in the least. He chuckled to himself, thinking it would leave evidence of their deed. He had only forgotten one thing.

Δ   Δ   Δ

Jeffery got used to Clarissa. He actually liked her very much. Soon, there were two robes available every morning. As he slipped the robe on her body, Jeffery would avert his eyes. Well, most of the time. When he could not help himself, he judged only her face to be homely.

Clarissa suspected she was pregnant from the first week. She did not have any real symptoms, just a general feeling. As the month went by, her feelings grew stronger and stronger. She could not tell whether the soreness in her breasts were real or imagined. She gagged at certain foods, but again could not tell whether what she was feeling was from her stomach or her head? "Could your mind make you have physical symptoms?" she wondered aloud.

It was late winter and she was looking forward to springtime. The only time she could remember when they made love without a rubber was at Longfellow Triangle. Of course, it could have broken. Or it could have leaked. Or the feelings could be absolutely nothing at all.

Was it the terror of being pregnant? Or could it be wishful thinking?

She loved John deeply, but they both had other plans. A bright future was available to each of them, but especially her.

She tried to remember when she last had her period. She looked at the calendar quizzically. She would wait a little longer. Could stress cause you to miss a period?, she thought--probably.

Her periods had always been fickle inconveniences. She was used to being late and early, at least in her own mind. When she was finally positive she had missed her period, she let it slip to John, "I may have a surprise for you."

He did not catch on to what she had said.

They talked more and more about their futures. She was headed to Georgetown. He was unsure. They talked about an advanced degree for him. He liked the idea of law school. She was suspicious it could be just to be close to her; not that she minded that idea much.

She decided she had better make a doctor's appointment to be tested. She knew rabbits did not really die because of a positive pregnancy test, but she could not resist one little joke to herself, "What's the big deal about sacrificing one little rabbit?" How will John react? She was not sure.

How about John's parents? Probably not well, but they would get over it.

How would her father take it? She wanted to have a family, but this was not exactly the way she had seen things turning out.

She would certainly want to name him either "Henry Wadsworth Longfellow Atwater" or "John Fitzgerald Kennedy

Atwater". After all, the two of them were as responsible for this predicament as John and her.

When the day came for her appointment, she called John.

"John, I need a lift to the doctor."

"Sure. What time?"

"Eleven."

"Any problem?"

"Probably just a little animal abuse. Nothing to worry about."

"What?"

Δ   Δ   Δ

While riding to the doctor's appointment, Clarissa told John she might be pregnant. He almost rear-ended the car in front of him.

Clarissa laughingly said, "Oh, you are going to make some father, dear!"

He was quiet the rest of the way, lost in his thoughts.

"Do you want me to go in with you?"

"No, I'd rather you not. This could take a while. I will probably want to get some lunch by myself. I'll grab a cab back."

"You sure?"

"Yes."

"Will you call me?"

"No, this is the last you are going to see of me. Ever. Of course I will call you."

"Dinner?"

"Sure."

All afternoon, his mind was reeling. It would be selfish to ask her to marry me. Should I encourage her to get an abortion? Should I encourage her to put the baby up for adoption? Oh, what have I done to the woman I love? He loved her deeply. He knew this was going to tie her down and limit her opportunities. She was so looking forward to Georgetown, now that was in jeopardy.

John decided he would do something he had hardly ever done before. He would cook her a lavish dinner in his apartment. "How hard can that be?"

She appreciated what he tried to do, but dinner was a disaster.

"Well, Okay, guess we order Chinese."

"No, let's go out--and get away from the smoke."

He did not know where to start in talking about their future. He did not know how to come across the right way when talking about abortion, adoption, or marriage. It all just came spilling out.

"Stop, stop, stop, John! First off, we are not sure that I am pregnant. It could be a week before the test results are back. Second: Why wouldn't you think I will not be thrilled to be your wife and the mother of your children?" Then she kissed him.

"I don't deserve you." He kissed her.

By graduation, with Clarissa showing, there was no longer putting off telling the parents. Radcliffe College commencement exercises were held at Sanders Theater on a Saturday. Graduating magna cum laude, Clarissa was beyond being just bright; she was brilliant and always focused on her studies, in spite of John.

She selected Georgetown University Law Center in the fall for her law degree, but the pregnancy put a crimp in her plans. She deferred for a semester to begin in the spring.

Junior was not surprised: He was pleased and delighted. He only knew a little about John, but could see the love he had for his daughter. He also had a string of letters Clarissa had written to him while she was away at college and knew of her love for John. Junior had been a lucky man to have had two great loves in his life. John's parents politely declined to attend Clarissa's graduation.

The following week's convocation in Tercentenary Theater in Harvard Yard was filled with flags, fanfare and music. There were nearly a thousand in attendance and the speakers were on a platform with a backdrop of massive columns and large red banners.

John was not graduating with honors. He had done well, but Clarissa had been too big a distraction the last two years.

After the ceremony, there were pictures and handshakes all around. Junior was introduced to John's parents. There were smiles and talk about what everyone was going to do next.

John grabbed Clarissa and held her facing his parents, "Mom and Dad, I have a surprise for you. I hope you will be pleased. We are expecting!"

There was stunned silence. Jack grabbed his wife's hand and left in a rage. They watched them storm off through the crowd at a quick pace.

Clarissa finally broke the silence, "Well, that seemed to go well!"

Δ   Δ   Δ

"You have screwed everything up!"

"Dad, I know you are mad, but--"

"You have screwed everything up! All my plans for you are down the toilet."

"All your plans for me? What about my plans?"

"Listen, stupid! I have a successful business. All you needed to do was keep your nose clean."

"You never wanted me anywhere near your business."

"Couldn't keep your dick in your pants, could ya."

"What?"

"All of this was yours for the taking. What, you think I would never retire?"

"No, you never wanted me involved."

"You must make her get an abortion."

"What are you talking about? No."

"What do you mean, no!"

"That is for Clarissa and me to decide. We have decided against that."

"Then you must put it up for adoption."

"It? It? He or she is not an 'it'!"

"It is as far as I am concerned."

"This is your grandchild we are talking about."

"You may be talking about it, not me."

"Why do you think you get to decide?"

"Why? Why? Because you apparently are too stupid to decide for yourself."

"Dad, you are not being reasonable."

"John, you are the one not being reasonable or sensible. What do you know about children or being a husband?"

"I will learn."

"You're not even smart enough to keep from getting a girl pregnant, and you think you can learn?"

"What? No. We want to get married!"

"You don't know what you want? You can't even decide what to wear without Jeffery!"

"What? This is our decision."

"You are too emotional to make a decision on your own. Marriage is out of the question."

"Out of the question? What do you mean, out of the question?"

"How are you going to support a wife and child?"

"I'll get a job!"

"What do you know how to do? Play golf?"

"What? No."

"You are a fool. You are so stupid not to see reason. You must not be my son!"

"What? What do you mean?"

"Are you too stupid to not know what that means? Who is going to support you and your expensive habits?"

"I'll support myself."

"You wouldn't know how! You'll starve without me."

"Why do you think so little of me?"

"You are no son of mine."

"What a hurtful thing to say!"

"You are no son of mine. There, I said it again, for the stupid boy in front of me who cannot seem to understand things the first time he hears them."

There was a long pause.

"So be it. If you want to disown me, so be it."

With that bitter word out of his mouth, John left.

Δ   Δ   Δ

Everything was taken away from John on June 1, 1960.

His car was repossessed. All belongings in the car were left on the sidewalk with a note lest John report it stolen. The lease on the apartment was canceled. While he was away, the apartment was emptied out, the furniture taken away and his clothing and personal items left on the pavement. His checking account was canceled. Clarissa helped him make good on bounced checks.

His country club membership was revoked. The business manager was embarrassed to have to raise it with John, "Of course, you may have lunch here one last time. We will all miss you." It did not matter to John.

Their wedding was scheduled for Saturday, July 2, 1960, beneath the maple tree at Clarissa's home in Baldwin. Most of their college friends and friends from the presidential campaign planned to come down from Boston and make a long weekend of it.

Jeffery agreed to serve as parent of the groom and best man. Dismissed by Jack, he felt a personal duty to see John through the wedding.

Junior's neighbors put up as many college students and

graduates as they could, and it turned into a four-day party.

For the wedding an arbor was set up, decorated with red roses. There were three bridesmaids and three groomsmen. Junior gave away the bride. John and Clarissa exchanged vows and rings in the shade of the giant maple tree.

There was a pig roast the following evening. Several boats were rented. There was a marathon softball game. People were in the water swimming. People just came and went at all hours of the day and night.

They took a photograph of the neighbors, their children, and their grandchildren. It was the first time they had all been together for a big event since Helena's death. They had lived and laughed together in their own little Eden on Long Island. They had shared tears and trials. They now enjoyed hosting the young people who came down from Boston for the wedding.

Clarissa's wedding also marked the final time they would all be together. This Fourth of July marked the beginning of the winter of their lives. Age was catching up with Junior's generation. There were fewer get togethers. More illnesses. More aches and pains. They soon faced their share of cancers, strokes and heart attacks. Hospitals and rest homes were in their not-too-distant future. Junior kept a framed enlargement of the photograph in his study for the rest of his life.

The finale of the weekend was fireworks at the waterfront on the Fourth. By the following morning, nobody wanted to leave. Most people lingered on through the late afternoon before a caravan of vehicles made its way north toward Boston.

Junior wanted to send the newlyweds on a honeymoon wherever they wished; they chose Cobh, Ireland.

JOHN

The day after the wedding, a friend from the presidential campaign, Richard Shelton, asked Clarissa if she would be interested in working with a group Kennedy wanted organized to look at "volunteer missionaries". She and John could still work on the Presidential campaign; this would just be a special extra project with dozen key people. He gave her just enough information to whet her appetite. The group would be meeting in Washington and Boston for the next three months. She said yes, provided she could start after her honeymoon. He agreed.

Kennedy believed a volunteer organization could defeat notions of the "Ugly American" and "Yankee Imperialism". He was fond of the quote attributed to Niccolò di Bernardo dei Machiavelli, "Keep Your Enemies Close and Your Friends Closer". He saw this as a good way of staying involved with friends and close to enemies. Quasi-governmental groups had been sent in to help stabilize battle-ridden areas after the Spanish-American and First World Wars. Both religious and nonreligious organizations have been sending volunteers overseas for decades.[xxxiii]

Kennedy wanted a game changer to the Cold War rhetoric coming out of the Nixon camp. Fear, innuendo, and chest thumping by both superpowers were unsustainable. Upping the ante would inevitably lead to war, even if only accidentally. It would not hurt to be engaged in the third world, to counter violent means being used to throw off governments left and right.

Clarissa and John thought of flying, but decided a cruise would be more romantic.

In preparation for their trip, Junior had given them a large manuscript titled, *The Felonies and Misdemeanors of Rory John Millwood, Senior.* It contained a detailed listing of sins of Rory--every detail Junior knew of or suspected were included. Deceptions and beatings were given in full, bloody detail. It was a no-holds-barred evaluation of her grandfather--honest to the last letter. Junior had done this, not to be hurtful, but to explain his past to his daughter. What he also wrote, but did not give her, was a volume titled *The Felonies and Misdemeanors of Rory John Millwood, Junior.*

She read about Grandfather Millwood, slowly and carefully, absorbing every detail. She wrote down a short list of names and last known addresses to take with her and returned the book to her father.

They sailed to Cobh, Ireland in July of 1960 and visited Cork, kissed the Blarney stone, and traveled to Killarney, Killorglin, and Dingle before returning. It was a leisurely trip with plenty of Murphy's, Toasties, Irish stew, and lamb chops.

In Cobh they looked up the local sites, including a list of places and people from her father's book. They tried to find family graves in the church graveyard, but were unsuccessful. They did find O'Rourke's Tavern, where Clarissa's grandfather had worked. There they heard stories of Rory and his passing from a massive heart attack in 1943 and of his wife's death a few years later.

Clarissa could not locate remaining cousins or uncles.

The cruise and their time traveling together was the most peaceful either of them had known. They were in love and enjoying each other in every possible way. As the ship left the harbor, John pulled Clarrisa close, kissed her and whispered, "I don't deserve you."

During her college years, events had not stressed her. She had been intensely analytical about current events, as if she were able to emotionally disassociate from them, in order to observe them under a magnifying glass. With the second trimester of her pregnancy, however, she had begun feeling panicked about world events. She decided she needed to check in with her counselors and her doctors to see if hormonal changes were triggering this and if there was anything that could be done to prevent it.

The presidential campaign seemed to be going well, as was exploratory work toward a volunteer mission's organization. Clarissa liked everything about the project and where this appeared to be headed if Kennedy was elected. She determined to focus so tightly on her work, that she would not have time to think about world events. Her work team observed and interviewed people associated with Reverend James Henry Robinson's Operation Crossroads Africa. It was the third summer Robinson had sent missionaries to work at a grassroots level in Africa. Many of the objectives of Robinson's program paralleled what the Kennedy team was looking to accomplish.

The biggest concern was involvement of the Central Intelligence Agency and Federal Bureau of Investigation. The work team asked blunt questions of the managers about CIA involvement. It was not a primary intent, but Kennedy would not preclude their involvement. As far as the FBI was concerned, the work group got a chuckle when they heard J. Edgar had "his people everywhere and no presidential demand to the contrary would be able to keep them out". The FBI comments were handled in a lighthearted but realistic way.

Completing their report on time, work team members were thanked for their hard work. The only disappointment for Clarissa was that they had not had a chance to meet in Washington. All meetings had been held at Kennedy's headquarters in Boston. It seemed the Democratic Party was not as convinced of the desirability of the program or political need to distance from the Nixon camp. Only Kennedy recognized that advantage.

When the November election came, Clarissa was exhausted and emotionally over the edge. She had seen the Doctor the week before. He prescribed tranquilizers for Election Day and she was ordered to bed. She ignored the order, of course, but John kept a close watch on her and nearly had to call for an ambulance. She swung from one mood to another as the counting progressed. It was too close to call for most of the night. Around 3:15 a.m. Eastern Time, Richard M. Nixon conceded defeat when the television networks had Kennedy with 260-267 of the 269 needed electoral votes required to win. The Electoral College vote would be Kennedy 303, Nixon 219, and Harry F. Byrd 15, while the popular vote was just 112,927 apart.

Exhaustion overtook Clarissa during the final month of her pregnancy. Her doctor ordered her to stay in bed. John was with her constantly. On December 5, 1960, Clarissa gave birth. The delivery took just under eight hours. She had been given medication to ease the pain and was loopy and tired. They had decided that if it was a boy he would be named John Michael Atwater, Junior. They wanted to call him 'Mikey'.

Δ   Δ   Δ

The side effect from the polio vaccination Clarissa had when she was a teenager was one of the rarest. Events around her once again triggered overpowering emotional distress. Mikey's birth had gone well, but soon thereafter, her pediatrician recommended she see a psychiatrist who diagnosed her with postpartum depression. She experienced sadness, fatigue, insomnia, crying episodes and irritability.

While John and Clarissa watched John F. Kennedy's Presidential Inauguration on television, Clarissa cried hysterically. It was so bad, her psychiatrist came to her home to treat her with sedatives.

He tried vitamin treatments and hormone supplements, without success. After three months, he could no longer discount the side effects of the polio vaccination from more than seven years before. He thought she was possibly becoming suicidal. He read everything he could get his hands on and then contacted Salk's laboratory at the University of Pittsburgh School of Medicine.

By that time, awards and accolades were rolling in for Jonas Salk. He had become a national hero and celebrity. He was preparing to build the Salk Institute campus overlooking the Pacific Ocean in La Jolla, California. Researchers associated with Salk were indeed interested in studying Clarissa's case. They poked, prodded, and ran extensive blood and urine tests. Nothing showed up. They could not collect a sufficiently detailed medical history to understand if she had illnesses or a diminished immune system when she had received the vaccination. They never identified anything specific that could be done for her.

All they could suggest was counseling and isolation. The counseling seemed to have worked to some degree when she was a teenager. The isolation was intended to get her away from distressing news that might trigger an episode. The only question was how she was to do that with a newborn baby!

They resisted making any changes until Mikey was a little older, but by the time he was seven months old, John and Clarissa were at the breaking point.

Clarissa moved back in with her father. They spent the end of the summer talking, sailing, and walking. They rarely turned on the television. Clarissa missed John and Mikey.

John was beside himself. How could he manage with an infant? Unable to work or ask his own parents for assistance, John turned to his father-in-law. Junior gave him advice on locating people to help, starting with a nearby church. Junior paid all the bills and told John never to worry about it--his full time job was taking care of Mikey until Clarissa was well enough to return. John was grateful and took to the work with all his energy. There were frequent visits from John and Mikey; Clarissa and Junior enjoyed their stays, no matter how brief.

She was better after five months and returned home for the Christmas Holiday. There were presents under the tree and Mikey's first birthday. They had a relaxing week between Christmas and New Year's, or so John thought.

Clarissa confided to John that she still felt very stressed and would be returning to Long Island shortly. He was heartbroken. But, he took her to the airport and Mikey waved good-bye to his mother once again. The frequent visits continued and John could see that Clarissa was getting better all the time. By June, he was hopeful she could soon return. He received a telephone call for her from R. Sargent Shriver's office in Washington and passed along the telephone number at his father-in-law's home, where she could be reached.

He came to regret it.

Δ   Δ   Δ

On March 1, 1961, Kennedy signed Executive Order 10924 officially creating the Peace Corp. Three days later, he appointed his brother-in-law R. Sergeant Shriver as its first director. His staff began recruiting volunteers by July, and Clarissa was on the short list based on her earlier committee work. She had expressed a strong desire to serve in the field.

She never disclosed her medical condition, other than to indicate she had experienced postpartum depression. Normal enough, the reviewers thought. She indicated it lasted two months. The staff was aware she was pregnant when she was doing the three-month committee evaluation. They were not sure where her interests lay now. They would consider a husband-and-wife team, but a toddler was a different story. Since these were the early days of the program, they might just consider throwing a pilot label on it. What was the worst that could happen? Three airline tickets back to the States was not a hard price if things went wrong.

The call she received was to explore her interest in going to Africa with one of the early teams. She said she would love to. They asked about her husband and child. She said she would be going alone.

"This will be a two-year commitment."

"That is fine."

"Are you sure?"

"Yes."

"You know, you will not be able to see your family at all during that time."

"I know."

"Why do you want to go then?"

"This is a once in a lifetime opportunity."

That was all they needed to hear.

A few days later, she was invited to the White House to a ceremony for a team from Operation Crossroads Africa. Many from the 'Volunteer Missionary' work group had been asked to attend. As these were friends and colleagues Clarissa knew and respected very much, she agreed to attend. She did not tell John she was going. She met John, Jackie, Robert, and Ethel Kennedy, Sergeant Shriver, and Reverend James H. Robinson.

She was to be in the third Peace Corp group to leave. On August 28, 1961, the first two teams of volunteers left for Ghana and Tanzania. She was scheduled to leave the following month. She was heading for Ethiopia. First, she had to tell John.

Δ   Δ   Δ

"NO WAY!"

"Yes, I am!"

"You can't."

"If you are not ready to come home to us, you are not ready to go to Africa."

"I am ready to go."

"Where?"

"Both places!"

"Bullshit!"

"You knew that one day I would want to go."

"Of course I did. Just--after you are well."

"What if I am never well?"

"You will be." He paused. "You make this major decision in your life, and you don't even consult me?"

"I knew what you would say."

"Damn right."

"I can't believe you are even considering this?"

"It is an opportunity I cannot pass up."

"Have you talked to your father?"

"No."

"Have you talked to your doctor?"

"No."

"Who have you talked to?"

"The White House."

"What? They have that much influence over you?"

"No."

"Is it another man?"

"No."

"Did you meet someone when you were working with that group?"

"No, John. There is nobody, but you."

"--and Mikey."

"And Mikey."

"You can be away from us for how long?"

"Two years."

"You can be away from Mikey and me for two years?"

"Yes."

"Do they know you are sick?"

"I'm not sick."

"Do they know you have been sick and this can be triggered by stressful events?"

"Of course, I told them everything."

"You did not! They would not let you go."

"Did so! Okay, John. Don't interrupt me. I am going to lay this out for you from the top. I was on that volunteer missionary task force to evaluate the prospects of developing this program, which has now been named 'The Peace Corp'. I know what they need to accomplish more clearly than anyone does. I expressed an interest in doing this from the beginning. I believe I can make a difference. I can make this world a better place before I die. I will be leading the third team out. We are going to Ethiopia. It is primarily an agricultural mission. I will be managing a team."

She paused. He started to say something, but she raised her hand. She spoke slowly and distinctly.

"John, you have already lost me. Do you understand that? You have already lost me. I am as good as dead to you. I have to conquer my demons now, or I never will. I am going to Africa for two years. It will be hard for all of us. I intend to return after my two years are up. You and Mikey mean more to me than anything else in the world. I love you both more than you can imagine. I will not be extending my stay, under any conditions."

She paused.

"Let's be clear. If I fail, I will not be coming home alive. Do you understand? If I fail, I will not be coming home alive. I come home well, or I come home in a box. This disease ends here. I will not let it destroy you, and I will not let it destroy Mikey. If it finishes the job on me, it finishes the job. No different from cancer or a heart attack. But if I fail, I cannot bear to let the two of you see me die in the way it will kill me."

He didn't like her logic, but he understood it.

Δ   Δ   Δ

Clarissa's departure was delayed one month.

Junior was less than enthused about her plan. However, he could see she was determined and nothing would stand in her way. He would especially miss her not being at home. He had gotten used to having a woman in the house. After what he had done to his two wives, he had resolved never to marry again. He certainly was responsible for Moira's death. Had he not tried to hide from his boss, he would not have dropped the lit cigar into the box bin below the cutting table. However, no tragedy is so simple.

If the waste bins had been empty, if the doors had swung out, if the water hoses had worked, if there were more stairs, or if the doors had not been locked it would not have been as bad. So many things aligned to cause a great tragedy.

Helena died in childbirth. That was hardly a rare occurrence. Junior felt she was too old and small to bear children. He had insisted on having his husbandly rights. He must have circumvented God's plan and Helena's life was the price. His sins had once again required a payment, and the price was steep.

John brought Mikey to Baldwin for his '5th of the month'

celebration, after a party with his friends in Boston. Mikey had been born on the 5th, and they celebrated his birthday each month. This was to be a combined birthday and going away party for Clarissa. It was a small affair with neighbors in the evening.

They drove up on Monday and that evening Junior had a long talk with John.

"How can I help?"

"Break her legs so she can't go?" They both looked at each other and grinned.

"It is inviting. But you know there is no stopping her."

"Yes."

"So how can I help?"

"I am not sure."

"How about if you move up here?"

"Dad, that is gracious, but--"

"No, it is selfish. I am going to miss her, of course. I've gotten use to having her around."

"Me, too."

"If you were to come up here, I would have Mikey to get to know better. It would take a big load off your shoulders."

"Maybe you should just take Mikey, not me."

"No, I think we all need each other."

They talked more and more.

"Mill, I've got to be honest with you. These last few months have been the hardest. I, I--" He paused. "I have met someone."

"I thought you might."

"No, it is not what you think!"

"What do I think?"

"We get together for coffee. We have not done anything."

"Yet."

"Yes, yet."

"Well, you will have to decide this one for yourself. I can understand what you have been through. I know the needs men have. You are facing two long years. You are welcome here if you want to continue with your marriage. You are welcome to leave Mikey with me if you think that path will be too hard."

John decided to move to Baldwin.

AFRICA

In her small rented room on the Blue Nile River in the Amhara region of northwestern Ethiopia, Clarissa began each day looking through her clothing to decide what to wear. It was already warm in the early morning in late spring. She washed using bowls of water she brought to her room before dinner the previous evening. She had been there six months.

She stood near the end of her bed, naked, looking through the items on wire coat hangers she brought with her. Soon, she promised herself, she would collect native clothing, but for now, there was no time for a shopping spree. Her work had gone well.

The team was making progress. There had been the small illnesses that accompany any foreign trip, but their adjustments had been good. Clarissa firmly believed in keeping busy and that working hard afforded less time to focus on negatives. She missed John and Mikey far more than she expected. She knew in going away for so long she was putting extraordinary demands on John. She told herself, she will remain faithful to him, but she would not expect the same from him. She didn't deserve his faithfulness for leaving him. She was here to slay (or be slain by) her dragon.

She handled each item, felt their textures, and delighted in their colors and patterns. She selected a house-dress that would be as comfortable as possible in the heat of the day. Mostly she wore tennis shoes. An old Dodger's baseball cap, given to her by a team member, fit snugly on her head, replaced the sunhats she loved, but were impractical on the plains of Africa. She carefully applied her make-up and put on her jewelry. As she slipped on her wedding ring each day, she thought of John and Mikey. Did she make a hasty decision? Would she be ready to face motherhood when she returned? She loved them both and she smiled about John's patience with her. Why couldn't she handle being with Mikey during those early months? Was it her immaturity or something else? Was she made to be a mother? Would she want to try again?

She left the room she rented from the missionary couple and walked the few yards into the village. She believed in the mission of the Peace Corp of making the world a better place. She wanted her team to demonstrate to the world that Americans were not all those ugly tourists.

She told her team, "We have much to offer our neighbors. Now we have to be realistic about what can be accomplished. Being present makes a statement of our commitment."

She worked hard making connections with the other volunteers who specialized in agriculture. She knew nothing about their field, just as they knew nothing about what she brought to the table--organizational management.

Day in and day out, she focused on the task at hand.

She repeatedly told her team, "Two years is a short time to establish the trust necessary to truly have an impact. But that is all we get. Two years--just four planting seasons to show our neighbors what improvements can be accomplished."

After dismissing her team from a meeting, she surveyed her surroundings. She thought to herself--but dare not say to her team--this all can be whisked away in one bad windstorm. This all can vanish overnight. All our success can whither under this burning sun.

That day they would be using water collected from their rooftop to irrigate their vegetable gardens. Saving water in this way was a new concept for the locals.

She wrote frequently. Getting letters through the local postal system was slow--it could take months to make it back to the states. She received little mail in return.

She said aloud, to nobody in particular, "So much to be done in two years. What then will I come home to?"

Δ   Δ   Δ

202 D. H. COOK

They celebrated the 5th day of every month as 'Mikey's Day'. Usually, they just had a special dessert, but occasionally there was a small present.

On October 5, 1961, Junior presented Mikey with two dogs, two goats, and two Shetland ponies.

"We need the goats for milk for Mikey."

John laughed, "Yeah, what do you need two dogs for?"

"To keep each other company."

"Why the ponies?"

"I like ponies, don't you?"

"Yes, but Mikey is not even two yet!"

"It is a blessing to learn things early--riding, skiing, swimming--"

"--golf. Dad, what are you going to bring home next?"

"I am trying to locate another pair."

"Janet, how do I get in touch with Maria and Marta?" Janet was Junior's long time housekeeper.

"Mr. Millwood, Maria is married and has a child of her own. Marta lives nearby."

"See if either of them would want to work for me again."

He was not surprised that Marta was ready to return. Raising Clarissa had been the best job she ever had. She and her sister stayed until Clarissa was well into her teen years. He hired her right away.

He was surprised when Maria also showed interest. "My sister said they would have to find a job out there for her husband before she could come back. And they would need a place to live," said Marta.

"What does her husband do?"

"He works for the phone company."

"How old are their children?"

"They just have one. A daughter, four, Little Angela."

"Would her husband want to work for me?"

"I can ask. Doing what?"

"Somebody has to keep you three in line," he said with a wink. "Plus take care of the goats, dogs, and horses. General handyman stuff. Live-in security."

"Live here, too? Oh my! All of us together again! I'll talk them into it!"

It did not take much talking. Maria and her husband jumped at the chance.

The house suddenly exploded with activity. It went from the sedate recovery place for Clarissa--quiet, restrained, peaceful--to a perpetual ruckus.

Junior moved out of the master bedroom and let Maria and her husband, Juan, move in. Angela had the next bedroom over, the Red bedroom. It was her favorite color. Janet stayed in the servant's quarters and Marta returned to her old room. Junior moved to the furthest bedroom away, the Orange bedroom.

John and Mikey occupied the Purple bedroom.

Juan was up early, milking the goats and tending the ponies and dogs. Junior did not give the goats names, but Juan called them, "Abbott" and "Costello". The dogs were "Jake" and "Happy", one a black Labrador retriever and the other a smooth-coat collie.

"Okay, Mikey, what are we going to call this horse?"

He petted his mane and said, "Preeeddy" And that is what they called him.

"Okay, what are we going to call this one?" He petted her mane and said, "Preeeddy."

"No, we can't give them the same name." When Mikey could not come up with another name, they started to call her 'Spitfire'.

Junior, now in his early seventies, presided over swimming in the bay behind the house, even during the dead of winter. Bonfires became a nightly activity year around. There were long walks, riding the horses (for Mikey and Angela), games, canoe rides, and boat trips. John and Junior would sneak out together for a round of golf. John showed unusual patience as he taught Junior. They became like father and son.

Fall turned to winter, then spring, then summer again. Their cycle of life was great fun and few responsibilities.

Junior began taking his little family to church each Sunday.

Angela was always welcome in any of their adventures, but she also liked to spend time alone in her room.

Mikey was a bundle of energy, who collapsed in his father's arms at the end of each day. They arose early and they went to bed early.

One night, John put Mikey down and joined Junior for a nightcap.

"You asked me about my wealth the other day and I--"

"Oh, I am sorry; I did not mean to pry."

"You were not prying. You deserve to know. We are living off of ill gotten gains." John became somber at the serious delivery of Junior's words. "I want you to read this."

"What is it?"

"My autobiography. After you have read it, I want it back. You are free to ask any questions you may have. You can also have my father's story. Clarissa has read it."

John looked at the cover: 'The Felonies and Misdemeanors of Rory John Millwood, Junior.'

Δ   Δ   Δ

Mail service to Ethiopia was spotty. Clarissa's letters did not make it out of the country before being pilfered. They never found any treasure, because they were not looking for the right type--the rich descriptions of work in the early days of the Peace Corp: beautiful valley where Clarissa worked; birds she observed; heat of the equatorial sun; blast furnace winds; difficulty of getting the natives to move from their time honored practices to modern agricultural methods.

She talked of the wonderful children with their sad eyes and distended stomachs from malnutrition. With each bloated stomach and scrawny, scraggly arm she saw, she recommitted to success of the projects she oversaw. She sounded like she was doing well. She had gone a long way to stare down her demons. She was growing up, allowing herself a chance to overcome her problems.

She missed John and Mikey terribly. It broke her heart when she stopped working long enough to think about them, so she rarely took a break, but she wrote weekly. Perhaps one in four letters made it to Baldwin, Long Island. About the same number were written to her. About the same proportion survived the gauntlet of the Ethiopian mail service, but they could also send mail through the missionary agency of her landlord. Those letters were carried personally to her.

John's letters were filled with stories of Mikey. How he was growing. How tall he was and how much he weighed. His antics. How Grandpa was spoiling him. How the women took care of them. Mikey's animals. He was a prince in his own capital city.

John never wrote about himself. He never told her how he felt. He wanted her back. He wanted her well. He was willing to stick out these two years with the hope things would be better.

Δ   Δ   Δ

In late September 1963, word of the 16th Street Baptist Church bombing by members of the Ku Klux Klan in Birmingham, Alabama reached across the sea to the Amhara region of Ethiopia.

In her small, rented room, Clarissa could not get her mind off the four, innocent girls ripped apart by twenty-two sticks of dynamite. She tossed and turned nearly all night and, finally, began to dream.

She was rushing to the entrance of the three-story church as people were fleeing and recognized she could not enter. Going around to the back of the building, where smoke was bellowing out of a gaping hole, she climbed over the crushed vehicles to look into the hole and fell into the basement.

She could see people lying everywhere, there was screaming, and pain. She looked at the four dead girls, or what was left of them. As if putting together a jigsaw puzzle, she mentally recognized various body parts spread around the room, brought them one-by-one to the right body and reassembled them. She found her tears had the power to heal. Quietly, one-by-one, she reassembled each of the four girls. Rescue workers and medical crews came rushing in to attend to the wounded. However, they ignored the four girls. They lay there for a long time, until the ambulances quit their mournful screeches.

All was empty in the basement. It was just Clarissa and the girls now. She helped Addie Mae Collins to her feet. Next, she helped Carol Denise McNair up. She pulled Carole Rosamond Robertson up to stand. Finally, Cynthia Diane Wesley came back to life. Each walked up the stairs and out of the basement.

Clarissa sat on the floor, exhausted and wondering why, if her tears were so powerful, she could not heal herself?

When she awoke, it was over. She did not panic. She did not explode with emotion. She had witnessed a terrible tragedy up close and had been able to handle it. In her mind, in a basement thousands of miles away, she had stared down the demon--she had won and was free.

The next month, she was scheduled to return home. She had made it. She was ready to come home at last.

Δ   Δ   Δ

Pan American World Airways B707-123 Clipper America from the Paris-Orly Airport to New York City's Idlewild Airport was scheduled to arrive at 9:15 p.m. on Halloween, 1963. It was four hours late. John complained, "Figures she would not make it back for another month!"

Junior booked four rooms at a local hotel for the night. Everyone came to see Clarissa. Angela and Mikey were beyond tired, sleeping soundly in their respective father's arms. Clarissa had been traveling 27 hours straight, but looked rested. Her flight from Ethiopia to Paris had been on a U. S. Government plane with minimal accommodations. It didn't matter. She was ready to come home. The flight from Paris to New York was on a commercial flight with wonderful amenities.

They were seated where they could watch her disembark. She was tanned and healthy. Her work had been physically demanding, and her bare arms proved it. Her skin was dark from the sun. She walked through the door looking refreshed and energized against the backdrop of dozens of grumpy businessmen getting off the plane.

She saw John and burst into a run. He almost forgot Mikey was in his arms as he jumped up from his seat. He handed Mikey off to his grandfather to meet her. She hugged and kissed everyone in rapid-fire fashion, including Juan, whom she had not yet met. She took sleepy Mikey in her arms and held him firm against her chest. This is what she had missed most. He was approaching three now and she hoped he could quickly adjust to her presence.

They retrieved her luggage and two limousines sped them to the hotel for the night. She and John talked the rest of the night. They tentatively made love in the dawn light, as if they had forgotten how. Slowly, deeply their fingers linked. Then they fell asleep.

It seemed like a few minutes later, when there was a knock from the adjoining suite, Mikey waiting to be with his parents. John opened the door and let him snuggle with them. There was no more sleeping after Mikey joined them. They lay there for a while, before Clarissa got up to take a shower and John and Mikey watched cartoons on television.

They ate breakfast with Junior at the hotel restaurant. A buffet disappointed everyone except Clarissa, who had not seen pineapples, grapefruits, watermelon, and cantaloupes in a long time.

"I only booked your room for one night. The rest of us will stay here an extra day. You go back and get reacquainted."

Janet insisted on going back with them to cook, but Junior told her clearly and directly, "Absolutely, NO!"

Junior had arranged for hot lunch, dinner, and breakfast the following day to be delivered and for care of the animals.

The young couple talked well into the night.

She told him all about Africa.

He told her all about Mikey. She had missed so much in taking off for the years when he was so young.

"I know it was selfish. But you also know it had to be done."

It was easy to avoid the elephant in the room; she looked great, but was she well?

Everyone returned home in early afternoon and Janet cooked BLTs. Mikey had fallen asleep on the ride home. He had enjoyed swimming in the big, indoor hotel pool with Grandpa, but his eyes stung from the chlorine.

During the next month, they talked about what was next for them. She asked if he was still interested in law school, and he said yes. "I can put off school until you are done."

He replied, "Or we could both attend at the same time."

"How would we manage with Mikey?"

"We would learn. We'll figure it out."

Juan came running in from the yard. He had been listening to music on his transistor radio. "Quick, turn on the TV!"

"What's all the commotion?" asked Junior.

From all through the house everyone came running to their one television to watch Walter Cronkite, "From Dallas, Texas, the flash, apparently official: President Kennedy died at 1 p.m. Central Standard Time. Two o'clock Eastern Standard Time, some 38 minutes ago."

The next three days were a blur for each of them. Around the clock, they stayed close to the television to watch a nation in mourning. John was deeply concerned about Clarissa and he observed her closely. Her reaction was like most people. There were tears, but not an overwhelming dread and sobbing. She watched closely and spoke of that June day she met him. They talked about the campaign and the bright future the nation felt was before them. Now, the leader struck down, what would happen to that future? What legacy would remain? Had these last three years been in vain?

Pleased his assassin had been caught so quickly, she felt robbed from knowing the truth by his being shot to death. She wept at the Sunday services. She watched the reporting that took place through until Monday morning.

Then she was done. It was sad. It was tragic. It was over. She had not gone over the edge, as she would have in the past. She passed a major test. One of the most traumatic moments in the Nation's history and she had survived.

She was too young to remember the day Franklin Roosevelt died, but people spoke of his death as a day when everyone remembered exactly where they were. This day, November 22, 1963 was another.

Δ   Δ   Δ

It did not take long for Clarissa and John's love to return. Junior suggested a date night one evening per week. "You need to get away from Mikey and have some fun together."

They typically went for coffee, and talked frankly about how it was being apart. What the experience had been for each of them. Clarissa was sad about the time she lost with Mikey. She appreciated John had stuck it out with her; she felt she had abandoned him, but he had not abandoned her. Through Christmas and spring, they did not pressure each other. They started talking more seriously about what was next for them, like how they would manage law school, and what they would do with Mikey, if they attended simultaneously. They also discussed first Clarissa, then John, attending law school. They talked about finances for the apartment and getting a loan from Junior.

Junior barked, "Absolutely no loan. My gift to you".

Clarissa had applied to Georgetown Law before suspending her application to join the Peace Corp. When she called to find out what the process was for restarting the application, she got the run around. She took the hint she needed to take another route when she got unexpected comments from a clerk, "Summacumwhat? Could you spell that?"

She contacted friends at the White House from her Harvard days whom she thought might know people at Georgetown Law. Washington is a wonderful town. Things can actually get done when you finally get to the right person. As the story came back, someone at the White House staff asked around to find who knew the President of Georgetown Law.

"I know him. I'll make that call!"

"Mary, get Georgetown on the phone."

"She is a Kennedy girl. Summa Cum Laude outta Harvard. Two

years with the Peace Corp. Jack himself would be calling you if he were alive. Now what do you think you can do for your old buddy from Texas?"

Of course, no one will ever know whether it was Lyndon Baynes Johnson who made that call. All they knew for sure was Clarissa received a call from Georgetown Law a few hours later asking how soon she wanted to start.

"The Fall semester. My husband, too."

"Your husband, too?"

"Yes."

"I'll have to get back to you." They called back later to apologize; they could not locate his application and asked for him to fill them out again. They would mail the forms. It would just be a formality; both were accepted for the fall semester.

John had never filled out an application. The school had broken every rule in accepting Clarissa and John Atwater to Georgetown Law. With the next step in their future defined, and a long wait until school began, they enjoyed a spring and summer of fun and romance. The three of them were inseparable. They became the family they had never been. They talked about looking at apartments in Washington. They decided the three of them would take a trip down to Georgetown, but thought better of it and left Mikey home with Grandpa.

Junior was not looking forward to them leaving. It also meant there was no real need for Maria and Marta. What would he do?

JADON

In September 1964, the Atwater Family moved to a small apartment near Georgetown University. There was a teenage girl, Patsy, who lived in their apartment complex, who cared for Mikey when they both were in class and for date night. They studied together each evening. They were like high school sweethearts-- studying, laughing, and playing.

Clarissa found classes that first year were easy, but John struggled. He had been out of the classroom for too long. With her help he got back on track.

"Okay, this time you ask the questions and I'll give the answers."

"Alright."

"But then after I give the answer, you have to find in the book where it is discussed."

"You know I hate that."

"I know you do, but you just have to learn to find the reference."

"And what do I get if I get it right?"

"A Hershey's Kiss."

"How about another kind of kiss?"

"Perhaps one with almond?"

"You know what kind I want."

"John, we always get carried away."

"Pleeeezzzz."

"Maybe later."

One afternoon, shortly before Christmas, Clarissa was in a particularly chipper mood. John noticed how beautiful she looked. It was their date night, but instead of going out, Patsy was taking care of Mikey at her house.

Clarissa had prepared a nice dinner and they opened a bottle of wine. They had decorated their Christmas tree that afternoon and the house smelled of pine. Mikey placed all the ornaments on the tree within his reach; a one-foot circle filled with ornaments and the rest of the tree bare. It was a beautiful thing.

They listened to long-play Christmas albums.

After dinner, she sipped her wine and casually mentioned, "Hey, I passed a test today." Of course, that was not unusual.

"I did not know you had an exam."

"Oh, yeah. Dr. Brandon."

"Who?" He could not remember a Brandon at the Law School.

"Dr. Brandon."

"What subject?"

"Hard knocks."

"What?"

"The School of Hard Knocks."

"What are you talking about?"

"Here." She handed him a slip of paper.

"What is this?"

"Lab report."

"What do you mean, lab report?"

"Am I not speaking English? Lab report."

She pointed to a sentence near the end, where it read the word 'POSITIVE'. "Yeah, see right here. Says you are going to be a father again!"

"What?"

"Congratulations, Dad."

"How did that happen?"

"What, do I have to show you? Actually, that might be fun!"

He was confused.

She continued, "When you play with fire, sometimes you get burned!" He laughed.

"Yep, you are trying to make law school difficult for me!"

"Yes, but are you happy?"

"Thrilled!"

"Really? How did this happen."

"I was amorous. You were lazy. No condom again. Voilà!"

"I see."

"I hope you see, 'cause you are gonna have to explain this birds and bees things to our children some day. You better figure it out for yourself soon."

He laughed again.

"But, John, are you happy?"

"I'm thrilled. And I'm thrilled that you're thrilled!   I don't deserve you."

As best the doctor could calculate, her due date was mid-July 1965.

"When do we tell Mikey and your Dad?"

"Soon."

"How about my folks?"

"Why don't you send them a letter?"

Δ   Δ   Δ

The day Jadon arrived was hot and sticky. Clarissa spent much of the morning in the water behind her father's house. While she was walking back toward the house to make lunch, her water broke.

On July 22, 1965, Jadon Thomas Atwater was born at Meadowbrook Hospital in East Meadow. The name was going to be Jack, until they received back a letter in response to John's overture to make peace with his own father. He kept his ears and eyes open concerning his father's business and personal dealings, and things had not gone well. His financial daring-do had caught up with him. Foreclosures and tax fines were killing him financially, while the embarrassment of it was killing his pride. John's mother had taken up with another man who was able to maintain her lifestyle. She was on a boat in the Mediterranean. He did not know how to contact her.

Jadon weighed in at 8 pounds, 4 ounces and eighteen inches long. He was a beautiful baby--the spitting image of his father. Because of the time they spent together while Clarissa was in Africa, Mikey was closest to John. With five years between the boys, they could not have been more opposite.

The only thing Mikey liked about the Georgetown Law years was his babysitter. He hated Washington. His parents took him to exhibits, museums, and on the National Mall. While they were interested in the history and pageantry, he could care less. He longed to be in Long Island with his grandfather, swimming and diving. He wanted to be with his animals. He hated city living. Mikey resented being away from his grandfather in a place he did not like. He was a moody and angry child.

He resented the attention his newborn brother received. He hated when his parents would go off to class for long periods. His father had less time for him. The neighbors began to wonder if there was something wrong with him. It was not right for a child his age to have the pent up anger he seemed to have.

Jadon was a good baby who settled in easily. By the time his parents' graduated, he had been walking for a year and was running around the house, pestering his brother. Junior came down on the train for the graduation ceremony. Clarissa and John had done well in school. Both planned on taking the summer off, and then get serious about finding work. John had two job prospects already, while Clarissa was exploring a political career.

"Clarissa, I would never have made it through law school without you. I don't deserve you."

As Washington heated, with oppressive temperatures and humidity, the Atwater's returned to Long Island, the water, and the calming sea breezes. That summer cemented the boys love for the water.

$$\Delta \qquad \Delta \qquad \Delta$$

John and Clarissa studied together for their bar exams during the summer and passed. In the late summer of 1967, John took a position at one of the two law firms he had been speaking with since graduation.

He loved the work, was good at it and threw himself at it like nothing he had done before, except maybe golf. He found applying himself to both ventures was a key to success. His hours at the office were pleasant, and he would have some homework each evening and on weekends. It was a bit like law school all over again--emotionally and mentally stimulating. He also found Clarissa was a good partner as he sorted through issues in his own mind and determined the best approach to problems.

The firm also loved that they had a premier golfer on their staff, talented and social, who could lose when needed. The golf membership at the recently opened Middle Bay Country Club was paid for by the firm, but it really belonged to John.

Golf excursions usually started with one of the senior partners opening the unlocked door without knocking and leaning into John's office.

"Mr. Atwater, would you mind taking Mr. Remington out for golf tomorrow afternoon."

Without looking up, John would reply, "Well, I don't know, Mr. Billingsly, I have a lot of work."

"I would consider it a personal favor."

"Will it help me make partner?"

"Of course we appreciate all the talents our staff brings to bear."

"Do I have to let him beat me?"

"Of course."

"Where does he score?"

"Mid-nineties on a good day."

"Perhaps I could cut my throat? Make it easier for him to beat me?"

"Whatever it takes."

"Tom, you are a real ass for asking me to do this again."

"Perhaps I am. But John, if I were really an ass, I would not rescue you by joining you for cocktails afterward."

"Dinner, too?"

"Not this time. You can make an excuse and get back to your family after one drink. I will have 'Miss Crumplebutt' set it up for you." (That was their nickname for John's new secretary. Her butt was anything but crumpled and she was the talk of the office).

"Okay. Remember the partnership."

"Remember to lose."

After graduation, Clarissa had felt restless. She went to the anti-Vietnam protests that sprung up on college campuses in New York City and got in touch with friends on Robert Kennedy's staff. They were people who had worked for his brother after their Harvard days and moved onto RFK's staff after John's assassination. Soon she was offered a job in a senior position in Bobbie Kennedy's New York City Senate office. She knew this would put demands on her family, but she was excited and felt she could manage.

KENNEDY

When Clarissa joined Kennedy's staff in September of 1967, it was running about as smoothly as a Senator's office ever runs. She had to deal with special requests, soothe egos, and handle mundane tasks--like requests for American flags flown over the Capitol Building, speeches to civic groups, military school recommendations, and proclamations galore.

Bobbie Kennedy was a premier organizer in his own right. President Kennedy had once remarked, "If I want something done and done immediately I rely on the Attorney General. He is very much the doer in this administration, and has an organizational gift I have rarely if ever seen surpassed."

To organize for the organizer was a demanding task. With her amazing memory, detailed approach, and ability to document each step (and locate all the wayward notes) Clarissa ably organized for The Organizer. It did not go without notice all the way through the chain of command, up to the Senator himself.

There were growing demands from the African-American community. Clarissa planned trips for RFK to see first-hand the abject poverty in the inner city. He was confident she would keep his schedule on track and handle whatever came up.

She loved his intensity. More than once, she steered him clear of disaster. Kennedy had once joked to a reporter, "If I find out who has called me ruthless I will destroy him".

She interrupted a particularly heated discussion once to defuse a situation, "Excuse us. Sir, we have an urgent development". She would point to some papers, while whispering in his ear, "This is not going to get you anywhere. Just take my pen, sign the pizza flier as if it were an official document, then say, 'Where were we?' and change the subject before they answer".

She organized trips to Bedford–Stuyvesant in Brooklyn and to Harlem, for him to see conditions, as Clarissa put it, "In the shadow of your own office".

Most politicians would spend twenty minutes in a photo opportunity and have gone home for cocktails. RFK was entranced by what he saw. He forcefully called the people he saw "the disaffected," "the impoverished," and "the excluded." Touched by the cycle of poverty, even in a place as prosperous as New York City, he told Clarissa he knew he could help break the cycle.

Clarissa could see first hand his outrage at what he experienced. He saw it as a systemic breakdown, no less than what he had experienced in the South during his days as Attorney General.

He spent more and more time in New York City through the fall and into the winter. He confided to Clarissa late one evening in February, he was considering a run for the White House. If so, was she willing to help?

She was.

"It would mean relocating to Washington."

She swallowed hard. "Okay."

Kennedy had been unsuccessful in getting Senator Eugene McCarthy of Minnesota to withdraw from the presidential race. While he lost the race in New Hampshire to Johnson, it was so close it actually boosted McCarthy's standing to a legitimate Democratic contender. Kennedy had mixed feelings. He had favored the war, as his brother did, but was not in favor of ground troops.

On the phone to a reporter he said, "We have to keep it contained. We have to remember it is not our war. We are helping. We are providing advisers. Air strikes inland. Navy blocking ports. A minimum of ground forces. Only advisers. Only advisers".

Johnson was not moving quickly enough to conclude the war. McCarthy had strong feelings about the war, but lacked the breadth of experience needed for all aspects of the job. The war was not the only large issue looming over the country. Kennedy felt he was best positioned to fend off the Republicans, who were saddling the Democrats with war and domestic economy issues.

Even though in January he had said he would not run, Kennedy declared his candidacy on March 16, 1968 in the Caucus Room of the old Senate Office Building, stating, "I do not run for the Presidency merely to oppose any man, but to propose new policies. I run because I am convinced that this country is on a perilous course, and because I have such strong feelings about what must be done, and I feel that I'm obliged to do all I can".

On the last day of March, Lyndon Johnson withdrew from the race.

By April, Clarissa had placed work before family again and was in Washington. John didn't know where this was leading, as he had not had an opportunity to have a serious talk with her. They seemed to have come so far. What this all would mean to their family and them as a couple, he just did not know.

When she had joined the Peace Corp he thought she really needed to be away and deal with her mental health. But going to Washington for the RFK campaign, without any discussion with him, without any consideration of her family, showed him she would continue in this irresponsible behavior as long as he allowed it. This would be the last time. John thought of the old idiom: "Fool me once, shame on you; fool me twice, shame on me".

She organized events, travel arrangements, and hotels for dozens of staffers all over the United States. She traveled with Kennedy continually and was a trusted adviser.

She had sent an advance team to California--a critical state and the most populous state in the Union. In many ways, Democratic national party politicians were either for Kennedys or against them. There was no gray. The three-way race between McCarthy, Humphrey, and Kennedy was too close and too dynamic to call. The political establishment fractured when Johnson withdrew.

Kennedy won in the Indiana and Nebraska primaries, but lost Oregon. KNX Radio in Los Angeles reported, "If Kennedy can beat McCarthy in California, he could very well knock him out of the race. This would lead to a one-on-one fistfight against Hubert Humphrey at the Chicago national convention in August."

Humphrey had come to the plate late, declaring his candidacy at the end of April 1968. His close attachment to Johnson was a liability. Having trouble getting out of the President's shadow, he avoided primaries, concentrating instead on winning delegates in all the non-primary states. While he may have had time to apply for the California primary, he did not have the horsepower to win. It was better to have not played than to lose.

Tuesday, June 4, 1968 was a beautiful day: Primary Election Day in California. Clarissa had events scheduled throughout the state. She had to get calls out to every Democrat likely to vote for Kennedy to make sure they were going to the polls. Feeding the right information was Clarissa's job. On the phone constantly she squashed doubts when exit polls hinted at adversity, and claimed victory with the slightest eyelash of truth. Supporters stampede to a winner—as does the media. All the television networks interviewed her throughout the day, and she portrayed cool confidence.

The children were allowed to stay up late to watch their mother being interviewed frequently throughout the day. Things were going well with the campaign and as the day stretched on, better news was coming out of the Kennedy camp.

John was taking the next day off. He had not seen or heard from his wife during the entire time she had been in Washington. He knew this was critical, but it only positioned Clarissa to be away longer. Success would lead to greater demands toward the nominating convention in August. Success there would lead to even demands toward the general election in November.

Only an election loss could bring his Clarissa back to him. Or so he thought.

Δ   Δ   Δ

Nobody was sure how Clarissa got home from California. She had been at The Ambassador Hotel in Los Angeles, and congratulated Bobby Kennedy on his victory in the early hours of Wednesday, June 5, 1968, as he whisked toward the hotel kitchen. The rest was a blur.

She came through the front door of the house in Baldwin on the evening of the seventh, without money, suitcases, or her purse. Nobody heard a taxi pull up. She walked straight to the shower and went to bed. She did not say hello to her family. She did not eat. On the floor in their bedroom John found her clothing--the yellow dress she had worn all election day when her children had seen her on television.

At mid-morning, she got up, showered again, dressed, and came to the kitchen to eat. John was waiting for her.

"Well, welcome home. Are you Okay?"

"No."

"Where are you going?"

"Saint Patrick's for Bobby's Requiem Mass."

"I'll take you."

She hugged him and held him tight. "Thank you."

"You better eat."

"Yes, I better."

"I did not hear you come in."

After breakfast, she returned upstairs to their bathroom, vomited, showered, and dressed again. When she came back down, she announced she was ready to go.

After Mass, they returned home, and she went to bed to watch the non-stop television coverage while Kennedy's body was transported to Arlington National Cemetery, in Virginia.

At his young age, Mikey only partially understood what had occurred. Mommy's boss had been killed. Mommy came home, but Mommy was still gone.

She stayed in bed for the next few days, having food delivered to her bedside, which she barely touched. She began crying hysterically and the wailing went on for days. Finally, John tried to reason with her. She told him she was too sick to talk about it.

He called the doctor, who came over and gave her sedatives, but they only temporarily masked the pain she was feeling. She was unable to function. Days turned into weeks, which turned into months, with little progress.

John was frustrated and angry. Mikey felt angry again. Jadon did not know why he could not visit his mother.

John's boss delivered a stern talk to John. This could not go on any longer. His work was suffering. He gave him an ultimatum.

Her doctor was at whit's end. He ordered an ambulance to take her to Bellevue for a mental evaluation. Diagnosed with post-traumatic stress disorder, mania, and depression, she experienced "clinically significant distress and impairment in all major domains of life activity; social, occupational, sexual, and other important areas of functioning" the report said. They prescribed twice-weekly counseling sessions and heavy medications. She ran through a staggering list of medications without effect until they got to morphine. She slept little and when she did, her dreams were distorted and terrifying. In each dream she played back that evening at The Ambassador, and she saw everything she could have done to prevent the assassination.

To the outsider, of course, everything she "could have done" was preposterous.

John could not talk to Clarissa about how he felt before. He had been excluded--cast away, ignored--when she moved to Washington to help on Bobby's Presidential campaign. She hadn't even tried to discuss it with him. She just disappeared—-leaving him to pick up the pieces with the boys. She never reached out to him to say, "Let me do this!" He felt small. Demeaned. He had not been able to talk to his own wife about how he felt then--now she was beyond reach. He grew bitter. He wanted out of the marriage, but divorce was out of the question--he liked Junior's money too much. The cycle of crisis had to stop. She had been a drain on his career and his emotions. He would not let her take advantage of him again. He thought out the perfect plan--get rid of Clarissa and get on with his life. Start dating again. Enjoy himself. Live another life. Let the boys make do on their own.

The meeting with the doctors took place in a conference room near her private room.

"We have stabilized her. During the last two days she has quit crying hysterically."

"Is she heavily sedated?"

"Yes, well no. Not as much as she was."

"What are the options?"

"I think she needs some more rest. Perhaps a few weeks. Then she could come home."

"Yes, we are in agreement that she is not a threat to herself or to those around her."

John asked, "What are the chances she will relapse?"

One doctor sighed and looked over to his colleague nervously. "The medications get her calmed down, giving her a chance to catch her breath, relax, and get ahold of herself. But she may never be cured."

The other doctor continued, "But there are scientific advances on the horizon. One day there may be a cure. We are hopeful."

"But, of course, there is no guarantee."

"We must be realistic. In the short term, there will be bad episodes."

"Will they require hospitalizations?

"Perhaps."

"Damn it, Dan, give him the truth! Probably. We don't know. But it is just as likely to get worse as well as better. We just don't know."

With the meeting with her doctors concluded, John opened the door to Clarissa's room. She lay in bed peacefully. She watched him, but he thought she was asleep. He thought about the living hell he was already in. He thought about a single phrase the doctor had used--"just as likely to get worse". He didn't know if he was up to it. He thought, what had he done to earn this hell. She saw the scowl on his face. He looked down at his feet and missed that she was raising her right hand to him. He reached into the room and turned out the light, while he muttered softly, "I--don't--deserve--you." The door swung shut.

John convinced Junior of the need for long-term care for Clarissa, in a controlled environment. Junior loved Clarissa so much, he would do anything for her. John would just need to guide him to the correct conclusion. He had earned enough trust from his father-in-law to pull it off.
"For her benefit," he would say. Junior just needed to be sufficiently convinced that what John was doing was the best for Clarrisa. Junior trusted John. He knew he loved her by the letters he had seen. He stood by her in the past. All cautions disappeared, when Junior heard the magic words, "for her benefit."

Δ   Δ   Δ

John immersed himself in his work and his pleasures. He designed a small dock leading off the sand and a diving platform out on the bay. Once Mikey was a strong enough swimmer, he had the area dredged to make sure it was safe for diving. As the boys got older, the diving platform was stabilized and raised to a greater height. While Jadon would cannon ball from the peak, Mikey preferred to dive headfirst into the gray-blue waters. An extravagant, complex dive was never the same if the feet entered the water first. Mikey practiced for hours on end. More than once, he needed to be rescued by boat from the diving platform when he was too exhausted to swim back. He would lay down on the deck of the platform, shivering, until his father sent someone in the small motor launch to collect him. After supper, immediately excused to his room, he slept the sleep of the dead until morning, then got up bright and early, famished for breakfast, only to go back for another day of diving.

One spring afternoon, Jadon heard a maniacal laugh. What was Mikey up to? He came down to the water to explore where it was coming from and found him at the stream. Mikey was on his knees, motionless. He was intently watching a bullfrog that was facing him on the bank near the stream.

"Whatcha doin'?"

He received no reply.

"Mikey, what doin'?"

That is when he saw the stick. He had a 1×3 left over from some construction project in his left hand. There was a large nail bent over and pointing out the end. Mikey held the nail point near the eyes of the frog. Motionless.

Mikey was whispering to the frog, but Jadon could not make out what his brother was saying. The bullfrog seemed powerless to jump away. That's when Mikey lunged.

Then he laughed.

"Pretty good, huh, Jade?"

Jadon didn't know what to say. When he lunged, he had pushed the nail between the eyes of the bullfrog and directly into its brain. There was little wiggling or writhing. Just a small ooze.

Mikey stood up with the bullfrog still attached to the nail and walked upstream to where the bank of the stream was steeper.

That is when Jadon saw what his brother was doing. He retched.

He walked over to the letter 'Y'. It was nearly complete. He shook the bullfrog off the nail and slid it over to the correct position.

"Two more to go."

The word, M-I-K-E-Y was spelled out on the bank. Most of the frogs were still wiggling.

That evening, John talked to both his sons about the frogs left on the bank. Mikey just gave his father a blank expression. He saw nothing wrong in killing the bullfrogs. "There just bullfrogs." It was a quiet spring.

Mikey's fourth grade teacher, Miss Dorothea saw in his troubled artwork, moodiness, and anger that he needed help. He behaved in class, for the most part, but never seemed to be happy. He grumbled at everything and everyone. After observing him for a few months, she sent him to the school nurse.

Mrs. Mauer, R.N. was sweet, smart, dedicated to her charges, and thorough. She did not wear the typical nurse attire of a white uniform, peaked hat, white stockings and shoes--she felt that might intimidate the children. She wore light sweaters, Capri's, and dark slippers. She insisted she not be called 'Nurse Mauer'; she went my 'Miss June'.

In her typical day, she handled stomachaches, headaches, and diarrhea without skipping a beat. She dealt with digestive tract, chickenpox, and influenza epidemics each year as if she had seen it all before. She had. Nothing would rattle her. She had dealt with her share of child abuse cases, including sexual abuse.

A dozen times a year she would be asked to look at a student for other reasons. It could be suspected speech, hearing, or sight issues. Or it could be unexplained behavioral problems in the classroom. She patiently ran her battery of physical, emotional, and mental tests on Mikey and recommended he be seen by the school district psychologist.

Dr. Mack came in later in the week. He wore a crew cut, thin gray tie, and short sleeve white shirt. He reviewed Mikey's Cumulative Education Folder from the district office, Miss June's test results, and notes from Miss Dorothea, before meeting with Mikey.

Dr. Mack easily recognized Mikey's anti-social behavior. In this first meeting, he did not have a feeling for a specific diagnosis. He suggested counseling for Mikey in order for him to get in touch with his feelings, but this was beyond the capabilities of the school district. He called John and set up a meeting.

They discussed Mikey's behavior in the classroom and he asked for John's observations at home.

"He has had some difficulties at home." He did not discuss his wife's illness with Dr. Mack.

"I have seen counseling do wonders in cases like this. Perhaps he will need medication as well. I suggest you send him to a psychiatrist for an evaluation. He may want you to work with a psychologist instead of him directly."

"That sounds fine."

"I have a few psychiatrists I have worked with in the past." Dr. Mack looked at the Atwater's home address in his folder.

"Actually, there is a new child psychiatrist near you. My wife has taken my children to him."

John took his name, address, and telephone number and as soon as he was back to his office, he called to make an appointment.

Maria led Mikey into the waiting room and to the receptionist. She had to knock on the window twice before Mrs. Clark answered.

"I have Mikey Atwater for his two o'clock appointment."

"What?" Mrs. Clark was hard of hearing. The Doctor liked her that way, so as not to hear much of what was occurring in his office.

"I have Mikey Atwater for his two o'clock."

"Are you Mrs. Atwater?"

"No, I am his caretaker."

"I see. Here are the insurance forms. Please have Mr. or Mrs. Atwater fill them out and return them in this envelope. Be seated."

She handed Maria the packet and closed the window.

The waiting room had teak wood furniture with yellow cushions. The tables had copies of comic books, *Reader's Digest*, and *Psychology Today*. There were cheap modern art prints on the walls in teak frames. The floor was off white linoleum with blue geometric shapes.

Dr. Pembroke was not new to psychiatry, but he was new to dealing with children. Pembroke had recently partnered with two other mental health professionals. Each would specialize in a single area of focus: children, adolescent, and adult. He thought this model completed the whole mental health life-cycle--deal with sick children, turn them into sick adolescents. Deal with sick adolescents, turn them into sick adults. Deal with sick adults. Make lots of money.

Pembroke did not particularly like children, but he did like young mothers. He was cynical about psychiatry and psychology. He recognized the benefits of talking things through, but felt the pharmaceutical part of mental health care was in its infancy.

His hobby in the evening after work was scotch and marijuana. He and his wife's hobby on the weekend were swinging with the neighbors and trying out hallucinogenic drugs; the better to understand what he was prescribing to his patients.

He wore sweater vests, long sleeve striped shirts, navy blue slacks with cuffs, cream-colored socks, and black wingtip shoes. He had oversized black frame reading glasses and smoked a pipe--he played with one or the other continually.

His desk was also teak and never had anything out of place. The teak "in and out" baskets were always bare and the desk was empty of papers whenever a patient was in the office. His college diplomas were framed and mounted on the wall behind his desk. Modern art was on his office walls; more expensive paintings than in his reception area. He had sculptures around the room. At first glance they just seemed like scrap pieces of clay. Upon closer examination, they were suggestive of certain parts of the female anatomy.

His partners kidded him in private, "I understand your previous practice specialized in sexually-repressed housewives."

"I heard you specialized in a new technique: 'Therapeutic Trysts.'"

"Oh, that's not new. As old as Freud."

Mrs. Clark slammed open the window and yelled, "Atwater. The Doctor will see you."

Maria opened the single door and stepped onto the orange, shag carpet where Dr. Pembroke had practiced his therapy with so many young women.

"This is Mikey Atwater, Dr. Pembroke. I am Maria, his caretaker. I will not be staying."

"Hello, Mikey. Please be seated. Thank you Maria." After sizing up Maria, he decided he would not be disappointed in her leaving.

Over the next two years, Dr. Pembroke saw Mikey weekly. He gave periodic written reports to John. They always said the same thing, Mikey is progressing. He is talking out his feelings. It is best that they continue with weekly sessions. They never gave John a clear understanding of Pembroke's diagnosis, prognosis, or cautioned him about likely behaviors. But John thought he saw where Mikey was headed. After two years, Mikey started resisting attending the sessions. His father paid for the missed appointments. Finally, Mikey quit going altogether. John thought perhaps he was following in his mother's path.

Each weekday afternoon, Maria picked up the children from school. Mikey was the first one in the door, dropping his textbooks and jacket on the floor of the mud room, and then bolting up to his bedroom to change into his swim trucks. Angela was next. She hung up her jacket or sweater, and took her homework to the kitchen table. Jadon and Marta came in last. Jadon asked about everyone's day and told everyone what he had learned in school. He hung up his jacket and brought any papers he had to the table. There were three glasses of milk and three short stacks of cookies on paper napkins waiting for them.

Mikey ate the snack as he went flying by to go out to the bay. Angela and Jadon sat together eating and drinking their snacks, talking quietly. When Angela was done, she took her homework to her room, and closed the door to play by herself and study until supper. Jadon usually went swimming.

Junior began following the boys down to the water after school. Sometimes he swam and other times he lay on the sand on a beach towel, where he could watch them.

"Why are you spying on us?" asked Mikey angrily.

Junior did not give him a reply.

Junior appreciated the graceful, beautiful dives Mikey performed. As soon as he finished with a dive, he would climb back onto the platform and climb up the ladder to start another.

Jadon swam around, gliding like a seal under the water, and occasionally followed his brother up the platform.

"Watch, Grandpa!"

Jadon did a cannonball, giggling to his hearts content.

"Did I get you wet?"

When Jadon became tired and cold, he wanted to snuggle with Junior. Junior would make him dry off, then let him curl up with his back again Junior's chest. His swimsuit would get the front of Junior's pants wet, but he never seemed to mind. Jadon talked, wiggled, and giggled, nesting in his grandfather's strong arms. When he began to settle down, Junior took Jadon's beach towel with one hand and pulled it to cover his grandson. Most days, Jadon nodded off to sleep.

When John got home, dinner was usually ready and he rang the wrought iron triangle shaped dinner bell mounted on the deck. Junior and Jadon collected their beach towels and walked hand in hand up to the house. Normally Mikey was not far behind them, but he often ignored the bell.

Juan was working in the yard one afternoon and saw Junior and Jadon snuggled together. He paused to watch them. Smiling, he took his gardening tools up to the shed. That evening he gave a slip of paper to Marta asking her to get rope and canvas to his specifications. He asked her if she would be willing to do some sewing.

He spent the next three days in his workshop. The following afternoon there was a present for Junior by the water. It was a redwood lounge chair, extra wide--big enough for both Junior and Jadon. The center was a web of ropes with a canvas cushion and two pillows. When Junior thanked him profusely, Juan blushed and beamed.

From the top of the platform, Mikey experienced perfect

balance and grace as he pushed himself high into the air. He entered the water with hardly a splash, while the streaming water caressed him as if long, sensuous, fingers were sliding down his body. The briefest split second felt like it extended all afternoon. As he pierced the surface of the water, he knifed through, until buoyancy returned him to reality, and he slowly swam up to the surface.

When he became older, the area coaches appreciated Mikey's obsession for training. His resistance to training for dives that resulted in entering the water feet first became a sore spot.

"Does it hurt when you go in feet first?"

"No."

"Then why won't you do those dives."

"They aren't fun."

"But they are the same. You are jumping through the air with the same aerobatics. They are no different."

"To me they are."

"How do you expect to be a champion if you only will do part of the established diving repertoire?"

"Why do you expect me to be a champion?"

"Because you have the physique, strength, grace--you have all the tools and abilities to be a champion. Why don't you want to be the best you can be?"

"Why should I?"

"It can be the pinnacle of accomplishments. A skill no one else can master. You could be in the Olympics."

"But I dive for myself."

"You can dive for yourself and for your country. And for your family. And for me."

"You dive for you and I'll dive for me."

One by one, coaches left exasperated at the thought of so much talent being lost. More than one coach walked away muttering, "There is something really wrong with that kid."

Jadon heard that maniacal laugh again one afternoon, and immediately knew it was Mikey. Curious, he followed the laugh to find Mikey had the High School Swimming Coach pinned to the ground.

"Do not ever come back here, you bastard. I don't like your school and I don't like you. If I ever see your face again here I will rip it apart and feed--"

"Mikey, what are you doing! Let him up."

Jadon ran over and pried Mike's hand off the coach's throat.

"Let go, Mikey!"

Mikey released his hold and rolled off the coach.

Rubbing his throat, he could barely get out, "What do you think you are doing, you crazy bastard?"

Jadon looked mortified, but Mikey just laughed.

Jadon helped the coach to his feet. He was white as a sheet.

"I come here to help you and you attack me? We'll see about this!"

Rubbing his throat, he ran to his car and drove straight to the Sheriff's Office.

"Now, Harold. You really want to press charges? Do you know how it is going to sound when people hear a high school freshman boy whipped your ass?" Cooler heads prevailed and no charges were pressed.

When Mikey was done with dinner after swimming and diving he was ready for bed.

"Do you have any homework?"

"No," he lied.

"Are you sure?

"Yes."

He often climbed the stairs, closed the door to his room, and was asleep within minutes. Junior, Jadon, and John spent their evenings in the family room and Angela would sometimes join them. John and Junior had a scotch or two. They read the newspaper or books, watched television, or talked.

Jadon loved to hear stories of when his grandfather was growing up in Ireland. He loved to hear about coming to America on a big boat and when Junior got bushwhacked by thieves! He loved to see the 'Africa pictures'. Junior would pull out the letters Clarissa had written from Ethiopia. While he read the letters, he gave Jadon the dozen faded Kodacolor prints she had sent home of her teammates, projects, natives, merchants, and wild animals at a nearby watering hole.

As the boys entered their teen years, they routinely visited their mother in the sanitarium. While Jadon was still a freshman, he asked Junior to take him to see his mother, explaining he was doing a report for school on Ethiopia and wanted to interview her to get more information. This came as a bit of a shock--visits to Clarissa were planned well in advance and well orchestrated by the staff.

The interview was arranged for the following week. The library had been prepared with three club style oxblood red leather chairs with cognac brown wood legs to match the paneling and cocktail table. The cocktail table held a large, silver platter of Oreo cookies, milk, tea, coffee, cream, sugar, small plates, cups and saucers, and cloth napkins.

Junior pulled up to the front door in his Rolls Royce and was greeted by a tall man in a business suit, "You must be Mister Millwood and Mister Atwater. Welcome." He hung up their sweaters and escorted them to the library.

"Please excuse me." He returned a minute later with Clarissa.

She was dressed for the interview in a dark green business suit, pearl earrings, matching pearl necklace, and high heels. She hugged her father and her son.

Jadon started right in asking questions. He took careful notes and his questions ranged all over the map. She gave him simple answers, but would tend to go into greater detail on areas of interest to her. This led to follow-up questions. After two hours, her mind began to wander.

She thought how proud she was of Jadon. How he had grown up. How smart he was. Then it hit her like a dagger to the heart-- oh, how much she had missed! Oh, how much she had thrown away! She began to cry uncontrollably.

Alarmed, Junior said, "Perhaps we have exceeded our welcome."

"No, really, I'll be fine in a minute."

"Jadon, do you have any final question for your mother?"

"Can I get the names and addresses of people you were with in the Peace Corp? So I can speak with them?"

Junior answered for her, "Certainly we'll get that for you", as he grabbed Jadon by the arm and lifted him from his chair. As if he had been waiting outside the room, the attendant who saw them in was standing at the doorway holding their sweaters.

"Thank you, but you will excuse us."

"No, please don't go!"

And with that, they were off.

"Please stay! Please stay! Oh, please--"

Junior was quiet on the drive home. He thought to himself, John is right to keep her there. She is sicker than I thought. She can't keep from breaking down at even simple conversation. He could not keep her breakdown out of his mind. After dinner he had a few more scotches than usual and was quiet. His thoughts turned to Mikey as he went off to bed that evening.

Mikey was a stormy sleeper. The clean bed sheets were always tossed everywhere. He dragged his naked body past the walk-in closet that got little use, and to the bathroom. The bathroom was always spotless--until he entered. He walked to the toilet, lifted the seat, and without using his hands to guide the stream, urinated. He would stand urinating and rubbing his eyes, wobbly, yawning.

When he was done, he backtracked past the packed but unused, custom designed dressing furniture, armoire, and bed stand, and searched for the jeans he had dropped on the floor before going to bed. There they were partially hidden by the satin sheets, just as he had left them; two leg holes open, the pant legs scrunched down. There were neat stacks of clean boxer shorts in the dresser drawers, but he could not be bothered. He put on the tee shirt and socks he cast aside last night. This would be day three if he were counting, so he would probably receive the subtle hint from the servants of fresh clothing on top of the dresser tonight. They had learned from Mikey's blistering temper to wait until they experienced his ripened aroma personally before leaving out fresh clothing.

Jadon's tutors described him as odd, but in a different way from his brother. He was not extremely sociable, though his smile was open and warm. Jadon tried to understand how everything worked. Waking up in the morning, he made his bed so you would not have known he had slept in it. He hardly moved when he slept. He showered, shaved, and brushed his teeth, putting everything away and hanging his towels up. The servants wondered where he had learned this trait: Certainly not from his brother.

Like his mother, he was an excellent student, ready to master any subject. He could be quite challenging to his tutors, blasting them for not knowing more about an obscure subject. He absorbed information like a sponge, but was not haughty about what he knew.

UNITED NATIONS

Until age fourteen, both boys were tutored at home. Mikey then went to the public high school in Baldwin for four years. He was a 'C' student, who never applied himself and never studied. A comment hand written into his permanent file told the whole story--"Does not seem to have an interest in anything". The swimming coach attempted to get him to join the team, but Mikey had no interest even there. When he graduated in 1977, he had no plans to attend college and when pressed by his father, took a job as a lifeguard for the local YMCA.

Jadon attended a private, preparatory school in Rhode Island and graduated at the head of his class in 1982. He loved the rural setting, which was similar to Long Island. He decided he wanted to attend Cornell University, liking its egalitarian roots and beliefs.

The college brochure said Cornell was the most educationally diverse member of the Ivy League. In Jadon's mind, it retained roots of the classical form from three centuries before.[xxxiv]

He tried to create, as much as possible, a classical coursework for himself. He earned a pre-law undergraduate degree in 1986. He immediately went for a law degree at Cornell, graduating with honors in 1989. His father sprung Clarissa from the sanitarium for the graduation ceremonies. She was markedly better by this time. John still wasn't considering bringing her home.

There had been rumors of John and his secretary's love affair for years. There was also speculation John was keeping his wife locked away for his own benefit. Jadon's grandfather attended the graduation, looking weak and frail in his late nineties.

That summer, John made partner at his law firm. He had done significant legal work but his golf actually hindered his advancement. He was seen from one frame of reference--golf host to clients.

$$\Delta \qquad \Delta \qquad \Delta$$

Days after his graduation, Jadon was mesmerized by a showdown in Tian'anmen Square, Beijing, People's Republic of China.[xxxv]

Since early May, pro-democracy protesters, predominantly students, angered over the closed nature of Chinese government had become increasingly vocal.

The match that lit the protest and led to massacre was the death of Hu Yaobang, the sixth General Secretary of the Communist Party of China, of a heart attack. He had resigned after being vilified by the government not for his pro-democracy and anti-corruption reforms, but for his laxity in government.

The image of the Unknown Rebel, nicknamed the Tank Man, standing before a column of Chinese Type 59 tanks forcibly removing protestors from Tian'anmen Square on June 4, 1989, was seared into Jadon's memory.

With his legal education completed, Jadon considered several options and made a curious choice. He believed the United Nations should have taken a greater stance in helping mediate conflicts that led to massacres and unrest, such as the one in China. He determined to work there. He wanted to become the United Nation's Tank Man.

With his mother's contacts dating back to her Peace Corp days, and his grandfather's money, he gained easy access to the United Nations. Two months later, he started there as a junior attorney and leased an apartment nearby. With intelligence and diligence, he moved up the ladder quickly.

During the next twenty years his claim to fame would become work done prosecuting war crimes in Darfur and Sudan. Based on his mother's experience, he loved the African people. He traveled to the Sudan and Ethiopia with her former Peace Corp associates. They were troubled by her long history of mental health issues, and willingly helped him. Becoming an attorney at the United Nations was not much of a problem. However, working the Darfur conflict created his first two great obstacles-- Jadon had neither prosecutorial experience nor seniority.

Senior attorneys coming to the UN brought their own staffs. Most junior attorneys sought the experience as stepping-stones to greater opportunities. He wasn't interested in polishing his political star or grandstanding. Darfur was what interested him.

A past professor talked to Jadon about this direction. "Are you sure you want to do this? It is not for the faint of heart. I have seen it a dozen times--the most inane political decision can derail your prosecution, and probably will. However, in the realm of high power international politics, this is not necessarily bad for some people. One can speak fervently about the 'injustice' of it all, slander an ardent critic, resign with righteous indignation, and still end up winning the end game, a plum opportunity--without losing the case. But that's not you. The only thing that can get in those peoples way is some maverick, do-gooder underling gumming up the works."

He left unsaid, that do-gooder who might risk it all could be Jadon.

The second great, new obstacle was also political in nature, but of a different kind. While the Darfur conflict was being discussed at the United Nations, the General Assembly convened a conference in Rome in June 1998 to finalize a treaty creating the International Criminal Court (ICC). The United States voted against the treaty. The ICC's jurisdiction, supposedly limited, covered genocide, crimes against humanity, war crimes, and crimes of aggression. It exercised jurisdiction only when national courts were "unwilling or unable" to investigate and prosecute crimes.

That may have sounded ideal, but "crimes of aggression" and "unwilling or unable" were very subjective. Over cocktails, the United States Ambassador to the United Nations whispered to Jadon, "In a forum that freely slanders the United States, and where our citizens routinely clamored for exiting the tribunal, putting Uncle Sam's head in a noose is not something we are going to let happen."

By 1989, Jadon had aged gracefully. His hair was long and prematurely gray. They called him the Silver Fox behind his back.

He was short with a good physique. He watched what he ate and drank, and exercised religiously.

His manservant laid out his clothes each day, but did not dress him. He enjoyed colorful attire. His costume on the golf links was most provocative--loud shirts and knickers with white golf shoes. He played against his father as often as he could.

At work, he wore expensive suits and pastel or dazzling, bright white dress shirts. He had a collection of ties featuring the US flag. His dress shirts always had French cuffs and he wore gold cuff links and rings. He carried an expensive pen in this shirt pocket, a hand-me-down from his grandfather, featuring The Seal of the Mayor of New York City.

He dated little as women were put off by his extreme focus on work. For breakfast, he sipped orange juice and tea. He drank coffee and champagne in social settings, and read newspapers religiously. When he walked into his office at the United Nations, all eyes turned his way. His assignment was considered career suicide because of the Bush administration's opposition to the court being established. He worked to prosecute crimes in spite of likely circumvention by his boss, Jean Luis Moreno.

He had a recurring dream almost every night in which the sun was brightly shining overhead. It was quiet, but he could hear the flapping of cloth in the wind. The cloths flapping in the wind were flags. Flags of all countries. Dozens and dozens of flags. Flags flapping around Jadon. Slapping Jadon's arms. Sliding across his face and body. His arms were raised and he felt the warmth of the sun beating down. Through a break in the flags, he noticed there were children, smiling, gaily dressed in native costumes, with flagpoles in their arms. Circling, joyous, singing. Randomly they began dancing.

Jadon saw rogues--mean, plotting, devious. He took some flags, rolled them into ropes, and bound all the rogues so they couldn't move. He led them away as they wept and cried out, but their voices couldn't be heard.

Jadon took more of the flags and rolled them into ropes. He drew people in toward himself. All the children were joyous, being collected together, respected, loved, and honored. They began singing. They sang songs in their own languages, which blended beautifully together with all the others.

Suddenly the remaining flags parted and they were near a podium at the United Nations. The children had become adults. Their costumes were still the same, only their size and age changed. He mounted the stage. As trumpets played, he mounted the podium. Clarrisa reached the microphone just before him, and introduced him as the new Secretary-General. As she completed the introduction, she turned to hand him a gavel. Jadon looked over the packed house of dignitaries, standing and applauding. He opened a general session of the United Nations as he heard chanting--"Tank Man, Tank Man, Tank Man".

JUNIOR

On Christmas Day 1989, the boys--at ages 29 and 24-- joined Junior and John to open presents. They sprung Clarissa for the day. Their large Christmas tree, selected by one of the servants, filled the room to the peak of the ceiling in the A-frame main portion of the house. Beyond the tree, through the picture windows, deer grazed in the back. Just a small amount of snow remained from a few days before, under overcast skies.

Junior was bundled up on a love seat, enjoying the fun. He was still fully alert and aware, having retained all his mental faculties. He'd had a few minor medical issues of late, was cold most of the time, and dozed off frequently.

They enjoyed hot cider and rolls for breakfast, while the boys opened their presents. It was jokingly expected they would behave as if they were still schoolchildren. Neither of them did, of course, but Jadon took the teasing in good nature. Mikey acted angry and bitter at the suggestion of opening presents marked: From Santa.

Clarissa was calm, quiet and good-natured, enjoying both the fire and the time with her family. John and Jadon enjoyed sitting around the fire, chatting. Junior dozed off. Mikey paced along the windows, alternating between being bored and about to attack the world. Occasionally he let out his maniacal laugh; at what, nobody knew.

If anyone needed the clothing their father had gotten them for Christmas, it was Mikey. He disappeared for long periods and did menial jobs most of the time. Anger eventually got the best of him and he either quit or was fired.

But he always found minimum wage jobs to keep him busy. It never seemed to bother prospective employers that he had left so many jobs. He never worried about where he lived, what he wore, or what he ate. The family stopped asking how he was doing and where he lived; he snapped at them for intruding and they never got an answer anyway. If they had an urgent need to contact him, they left a message at a number he gave them, and he eventually got back to them.

He never disclosed where he lived when he was away from Baldwin House or where he worked. His father paid for a medical and dental insurance policy, but if he ever used it, he was not saying.

It was a quiet, relaxed morning. They were planning a late brunch of egg soufflé, ham with pineapple, Champagne, and coffee. When they tried to wake Junior for brunch, he was gone. He lived to be three months short of his one-hundredth birthday.

Two days later, they buried him under the maple tree that he loved so much. He was at last at rest with his two wives and little Ruth.

The family never seriously discussed what they would do with the house after Junior passed away. John talked about keeping it as a vacation house, but it was much too big. He wanted to move to Manhattan to be near his work (and perhaps his lover). Jadon loved the house, but found his apartment near the United Nations more convenient. He did not want to move back, but he did not want to sell the house either.

Mikey did not care one way or the other about the house, until told he would not be able to come back there to swim. "Oh, we can't sell it, then."

The path of least resistance was to do nothing, which is exactly what they did. When John moved, he had the bedrooms sealed. He let go of the staff, except for a caretaker/security man and his wife. He hoped that one day Jadon would want to return to raise a family. He did not think he would ever let Clarissa return, though he knew she was much better. She never pressed the issue. She figured there was probably another woman in his life. She told herself, when he is ready he will invite me back. Until that day, she accepted her penance for all she had done.

Δ   Δ   Δ

Clarissa had lived in the same private sanitarium for more than two decades. There were no crazy people running around the halls. No evil nurses. She was the only resident. It was originally a private home on an 800-acre estate on Long Island. The house was not exceptionally large, but there were elaborate gardens (and a winery in its heyday). There were two live-in nurses, a psychiatrist who came by weekly, and a resident psychologist, who worked there during the week, meeting with Clarissa as often as she requested.

The psychiatrist had taken her off all medications in 2000. His official medical notes read: *She is making excellent progress.* The psychiatrist's personal notes would have said: *This lady ain't sick.* That paralleled every other staff member's observation.

She had long ago worked through her problems. Yes, there was a medical component to it, but that was not her real issue. She had succeeded in her education and she pushed her career hard. After the Peace Corp success, she felt invincible. She had to push her career again to extraordinary levels. She only saw it in herself in hindsight. She thought to herself: how self-centered and strong-willed can a person be? It had all come tumbling down with Robert Kennedy's assassination--and cost her her husband and her sons.

She thought to herself, doesn't everyone deserve a second chance? Then she realized she had her second chance already, and had blown it. To ask for a third chance seemed to require her to be even more self-centered and more strong-willed. She wouldn't do that. It ran contrary to what she knew was right. She did not deserve it. She would not ask ever again.

She knew she still had a choice. She could become the tragic victim--"Poor, pathetic, sick Clarissa"--or she could bear up under it, waiting, and hoping.

For nearly thirty years she had spent her time gardening, cooking, tending her dogs, walking through the park-like setting, reading, and writing.

She did not ask, and they did not ask her, if she would like to be released. When Junior was alive, he trusted John to do the right thing for his daughter. He continued to pay, in cash, their exorbitant fees each month.

Everyone knew she was well—and that there was too much

money at stake. Doctors knew from the beginning they were expected to play along and administrators knew not to ask.

Nobody was her advocate. She did not want one. She hoped one day to be asked to return home. Until then, this was her lot in life. Her husband visited her periodically. He asked how she was. He asked if she needed anything. However, he never asked her to come home, except on Christmas Day.

When her father passed away, he was worth $400,000 on paper. His money was well hidden, and in excess of $100 million. His trust funds provided for a well-paid team of accountants, tax lawyers, and the best investment people money could buy. Everyone in the family had 'the phone numbers' if they needed money for any reason and at any time. There were dozens of unlisted off-shore accounts. There was nothing in the way of a paper trail for his ill-gotten gains. There was nothing to tie him to the accounts that were not in a safe location outside of the United States, in a jurisdiction that had no interest in turning things over to the United States.

When cash was needed, cash was delivered. Cash only. It appeared the next day on the doorstep. Junior had lived a simple life. He had not flaunted his wealth or raised suspicions at the Internal Revenue Service. His methods did raise some questions when multiple individuals showed up to hand large amounts of cash to Cornell University for Jadon's schooling. Each transaction was under the dollar amount required for reporting to the IRS (the school clearly understood reporting was undesirable). Each transaction received a cash receipt. When there was a discrepancy in his account, created by a minor clerical mistake (and once by a lost key) a person was dispatched to resolve it.

Junior's secret accounting and legal team were fully aware of the situation with Clarissa. They had clear instructions on how to handle it. They knew more about the whereabouts of Mikey, his living conditions, and his employment status than his family. They were handsomely paid for their discretion, attentiveness, and loyalty to the family. The arrangement continued after Junior's death, and if they kept things clean, into perpetuity.

Clarissa loved to garden her vegetables. Each week brought something new to be planted, rearranged, pruned, or watered. This day she carefully tended her pumpkins. Everything she grew ended up on her dinner table and the tables of the staff of the sanitarium. Of course, they never called it a sanitarium. She was no longer ill. They still saw to her every need, but her house had unique features and carefully guarded secrets--there were no telephones in plain view, televisions, radios, newspapers, or magazines. None where Clarissa could access them or where she knew there was one. In the staff lounge, off limits to Clarissa, there was a hidden large television, so she would not be exposed to world events that could trigger distress.

The outside world was a carefully guarded secret. Over time, she overheard comments and figured things out. By the mid-80's she figured out the Vietnam War was over. She never heard of Presidents Carter, Reagan, or the first Bush. The Iran Hostage crisis, fall of the Berlin Wall, and breakup of the Soviet Union never occurred, as far as she was aware. She only knew of President Clinton, because of someone's offhanded giggling remarks to another staff member about Monica Lewinsky.

Her pumpkins were coming along nicely and she figured she was three weeks away from harvest. Her dogs were sleeping comfortably nearby as she puttered in her garden. On a Tuesday morning, she noticed a large cloud of smoke coming from the west. She stood watching the billowing clouds.

"I hear a local farmer was burning leaves, and it got out of control."

Clarissa just looked at him. "Bullshit. Charles, John would be disappointed in you. You are going to have to lie better than that."

"Ma'am?"

"Why are so many of the staff missing?"

"Oh, they are just busy."

"No they are not."

"Will any of you tell me the truth?"

There was a long pause.

She continued, "Your face gives it away, Charles. It is big, isn't it?"

He did not respond.

"When will Doctor Lee be in?"

"I can arrange it for tomorrow."

"You know I am not stupid."

"Of course not, Clarissa."

"I am over sixty years old and have lived here half my life. You have kept things from me and I have played along, but you can't keep everything from me. Something big has occurred."

"We both know how these things disturb you."

"They used to disturb me. But I have been better. I have been off the medication for over a year. I have been prisoner now for, how long has it been, thirty-some years."

Doctor Lee remained stoic.

"I have actually been well now for twenty-five of those years."

He still did not say anything, but they both knew it was true.

By the end of the week, she was still working in the garden. The continuous sounds of sirens in the distance had dissipated by Friday. Clarissa could sense the stress on every one; nurses, kitchen staff, maids, Doctors Lee and Kim. "I would like to see both of my Doctors together, now, today."

"A large cloud of smoke on Tuesday, sirens continually in the distance for the last three days. Oh, and no airplanes in the sky since Tuesday. The staff is so stressed you can cut the tension with a knife. I know you will not tell me anything. That is the game we have played around here for more than thirty years. But, for God-sakes, I am a mother. You have to tell me one thing. It wasn't the United Nations building was it?"

The doctors looked at each other, but did not respond. She could tell that they would, however. Soon.

Jadon called. He had been told what he could say, which was not much. They just wanted him to call so she could hear his voice--to let her know he was alive. He would be careful, but he had decided to tell her the truth and speak beyond their instructions. They would listen in, of course, but he didn't care.

She was sitting in her favorite chair after dinner on Friday evening. They brought a telephone to her on a silver platter, and plugged the phone into a hidden receptacle. It was a pink Princess phone from the sixties, with a special feature--no dial. She laughed to herself when she saw it, thinking, I couldn't call out even if I had found the damn phone. She raised the receiver to her ear, "Hello?"

"Mother. It's Jadon."

She sighed. The doctors noticed the relief on her face.

They talked quietly to each other. Small talk. Then it turned serious, "Are we at war?"

"No. At least not yet. America was attacked."

"Where?"

"Manhattan. Pentagon. And a plane went down in Pennsylvania."

"How many are dead?"

"They really don't know yet."

She gasped. She was thinking a million, but said, "A thousand?"

"More."

"Tens of thousands?"

"Maybe. They are estimating under ten."

"Is your father alright?"

"Yes."

"What about you brother?"

"Yes."

"Thank God."

Δ   Δ   Δ

The year after Junior's death, John had moved into an apartment on the lower east side of Manhattan. It was modest, but convenient for his work. If he played golf at the country club, and he was not staying for a client's dinner, he could sit by himself on the pier at the Baldwin House with a glass of wine, until sunset. In the cool of the evening, it was pleasant on the bay, with a small amount of boat traffic. The trees around him absorbed all outside noises, leaving only peace. He watched the birds in the cool breeze as they swooped down looking for fish and insects. He was able to collect his thoughts and reflect on his life. This home on Long Island meant so much to him. He thought about the good times on the water with the boys. How different they were. He thought about Junior a great deal. Junior had been a good father-in-law, who supported them through all the hard times and never complained or gave advice on John's parenting. He was generous and loving to John and the boys.

What a contrast he was to the confession he had written. It was hard to picture things he had done, but John never doubted they were true. He thought about Clarissa as little as he could. He suspected she was well enough to come home and live with him. He knew he was being selfish. He enjoyed the company of women and not just in a sexual way. It's clear he liked women, but mostly at arm's length. The dinners and walks where he could talk about things were refreshing, but he chose women who would be discrete--enjoy just talking, walking, playing golf, quiet dinners, an occasional roll in the hay, no strings attached. Women who had something to lose if their dalliances became known. Usually married women. He bought them toys, mostly jewelry, and he broke things off when he felt himself becoming too attached.

He had only misjudged two of his choices. One resulted in a child; her husband never knew the child was not his. The other required a call to Junior's "spy network"--the last he heard she had died in Switzerland.

Mostly he needed women to talk to: He could not talk with Clarissa about many things. He had built a barrier against her.

He had to admit Mikey was a puzzle and a disappointment. He could call Junior's 'spy network', as John called Junior's legal/financial team, and get a pinpoint accurate description of his location and activities any time he wished.

He wondered, what had gone wrong? Why did he give up on life at such an early age? Why was he deeply affected by his mother's illness and absences? Why hadn't he outgrown it? Where did I fail him?

Many times, he left the dock to visit Clarissa at the sanitarium. She was always happy to see him and they had good visits. As much as he tried, he could not get over his love for her. He felt guilty about this arrangement, which he perpetuated just so he could be with his mistresses. His liaisons were a series of shallow arrangements. He was spending a lot of money keeping Clarissa locked away. Money that did not even belong to him. He had kept Clarissa locked up for more than thirty years. He was getting too old to keep playing these games. She never asked to come home. He never let her out.

John, Jadon and Mikey kept the Baldwin house as a vacation home for several years, but it was not getting enough use to warrant them keeping it. Still, the path of least resistance was to pay the property taxes, its upkeep, and for a caretaker.

Mikey swam and dove there nearly every day, except in the worst of weather. He never used the house. He never came in to say hello to the caretaker or his wife.

By late 2010, the caretaker was ill and wanted to retire. He notified John of his decision and indicated he would stay around for another month to teach the ropes to his replacement, but his date of retirement was firm. John never responded nor did he look for a replacement. The day after the caretaker retired, John received keys to the house in a Federal Express envelope and a long list of things that would need to be done to the house to take it out of moth balls, with a forwarding address in West Palm Beach.

John could not decide to vacate the Long Island house entirely. They certainly needed to clean the place out. The boys still had stuff there from their youth and John needed help with Grandpa's stuff. Maybe, once emptied, he could part with it.

Δ   Δ   Δ

John finally got the boys together to come clean out the Baldwin House. He invited them up over Christmas. Jadon was happy to be away from the United Nations. He needed to unwind from the intense political battles that were raging. Every two-steps forward was met with one-step back. His boss was the biggest problem. He did not seem to have a heart for the real problems they were dealing with. He never could see the life stories that were taking place behind the headlines. People were dying. People were suffering. Yet he was mostly worried about keeping the leadership unruffled and untainted.

Mikey was like a long-tailed cat in a room full of rocking chairs--intense, and taking offense at the slightest provocation. John wondered if Mikey was headed for the same fate as Clarissa. Perhaps they should be locked up together soon?

Would crazy Mikey cause Clarissa to relapse? Probably. But what did John care? He had his own life now and with Junior dead he had all that wealth to himself. He could toss the keys to the sanitarium into the East River and never have to think about either of them again.

By the end of the week, each of the boys had packed or tossed out their personal belongings. Neither wanted to keep much from their childhood, but for different reasons. Jadon did not have much space in his apartment. He had already taken the most important things from his life--fond memories of a good childhood. Despite family trouble and adversity, it was still good.

Mikey did not want to keep anything, because he did not care. His father forced him to come, forced him to look through all this crap. He did not have any use for any of it. They were just reminders of a bad life. His mother never loved him. She ran off to Africa rather than deal with him. She ran off to Washington. Then she ran out to a sanitarium to get away from him. Anything they gave him was to compensate for her being away--a peace offering, where there was no peace. He did not accept them then and he sure as hell was not going to accept them now. It could all go into the dumpster, for all he cared. And it did.

They would work a while, then take walks or swim in the

freezing bay, or nap. They took a break on New Year's Day 2011. Jadon and John watched a little football. Mikey just stared out the window. They talked about visiting Clarissa, but never bothered. John hired someone to bring in meals, and New Year's Day was a feast. They picked at the food all day long.

On January 2, John announced it was time to tackle Junior's things. He wanted them to keep anything that had meaning for them. He advised them to look through them carefully. They weren't in a rush. There were notebooks, letters, cards, awards, plaques, trophies, and letters of commendation. There were the boy's old report cards and pictures from their youth; photos of dogs, faithful companions from years past; unmarked photographs of people long forgotten.

Jadon asked, "Dad, what is that marker out back with Grandma? The 'Ruth' one".

Mikey burst in, "Probably his bastard daughter." His maniacal laugh gave them both the creeps. They thought he had not been listening.

"No, Ruthie was the daughter of a good friend. They may have been lovers, I do not remember. She was not his. He thought he may have contributed to her death."

"Really? Where did you get that?," asked Jadon.

"He wrote about it. He wrote about many disturbing things. He had a prior life. A life we never knew about and couldn't imagine. He wrote about himself and he wrote about his father. Two volumes. I am not sure if it was fictional or not, but if they were true, there were many incriminating details in both books. I doubt he wanted you to see them before, but you might as well see them now."

John went to the bookcase and found the special compartment where Junior kept them--out of the way from most books, but also a place where they would not get lost, even once he was gone. He handed one volume to each of his sons.

Both sat for hours mesmerized by the two volumes, detailing two lives.

Jadon found the writings about Senior interesting, but he had not known him or the circumstances in which he lived. It was like reading a novel about an explorer from long ago--interesting, but not particularly relevant. There was nothing to be done with the information. For him the writing about Junior was disturbing. It was also disorienting. Here was the secret life of a man he had known. However, the man portrayed here and the one he knew were so different he could not reconcile how it could be the same man. Again, he came away not entirely disbelieving it as fiction, but unknowing how to respond.

Mikey, on the other hand, absorbed the details. He was awakened by what he read. He saw here his own feelings and his own hidden life. He knew his mother and he were being punished for the sins of the past. So this was how God was getting vengeance on the Millwoods! He was stomping out every vestige of sin and wrongdoing. His grandfather had killed hundreds; it was time for God to repay. He had spared his father and his brother.

Mikey was willing to get back his mother's sanity, for the right price. God was waiting for the necessary sacrifice on their behalf. What could he do?

$$\Delta \qquad \Delta \qquad \Delta$$

Jadon had carefully read the two volumes and set them aside. They were disturbing. Mikey could not put them down. Late in the evening, John tried to get them away from him, but he raged, "Get away from me!" and retreated to his bedroom. He read them all night, slowly running through each detail. He read and he reread. He spent most of the time on his grandfather's volume. It explained so much, in his mind. His eyes were sore from the hours spent looking over the material. His eyes were being opened. About four in the morning, spent and exhausted, he fell asleep.

Mikey dreamed he was falling from the sky and dropping feet first into the ocean.

As his feet pierced the surface, it felt warm. He realized he was landing in an ocean of liquid chocolate. In slow motion, the velocity of his fall took his head under the water and then he realized something was wrong. Dreadfully wrong. It was not chocolate at all but old, dirty, warm motor oil. He was in the Gulf of Mexico, where he had been working on a BP oilrig. It had exploded in a fiery ball and he had been propelled away, mile after mile, catapulted end over end. He popped to the surface and tried to wipe his eyes and mouth, but everything was covered with dirty oil. His eyes covered, his hands covered. He struggled to look in each direction and could not see land. His eyes stung and the smell was overwhelming. He did not know which way to swim. The oil was heavy and pulling him down. He struggled to move and with every effort, he was straining against the thick, black, smelly oil. He couldn't make any progress. He swam and swam, getting nowhere. He was being pulled down, deeper and deeper. He was sputtering oil out of his mouth, choking with oil. He struggled just to keep his head above the surface. He struggled to bob to the surface to spit out the dirty oil. He was swallowing oil. He realized he could not escape from drowning. He wanted to give up, just to let himself sink below the surface, gasp the oil into his lungs, and be done with it all.

He woke up gasping for air. He realized God was trying to kill him as a debt for the family's sins. A debt was owed so others may live.

Δ   Δ   Δ

Mikey saw the whole ugly landscape of disasters his family had caused and how they had benefited from the deaths!

He lay in a bed, in comfort, surrounded by the beauty of nature. All this wealth, privilege, and comfort was at the cost of other people. His great-grandfather and grandfather had killed many. Each family member's life was a lie. Everything the family represented was untrue, devious, unearned, and undeserved. It was all there in black and white--the words penned by his own grandfather. The family history was of scheming and squashing enemies. They had stepped on the backs of the innocent to reach the heights of fame and fortune. They had gotten law degrees at prestigious universities, but their lives had been about injustice. They nearly attained the White House, through deception and misdeeds. They were at the United Nations exposing moral debauchery that caused millions to die, while their own debauchery lay hidden.

Mikey felt unclean. His family deeds were now reaching into his body; strangling the life out of him, it had wrapped fingers around his soul, and would not let go. Was there no way to atone for the family sin? Was there no way to come clean? How could he redeem his family?

His mother was so sick; being killed by her sins and the sins of her father. His father had turned on her. He kept her locked up, in her personal jail, with a lock on the door and the key around his neck. There was no reason for her to be there any longer. Couldn't everyone see what he was doing? I can free her.

His little brother is the innocent one here. He does not know the good he can do. He needs to break through to complete his destiny in life. He can prosecute those war crimes and bring evil men to justice, but he must be freed in order to do that. He cannot have blood on his own hands, and still bring the evil doers to justice. When he raises his hand in the courtroom to point out those that are guilty, there cannot be blood dripping from his own hand.

Mikey started to put a plan into action. He thought about this \for hours. It had to start at the Triangle. He had to announce it to the world in the most dramatic way possible. He had to show God his sacrifice to redeem his family. He knew that the Asch Building was now the Brown Building of Science at New York University. The place of his grandfather's greatest murders was now a place of science and learning. He needed to think about this a bit. Perhaps he could get a job at NYU. He did not have the science background to work there, but somehow he must get in. Could he work for a company that contracts for janitorial service? Could he work for a security company? Where would he gain fullest access to the facility?

Soon after New Year's Day, Mikey walked through the Waverly Building entrance. He thought this was a long shot and had already thought of two other ways of getting in.

Waverly and Brown buildings share a city block with the Silver Center at New York University. In the middle of the building, just west of the Waverly elevators, sat John Roosevelt Peters, Manager of Security Services. He was not happy to be there.

Over the Christmas holiday, there had been malicious mischief in the Waverly Building and after he had fired three employees that morning, he was instantly short staffed.

Until he could hire replacements he had three options. Hire a security company to come in (and blow his budget). Have the remaining staff work overtime (and blow his budget). Or personally staff one of the Centers security desks until he could hire replacements. He chose to staff the least trafficked desk.

"I would like an employment application."

Peters looked him over. He was well-built; just what he was looking for. "Are you the guy Ralph was talking about?"

Mikey didn't know anyone named Ralph, but replied, "Yes."

"I can't make it a permanent position."

"Okay."

"But I am short handed and can expedite things for a

temporary position. When could you start?"

"Now."

"We can make it week-to-week. If things work out, I may be able to make it permanent."

"Okay."

"I assume Ralph has told you all about the position?"

"Yeah."

"Any questions?"

"No."

"Have you ever done work like this?"

"Yes."

"What were you, a wrestler?"

"Swimmer. Diver."

"You look like you are in good shape, not that it requires much." Peters laughed and patted his stomach. "Basically you just sit here and make sure everyone has a badge from the school. You also answer questions if tourists wander in. Generally they come over from the park, looking for a restroom. Once an hour, you rotate. And one of you walks all the halls and stairways to the top of the Silver. All three buildings. If anything happens, you go and chase people away that shouldn't be there."

"Okay."

Peters thought, well, if he is a friend of Ralph's, he must be Okay. "Think this is something you would want to do for a few weeks? It's a couple bucks an hour over minimum wage."

"Yeah."

He handed him an application. "Fill this out. Come back here at 8 a.m. tomorrow. Bring your social security card and we'll get you a drug test."

It was almost too easy. He thought, I need to be on my best behavior. The evening he received the master key he had a duplicate made.

3C

Each year since 1911, community activists, labor unions, and the fire department had stoked embers of that original fire. They have made sure the lives lost were not lost in vain.[xxxvi]

In the early days, trade unions were the standard bearers showing the world what had occurred.

Legislative hearings about the fire lingered and sputtered. Outrage waned. Humane workplace regulations mired in committee hearings. Nothing was having an impact on people at greatest risk. By an eyelash, the fire led to legislation improving industrial safety standards. Great advances in labor law and public safety rose from the ashes. Alfred E. Smith rode to the steps of the White House on the issue; but not in, due to prejudice over his Catholicism. Even today, these advances are worth celebrating.

Since the fiftieth anniversary of the fire, there have been annual commemorations on Washington Place, in front of the Brown Building of Science on New York University campus. Hundreds have attended to watch as city firefighters on Turnable Ladder Trucks laid wreaths on the Brown Building. They listened to speeches, choirs, drums and cranky public address systems, echoing against the buildings on Washington Place.

The building still stands--ten-stories high (135 feet tall) located just east of Washington Square Park. As it was designed to do, it survived the horrific fire. But it could not escape the stigma; the shadows that followed it made it difficult to lease. It was renamed The Greenwich Building, but still could not dodge its past. Frederick Brown, real estate speculator and philanthropist, bought the building and donated the structure to the University in 1929.

Except for the ground floor, the exterior is mostly as it stood one hundred years ago. The building is plain. Symmetrical, unevenly spaced windows face Greene Street and Washington Place, with small ledges and vertical brickwork where employees clung for the last few seconds of their lives. The top floor carries fluted, Ionic pilasters and arches, as if to dress up the original executive workspace.

Refurbished into state-of-the-art science and technology space during the 1962 renovation, little of the original interior exists today. Of course, pillars and the twelve-foot ceilings can still easily be seen. Ironically, one of the original, narrow, 33-inch stairways still exists--turned into an extra fire escape route should the nearly six foot wide staircases added in the 1962 renovation prove inadequate.

Greene Street still displays rutted cobblestones, where fire wagons helplessly stood on a warm Saturday afternoon nearly a hundred years earlier.

As the centennial anniversary of the tragedy approached, an exhibition of the fire, graduate courses at two universities, better commemorative plaques, artwork, and a larger celebration was planned by the all-volunteer organization, The Triangle Waist Factory Fire Centennial Commemoration Cooperative (known as "3C") was hoping five hundred people would attend.

Δ Δ Δ

The 3C had applied with the city to block off Washington Place from Greene Street to University Place.

On the east end, in front of the Brown Building of Science, they planned risers for a choir and a platform for an orchestra. In the center of the platform, a podium for speakers was designed facing seating for six-hundred.

Behind the seating, exhibit space was designated for various groups, including labor unions, New York Fire Department, New York University and other colleges, artists, and political organizations.

They planned to set up a stage on the far west end of the street, in front of NYU's Silver Center Main Building (formerly the American Book Building) next to Washington Square Park, where actors would reenact principals in the tragedy--the owners of the factory, Alfred E. Smith, Socialist/Progressive speakers, and Union Dignitaries of the age.

Between the exhibits and the stage, food vendors would offer plentiful fare.

The 3C researched families affected by the tragedy and had looked for four families to represent the hardships and the successes that came out of the tragic fire. A family who had lost three members was first chosen. In another family, a descendent became a prominent member of the labor movement. A third family had a prominent scientist who had been inspired to learn more about building science and how to make structures not only fireproof, but also safe for the occupants.

The last family was the Millwoods. The archives included references to how R. J. Millwood had been instrumental in implementing legislation Alfred E. Smith proposed and brought into being. He had escaped the fire personally but lost his dear, beloved wife. He achieved prominence in city government as a guardian to the memory of the victims of the Triangle Waist Company factory fire. He achieved high office as right hand man to the Mayor.

Through the Society page in one of the New York City newspapers, they located Jadon Atwater, Junior Millwood's grandson--a United Nation's dignitary and the perfect candidate to speak at the centennial.

Δ   Δ   Δ

The 3C aimed high. They sent a delegation to ask Mayor Michael Bloomberg to serve as their Master of Ceremonies and were granted an audience.[xxxvii]

Bloomberg had questions. "I need to know, who will be speaking? What will their speeches entail? Who are the neighborhood organizers?"

Here was an opportunity to host a diverse group of citizens in recognition of a significant event in the country's history. To honor the lost souls from the tragedy was to honor the progress his city had made.

He excused the 3C with handshakes all around, "Thank you for coming. A staff member will get more details. I will give you my answer then."

"Thank you for spending time with us. We hope you will consider our request favorably." They appreciated he had taken time to meet with them.

His advisers would take a good look at the list. His representatives in the Police and Fire Departments would give their opinions. His public relations group would provide their advice. Only then would he send a letter formally accepting their offer. As they left, he thought to himself, what could possibly go wrong?

Δ   Δ   Δ

At the United States Department of Labor, Hilda Solis' staff monitored the workings of labor unions. It had come up on a tickler in March 2010 that the one-hundredth anniversary of the Triangle Waist Company factory fire was a year away. The staffer assigned was not intimately familiar with the fire, so she did some research. What she found was amazing. This event was a pivotal piece of labor history.

"It sparked legislative activity that effects us today." She told her boss, "We all owe a great debt to the work that was done in the aftermath of the fire".

She also thought this event could be a good political opportunity for the Secretary of Labor.

The staffer contacted the New York City Mayor's Office to see what was being planned. Not much had occurred by that point. There were a few things in the works, like most years, and a couple add-on activities, such as an exhibit and classes at New York University.

She asked to be kept posted if the centennial celebration grew to a place where the Secretary of Labor might be asked to make an appearance.

Her contact in the Mayor's Office just laughed. "Maybe they'll get two hundred people out for it. Three hundred if they offer free beer to the college students."

She hung up expecting never to hear about it again.

Three months later, she received a surprise phone call.

"The mayor is going to emcee the Triangle thing?"

"The what?"

"The Triangle Waistshirt or Waistcoat fire. You know the factory fire we talked about some time ago."

"Oh, uh huh."

"Anyway, he is going to appease the trade unions and community groups by being master of ceremonies."

"Where?"

"In front of the building where the fire happened."

"How many are they expecting?"

"Four to five hundred."

"Really."

"Who is handling the invites?"

"Some community group. Call themselves '3C'."

"I doubt the boss will want to come, but just in case, can you get her on the podium."

"Speaker or dignitary?"

"Let's assume speaker, if she wants. I'd leave it up to her."

"Not a big deal. The mayor can get whatever he wants on this."

"Great. I'll write up a brief. It's doubtful she'll come, but you never know."

Upon reading the brief, Secretary Solis was not particularly impressed. But it was New York City, and that was never bad duty. The Mayor was playing emcee, so that was a plus. In politics, you never know when you might need a job, she thought.

She toyed with it, before putting it into the "maybe" pile. A few weeks later, she was scanning her schedule for months in advance with her secretary. "I wouldn't bother speaking at the event." She thought to herself she did not have any high profile appearances in March.

"It wouldn't hurt to have a photo op with the mayor and the New York City labor union folks."

Still it was only 400-500 people. She reluctantly stuck it in the "yes" pile.

She whispered to her assistant, "There are so many places to eat and shop it can't be an entire loss." They both smiled.

It is customary at the White House for the chief of staff's office to maintain a synopsis of calendars for cabinet members--primarily to know what everyone is doing and when people would not make cabinet meetings.

White House Chief of Staff Rahm Emanuel asked for more

information on the Triangle Waist Company event. Although he had some knowledge of the fire, he was not sure why the Secretary of Labor was bothering.

Things were not pretty for the President. He was being attacked from the right for spending too much; that was to be expected, and not too bothersome. But even James Carville was blasting him. He was being attacked from the left for not being more progressive. He was being blamed for the slow response to the BP disaster in the Gulf of Mexico. His team was accused of being disorganized. He was being blasted for his efforts in the Middle East. He was losing Senators and Representatives left and right. With mid-term elections six weeks away, it was not looking pretty.

Emanuel received the additional information he requested--his eyes brightened. He stuck the material in his pile marked "Axelrod". He had his differences with the senior adviser to the President, David Axelrod, and was looking forward to leaving the White House soon. The right opportunity was looking promising. Getting away from Washington was a bonus. A week from Friday he was announcing his resignation to run for Mayor of Chicago.

"Well, it shows support for the labor unions."

"Yes and a solid social cause."

"Shows respect for the victims. Moves us off that Arlington thing." He was speaking of the President skipping the speech at Arlington National Cemetery the previous Memorial Day.

"How hard can this be?"

"How big is it gonna be?"

"Six hundred is what they have planned."

"With POTUS, it goes to twenty grand, easy."

"Can we get it moved to Yankee Stadium?"

"With our luck, the Yankees will be playing the Nationals."

"Will Strasberg be back to pitching by then? Is he a Democrat?"

"You are brutal."

"Yankee Stadium would be too big. But, ya know, this place is right next to Washington Square Park. They could probably get four to five grand in there if they had to."

"Forget the numbers. Have you been there? They have our answer to Paris' Arc de Triomphe there."

Axelrod spun around his chair to do an image search on the Internet. He read the text next to the image, "At the Centennial of Washington's first inauguration as President of the United States, a wooden Memorial Arch was constructed in Washington Square Park. In May of 1895, a seventy-seven foot tall marble arch was christened on the north side of the park. Two large sculptures of Washington were later added on the north side of the monument."

They looked at the images on the computer screen.

Emanuel said, "A softball event, focused on labor unions and social issues, and a great television visual backdrop. Lay a wreath, say a few words, and pump up the progressives in Greenwich Village".

"The upside is so-so, but I don't see any downsides."

"I'll ask the boss."

SECRET SERVICE

When the leadership of the 3C heard the Mayor was inviting the Secretary of Labor, they were ecstatic!

"Think he will really come?"

They missed on two points. The Secretary of Labor was a woman and she had asked the mayor if she could attend.

They were amazed when rumors started flying that the President might attend. Of course, everyone thought it was a rumor.

The mayor already knew better. "Shit! Any chance of backing out?"

"Not now."

"Do you know what this means?"

"Of course, our little group of citizens meaning to honor a few victims is about to get trampled."

"Yep."

"They are not gonna know what hit them."

"Did you ask the White House who he thinks is paying for all this?"

The Secret Service hijacked a conference room on the sixth floor of the Bobst Library at New York University for a planning meeting with a handful of White House staffers. They also invited school and city officials.

"How about the little R's?" He was referring to Renaissance (Michelle), Radiance (Malia), and Rosebud (Sasha).

"No, just Renegade (Barack Obama) is going to the party."

"Okay. We'll get satellite photos and surveillance video, and talk to you next Monday."

The Mayor exploded, "Let's not go crazy here. I can answer that one: No, you are not asking NYU to shut down for the day. Look, the thing is taking place late in the day. Most classes will be over. Most students will either be trying to get into the event or staying as far away as possible."

"I don't know," responded the Secret Service Agent.

"I do. Look, I am letting you lock down twenty blocks around the school. Metal detectors. Landing spot for Marine One. Security area at Kennedy for Air Force One. Police on four motorcade routes. You are getting your snipers on all the surrounding buildings and the trees in the park, counter snipers everywhere, canine explosive detection units, and emergency response teams. We are even stopping phase 2 construction in the park immediately. You can do whatever you want with the Coast Guard patrols; just don't block any boat traffic. I do not think you are going to need it. You know, we have a pretty damn good counter-terrorism group right here. My non-negotiables are increased railroad security and more extensive road closures. Those two are over the top. Oh, and I almost forgot, I'm buying him and his entourage lunch at the Mayor's mansion. What more do you want?"

The 3C leaders freaked out as they listened to the Secret Service team and representatives from the mayor's office run through the details.

Their little program was slipping away. It had been moved from in front of the Brown Building to the arch at Washington Square Park. Seating had gone from five hundred to five thousand in a big triangle shape around the fountain. Invitations were at the prerogative of the White House, though they were encouraged to submit a small list who would be investigated by the FBI, Secret Service, and White House staff. Television cameras and the press would be placed behind the fountain. The whole block would be secured with two entrances to the park through metal detectors--one for attendees and one for dignitaries. The dog park was to be taken over for exclusive use by bomb smelling K-9 units. The vendors and art exhibits were left on the street away from the President.

The solemn little commemoration began to feel like a national convention. There were requests by the White House to reduce the number of speakers, to eliminate any Republicans, Tea Party, or Independents. Larger labor unions, not involved with garment workers, were pressing to be included on the podium as speakers.

As they left, one agent remarked, "Be happy it's not a 'NIS-EE'. Do you know what a National Special Security Event is?"

"No."

"Well, if you get enough important people together--like the President and the whole line of succession. Or a large group of folks that would make it especially attractive to terrorists, like the Super Bowl. Or something of special significance, like a historical event or like the G8 Summit, they declare it a 'NIS-EE'."

"So."

"Do you know how many people there are in the Secret Service?"

"No."

"Over six grand."

"My gosh!"

"And a 'NIS-EE' means they all come to dinner. When a NSSE is declared, the Secret Service takes over everything and a dozen other federal agencies jump into the game. You'll be filling out forms in triplicate four weeks in advance in order to get permission to take a crap."

"If the Secret Service had their way, they would build a forty-mile wide moat around the Castle (White House), rimmed by heavy artillery", whispered one White House staffer under her breath.

Overhearing her comment, a 3C leader sitting next to her replied, "Right now, they were doing their best to do that in the middle of Manhattan."

Δ   Δ   Δ

As with everything Jadon did, he took writing this speech seriously. He wanted to know more about Moira and honor a woman he never met, but had spent time by her grave near the large maple tree at the Baldwin House. He wished to know more of Moira. Of course, the speech was going to need to be delicately handled. He had his grandfather's confession to having started the fire. This fact was not relevant to his speech or the special memorial, but it nagged at him. His grandfather was being portrayed as some kind of hero and he would not have wanted that. As far as Junior was concerned, what happened happened; there was no use hurting more people in what could never be undone.

This event was not about the Millwoods. It was about a tragedy and all the good that arose from the ashes. He visited websites and talked to his parents. He contacted Dr. Lynne P. Brown at New York University and toured the facility with Regina Drew and Maria Skouras to get a greater sense of the building itself and what the victims had faced.

He poured over old newspaper articles from the day of the fire to beyond the trial of the owners of the Triangle Waist Company. He read the newspaper editorials and was disgusted to see the owners paid $75 per victim for funeral expenses (under eleven thousand dollars in total), while receiving two hundred thousand dollars in the insurance settlement. They were acquitted of criminal culpability through the handiwork of a slick lawyer.

With the help of his staff, he honed and tuned it, until he had a speech to be proud of--it honored the victims and challenged the audience to redouble their efforts in fighting for social justice.

When it was nearly done, a White House staffer asked whom he would like to invite to attend. This was a courtesy extended to all speakers. He thought his parents would enjoy the speech. His mother would be interested in learning more about Junior's first wife. He did not know if his father would permit his mother to attend. His father told him about the times he spent out at the sanitarium visiting her and Jadon could tell his father still loved her. He doubted his brother would come, but he added all three of their names to the list the White House requested.

The speech was very good.

Δ   Δ   Δ

The morning of March 23 was bright and clear without a cloud in the sky. Mikey reported to his workstation promptly at 7:30 a.m. He wore his tan security-shirt and brown pants. Students were already wandering in for their 8 o'clock classes.

Chester lifted off the chair in the security stand at the main entrance to the Silver Center while he said, "Good Morning". He got no reply from Mikey, which was not unusual. Mikey had a lot on his mind. Chester had just completed his shift. He was ready for breakfast, a hot shower, and bed. He was not looking for small talk.

Students wandered by while Mikey was expressionless. Every hour he rotated to another security station in the Silver Center complex. After four hours, it was his turn to wander the halls and have his lunch break. He started on the ground floor and walked the halls of the Silver, Waverly, and Brown buildings. He made sure that all doors that should be locked were and all doors that should be unlocked were. There was no graffiti or piles of trash, and fire exits were not blocked. He made sure students were not getting into trouble. He took his time as he wandered the halls, using a different staircase every time he ascended to the next floor.

All was in order. When he got to the tenth floor, he checked the roof access. He tried his key in the door. It unlocked. He relocked it. He was now free to get his lunch. As he walked to the cafeteria, he thought how much he would miss this place.

Mikey got off work at five. He thought how much he wanted to take a swim after work, the way he did most nights. However, tonight's swim was to be special. He got into his VW Beetle, exited the parking lot, and began driving toward Baldwin.

Just before midnight, Mikey drove back. He dropped off something at the corner of the Brown Building, before entering the Silver Center. Chester was at the main security desk. "I didn't expect to see you this early." Mikey scanned his badge and walked in without saying a word. Chester thought, must have something to do with that letter. Mikey went to the Brown Building and let himself into a conference room on the eighth floor. He was careful to lock the door behind him. He lay on the floor and tried to sleep. Dawn felt like an eternity away.

Δ   Δ   Δ

All staff members working at the Brown Building of Science had received a letter telling them the Secret Service would begin securing the building at 8:00 on the morning of March 24, 2011.

As dawn broke over the city that day, Mikey knew his Olympic moment had come. It was the moment he trained for all his life.

He visualized his dive and heard Bob Costas' voice announcing his name. He saw the NBC graphics below his image on the television screen: John Michael 'Mikey' Atwater of Baldwin, NY. He was so focused on his dive, he only heard a smattering of Costas' monologue in the background as he went through his motions. He took off his security uniform and tossed it to the deck. Standing there in red, white, and blue swim trunks, he paused before mounting the platform. "--now preparing for the dive of his life--" He stood and closed his eyes, watching his dive unfold in slow motion. He saw beautiful balance and grace as he pushed himself high into the air. "This is to redeem his family."

He saw the pinnacle of the arc as gravity pulled him downward. He saw his arms stretching forward to cut into the water. "--with this dive he is paying the ultimate price--" He saw his body in perfect, vertical form. He saw himself entering the water with hardly a splash. "--he is freeing his family of their sins--"

He felt the streaming water caressing him as he slid through the surface. Those long fingers he had experienced so many times before were sliding along his body in slow motion. "--he is sacrificing himself that his parents and his brother might be redeemed--" He felt the sensuous caresses of Mother Nature. He knifed through the surface and reached a moment of suspension, where he was weightless. "Greater love hath no man than this--" It seemed to take an eternity. He was at the point where the force of inertia from his dive matched the buoyancy of his body in the water.

He turned his body around to face upward. "--that a man lay down his life for his friends." He could see the sun above him and he clawed toward heaven to pierce the calm surface and gasp for breath. He was ready to make his dive--it would be done in a few seconds.

At the top of the Brown Building, they found his security-clothing scattered about. He had carefully climbed in the dawn over the ventilation equipment, over the additional science monitors and laboratory paraphernalia, to the cornice at the southeast corner of the building.

At the corner of the building on the sidewalk, where Washington Place meets Greene Street, they found three items. Each was individually and carefully wrapped in heavy plastic. The three items were stacked one upon the other--one letter and two books.

△   △   △

Jadon was wearing sweats and a tee shirt. He had just finished his morning workout--an hour of rowing and weight lifting. The door to his balcony was open. It was a lovely morning, bright and sunny. In his left hand, he had a glass of orange juice, and his right hand held a mug of tea. His newspapers had already been laid out for him on the balcony table. He grabbed the sports page of *The New York Times* first. Each day, before work, he read five newspapers: *New York Daily News*, *New York Post*, *The New York Times*, *The Washington Post*, and *The Washington Times*. With all the duplications in stories, it took him just over an hour. He took *The Wall Street Journal* with him to read during lunch. His manservant replenished his tea as needed.

He quickly shaved, showered, and dressed. He loved it when he walked into the United Nations and overheard whispers of "Silver Fox". He was quite the presence.

"You have a nine o'clock with Mr. Moreno."

"Thank You." He hardly needed the reminder. He dreaded this weekly meeting with his boss. Jean Luis Moreno was a consummate politician--a progress-killer. He protected the status quo at all costs. He was there to make sure the Secretary-General was not surprised. If nothing ever happened, there could never be a surprise.

The meeting with Moreno was as dreadful as ever. He wanted reports on everything, no matter how menial. Next week's meeting would be the same--report progress followed by new assignments to report on progress, to make sure there was not any.

When Jadon protested, Moreno claimed his English wasn't that good.

Jadon had once even protested to Secretary-General of the United Nations, Ban Ki-moon. He got a chuckle and a sympathetic handshake.

"Jadon, you are doing great. You know he is just trying to protect the institution. Just bear this, as you have been doing. When the right issue comes up and you need to bypass Jean Luis, give me a call."

Ban's vote of confidence helped.

Jadon and Ban had a close connection since the Darfur conflict. At Jadon's prompting, Ban had pressured Sudanese President Omar al-Bashir to allow UN peacekeeping troops to enter Sudan. They had celebrated the success together over champagne one evening at Jadon's apartment.

Jadon walked out of his meeting with Moreno with a massive headache. His secretary followed him into his office carrying a mug of tea and two ibuprofen.

"Sir."

"Oh, thank you. How did you--"

"You always have a headache after your meeting with him."

He laughed. He popped the pills into his mouth and took a swig of the tea.

"Your meeting at eleven with Mr. Shaw has been rescheduled. So you have a free hour. Lunch is with Mr. Rawden. One-thirty staff meeting in the Gray Conference Room."

"Thank you. No calls until Rawden comes by."

She pulled the door shut as he laid down on the couch.

He rested a while and then read *The Wall Street Journal.*

After his staff meeting, Jadon asked his secretary to bring in his appointment calendar. There was something he was forgetting, but he could not place his finger on it.

He had a number of telephone calls to make before the end of the day. He had to check the status of a few cases.

At a quarter until six, his secretary opened his door. He was standing behind his desk, reading intently. "If there isn't anything else, Sir, I will be leaving."

"Thank you, Marilyn, that will be all."

After a big lunch with Roger Rawden, he was planning just a salad for dinner. He reached into his pants pocket to see what cash he had. He flipped open his money clip. He had more cash than he thought. He counted the bills and when he got to the middle of the folded over bills, he saw the claim slip.

He turned to look at the clock.

"Shit!" He grabbed his coat and left the office running, passing Marilyn before she had gotten to the elevator.

Δ   Δ   Δ

How could he have forgotten? He beat himself up. He would have sent one of his assistants, but by the time he did that, they would probably have closed. He ran through the streets dodging traffic. There were a few horn beeps and a few drivers flipped him the bird. Most could see he was in a hurry and didn't bother. The dry cleaners closed at 6 sharp. He grabbed the door as the proprietor was about to close it and slip his key into the lock. The clerk said, "You're in luck; I haven't cashed out the register." (He was thinking and wishing he was saying, "Too late, Asshole!") Jadon handed him his claim receipt. "Thanks!"

This was his favorite suit, which he had worn the day before when a waitress slid a whole container of bleu cheese dressing onto his trousers. Though he was not generally superstitious, he considered it his lucky suit--a bespoke double-breasted, navy blue, pin-striped suit made from choice worsted wool. It was the ideal suit for television.

A few minutes later, the man returned. "Heavy starch on the shirt. Suit coat, suit pants, tie. That will be $16.25."

Just then, Jadon's cell phone rang. He tossed down a hundred dollar bill, thankful he had made it and the clerk was not a prick about him being a few minutes late. He mouthed, "Keep it!"

The man looked in amazement, smiling to himself.

"Hello."

"Mr. Atwater?"

"Speaking." He wondered how a stranger had his personal cell phone number.

"My name is Detective Lieutenant Bill Wilkinson."

Earlier that day, March 24, 2011, Bill had completed his investigation at the scene. The body had been transported by ambulance to the First Avenue Office of the Chief Medical Examiner. There was no need for speed or siren. The body was taken through the loading bay on 30th Street and Wilkinson caught up with it as the Doctor watched the attendants peel back the body bag.

"What are you doing to me, Bill? Nice Speedo, huh?"

"Sorry, I don't dress 'em, just investigate."

"Anything suspicious?"

"No."

"Do you think you could have mangled him more for me, Bill? You gotta take better care of my precious bodies before you deliver 'em."

He paused to look at the mangled pile of flesh. Unrecognizable.

She continued, "Diving head first from 100 feet up will do that to your scalp. Note?"

"Yeah. Kinda bizarre. Letter to God and two, old handwritten books near impact point. Confessions or something, by somebody else. Perhaps all fiction. Clothing scattered around from where he jumped. Security badge. I'm gonna grab an office and be here a while."

"Dove."

"What?"

"Dove. He dove. He did not jump. He dove. He intentionally went headfirst into the pavement."

"Jezz-us. Nut case?"

"Probably. We'll run the biologicals. Maybe we'll get some tox, but I am guessing straight nut case. With no evidence of foul play, I think we are looking at a suicide. Did he have a wallet?"

"In his Speedos?"

She had to smile and shake her head. He got her this time.

He knew it too, so he went on, "Wallet was with the clothing on the roof. Telephone number and name of next of kin, well, his brother at least, was with the suicide note. He sure planned this thing out."

"I guess."

"I wonder if he planned on the President being there tomorrow?"

"What?"

"The President. He is going to be there tomorrow. Some commemoration. Triangle Waist Company factory fire."

He held up a flier about the event.

"Secret Service was setting up while we were investigating. They wanted our boy, your little mess, off the street pronto and the street washed down immediately."

"So how did he get onto the roof?"

"Easy. He worked there--security."

Δ   Δ   Δ

Detective Wilkinson escorted Jadon into the viewing room. He was reluctant to pull back the curtain. The room was harshly lit, with a wastebasket, chairs, bottled water, and Kleenex. It smelled of formaldehyde and antiseptic. Out of curiosity, Dr. Simonton, bespectacled and wearing a lab coat, strolled into the autopsy room to see the handsome, immaculately dressed man who had been summoned to try to identify the body.

"We have positioned the body as best we could. There is great distortion due to the impact. He dove from a considerable height."

"Where?"

"What?"

"Where did he dive from?"

"Top of the Brown Building at NYU, where he worked."

"It is likely it is him."

Astonished, Wilkinson asked, "What? How would you know that?"

"Our family has a history with that building. Go ahead and open the curtain. Let's get this over with."

Wilkinson opened the curtain. They had unwrapped the plastic from the body in the cold basement.

There was no way to identify the body in its present state.

"He has a birthmark on his left side. There it is."

There was no way he could have identified the body from that birthmark, it was too mangled.

Wilkinson studied Jadon's face. He did not kill him. He knows, maybe instinctively, the body belongs to his brother. He had no doubt.

"I'm sorry for your loss."

"He was very ill."

"I have something he wanted you to have."

They walked back to the office where Wilkinson had been reviewing the suicide note and the two books for most of the day.

"Technically, I should probably be keeping all this stuff. And I should not be giving this to you at all." He handed him a photocopy of the suicide note. He kept the original.

"His suicide note and these two books were individually wrapped in heavy plastic. I guess he was worried about them being splattered. They were stacked together, with the note on top. It is at my discretion to determine whether the note and the books have anything to do with each other, and the suicide."

He paused.

"I am ruling the books don't and releasing them to you as next of kin. But we are not gonna bother with any paperwork on this, got me?"

Jadon nodded.

"I read through some of the two books. It is either a fiction or confessions to a bunch of highly indictable crimes."

Jadon nodded again.

"Since the subject of the stories was your grandfather and great-grandfather, and they are both unavailable to defend themselves, I am going to assume it is all fictions and fantasies. I don't want any crap from having done this. Got me?"

"Okay." Jadon did not know what to say next.

"You are free to take these books with you, or you are welcome to stay here in this office. I don't need it until tomorrow."

"Why?"

"What?"

"Why? Why are you doing this? Why are you giving me these two books?"

He stepped back and answered quietly, "I believe, no matter how disturbed they are we should grant a person's last wish. You'll read about it in that copy I gave you. He wanted you to have the books. Said you might need them for your speech tomorrow."

"What?"

"For your speech tomorrow."

"Shit."

Δ   Δ   Δ

Jadon sat at the morgue through the night and into the day reading. Slowly, carefully, he read through both volumes. Then he read the letter. He digested Mikey's words. Now he understood what Mikey was doing, or at least what Mikey thought he was doing.

Tears streamed down Jadon's face. He walked by the curtained room where he had last seen Mikey and affectionately knocked on the window as he went by.

At about three that afternoon, Jadon fetched his suit and asked if there was somewhere he could wash up. Of course, they had a full locker room and shower facility. He showered quickly and dressed. He asked to borrow a hairbrush. A friendly man returned quickly and handed him the brush, "Don't worry; it hasn't been used on a stiff. It's mine."

He ran out the main door and immediately hailed a cab. He emptied his pocket of the speech he worked so hard to create, dumped it into a trashcan, and walked to the cab.

He told the cabbie, "Washington Square Park."

"Are you crazy? Do you know what is going on there today? Do you know who is speaking there?"

"Yes, I am."

He tossed three one-hundred dollar bills through the cab's security window and gave the driver his credentials and identification. He told the driver to come in from the north side of the park through the barriers and blockades to the Washington Arch Security Area.

CENTENNIAL

President Obama flew to JFK that morning, arriving shortly after noon. He was whisked by Motorcade to Gracie Mansion. They cordoned off much of Carl Schurz Park to accommodate the luncheon. It was scheduled for 1 p.m., but Presidential entourages are known for being late. They needed, however, to be at Washington Square Park well ahead of the ceremonies, scheduled for 4:30 p.m. (shortly before the time the fire had begun exactly one-hundred years earlier).

The luncheon was small, by Presidential standards. Time permitted photographs and introductions with business, union, and civic leaders who had not been invited to attend either the luncheon or the ceremony.

Before leaving for the ceremony, there was one last task. Obama had agreed to meet with Federal and New York and New Jersey State agencies to encourage settlement of the Access to the Region's Core (ARC) tunnel dispute. Reminiscent of the wrangling that proceeded *The Mill* and *The Thomas* scraping the bottom out of New York Harbor more than a century before, a billion dollar per mile project to burrow under the Hudson River between New Jersey and Manhattan was stalled--mired in lawsuits, political wrangling, finger pointing, and out of control cost overruns. One thing wasn't in dispute--the vital transportation corridor doubling commuter capacity was desperately needed. Once again, governments had failed and the economic fallout to the region could be devastating.[xxxviii]

Promptly at 3:30, the motorcade left from Gracie Mansion, drove to Washington Square Park using one of the four secure routes, and parked along the blocked-off north entrance to the Washington Square Arch.

The President and his detail bypassed the special security station set up near that point and the President was led out to the crowd who had assembled two hours earlier. Tickets were difficult to obtain and the 3C understood the trade-offs that occurred when a President attended your humble, little event. Originally, their thought was five hundred metal folding chairs. Now the plaza was filled with equipment, barriers, bunting, Secret Service Agents, K-9 patrols, electronic monitors, television cameras, and five thousand guests they had not invited.

Mayor Bloomberg seemed to enjoy the sunshine in the park and the chance to talk with old friends. His duties had been well-crafted and he played the gracious host in recognizing a seminal event in the cities history. When the time came to begin, an assistant led the Mayor to the podium, and his handlers escorted the President to his seat.

At precisely 4:30 p.m. on Friday, March 25, 2011, the mayor welcomed all in attendance to the occasion, introduced the President, dignitaries, and speakers, and asked all to rise for the playing of the National Anthem.

A twenty-person ensemble of The Greenwich Village Orchestra--mostly brass and percussion, with a few strings--played a rousing anthem to the somber crowd. The mayor led the assembled guests in the "Pledge of Allegiance." Television cameras scanned the crowd and pulled away to show shots of the Square, the massive arch, fountain, bunting, long streams of red, white, and blue balloons reaching far into the sky, the President, the Mayor, and the large crowd in the triangle shaped seating area.

The Mayor invited Rabbi Ruth Sarah Cohen of Chabad House to give the invocation. The President and Mayor placed wreaths at the foot of the podium, but were cut off when a bell was first struck. The bell was struck every twelve seconds for the next thirty-minutes, from precisely 4:45 until 5:15 p.m. (the thirty minutes the fire had raged). After striking the bell, two readers at each side of the stage alternated reading a single name slowly and precisely: from 'Lizzie Adler' through 'Berta Wondross', as each of the 146 victims was recognized, in alphabetical order. Hauntingly, six times at the end, the audience heard "Known Only to God" for souls never identified.[xxxix]

Mayor Bloomberg asked the Brooklyn Tabernacle Choir to sing two hymns. They sang "Nearer My God to Thee" and "Amazing Grace". As the television panned the podium, one dignitary's seat stood empty. Two union leaders were next.

The first talked about the great things the unions had done and how everyone needed to join with them to guarantee better wages. The second union speaker talked as if she had an audience of one: Barack Obama. It was all about what the unions had done to get him elected and how they expected payback. The crowd hissed impatiently and squirmed in their seats.

The Mayor introduced a local Fire Captain, who nervously talked about the need for maintaining fire safety, funding a well-prepared, professional firehouse, the losses of 9/11, and the Fireman's Pension Fund. There was no applause at all when he finished and stepped away from the microphone.

Next, it was time for the four families to speak.

Δ   Δ   Δ

Police were everywhere and motioned for the taxi driver to stop.

They looked inside, "We have been told to expect you."

They told the driver to pass through to the next checkpoint. They barely got through the second checkpoint, before the Mayor's Assistant opened the car door, grabbed Jadon by the sleeve, and tugged him through the metal detector.

"Sorry I am late."

"Glad you finally made it. Thought I was going to have to do a little soft-shoe myself."

Instead of going to his assigned seat on the podium, Jadon walked to the VIP area where his mother and father had been seated. He kissed and hugged them both. Then he noticed the empty chair that had been reserved there for Mikey. He spoke to them quietly, calmly. The television caught the images but not the sound. Clarissa's hand came up to her mouth. She looked shocked. She pulled out a handkerchief from her oversized bag. John stiffened stoically. Jadon placed one hand on each of their shoulders. Clarissa reached over, grabbed John by the hand, and looked into his eyes. Jadon spent a few more minutes with his parents before he turned and slowly walked to the podium to take his seat.

The Mayor had just invited a representative from the second family to come forward to say a few words. He gave Jadon a where-the-hell-have-you-been glare, but when he caught his eye he could tell some tragedy had occurred.

He mouthed the words, "You Okay?" Jadon nodded in reply. While the second family representative got up to speak, Jadon took his seat. He was lost in his thoughts and could not follow what the others said. He was jarred when he heard Mayor Bloomberg announce his name.

He slowly rose to polite applause. He did not know quite where to start, so he broke right in: "Many of you are unaware of a suicide that occurred near here yesterday morning. It was the death of the last victim of the Triangle Waist Company factory fire. The victim was my brother."

The crowd sat, stunned as Jadon recounted how his grandfather accidentally started the fire. How his wife had been among the victims. How he had kept it secret, all those years and how he had prospered afterward.

Pulling Mikey's note from his coat pocket, he started to read it,

"Dear God, I know we have all done bad. My grandfather was the worst, but I am no better. We gotta stop this thing, God--You and me. It has gone on long enough. My family has suffered for what our grandfather did. So I will make you a deal. I'll give my life as a sacrifice, if you will free my mother, my father, and my brother."

Jadon broke down and could not read any further.

Father Victor DePaolo, the Director of Campus Ministry at The Catholic Center at NYU came up to Jadon from behind, helped him to his seat, and returned to the microphone.

Δ   Δ   Δ

Father Vic, who was there to give a closing benediction, turned around and faced the audience as he collected his thoughts.

"Finally, something honest said today. I have been listening to all these speeches and am, well, appalled. I am hoping our President's speech will not continue in this disappointing vain. But here we finally have something honest said. Thank you,

Jadon.

"Jadon, on behalf of God, I accept Mikey's request. I do not have the authority to do so, but the loving, caring Heavenly Father I know, who is all wise, will know how to redeem this situation.

"God looks at the heart of man. In Mikey, He would have seen a sincere, if misguided, effort to atone for his grandfather's sins. I wish I could have told Mikey that God does not work that way. Nor does God punish us for the sins of our ancestors. All sacrifices necessary to appease God the Father have already been made and accepted. There is no longer anything yet to be done.

"So, in the Name of the Father, I free your family, as Mikey asked. From this point forward, God will not punish you for what your grandfather did. Any of you. Or your descendents. I know He won't."

He looked at the other speakers on the podium. "When were we going to get around to honoring the dead today? Their deaths have been in vain if the speeches we have heard so far today are any indication. Shouldn't their lives mean something to us, even today?

"We have heard speeches about how bad the Triangle owners were. We have heard how corrupt the Government was. We have heard about the sins of this grandfather. However are we any better, here, one-hundred years later?

"We hate the greed of the managers of Enron, but we do not look at how we profited from these rising stock prices. No, we punish the stock manipulators only after the stocks plummet. We turn the other way when stocks soar by manipulation.

"My own house is not clean: How many of my brothers claimed celibacy while raping young boys. Where was I? I was looking the other way.

"Do you seriously think God would leave us with a moral compass, when we cast the Ten Commandments out of our classrooms?

"The labor unions talk about social justice, but it seems to be limited to the wages, deals, and concessions of their own members. We buy our clothing at discount stores, while forcing their creation on boys and girls in third world countries at slave wages and inhumane conditions, much like the workers we were to honor here today, just to keep prices low. Where is our outrage for social justice for them? What justice did we hear from these union leaders that does not benefit them personally?

"Your President will get up here in a few minutes. He may give platitudes, but like all the others, he will have no answers. Let him explain to us what John Kennedy said about 'Asking not what your country can do for you--' He is turning that around and turning us into a country of beggars in the process. Beggars who can only ask 'of' their government.

"Technology has not provided answers. We have some of the most advanced technologies doing the most meaningless things. Do we really think 'twittering' and 'texting' is the answer? When will we put away our video games, our internet obsessions--gambling and pornography--that only expose our selfishness.

"When will we be called to overcome our victim-hood? We set low expectations for ourselves, and then fail to meet them. When will we stand up on our own two feet? When will we step up to a better expectation of ourselves?

"The answers do not come from our government or organizations. We do not have to look far to find answers, but we do have to look in the right place. The answer comes from within us.

"Proverbs says, 'Evil men do not understand justice, But those who seek the LORD understand all'.

"Things will become better when we look beyond ourselves to make things better for our neighbors. We can do better than our forefathers have done.

"I am afraid we have to give ourselves a failing grade on the progress we have made in the last hundred years, but we can make the next one hundred years better. We will not do it by being either lazy or selfish, always looking for the easy answer and the silver bullet. We will have to change first.

"Jesus did it best, but Mohandas Gandhi said it in terms I can understand: 'Be the change you want to see in the world.'

"But will we have the courage to change?

"When will we be the people we can be? Are we willing, individually, to change?

"Shouldn't this event, this commemoration today, change us?"

Δ   Δ   Δ

The words had just tumbled out. When Father Vic was done, he walked back to his seat. The audience sat stunned. Then one person stood and applauded. More joined in. Then all were on their feet applauding. Even the speakers finally stood up, each of them looking down, embarrassed to still be seated.

After the Father's speech, there was really nothing left to say.

The Presidents handlers motioned for the Mayor to skip the President. But Obama stood and walked over to the Mayor, shook his hand warmly, looked him in the eyes, smiled and whispered, "When they put that Presidential Seal on the podium, there is no escaping."

Bloomberg turned to the microphone and said, "Ladies and Gentlemen, the President of the United States, Barack Obama."

"In memory of those who perished one hundred years ago today--"

Δ   Δ   Δ

When the President was finished with his brief remarks, the Mayor called Father Vic back to the podium for the benediction. The ceremony was over.

The President was hurried out and the motorcade retreated to the airport for a quick departure. The mayor lingered at the podium watching the crowd. He was proud of his city. The last thing he said to no one in particular, "Something special occurred here today".

Many who walked away from Washington Square Park that early evening carried away a personal challenge to change. The deaths were once again starting a revolution. John and Clarissa still held hands. With the President gone, many of the guests in the VIP area, talked about Father Vic's words.

Jadon returned to his parents. They had a son and brother to bury. They all knew where it would be: in the shade of the maple tree, near the water. Jadon said, "He had a troubled life. May he find peace and rest near the water."

Clarissa said, "Yes, of course. It was the only place he ever found peace."

They were all quiet, before she continued.

"I don't know how much money Dad had, but it is time to put it to work. Give it all away, where it will do some good".

Jadon also thought what he must do. He must make the United Nations more effective in confronting wrongdoing. He must stand up to the political wrangling. Maybe he would not succeed; at least he needed to take a stand.

John thought about the change he needed to make. It was long overdue. "Clarissa, do you want to come home again? Back to Baldwin House? Back with me?"

She hugged him, kissed him and whispered a reply she had dreamed of making for a long time, "I don't deserve you."

THE END

Irish Terms and Slang
Aunt Flo and Cousin Red = menstruation, menstrual cycle
Bottle of water = daughter
Clap = see
Irish Disease = small penis
Langer = bastard

Uncommon English Words
Aigrettes = a plume or tuft of feathers of a heron
Bespoke = the highest level of custom men's suits
Menservants = plural of manservant

ENDNOTES

[i] *The Thomas* and *The Mill* were both 300 feet long, weighed 2,525 gross tons and could be filled to capacity with sand, silt, and mud in around an hour. They would lick down to 40 feet below the surface, a channel which ran two thousand feet in from the ocean. The dredging was necessary to accommodate the "Big Four" being built on the other side of the ocean.

[ii] Maryland Steel later became Bethlehem Steel.

[iii] By the end of the nineteenth century (after a series of purchases, industry consolidations and divestitures) White Star owned and operated the world's premier fleet of luxury ocean liners.

Ismay ordered the construction of *The Oceanic*, to be followed by her twin sister ship, *The Olympic*. *RMS Oceanic*, at 17,272 gross tons, was truly the "Queen of the Ocean", costing an astounding one million pounds sterling to build. Her bridge and superstructure had a sleek, fluid design and she sliced through the water at the unprecedented cruising speed of 16 knots. She accommodated 1,700 passengers with a crew of 349. Speed across the Atlantic was still the game and Ismay was at the top of his, when be began experiencing chest pains. He underwent multiple unsuccessful gallstone surgeries. The pain was not gallstones--he was having a series of heart attacks, which killed him on November 23, 1899.

With his death, the course of shipping history took an abrupt turn. His son, Joseph Bruce Ismay, took the helm of the company and recognized something his father had already observed and to which he had begun to respond. Further increasing the speed of transatlantic ocean liners was economically unsustainable. In the 1860's it took twelve days to cross the Atlantic, down from six weeks just two decades earlier. It would take another forty years of technology to shave an additional three days off transit times. While ordering *The Olympic* and *The Oceanic* for speed, Thomas Ismay protected his bet by ordering an entirely different type of ship, *The Celtic*, for economy and capacity.

His son (known as J. Bruce) eventually canceled the order for the remaining high-speed ship and shifted the company's attention entirely to economy and capacity. He expanded construction of new monsters of the high seas. His ships became known as "The Big Four". Gross tonnage grew by 22%, while the number of passengers increased 65% (to 300 First Class, 160

Second and 2,350 Third Class "steerage" passengers on the Cedric).

While Thomas' ships were luxurious, J. Bruce would take first-class to a completely new level. Thomas' "floating palaces" gave way to J. Bruce's "floating towns". J. Bruce's moniker, "Nothing but the very finest" was certainly true, even if it only really applied to First Class.

To reflect their new direction, White Star Line's slogan was changed to "Comfort, safety and size." The race for speed had all but disappeared.

For all his insights in building a series of massive, opulent luxury liners, J. Bruce is mostly remembered for being on the last lifeboat to leave his final creation, the *RMS Titanic*. Unjustly branded a coward he resigned his position as Managing Director of the White Star Line to live in obscurity.

The decision to increase the size of ships by massive proportions played a central role frequently lost in that disaster. Board of Trade regulations required ships of more than 10,000 tons to have sixteen lifeboats. The *Titanic* provided more (20) and larger lifeboats than legally required. When the regulation was enacted (in 1894), the largest passenger vessel was the RMS Lucania at 12,952 Gross Register Tonnage. (By comparison, the largest cruise ships today are the Royal Caribbean's *Allure of the Seas* and *Oasis of the Sea* with 225,282 gross tonnage each. The *Allure* is two inches longer than her sister). The regulations had not kept up with the bloating vessels.

[iv] Since the Napoleonic Wars, Cork Harbour has been recognized for its strategic location. The British built fortifications first to protect the city, next to protect the anchorages near the city, then throughout the harbor, all the way out to the sea. From these anchorages, the Royal Navy guarded the southern entrance to the English Channel and blockaded all French ports. For ten years after Irish independence, some defenses remained under control of the British Royal Navy.

Even in peacetime, the Royal Navy provided bustling industry to Queenstown. There was always need for cloth, milk, meals, drink, mending, and companionship.

[v] Thanks to Mr. Beamish, Mr. Crawford and Mr. Murphy the second liquid was plentiful, foamy beer and ale.

In 1792, William Beamish and William Crawford had purchased from Edward Allen a brewery in Cramer's Lane that had brewed porters at that location since at least 1650. In their first year, they produced twelve thousand barrels of 'Beamish & Crawford's Cork Porter'. They went on to become the largest brewery in Ireland.

In 1854, James Murphy purchased The Foundling Hospital, on Leitrim Street in Cork, as the site for a brewery. It had plentiful water and was situated adjacent to a place venerated for its water, a 'Holy Well' from which the Brewery derived its name: Lady's Well Brewery. Many still worship these waters in a different form--Murphy's Irish Stout.

vi A butt is another name for a cask. Scuttling is the act of allowing water to seep in (as in scuttling a ship to sink her by allowing water into the hull). A Scuttle Butt was where fresh water flowed into the cups of thirsty sailors when they worked on deck. It was the central drinking water supply for the crew, and they gathered there periodically to have a drink and a word with each other. In the same way workers today stand around the coffee machine to have a drink and a word with each other, sailors shared rumors--or the scuttlebutt.

vii Royal Mail Ships (usually abbreviated as RMS) are seagoing vessels under contract with the British Royal Mail (and in those days typically had a reciprocal agreement with the United States Post Office). They proudly still fly the pennant of the Royal Mail when sailing and, therefore, expect the Royal Navy to come to their assistance at the least difficulty.

viii Steerage got it name from the area of sailing ships where the steering apparatus was contained. In the 1860's, the complex sets of ropes, cables, and pulleys of block and tackle (attributed to Archimedes of Syracuse) gave way to steam power. Steering engines (steam-powered mechanical amplifiers) were created to drive the rudder position in response to the changing wheel positions. The larger the ship was the greater the need was for mechanical assistance to move the rudder. In 1863, the Royal Navy used 78 men to haul block and tackle gear to turn the rudder of a 10,690-ton ship, the *HMS Minotaur*. The expenditure of labor and space requirements for this task was enormous. While the steering engines were large and noisy, the removal of the block and tackle arrangement left cavernous unused areas in the bottom of ships. Ship design was not changed accordingly; the space was re-purposed.

Steerage was no bargain. It cost half that of a Second-Class ticket and carried with it a sixth of the deck space, even less of the total living space, and subhuman sanitation. Even as the ships got bigger and more luxurious for first-class, the conditions got worse in steerage. More people survived steerage by the turn of the Twentieth Century than forty years earlier based on better screening of passengers, and little more. The better screening was solely for the economic benefit of the steamship companies, which had to pay for rejected passengers return.

[ix] There were as many theories on preventing seasickness as there were people on the ship: wives tales, home remedies, patent medicines, and narcotics were used. One thing there was not on the ship--one person who had not carried something on-board to ease the distress and discomfort. Many people died of dehydration in steerage. The sour odor of vomit permeated the spaces and lingered from voyage to voyage. There was no place a man could bury his head to get away from the stench. When seas were rough, the small amount of deck space allotted to steerage was off limits. Dying on the ship was the second most preferred method of relief from seasickness, though some welcomed it and slipped up to the deck to make their own burial at sea without the flags, Bible reading, hymns, and commotion. The preferred method for ending seasickness was two days on dry land, which would not come for another ten days in dreadful conditions. Many passengers stood on Ellis Island wondering when the island was going to quit rocking.

[x] About two percent of immigrants became trapped on the Island of Tears or returned to their home ports. For them the experience could be dreadful. For the remaining ninety-eight percent, their tears might have been tears of joy. Processing became more efficient as time went on, though the sheer volume of immigrants delayed processing considerably. The year Junior arrived in New York in this story (1906) more than a million people were processed at Ellis Island.

[xi] The list of 29 questions varied over time. Here is a composite from various sources. It is unclear how questions 1 and 13 were different. From looking at various samples, it appears the twenty-nine questions were numbered differently as well--such as splitting question #26 or combining #23 and #24. Dollar amounts in #15 changed over time from $30 to $50. The most important questions are in bold.

1. Identification on Ship Manifest. (Number on List)
2. **Family Name/Given Name**
3. Age. Years Months
4. Sex
5. Married – Single

6. **Occupation**
7. Able To Read Write
8. Nationality
9. Race
10. Last Residence: Country City/Town
11. Name & complete address of nearest relative or friend in country from whence alien came
12. Final Destination, State City/Town
13. No. on list.
14. Weather having a ticket to such a final destination
15. **Whether in possession of $30**
16. **Whether ever in U.S. before Yes/No How Long Where?**
17. Whether going to join a relative or friend; if so, list name and complete address.
18. Ever in prison, almshouse, institution for care of the insane or supported by charity?
19. If so which?
20. Whether a Polygamist
21. Whether an Anarchist
22. **Whether coming with offer, promise, or agreement of labor?**
23. **Condition of Health**
24. Deformed or Crippled
25. Height: Feet/Inches
26. Color of Hair and Eyes
27. Complexion
28. Marks of Identification
29. Place of Birth: Country City/Town

[xii] Samuel Ellis' Oyster Island is unfairly referred to as the "Island of Tears".

New York State operated the Emigrant Landing Depot at the Castle Garden, formerly the West Battery Fort, in lower Manhattan. Today it is the site of Castle Clinton (named after Mayor Dewitt Clinton) in Battery Park. In 1890, the United States Department of Immigration assumed operation of the landing depot and began planning to replace the facility. An island across the harbor was selected and on January 1, 1892 the premier federal immigration station was opened---Ellis Island. Man-made landfill, gained through construction excavations and immigrant ship ballast, was added to a dollop of land comprised of oyster shells and sand. An island of 3½ acres grew by 24 acres to become the base for thirty-three buildings in the Ellis Island complex.

Contrary to myth, it was efficient, well-organized, and properly administered. As long as documentation was in order and the immigrants' answers aligned, most stays on Ellis Island were counted in hours, not days or weeks. Most people were processed in their native language by staffs of previous immigrants from their home country. Prejudice was no greater than was common to the era and graft and corruption was minimal.

[xiii] Indentured servitude had been outlawed through passage of the thirteenth amendment to the United States Constitution. There had been a long-standing tradition since before the Revolutionary War of earning passage from Europe in exchange for labor for a fixed period. Widespread abuses, such as adding on exorbitant fees for room and board, created de facto slavery as immigrants found they could never earn enough to release themselves from debt. Arrangements attempting to circumvent the law were quickly found out through a few questions in the Registry Department.

[xiv] William Alciphron Boring (1859-1937) and Edward Lippincott Tilton (1861-1933) studied architecture together at Paris' École des Beaux-Arts. They won a competition to design the reception and inspection center. The building they designed was immense (388 feet long by 164 feet wide and 57 feet to the balustrade handrails and 126 feet to the dome finials). It was intentionally grandiose. It was criticized as being "bloated" and heavy-handed, which likely pleased Boring and Tilton. They intended the building to be easily seen and recognized from a distance with an attractive sense of overlooking the busy harbor. Their work was honored with gold medals for Architecture at the Exposition Universelle, Paris (1900), and Pan-American Exposition, Buffalo (1901); and a silver medal at the Louisiana Purchase Exposition, St. Louis (1904).

[xv] The Great Hall is 189 feet by 102 feet wide with a 60-foot vaulted ceiling.

[xvi] The United States Public Health Service conducted most of their medical exams as the immigrants climbed up the stairs to U.S. Marine Hospital Number 43. Senility and mental defect were often determined by what the immigrants said--to themselves.

Following the six-second medical examination, rejected immigrants were marked with a letter to indicate the medical condition for which they were being denied entry:

B – Back
C - Conjunctivitis
CT – Trachoma
E – Eyes
F – Face
FT – Feet
G – Goiter
H – Heart
K – Hernia
L – Lameness
N – Neck
P – Physical and Lungs
PG – Pregnancy
S – Senility
SC – Scalp (Favus)
SI – Special Inquiry
X – Suspected Mental defect
X (circled) – Definite signs of Mental defect

[xvii] Under custom of the Anglican Church, Irish immigrants were assumed to have entered into common law marriages and were encouraged to marry in the Church to legitimize their marriages. The custom of announcing a wedding for three Sundays before the ceremony was routinely waved, as was the acquiring of a wedding license ahead of time, if the pastor could determine there were no legal, moral, or religious reasons the couple should not be married.

The American Episcopal Church had been organized around the time of the American Revolution when Church of England clergy was required to swear allegiance to the British monarch. They continued to follow the customs of the Anglican Church in most matters.

[xviii] Cooper Union for the Advancement of Science and Art opened fifty-one years earlier by the Christian industrialist and philanthropist, Peter Cooper. Just as he had spoken out against social injustice, the institution he presented to New York City would become a major platform against social injustice and for free speech.

[xix] Nobody who jumped that day survived. One who jumped into the firefighter's nets nine stories below made it to the hospital and awoke from her coma shortly before she died. Another one lingered for four days, never out of a coma.

[xx] Garment companies were eager to move from old quarters on

Broadway to take advantage of low fire insurance rates for new buildings. Investor Joseph J. Asch had purchased three lots for $280,000 and built the Asch building on the corner of Washington Place and Greene Street for $400,000 (with a mortgage of $105,126). The building's skeleton frame was of protected cast-iron columns and steel girders and floor beams, with hollow tile floor arches. It had terra cotta fireproofing, with two freight and two passenger elevators.

On each floor, hoses were connected to a standpipe, linked to a roof tank filled with water. The building was ten stories high with a 101' x 100' footprint. Nine of the ten floors were manufacturing space (the first floor was retail). On each floor up to two hundred people spent nearly all their waking hours toiling at a sewing or cutting machine. High-rise loft buildings with small electric generators for building-wide power were a model of efficiency for New York City and the country. The close proximity of the workers made flow of partially completed garments easy.

Max Blanck and Isaac Harris (the "Shirtwaist Kings") signed a thirty-month lease for the eighth floor space and soon thereafter signed an additional lease, giving them the top three floors of the building. As uneducated, first generation immigrants, they routinely ignored labor laws designed to protect children and women to run a highly profitable business. They quickly became very wealthy.

[xxi] A Presidential Commission reported 955 passengers and two crewmembers lost their lives in that disaster.

[xxii] Triangle Waist Company occupied the top three floors of the Asch Building on the corner of Washington Place and Greene Street, near Washington Square Park.

[xxiii] The opening paragraphs of the March 28, 1911 New York Times article demonstrates the finger pointing: "City, country, and state officials were involved yesterday in the discussion of responsibility for the conditions existing in the ten-story loft building at University Place and Green Street, where Saturday evening's fire cost 142 lives, the latest victim dying in a hospital yesterday. Responsibility for the inadequate fire escape facilities was charged directly to the Building Department. In its defense Borough President McAneny issued a statement last night. He held that the Department was in no way to blame for the disaster and there was not the slightest grounds for accusing Supt. Miller. The efforts to hold him responsible he characterized as "outrageously unfair." Mr. McAneny said the plans for the

Washington Place building were filed eleven years ago and were accepted as complying with the law. This fact urged, contended that its Inspectors never had time to look at buildings except those in process of construction, and that several of its small force of Inspectors were grossly incompetent. District Attorney Whitman engaged two engineers yesterday to examine the building with a special view of determining official culpability, and their report will be ready when the April Grand Jury begins the investigation. Certain paragraphs in the State labor law were quoted by District Attorney Whitman to show that responsibility for proper fire protection in factories, especially in the matter of fire escapes, devolved upon the State Labor Commission. But State Labor Commissioner's Williams refused to accept this interpretation pointing to the fact that a decision of the Appellate Division in 1903 settled the fact that the Building Department has complete control over fire escapes in New York City." *[Note: reproduced here as published without correction]*

[xxiv] New immigrants had no set expectations as to hours, wages, or working conditions. There was also the language issue; dozens of languages other than English were used on the factory floors. It was difficult to mobilize a force when they could not understand what was being said.

The union's failure to gain closed shop status meant they were toothless. When the strike had expanded across the garment industry, it achieved twenty-percent higher wages and a 52-hour workweek. The new agreements had helped current workers, but did not establish a basis for negotiation with the over 1,200 factory company managements. The strike succeeded only because the Cutter's flexed their muscle. Repeating this success was difficult.

The unions allowed themselves to align closely with socialist and communist elements. It was easy for the owners to "paint them red" and drive away public sympathy with well-placed quotes in friendly newspapers.

Owners kept taking arbitrary, unilateral action against employees. All that was necessary was for them to brand the employees 'troublemakers' and show them the door. To take their place, there was a steady stream of new immigrants coming to America, who had never been involved with unions before.

[xxv] By 1911, even small-to-medium-sized towns had gas plants to provide for their needs. New York City had a great need for coal gasification to feed the ever-growing population. Within a mile of

Bellevue Hospital lay one of the world's largest Manufactured Gas Plants. They stored their inventory in large tanks on the rooftops of buildings in the area, to feed factories, homes, and tenements. A penny in the meter allowed gas to flow to furnaces and stoves in the home.

[xxvi] A group of hooligans, named the Gas House Gang reportedly committed 30-40 armed robberies per night in their heyday. They headquartered at 35th Street and 3rd Avenue.

[xxvii] Tim Sullivan was into extortion, graft, prostitution, and influence peddling along with his legitimate businesses, which included real estate and the theater. For Tim, there was never much of a line between legitimate and illegitimate businesses. And there was absolutely no line between government and private enterprise. Tim was known for giving away food and clothing all across his territory. That the food and clothing he was giving away were not his was of no concern.

In 1902, the Democratic Party (known as 'Tammany Hall' for the building they occupied and the society that formed their union) on paper had broken all direct links with organized crime. The criminal element the party controlled went underground and grew extensively. From the Lower East Side to China Town to Coney Island, the underground links all led to "Big Tim". He was the first ward representative able to control criminal activity; enabling criminal street gangs while eliminating competitors.

[xxviii] The true cause of Tim Sullivan's death was never determined. Since he was found on the railroad tracks, it was assumed he was killed by the train. That is highly unlikely. A few days later, New York Mayor William Jay Gaynor mysteriously died as he lay in a deck chair on the RMS Baltic 400 miles off the Irish Coast. Heart attack? Lingering effects from an assassination attempt three years earlier? It is unknown whether there was any connection between the two deaths.

[xxix] Tammany Hall collected large sums of money from garment manufacturers (as well as all other businesses in New York City). Graft was collected for permitting variances and favors and for finding (or making) patronage jobs with the city.

[xxx] New York City Health Department records show that malnutrition of children in the five boroughs was worse than any other place in the country. All the while, Tammany kept milk prices artificially high to benefit the dairymen--and maintain their kickbacks. When children died, Tammany came in to pick up the funeral tab for the bereaved families, in exchange for

promises of votes. Tammany played both sides against the middle everywhere it could.

xxxi Joseph-Francois Mangin had also designed New York City Hall six years earlier.

xxxii Today there are treatments, but still no cure, for polio.

Egyptian paintings and carvings (from around 1403 B.C.) depict otherwise healthy people with withered limbs, probably from polio.

Poliomyelitis was first recognized as a distinct condition by German orthopedist Dr. Jakob Heine in 1840. Its causative agent, (polio-virus) was identified by Austrian biologist and physician, Nobel Laureate Karl Landsteiner and his fellow Austrian physician Dr. Erwin Popper in 1908.

In Europe in the 1880s, major polio epidemics began to occur. Widespread localized outbreaks appeared in the United States soon thereafter.

Polio was epidemic twice in the twentieth century in the United States. In 1916, an epidemic polio infection broke out in Brooklyn, New York. That year, over 27,000 cases resulted in over 6,000 deaths in the United States with more than 2,000 deaths in New York City.

By 1950, near the peak in the United States, incidence shifted from infants to children aged five to nine years, when the risk of paralysis is greater. If the central nervous system was spared, the prognosis of survival was excellent. Mortality rate was about 5%. Most United States hospitals in the 1950's had no iron lungs for patients unable to breathe without mechanical assistance. Many children were condemned to death as a result. In 1977 there were 254,000 persons living in the United States who had been paralyzed by polio.

Any vaccine, even one that might have limited success, would have been a Godsend. This vaccine was a huge success. Within four years of the start of the Salk vaccine trials the disease had fallen nearly 90% in the United States. In 1985 the Pan American Health Organization (PAHO) launched a massive vaccination effort. The last verified case of polio in the Western Hemisphere was identified August 23, 1991 in a two-year old boy named Luis Fermín Tenorio Cortez, in Junín, Peru.

In October 2010, Polio unexpectedly broke out in the Congo and quickly spread to neighboring countries. This led the World Health Organization and U.N. Children's Fund to conduct a massive immunization campaign targeting 3 million Africans a month later. Polio had been considered eradicated in the Congo in 2000.

xxxiii At the conclusion of the Second World War, there were discussions of creating a volunteer organization to assist developing countries. In 1952, shortly before his death at 49 years of age, Senator Brien McMahon proposed a new form of 'army'-- an army of missionaries for democracy. The idea fell flat. In 1959, serious attention was given to Congressman Henry S. Reuss' idea of a 'Point Four Youth Corp'. The following year Reuss and Senator Richard L. Neuberger called for a non-governmental study on the "advisability and practicability" of such a quasi-governmental organization.

xxxiv The Morrill (Land Grant) Act of 1862 allowed federally owned lands to fund colleges and universities, with an eye toward agriculture and engineering. Legislation introduced the previous year had been vetoed, so when Justin Smith Morrill reintroduced the legislation, he cleverly included provisions for military studies and based the size of grant on the number of senators and representatives each state had in Congress. The tipping point for the legislation was when rural Southern states, which had not supported the legislation, seceded from the Union. President Abraham Lincoln signed the bill into law on July 2, 1862.

Cornell University was founded by Ezra Cornell and Andrew Dickson White in 1865 as New York State's land-grant institution on the southern shore of Cayuga Lake, in central New York. The former Indian Territory contains beautiful gorges, streams, waterfalls, and lakes.

xxxv The square is the largest public square in any city in the world. Named after The Tian'anmen (which literally means Gate of Heavenly Peace) and built during the Ming Dynasty in 1417, it once defined the Northern border of the square. The gate, subsequently destroyed, led into the Forbidden City. The square, originally built in 1651, has been enlarged to four times its original size over the years. It was cemented over in 1958.

xxxvi The International Ladies' Garment Workers' Union (ILGWU), largest union to have a principally female membership, along with the New York Fire Department has kept the memory of the tragedy alive. The ILGWU merged with the Amalgamated Clothing and Textile Workers Union to form the Union of Needletrades, Industrial and Textile Employees (UNITE) and later with the Hotel Employees and Restaurant Employees Union (HERE) to form their current union, UNITE HERE.

xxxvii At times, Mayor Michael Bloomberg's relations with labor unions have been cool. Unlike most politicians in New York State, he never pandered to the unions. In 2002, transit workers threatened to strike, and Bloomberg rode a bike through the city showing everyone how he would deal with the strike by finding an alternate means of transportation. It was not that he was anti-union or antagonistic. He saw the strike as holding the public hostage while the city was facing difficult times because of the economic downturn resulting from the attack of September 11th.

"Everyone needs to do his or her part. Fair is fair. Wage increases will cause fare increases--this is not the time for either."

xxxviii Access to the Region's Core (ARC) commuter rail project began in 1995 by identifying 137 alternatives. The first major tunneling contract was awarded fifteen years later on May 5, 2010. The 8.8-mile rail project was to tunnel under the Hudson River between Secaucus, New Jersey and Midtown Manhattan, doubling commuter capacity.

Under the 2009 Federal Transit Administration cost projections, multiple federal government agencies would pay $4.45 billion, Port Authority of New York and New Jersey (PANYNJ) would pay $3 billion, and New Jersey would pay $1.25 billion.

On October 27, 2010, New Jersey Governor Chris Christie killed the project. New Jersey state transportation officials projected cost overruns--"unforeseen" and "out of the state's control"--would be at least $2.5 billion.

In January 2011, New Jersey lawyers rejected Federal Transit Administration demands to repay $271 million, claiming it was "far more" than the $51.5 million it had been advanced under New Starts transit-funding program.

xxxix The most respected list of victims was identified in David Von Drehle's towering work, *Triangle: The Fire That Changed America*. In a HBO production (March, 2011) titled *Triangle: The Unidentified*, producer and historian Michael Hirsch claims to have identified the remaining six victims using genealogical investigative techniques.

www.ingramcontent.com/pod-product-compliance
Lightning Source LLC
Chambersburg PA
CBHW021509240626
47154CB00002B/562